A *New York Times* Bestseller • A *Los Angeles Times* Bestseller •
A *Washington Post* Bestseller • A *Publishers Weekly* Bestseller •
A Selection of the *Today Show* Book Club • A Book Sense 76
Selection • A Selection of the Quality Paperback Book Club •
A Selection of the Book-of-the-Month Club

Praise for
THE TIME
TRAVELER'S
WIFE

"[A] time-travel love story par excellence . . . It will be a hard-hearted reader who is not moved to tears by the dangers Henry and Clare ultimately face, and by the author's soaring celebration of the victory of love over time." —*Chicago Tribune*

"As Clare and Henry take turns telling the story, revealing the depth of their bond despite everything, a sci-fi premise becomes a powerfully original love story." —*People* (Top Ten Books of the Year)

"Spirited . . . Niffenegger plays ingeniously in her temporal hall of mirrors." —*The New Yorker*

"Readers will recall in *Love in the Time of Cholera* a love that works despite all travails and impediments . . . Marquez, like Niffenegger here, means to tell us that for such exalted love there is no tragedy and never any constraints." —*The Washington Post Book World*

"Niffenegger's inventive and poignant writing is well worth a trip." —*Entertainment Weekly*

"Moving, razor-edged prose . . . Niffenegger writes with the unflinching yet detached clarity of a war correspondent standing at the sidelines of an unfolding battle."   —*USA Today*

"A singular tale of a charming man with a funny condition (he slips in and out of time) and the woman who loves him. The setting, the city of Chicago, is luminous."   —*San Francisco Chronicle*

"As if love weren't complicated enough, debut author Niffenegger dreams up a happy couple plagued by a peculiar problem. . . . It is to Niffenegger's credit that she avoids cheap shots and develops her innovative concept in some exceptionally strange and witty ways."
—*Time Out New York*

"Contrary to appearances, *The Time Traveler's Wife* is a very old love story: wonky, sexy, incredible . . . charmingly, inventively retold and none the worse for it."   —*The Times* (London)

"An extraordinary novel with a unique premise . . . Niffenegger compassionately develops her unique characters, with the grace to accept their difficult circumstances, as well as their blessings. Don't be deceived by the easy charm of Henry and Clare's relationship; they will draw you into their small circle, make you complicit with their dreams and disappointments. They will break your heart."
—Curledup.com

"To those who say there are no new love stories, I heartily recommend *The Time Traveler's Wife*, an enchanting novel, which is beautifully crafted and as dazzlingly imaginative as it is dizzyingly romantic."
—Scott Turow, author of *Reversible Errors* and *Presumed Innocent*

"Haunting, original, and so smart it took my breath away . . . in short, the rare kind of book that I finish and jealously wish that *I'd* written."
—Jodi Picoult, author of *Plain Truth* and *Second Glance*

"An odd and enchanting love story. Most of us meet the person we love when we are adults, when the children we were are long gone. Henry and Clare—through the decidedly mixed blessing of Henry's Chrono-Displacement Disorder—have it both ways. It is a story of intense devotion filtered through time—of two people who share the best and worst of growing up as soulmates in a world that can change in an instant."
—Charles Dickinson, author of *A Shortcut in Time*

"Audrey Niffenegger imagines this story of an accidental time-traveler and the love of his life with grace and humanity. Fiercely inventive, slyly ambitious, and lovingly told, *The Time Traveler's Wife* sparkles as it fearlessly explores the delicate interplay of love and time. This novel is a joy."
—Anne Ursu, author of *The Disapparation of James* and *Spilling Clarence*

"A soaring love story illuminated by dozens of finely observed details and scenes, and one that skates nimbly around a huge conundrum at the heart of the book . . . Leaves a reader with a sense of life's riches and strangeness."
—*Publishers Weekly* (starred review)

"Intricately woven . . . Exceedingly literate."
—*Kirkus Reviews*

"Compelling . . . Skillfully written with a blend of distinct characters and heartfelt emotions that hopscotch through time, begging interpretation on many levels."
—*Library Journal* (starred review)

AUDREY NIFFENEGGER

....

THE TIME
TRAVELER'S
WIFE

A HARVEST BOOK • HARCOURT, INC.

Orlando   Austin   New York   San Diego   Toronto   London

Copyright © 2003 by Audrey Niffenegger

www.HarcourtBooks.com

First published by MacAdam/Cage, 2003

Library of Congress Cataloging-in-Publication Data
Niffenegger, Audrey.
The time traveler's wife/Audrey Niffenegger.—1st Harvest ed.
p.   cm.
ISBN 0-15-602943-X
1. Librarians—Fiction.   2. Time travel—Fiction.   3. Married
people—Fiction.   4. Women art students—Fiction.   I. Title.
PS3564.I362T56   2003b
813'.54—dc22   2004003577

Text set in Minion
Designed by Linda Lockowitz

Printed in the United States of America
First Harvest edition 2004

V U T S R Q P O N M

Permissions Acknowledgments begin on page 541 and constitute a
continuation of the copyright page.

Clock time is our bank manager,
tax collector, police inspector;
this inner time is our wife.

—J. B. PRIESTLEY,
Man and Time

Love After Love

The time will come
when, with elation,
you will greet yourself arriving
at your own door, in your own mirror,
and each will smile at the other's welcome,

and say, sit here. Eat.
You will love again the stranger who was your self.
Give wine. Give bread. Give back your heart
to itself, to the stranger who has loved you

all your life, whom you ignored
for another, who knows you by heart.
Take down the love letters from the bookshelf,

the photographs, the desperate notes,
peel your own image from the mirror.
Sit. Feast on your life.

—Derek Walcott

FOR

E LIZABETH H ILLMAN T AMANDL

MAY 20, 1915–DECEMBER 18, 1986

AND

N ORBERT C HARLES T AMANDL

FEBRUARY 11, 1915–MAY 23, 1957

CLARE: It's hard being left behind. I wait for Henry, not knowing where he is, wondering if he's okay. It's hard to be the one who stays.

I keep myself busy. Time goes faster that way.

I go to sleep alone, and wake up alone. I take walks. I work until I'm tired. I watch the wind play with the trash that's been under the snow all winter. Everything seems simple until you think about it. Why is love intensified by absence?

Long ago, men went to sea, and women waited for them, standing on the edge of the water, scanning the horizon for the tiny ship. Now I wait for Henry. He vanishes unwillingly, without warning. I wait for him. Each moment that I wait feels like a year, an eternity. Each moment is as slow and transparent as glass. Through each moment I can see infinite moments lined up, waiting. Why has he gone where I cannot follow?

HENRY: How does it feel? *How does it feel?*
Sometimes it feels as though your attention has wandered for just an instant. Then, with a start, you realize that the book you were holding, the red plaid cotton shirt with white buttons, the favorite

black jeans and the maroon socks with an almost-hole in one heel, the living room, the about-to-whistle tea kettle in the kitchen: all of these have vanished. You are standing, naked as a jaybird, up to your ankles in ice water in a ditch along an unidentified rural route. You wait a minute to see if maybe you will just snap right back to your book, your apartment, *et cetera*. After about five minutes of swearing and shivering and hoping to hell you can just disappear, you start walking in any direction, which will eventually yield a farmhouse, where you have the option of stealing or explaining. Stealing will sometimes land you in jail, but explaining is more tedious and time-consuming and involves lying anyway, and also sometimes results in being hauled off to jail, so what the hell.

Sometimes you feel as though you have stood up too quickly even if you are lying in bed half asleep. You hear blood rushing in your head, feel vertiginous falling sensations. Your hands and feet are tingling and then they aren't there at all. You've mislocated yourself again. It only takes an instant, you have just enough time to try to hold on, to flail around (possibly damaging yourself or valuable possessions) and then you are skidding across the forest-green-carpeted hallway of a Motel 6 in Athens, Ohio, at 4:16 a.m., Monday, August 6, 1981, and you hit your head on someone's door, causing this person, a Ms. Tina Schulman from Philadelphia, to open this door and start screaming because there's a naked, carpet-burned man passed out at her feet. You wake up in the County Hospital concussed with a policeman sitting outside your door listening to the Phillies game on a crackly transistor radio. Mercifully, you lapse back into unconsciousness and wake up again hours later in your own bed with your wife leaning over you looking very worried.

Sometimes you feel euphoric. Everything is sublime and has an aura, and suddenly you are intensely nauseated and then you are gone. You are throwing up on some suburban geraniums, or your father's tennis shoes, or your very own bathroom floor three days ago, or a wooden sidewalk in Oak Park, Illinois, circa 1903, or a tennis court on a fine autumn day in the 1950s, or your own naked feet in a wide variety of times and places.

How does it feel?

It feels exactly like one of those dreams in which you suddenly realize that you have to take a test you haven't studied for and you aren't wearing any clothes. And you've left your wallet at home.

When I am out there, in time, I am inverted, changed into a desperate version of myself. I become a thief, a vagrant, an animal who runs and hides. I startle old women and amaze children. I am a trick, an illusion of the highest order, so incredible that I am actually true.

Is there a logic, a rule to all this coming and going, all this dislocation? Is there a way to stay put, to embrace the present with every cell? I don't know. There are clues; as with any disease there are patterns, possibilities. Exhaustion, loud noises, stress, standing up suddenly, flashing light—any of these can trigger an episode. But: I can be reading the Sunday *Times,* coffee in hand and Clare dozing beside me on our bed and suddenly I'm in 1976 watching my thirteen-year-old self mow my grandparents' lawn. Some of these episodes last only moments; it's like listening to a car radio that's having trouble holding on to a station. I find myself in crowds, audiences, mobs. Just as often I am alone, in a field, house, car, on a beach, in a grammar school in the middle of the night. I fear finding myself in a prison cell, an elevator full of people, the middle of a highway. I appear from nowhere, naked. How can I explain? I have never been able to carry anything with me. No clothes, no money, no ID. I spend most of my sojourns acquiring clothing and trying to hide. Fortunately I don't wear glasses.

It's ironic, really. All my pleasures are homey ones: armchair splendor, the sedate excitements of domesticity. All I ask for are humble delights. A mystery novel in bed, the smell of Clare's long red-gold hair damp from washing, a postcard from a friend on vacation, cream dispersing into coffee, the softness of the skin under Clare's breasts, the symmetry of grocery bags sitting on the kitchen counter waiting to be unpacked. I love meandering through the stacks at the library after the patrons have gone home, lightly touching the spines of the books. These are the things that can pierce me with longing when I am displaced from them by Time's whim.

And Clare, always Clare. Clare in the morning, sleepy and crumple-faced. Clare with her arms plunging into the papermaking vat, pulling up the mold and shaking it so, and so, to meld the fibers. Clare reading, with her hair hanging over the back of the chair, massaging balm into her cracked red hands before bed. Clare's low voice is in my ear often.

I hate to be where she is not, when she is not. And yet, I am always going, and she cannot follow.

I

....

THE MAN
OUT OF TIME

Oh *not* because happiness *exists,*
that too-hasty profit snatched from approaching loss.

· · · · · · · · · · · · ·

But because truly being here is so much; because everything here
apparently needs us, this fleeting world, which in some strange way
keeps calling to us. Us, the most fleeting of all.

· · · · · · · · · · · · ·

. . . Ah, but what can we take along
into that other realm? Not the art of looking,
which is learned so slowly, and nothing that happened here. Nothing.
The sufferings, then. And, above all, the heaviness,
and the long experience of love,—just what is wholly
unsayable.

— from *The Ninth Duino Elegy,*
Rainer Maria Rilke,
translated by Stephen Mitchell

FIRST DATE, ONE

•••••••••••••••••••••••••••••••••

Saturday, October 26, 1991 (Henry is 28, Clare is 20)

CLARE: The library is cool and smells like carpet cleaner, although all I can see is marble. I sign the Visitors' Log: *Clare Abshire, 11:15 10-26-91 Special Collections.* I have never been in the Newberry Library before, and now that I've gotten past the dark, foreboding entrance I am excited. I have a sort of Christmas-morning sense of the library as a big box full of beautiful books. The elevator is dimly lit, almost silent. I stop on the third floor and fill out an application for a Reader's Card, then I go upstairs to Special Collections. My boot heels rap the wooden floor. The room is quiet and crowded, full of solid, heavy tables piled with books and surrounded by readers. Chicago autumn morning light shines through the tall windows. I approach the desk and collect a stack of call slips. I'm writing a paper for an art history class. My research topic is the Kelmscott Press *Chaucer.* I look up the book itself and fill out a call slip for it. But I also want to read about papermaking at Kelmscott. The catalog is confusing. I go back to the desk to ask for help. As I explain to the woman what I am trying to find, she glances over my shoulder at someone passing behind me. "Perhaps Mr. DeTamble can help you," she says. I turn, prepared to start explaining again, and find myself face to face with Henry.

I am speechless. Here is Henry, calm, clothed, younger than I have ever seen him. Henry is working at the Newberry Library, standing in front of me, in the present. Here and now. I am jubilant. Henry is looking at me patiently, uncertain but polite.

"Is there something I can help you with?" he asks.

"Henry!" I can barely refrain from throwing my arms around him. It is obvious that he has never seen me before in his life.

"Have we met? I'm sorry, I don't. . . ." Henry is glancing around us, worrying that readers, co-workers are noticing us, searching his memory and realizing that some future self of his has met this radiantly happy girl standing in front of him. The last time I saw him he was sucking my toes in the Meadow.

I try to explain. "I'm Clare Abshire. I knew you when I was a little girl . . ." I'm at a loss because I am in love with a man who is standing before me with no memories of me at all. Everything is in the future for him. I want to laugh at the weirdness of the whole thing. I'm flooded with years of knowledge of Henry, while he's looking at me perplexed and fearful. Henry wearing my dad's old fishing trousers, patiently quizzing me on multiplication tables, French verbs, all the state capitals; Henry laughing at some peculiar lunch my seven-year-old self has brought to the Meadow; Henry wearing a tuxedo, undoing the studs of his shirt with shaking hands on my eighteenth birthday. Here! Now! "Come and have coffee with me, or dinner or something. . . ." Surely he has to say yes, this Henry who loves me in the past and the future must love me now in some bat-squeak echo of other time. To my immense relief he does say yes. We plan to meet tonight at a nearby Thai restaurant, all the while under the amazed gaze of the woman behind the desk, and I leave, forgetting about Kelmscott and Chaucer and floating down the marble stairs, through the lobby and out into the October Chicago sun, running across the park scattering small dogs and squirrels, whooping and rejoicing.

HENRY: It's a routine day in October, sunny and crisp. I'm at work in a small windowless humidity-controlled room on the fourth floor of the Newberry, cataloging a collection of marbled papers that has recently been donated. The papers are beautiful, but cataloging is dull, and I am feeling bored and sorry for myself. In fact, I am feeling old, in the way only a twenty-eight-year-old can after staying up half the night drinking overpriced vodka and trying, without success, to win himself back into the good graces of Ingrid Carmichel. We spent the entire evening fighting, and now I can't even remember what we were fighting about. My head is throbbing. I need coffee. Leaving the marbled papers in a state of controlled chaos, I walk through the office and past the page's desk in the Reading Room. I am halted by Isabelle's voice saying, "Perhaps Mr. DeTamble can help you," by which she means "Henry, you weasel, where are you slinking off to?" And this astoundingly beautiful amber-haired tall slim girl turns around and looks at me as though I am her personal Jesus. My stomach lurches. Obviously she knows me, and I don't know her. Lord only knows what I have said, done, or promised to this luminous creature, so I am forced to say in my best librarianese, "Is there something I can help you with?" The girl sort of breathes "Henry!" in this very evocative way that convinces me that at some point in time we have a really *amazing* thing together. This makes it worse that I don't know anything about her, not even her name. I say "Have we met?" and Isabelle gives me a look that says *You asshole.* But the girl says, "I'm Clare Abshire. I knew you when I was a little girl," and invites me out to dinner. I accept, stunned. She is glowing at me, although I am unshaven and hung over and just not at my best. We are going to meet for dinner this very evening, at the Beau Thai, and Clare, having secured me for later, wafts out of the Reading Room. As I stand in the elevator, dazed, I realize that a massive winning lottery ticket chunk of my future has somehow found me here in the present, and I start to laugh. I cross the lobby, and as I run down the stairs to the street I see Clare running across Washington Square, jumping and whooping, and I am near tears and I don't know why.

Later that evening:

HENRY: At 6:00 p.m. I race home from work and attempt to make myself attractive. Home these days is a tiny but insanely expensive studio apartment on North Dearborn; I am constantly banging parts of myself on inconvenient walls, countertops and furniture. Step One: unlock seventeen locks on apartment door, fling myself into the living room-which-is-also-my-bedroom and begin stripping off clothing. Step Two: shower and shave. Step Three: stare hopelessly into the depths of my closet, gradually becoming aware that nothing is exactly clean. I discover one white shirt still in its dry cleaning bag. I decide to wear the black suit, wing tips, and pale blue tie. Step Four: don all of this and realize I look like an FBI agent. Step Five: look around and realize that the apartment is a mess. I resolve to avoid bringing Clare to my apartment tonight even if such a thing is possible. Step Six: look in full-length bathroom mirror and behold angular, wild-eyed 6'1" ten-year-old Egon Schiele look-alike in clean shirt and funeral director suit. I wonder what sorts of outfits this woman has seen me wearing, since I am obviously not arriving from my future into her past wearing clothes of my own. She said she was a little girl? A plethora of unanswerables runs through my head. I stop and

breathe for a minute. Okay. I grab my wallet and my keys, and away
I go: lock the thirty-seven locks, descend in the cranky little elevator, buy roses for Clare in the shop in the lobby, walk two blocks to
the restaurant in record time but still five minutes late. Clare is already seated in a booth and she looks relieved when she sees me.
She waves at me like she's in a parade.

"Hello," I say. Clare is wearing a wine-colored velvet dress and
pearls. She looks like a Botticelli by way of John Graham: huge gray
eyes, long nose, tiny delicate mouth like a geisha. She has long red
hair that covers her shoulders and falls to the middle of her back.
Clare is so pale she looks like a waxwork in the candlelight. I thrust
the roses at her. "For you."

"Thank you," says Clare, absurdly pleased. She looks at me and
realizes that I am confused by her response. "You've never given me
flowers before."

I slide into the booth opposite her. I'm fascinated. This woman
knows me; this isn't some passing acquaintance of my future hegiras.
The waitress appears and hands us menus.

"Tell me," I demand.

"What?"

"Everything. I mean, do you understand why I don't know you?
I'm terribly sorry about that—"

"Oh, no, you shouldn't be. I mean, I know . . . why that is."
Clare lowers her voice. "It's because for you none of it has happened
yet, but for me, well, I've known you for a long time."

"How long?"

"About fourteen years. I first saw you when I was six."

"Jesus. Have you seen me very often? Or just a few times?"

"The last time I saw you, you told me to bring this to dinner
when we met again," Clare shows me a pale blue child's diary, "so
here,"—she hands it to me—"you can have this." I open it to the

place marked with a piece of newspaper. The page, which has two cocker spaniel puppies lurking in the upper right-hand corner, is a list of dates. It begins with September 23, 1977, and ends sixteen small, blue, puppied pages later on May 24, 1989. I count. There are 152 dates, written with great care in the large open Palmer Method blue ball point pen of a six-year-old.

"You made the list? These are all accurate?"

"Actually, you dictated this to me. You told me a few years ago that you memorized the dates from this list. So I don't know how exactly this exists; I mean, it seems sort of like a Mobius strip. But they are accurate. I used them to know when to go down to the Meadow to meet you." The waitress reappears and we order: Tom Kha Kai for me and Gang Mussaman for Clare. A waiter brings tea and I pour us each a cup.

"What is the Meadow?" I am practically hopping with excitement. I have never met anyone from my future before, much less a Botticelli who has encountered me 152 times.

"The Meadow is a part of my parents' place up in Michigan. There's woods at one edge of it, and the house on the opposite end. More or less in the middle is a clearing about ten feet in diameter with a big rock in it, and if you're in the clearing no one at the house can see you because the land swells up and then dips in the clearing. I used to play there because I liked to play by myself and I thought no one knew I was there. One day when I was in first grade I came home from school and went out to the clearing and there you were."

"Stark naked and probably throwing up."

"Actually, you seemed pretty self-possessed. I remember you knew my name, and I remember you vanishing quite spectacularly. In retrospect, it's obvious that you had been there before. I think the first time for you was in 1981; I was ten. You kept saying 'Oh my god,' and staring at me. Also, you seemed pretty freaked out about the nudity, and by then I just kind of took it for granted that this old nude guy was going to magically appear from the future and demand clothing." Clare smiles. "And food."

"What's funny?"

"I made you some pretty weird meals over the years. Peanut butter and anchovy sandwiches. Pâté and beets on Ritz crackers. I think partly I wanted to see if there was anything you wouldn't eat and partly I was trying to impress you with my culinary wizardry."

"How old was I?"

"I think the oldest I have seen you was forty-something. I'm not sure about youngest; maybe about thirty? How old are you now?"

"Twenty-eight."

"You look very young to me now. The last few years you were mostly in your early forties, and you seemed to be having kind of a rough life. . . . It's hard to say. When you're little all adults seem big, and old."

"So what did we do? In the Meadow? That's a lot of time, there."

Clare smiles. "We did lots of things. It changed depending on my age, and the weather. You spent a lot of time helping me do my homework. We played games. Mostly we just talked about stuff. When I was really young I thought you were an angel; I asked you a lot of questions about God. When I was a teenager I tried to get you to make love to me, and you never would, which of course made me much more determined about it. I think you thought you were going to warp me sexually, somehow. In some ways you were very parental."

"Oh. That's probably good news but somehow at the moment I don't seem to be wanting to be thought of as parental." Our eyes meet. We both smile and we are conspirators. "What about winter? Michigan winters are pretty extreme."

"I used to smuggle you into our basement; the house has a huge basement with several rooms, and one of them is a storage room and the furnace is on the other side of the wall. We call it the Reading Room because all the useless old books and magazines are stored there. One time you were down there and we had a blizzard and nobody went to school or to work and I thought I was going to go crazy trying to get food for you because there wasn't all that much food in the house. Etta was supposed to go grocery shopping when the storm hit. So you were stuck reading old *Reader's Digest*s for three days, living on sardines and ramen noodles."

"Sounds salty. I'll look forward to it." Our meal arrives. "Did you ever learn to cook?"

"No, I don't think I would claim to know how to cook. Nell and Etta always got mad when I did anything in their kitchen beyond getting myself a Coke, and since I've moved to Chicago I don't have anybody to cook for, so I haven't been motivated to work on it. Mostly I'm too busy with school and all, so I just eat there." Clare takes a bite of her curry. "This is really good."

"Nell and Etta?"

"Nell is our cook." Clare smiles. "Nell is like *cordon bleu* meets Detroit; she's how Aretha Franklin would be if she was Julia Child. Etta is our housekeeper and all-around everything. She's really more almost our *mom;* I mean, my mother is . . . well, Etta's just always there, and she's German and strict, but she's very comforting, and my mother is kind of off in the clouds, you know?"

I nod, my mouth full of soup.

"Oh, and there's Peter," Clare adds. "Peter is the gardener."

"Wow. Your family has servants. This sounds a little out of my league. Have I ever, uh, met any of your family?"

"You met my Grandma Meagram right before she died. She was the only person I ever told about you. She was pretty much blind by then. She knew we were going to get married and she wanted to meet you."

I stop eating and look at Clare. She looks back at me, serene, angelic, perfectly at ease. "Are we going to get married?"

"I assume so," she replies. "You've been telling me for years that whenever it is you're coming from, you're married to me."

Too much. This is too much. I close my eyes and will myself to think of nothing; the last thing I want is to lose my grip on the here and now.

"Henry? Henry, are you okay?" I feel Clare sliding onto the seat beside me. I open my eyes and she grips my hands strongly in hers. I look at her hands and see that they are the hands of a laborer, rough and chapped. "Henry, I'm sorry, I just can't get used to this. It's so opposite. I mean, all my life you've been the one who knew everything and I sort of forgot that tonight maybe I should go slow." She smiles. "Actually, almost the last thing you said to me before you left was 'Have mercy, Clare.' You said it in your quoting voice, and I guess now that I think of it you must have been quoting me." She continues to hold my hands. She looks at me with eagerness; with love. I feel profoundly humble.

"Clare?"

"Yes?"

"Could we back up? Could we pretend that this is a normal first date between two normal people?"

"Okay." Clare gets up and goes back to her side of the table. She sits up straight and tries not to smile.

"Um, right. Gee, ah, Clare, ah, tell me about yourself. Hobbies? Pets? Unusual sexual proclivities?"

"Find out for yourself."

"Right. Let's see . . . where do you go to school? What are you studying?"

"I'm at the School of the Art Institute; I've been doing sculpture, and I've just started to study papermaking."

"Cool. What's your work like?"

For the first time, Clare seems uncomfortable. "It's kind of . . . big, and it's about . . . birds." She looks at the table, then takes a sip of tea.

"Birds?"

"Well, really it's about, um, longing." She is still not looking at me, so I change the subject.

"Tell more about your family."

"Okay." Clare relaxes, smiles. "Well . . . my family lives in Michigan, by a small town on the lake called South Haven. Our house is in an unincorporated area outside the town, actually. It originally belonged to my mother's parents, my Grandpa and Grandma Meagram. He died before I was born, and she lived with us until she died. I was seventeen. My grandpa was a lawyer, and my dad is a lawyer; my dad met my mom when he came to work for Grandpa."

"So he married the boss's daughter."

"Yeah. Actually, I sometimes wonder if he really married the boss's house. My mom is an only child, and the house is sort of amazing; it's in a lot of books on the Arts and Crafts movement."

"Does it have a name? Who built it?"

"It's called Meadowlark House, and it was built in 1896 by Peter Wyns."

"Wow. I've seen pictures of it. It was built for one of the Henderson family, right?"

"Yes. It was a wedding present for Mary Henderson and Dieter Bascombe. They divorced two years after they moved in and sold the house."

"Posh house."

"My family is posh. They're very weird about it, too."

"Brothers and sisters?"

"Mark is twenty-two and finishing pre-law at Harvard. Alicia is seventeen and a senior in high school. She's a cellist." I detect affection for the sister and a certain flatness for the brother. "You aren't too fond of your brother?"

"Mark is just like Dad. They both like to win, talk you down until you submit."

"You know, I always envy people with siblings, even if they don't like them all that much."

"You're an only child?"

"Yep. I thought you knew everything about me?"

"Actually I know everything and nothing. I know how you look without clothes, but until this afternoon I didn't know your last name. I knew you lived in Chicago, but I know nothing about your family except that your mom died in a car crash when you were six. I know you know a lot about art and speak fluent French and German; I had no idea you were a librarian. You made it impossible for me to find you in the present; you said it would just happen when it was supposed to happen, and here we are."

"Here we are," I agree. "Well, my family isn't posh; they're musicians. My father is Richard DeTamble and my mother was Annette Lyn Robinson."

"Oh—the singer!"

"Right. And he's a violinist. He plays for the Chicago Symphony Orchestra. But he never really made it the way she did. It's a shame because my father is a marvelous violin player. After Mom died he was just treading water." The check arrives. Neither of us has eaten very much, but I at least am not interested in food right now. Clare picks up her purse and I shake my head at her. I pay; we leave the restaurant and stand on Clark Street in the fine autumn night. Clare is wearing an elaborate blue knitted thing and a fur scarf; I have forgotten to bring an overcoat so I'm shivering.

"Where do you live?" Clare asks.

Uh oh. "I live about two blocks from here, but my place is tiny and really messy right now. You?"

"Roscoe Village, on Hoyne. But I have a roommate."

"If you come up to my place you have to close your eyes and count to one thousand. Perhaps you have a very uninquisitive deaf roommate?"

"No such luck. I never bring anyone over; Charisse would pounce on you and stick bamboo slivers under your fingernails until you told all."

"I long to be tortured by someone named Charisse, but I can see that you do not share my taste. Come up to my parlor." We walk north along Clark. I veer into Clark Street Liquors for a bottle of wine. Back on the street Clare is puzzled.

"I thought you aren't supposed to drink?"

"I'm not?"

"Dr. Kendrick was very strict about it."

"Who's he?" We are walking slowly because Clare is wearing impractical shoes.

"He's your doctor; he's a big expert on Chrono-Impairment."

"Explain."

"I don't know very much. Dr. David Kendrick is a molecular geneticist who discovered—will discover—why people are chrono-impaired. It's a genetic thing; he figures it out in 2006." She sighs. "I guess it's just way too early. You told me once that there are a lot more chrono-impaired people about ten years from now."

"I've never heard of anyone else who has this—impairment."

"I guess even if you went out right now and found Dr. Kendrick he wouldn't be able to help you. And we would never have met, if he could."

"Let's not think about that." We are in my lobby. Clare precedes me into the tiny elevator. I close the door and push eleven. She smells like old cloth, soap, sweat, and fur. I breathe deeply. The elevator clangs into place on my floor and we extricate ourselves from it and walk down the narrow hallway. I wield my fistful of keys on all 107 locks and crack the door slightly. "It's gotten much worse during dinner. I'm going to have to blindfold you." Clare giggles as I set down the wine and remove my tie. I pass it over her eyes and tie it firmly at the back of her head. I open the door and guide her into the apartment and settle her in the armchair. "Okay, start counting."

Clare counts. I race around picking underwear and socks from the floor, collecting spoons and coffee cups from various horizontal surfaces and chucking them into the kitchen sink. As she says "Nine hundred and sixty-seven," I remove the tie from her eyes. I have turned the sleeper-sofa into its daytime, sofa self, and I sit down on it. "Wine? Music? Candlelight?"

"Yes, please."

I get up and light candles. When I'm finished I turn off the overhead light and the room is dancing with little lights and everything looks better. I put the roses in water, locate my corkscrew, extract the cork, and pour us each a glass of wine. After a moment's thought I put on the EMI CD of my mother singing Schubert lieder and turn the volume low.

My apartment is basically a couch, an armchair, and about four thousand books.

"How lovely," says Clare. She gets up and reseats herself on the sofa. I sit down next to her. There is a comfortable moment when we just sit there and look at each other. The candlelight flickers on Clare's hair. She reaches over and touches my cheek. "It's so good to see you. I was getting lonely."

I draw her to me. We kiss. It's a very . . . compatible kiss, a kiss born of long association, and I wonder just exactly what we've been doing in this meadow of Clare's, but I push the thought away. Our lips part; usually at this point I would be considering how to work my way past various fortresses of clothing, but instead I lean back and stretch out on the sofa, bringing Clare along with me by gripping her under the arms and pulling; the velvet dress makes her slippery and she slithers into the space between my body and the back of the sofa like a velvet eel. She is facing me and I am propped up by the arm of the sofa. I can feel the length of her body pressing against mine through the thin fabric. Part of me is dying to go leaping and licking and diving in, but I'm exhausted and overwhelmed.

"Poor Henry."

"Why 'Poor Henry?' I'm overcome with happiness." And it's true.

"Oh, I've been dropping all these surprises on you like big rocks." Clare swings a leg over me so she's sitting exactly on top of my cock. It concentrates my attention wonderfully.

"Don't move," I say.

"Okay. I'm finding this evening highly entertaining. I mean, Knowledge is Power, and all that. Also I've always been hugely curious to find out where you live and what you wear and what you do for a living."

"Voilà." I slide my hands under her dress and up her thighs. She's wearing stockings and garters. My kind of girl. "Clare?"

"Oui."

"It seems like a shame to just gobble everything up all at once. I mean, a little anticipation wouldn't hurt anything."

Clare is abashed. "I'm sorry! But, you know, in my case, I've been anticipating for years. And, it's not like cake . . . you eat it and it's gone."

"Have your cake and eat it too."

"That's my motto." She smiles a tiny wicked smile and thrusts her hips back and forth a couple times. I now have an erection that is probably tall enough to ride some of the scarier rides at Great America without a parent.

"You get your way a lot, don't you?"

"Always. I'm horrible. Except you have been mostly impervious to my wheedling ways. I've suffered dreadfully under your regime of French verbs and checkers."

"I guess I should take consolation in the fact that my future self will at least have some weapons of subjugation. Do you do this to all the boys?"

Clare is offended; I can't tell how genuinely. "I wouldn't dream of doing this with *boys*. What nasty ideas you have!" She is unbuttoning my shirt. "God, you're so ... young." She pinches my nipples, hard. The hell with virtue. I've figured out the mechanics of her dress.

The next morning:

CLARE: I wake up and I don't know where I am. An unfamiliar ceiling. Distant traffic noises. Bookshelves. A blue armchair with my velvet dress slung across it and a man's tie draped over the dress. Then I remember. I turn my head and there's Henry. So simple, as though I've been doing it all my life. He is sleeping with abandon, torqued into an unlikely shape as though he's washed up on some beach, one arm over his eyes to shut out the morning, his long black hair splayed over the pillow. So simple. Here we are. Here and now, finally now.

I get out of bed carefully. Henry's bed is also his sofa. The springs squeak as I stand up. There's not much space between the bed and the bookshelves, so I edge along until I make it into the hallway. The bathroom is tiny. I feel like Alice in Wonderland, grown huge and having to stick my arm out the window just so I can turn around. The ornate little radiator is clanking out heat. I pee and wash my hands and my face. And then I notice that there are two toothbrushes in the white porcelain toothbrush holder.

I open the medicine cabinet. Razors, shaving cream, Listerine, Tylenol, aftershave, a blue marble, a toothpick, deodorant on the top shelf. Hand lotion, tampons, a diaphragm case, deodorant, lipstick, a bottle of multivitamins, a tube of spermicide on the bottom shelf. The lipstick is a very dark red.

I stand there, holding the lipstick. I feel a little sick. I wonder what she looks like, what her name is. I wonder how long they've been going out. Long enough, I guess. I put the lipstick back, close the medicine cabinet. In the mirror I see myself, white-faced, hair flying in all directions. *Well, whoever you are, I'm here now. You may be Henry's past, but I'm his future.* I smile at myself. My reflection grimaces back at me. I borrow Henry's white terrycloth bathrobe from the back of the bathroom door. Underneath it on the hook is a pale blue silk robe. For no reason at all wearing his bathrobe makes me feel better.

Back in the living room, Henry is still sleeping. I retrieve my watch from the windowsill and see that it's only 6:30. I'm too restless to get back into bed. I walk into the kitchenette in search of coffee. All the counters and the stove are covered with stacks of dishes, magazines, and other reading material. There's even a sock in the sink. I realize that Henry must have simply heaved everything into the kitchen last night, regardless. I always had this idea that Henry was very tidy. Now it becomes clear that he's one of those people who is fastidious about his personal appearance but secretly slovenly about everything else. I find coffee in the fridge, and find the coffee maker, and start the coffee. While I wait for it to brew, I peruse Henry's bookshelves.

Here is the Henry I know. Donne's *Elegies and Songs and Sonnets*. *Doctor Faustus*, by Christopher Marlowe. *Naked Lunch*. Anne Bradstreet, Immanuel Kant. Barthes, Foucault, Derrida. Blake's *Songs of Innocence and Experience*. *Winnie the Pooh*. *The Annotated Alice*. Heidegger. Rilke. *Tristram Shandy*. *Wisconsin Death Trip*. Aristotle. Bishop Berkeley. Andrew Marvell. *Hypothermia, Frostbite and Other Cold Injuries*.

The bed squeaks and I jump. Henry is sitting up, squinting at me in the morning light. He's so young, so *before*—. He doesn't know me, yet. I have a sudden fear that he's forgotten who I am.

"You look cold," he says. "Come back to bed, Clare."

"I made coffee," I offer.

"Mmm, I can smell it. But first come and say good morning."

I climb into bed still wearing his bathrobe. As he slides his hand under it he stops for just a moment, and I see that he has made the connection, and is mentally reviewing his bathroom *vis-à-vis* me.

"Does it bother you?" he asks.

I hesitate.

"Yes, it does. It does bother you. Of course." Henry sits up, and I do, too. He turns his head toward me, looks at me. "It was almost over, anyway."

"Almost?"

"I was about to break up with her. It's just bad timing. Or good timing, I don't know." He's trying to read my face, for what? Forgiveness? It's not his fault. How could he know? "We've sort of been torturing each other for a long time—" He's talking faster and faster and then he stops. "Do you want to know?"

"No."

"Thank you." Henry passes his hands over his face. "I'm sorry. I didn't know you were coming or I'd have cleaned up a little more. My life, I mean, not just the apartment." There's a lipstick smear under Henry's ear, and I reach up and rub it out. He takes my hand, and holds it. "Am I very different? Than you expected?" he asks apprehensively.

"Yes . . . you're more . . ." *selfish*, I think, but I say, ". . . younger."

He considers it. "Is that good or bad?"

"Different." I run both hands over Henry's shoulders and across his back, massaging muscles, exploring indentations. "Have you seen yourself, in your forties?"

"Yes. I look like I've been spindled and mutilated."

"Yeah. But you're less—I mean you are sort of—more. I mean, you *know* me, so. . . ."

"So right now you're telling me that I'm somewhat gauche."

I shake my head, although that is exactly what I mean. "It's just that I've had all these experiences, and you . . . I'm not used to being with you when you don't remember anything that happened."

Henry is somber. "I'm sorry. But the person you know doesn't exist yet. Stick with me, and sooner or later, he's bound to appear. That's the best I can do, though."

"That's fair," I say. "But in the meantime. . . ."

He turns to meet my gaze. "In the meantime?"

"I want. . . ."

"You want?"

I'm blushing. Henry smiles, and pushes me backward gently onto the pillows. "You know."

"I don't know much, but I can guess a thing or two."

Later, we're dozing warm covered with midmorning October pale sun, skin to skin and Henry says something into the back of my neck that I don't catch.

"What?"

"I was thinking; it's very peaceful, here with you. It's nice to just lie here and know that the future is sort of taken care of."

"Henry?"

"Hmm?"

"How come you never told yourself about me?"

"Oh. I don't do that."

"Do what?"

"I don't usually tell myself stuff ahead of time unless it's huge, life-threatening, you know? I'm trying to live like a normal person. I don't even like having myself around, so I try not to drop in on myself unless there's no choice."

I ponder this for a while. "I would tell myself everything."

"No, you wouldn't. It makes a lot of trouble."

"I was always trying to get you to tell me things." I roll over onto my back and Henry props his head on his hand and looks down at me. Our faces are about six inches apart. It's so strange to be talking, almost like we always did, but the physical proximity makes it hard for me to concentrate.

"Did I tell you things?" he asks.

"Sometimes. When you felt like it, or had to."

"Like what?"

"See? You do want to know. But I'm not telling."

Henry laughs. "Serves me right. Hey, I'm hungry. Let's go get breakfast."

Outside it's chilly. Cars and cyclists cruise along Dearborn while couples stroll down the sidewalks and there we are with them, in the morning sunlight, hand in hand, finally together for anyone to see. I feel a tiny pang of regret, as though I've lost a secret, and then a rush of exaltation: now everything begins.

A First Time for Everything

●●●●●●●●●●●●●●●●●●●●●●●●●●●●●●●

Sunday, June 16, 1968

HENRY: The first time was magical. How could I have known what it meant? It was my fifth birthday, and we went to the Field Museum of Natural History. I don't think I had ever been to the Field Museum before. My parents had been telling me all week about the wonders to be seen there, the stuffed elephants in the great hall, the dinosaur skeletons, the caveman dioramas. Mom had just gotten back from Sydney, and she had brought me an immense, surpassingly blue butterfly, *Papilio ulysses,* mounted in a frame filled with cotton. I would hold it close to my face, so close I couldn't see anything but that blue. It would fill me with a feeling, a feeling I later tried to duplicate with alcohol and finally found again with Clare, a feeling of unity, oblivion, mindlessness in the best sense of the word. My parents described the cases and cases of butterflies, hummingbirds, beetles. I was so excited that I woke up before dawn. I put on my gym shoes and took my *Papilio ulysses* and went into the backyard and down the steps to the river in my pajamas. I sat on the landing and watched the light come up. A family of ducks came swimming by, and a raccoon appeared on the landing across the river and looked at me curiously before washing its breakfast and eating it. I may have fallen asleep. I heard Mom calling and I ran back up the stairs, which were slippery with dew, careful not to drop the butterfly. She was annoyed with me for going down to the landing by myself, but she didn't make a big deal about it, it being my birthday and all.

Neither of them were working that night, so they took their time getting dressed and out the door. I was ready long before either of them. I sat on their bed and pretended to read a score. This was around the time my musician parents recognized that their one and only offspring was not musically gifted. It wasn't that I wasn't trying; I just could not hear whatever it was they heard in a piece of music. I enjoyed music, but I could hardly carry a tune. And though I could read a newspaper when I was four, scores were only pretty black squiggles. But my parents were still hoping I might have some hidden musical aptitude, so when I picked up the score Mom sat down next to me and tried to help me with it. Pretty soon Mom was singing and I was chiming in with horrible yowling noises and snapping my fingers and we were giggling and she was tickling me. Dad came out of the bathroom with a towel around his waist and joined in and for a few glorious minutes they were singing together and Dad picked me up and they were dancing around the bedroom with me pressed between them. Then the phone rang, and the scene dissolved. Mom went to answer it, and Dad set me on the bed and got dressed.

Finally, they were ready. My mom wore a red sleeveless dress and sandals; she had painted her toenails and fingernails so they matched her dress. Dad was resplendent in dark blue pants and a white short-sleeved shirt, providing a quiet background for Mom's flamboyance. We all piled into the car. As always, I had the whole backseat to myself, so I lay down and watched the tall buildings along Lake Shore Drive flicking past the window.

"Sit up, Henry," said Mom. "We're here."

I sat up and looked at the museum. I had spent my childhood thus far being carted around the capital cities of Europe, so the Field Museum satisfied my idea of "Museum," but its domed stone facade was nothing exceptional. Because it was Sunday, we had a little trouble finding parking, but eventually we parked and walked along the lake, past boats and statues and other excited children. We passed between the heavy columns and into the museum.

And then I was a boy enchanted.

Here all of nature was captured, labeled, arranged according to a logic that seemed as timeless as if ordered by God, perhaps a God who had mislaid the original paperwork on the Creation and had requested the Field Museum staff to help Him out and keep track of it all. For my five-year-old self, who could derive rapture from a single butterfly, to walk through the Field Museum was to walk through Eden and see all that passed there.

We saw so much that day: the butterflies, to be sure, cases and cases of them, from Brazil, from Madagascar, even a brother of my blue butterfly from Down Under. The museum was dark, cold, and old, and this heightened the sense of suspension, of time and death brought to a halt inside its walls. We saw crystals and cougars, muskrats and mummies, fossils and more fossils. We ate our picnic lunch on the lawn of the museum, and then plunged in again for birds and alligators and Neanderthals. Toward the end I was so tired I could hardly stand, but I couldn't bear to leave. The guards came and gently herded us all to the doors; I struggled not to cry, but began to anyway, out of exhaustion and desire. Dad picked me up, and we walked back to the car. I fell asleep in the backseat, and when I awoke we were home, and it was time for dinner.

We ate downstairs in Mr. and Mrs. Kim's apartment. They were our landlords. Mr. Kim was a gruff, compact man who seemed to like me but never said much, and Mrs. Kim (Kimy, my nickname for her) was my buddy, my crazy Korean card-playing babysitter. I spent most of my waking hours with Kimy. My mom was never much of a cook, and Kimy could produce anything from a soufflé to *bi bim bop* with panache. Tonight, for my birthday, she had made pizza and chocolate cake.

We ate. Everyone sang Happy Birthday and I blew out the candles. I don't remember what I wished for. I was allowed to stay up later than usual, because I was still excited by all the things we'd seen, and because I had slept so late in the afternoon. I sat on the back porch in my pajamas with Mom and Dad and Mrs. and Mr. Kim, drinking lemonade and watching the blueness of the evening sky, listening to the cicadas and the TV noises from other apartments. Eventually Dad said, "Bedtime, Henry." I brushed my teeth and said prayers and got into bed. I was exhausted but wide awake. Dad read to me for a while, and then, seeing that I still couldn't sleep, he and Mom turned out the lights, propped open my bedroom door, and went into the living room. The deal was: they would play for me as long as I wanted, but I had to stay in bed to listen. So Mom sat at the piano, and Dad got out his violin, and they played and sang for a long time. Lullabies, lieder, nocturnes; sleepy music to soothe the savage boy in the bedroom. Finally Mom came in to see if I was asleep. I must have looked small and wary in my little bed, a nocturnal animal in pajamas.

"Oh, baby. Still awake?"

I nodded.

"Dad and I are going to bed. Are you okay?"

I said Yes and she gave me a hug. "It was pretty exciting today at the museum, huh?"

"Can we go back tomorrow?"

"Not tomorrow, but we'll go back real soon, okay?"

"Okay."

"G'night." She left the door open and flipped off the hall light. "Sleep tight. Don't let the bedbugs bite."

I could hear little noises, water running, toilet flushing. Then all was quiet. I got out of bed and knelt in front of my window. I could see lights in the house next door, and somewhere a car drove by with its radio blaring. I stayed there for a while, trying to feel sleepy, and then I stood up and everything changed.

Saturday, January 2, 1988, 4:03 a.m./ Sunday, June 16, 1968, 10:46 p.m. (Henry is 24, and 5)

HENRY: It's 4:03 a.m. on a supremely cold January morning and I'm just getting home. I've been out dancing and I'm only half drunk but utterly exhausted. As I fumble with my keys in the bright foyer I fall to my knees, dizzy and nauseated, and then I am in the dark, vomiting on a tile floor. I raise my head and see a red illuminated EXIT sign and as my eyes adjust I see tigers, cavemen with long spears, cavewomen wearing strategically modest skins, wolfish dogs. My heart is racing and for a long liquor-addled moment I think *Holy shit, I've gone all the way back to the Stone Age* until I realize that EXIT signs tend to congregate in the twentieth century. I get up, shaking, and venture toward the doorway, tile icy under my bare feet, gooseflesh and all my hairs standing up. It's absolutely silent. The air is clammy with air conditioning. I reach the entrance and look into the next room. It's full of glass cases; the white streetlight glow through the high windows shows me thousands of beetles. I'm in the Field Museum, praise the Lord. I stand still and breathe deeply, trying to clear my head. Something about this rings a bell in my fettered brain and I try to dredge it up. I'm supposed to do something. Yes. My fifth birthday . . . someone was there, and I'm about to be that someone . . . I need clothes. Yes. Indeed.

I sprint through beetlemania into the long hallway that bisects the second floor, down the west staircase to the first floor, grateful to be in the pre-motion-detector era. The great elephants loom menacingly over me in the moonlight and I wave to them on my way to the little gift shop to the right of the main entrance. I circle the wares and find a few promising items: an ornamental letter opener, a metal bookmark with the Field's insignia, and two T-shirts that feature dinosaurs. The locks on the cases are a joke; I pop them with a bobby pin I find next to the cash register, and help myself. Okay. Back up the stairs, to the third floor. This is the Field's "attic," where the labs are; the staff have their offices up here. I scan the names on the doors, but none of them suggests anything to me; finally I select at random and slide my bookmark along the lock until the catch pushes back and I'm in.

The occupant of this office is one V. M. Williamson, and he's a very untidy guy. The room is dense with papers, and coffee cups and cigarettes overflow from ashtrays; there's a partially articulated snake skeleton on his desk. I quickly case the joint for clothes and come up with nothing. The next office belongs to a woman, J. F. Bettley. On the third try I get lucky. D. W. Fitch has an entire suit hung neatly on his coat rack, and it pretty much fits me, though it's a bit short in the arms and legs and wide in the lapels. I wear one of the dinosaur T-shirts under the jacket. No shoes, but I'm decent. D. W. also keeps an unopened package of Oreo cookies in his desk, bless him. I appropriate them and leave, closing the door carefully behind me.

Where was I, when I saw me? I close my eyes and fatigue takes me bodily, caressing me with her sleepy fingers. I am almost out on my feet, but I catch myself and it comes to me: a man in silhouette walking toward me backlit by the museum's front doors. I need to get back to the Great Hall.

When I get there all is quiet and still. I walk across the middle of the floor, trying to replicate the view of the doors, and then I seat myself near the coat room, so as to enter stage left. I can hear blood rushing in my head, the air conditioning system humming, cars whooshing by on Lake Shore Drive. I eat ten Oreos, slowly, gently prying each one apart, scraping the filling out with my front teeth, nibbling the chocolate halves to make them last. I have no idea what time it is, or how long I have to wait. I'm mostly sober now, and reasonably alert. Time passes, nothing happens. At last: I hear a soft thud, a gasp. Silence. I wait. I stand up, silently, and pad into the Hall, walking slowly through the light that slants across the marble floor. I stand in the center of the doors and call out, not loud: "Henry."

Nothing. Good boy, wary and silent. I try again. "It's okay, Henry. I'm your guide, I'm here to show you around. It's a special tour. Don't be afraid, Henry."

I hear a slight, oh-so-faint noise. "I brought you a T-shirt, Henry. So you won't get cold while we look at the exhibits." I can make him out now, standing at the edge of the darkness. "Here. Catch." I throw it to him, and the shirt disappears, and then he steps into the light. The T-shirt comes down to his knees. Me at five, dark spiky hair, moon pale with brown almost Slavic eyes, wiry, coltish. At five I am happy, cushioned in normality and the arms of my parents. Everything changed, starting now.

I walk forward slowly, bend toward him, speak softly. "Hello. I'm glad to see you, Henry. Thank you for coming tonight."

"Where am I? Who are you?" His voice is small and high, and echoes a little off the cold stone.

THE TIME TRAVELER'S WIFE

"You're in the Field Museum. I have been sent here to show you some things you can't see during the day. My name is also Henry. Isn't that funny?"

He nods.

"Would you like some cookies? I always like to eat cookies while I look around museums. It makes it more multisensory." I offer him the package of Oreos. He hesitates, unsure if it's all right, hungry but unsure how many he can take without being rude. "Take as many as you want. I've already eaten ten, so you have some catching up to do." He takes three. "Is there anything you'd like to see first?" He shakes his head. "Tell you what. Let's go up to the third floor; that's where they keep all the stuff that isn't on display. Okay?"

"Okay."

We walk through darkness, up the stairs. He isn't moving very fast, so I climb slowly with him.

"Where's Mom?"

"She's at home, sleeping. This is a special tour, only for you, because it's your birthday. Besides, grown-ups don't do this sort of thing."

"Aren't you a grown-up?"

"I'm an extremely unusual grown-up. My job is to have adventures. So naturally when I heard that you wanted to come back to the Field Museum right away, I jumped at the chance to show you around."

"But how did I get here?" He stops at the top of the stairs and looks at me with total confusion.

"Well, that's a secret. If I tell you, you have to swear not to say anything to anyone."

"Why?"

29

"Because they wouldn't believe you. You can tell Mom, or Kimy if you want, but that's it. Okay?"

"Okay. . . ."

I kneel in front of him, my innocent self, look him in the eyes. "Cross your heart and hope to die?"

"Uh-huh. . . ."

"Okay. Here's how it is: you time traveled. You were in your bedroom, and all of a sudden, poof! you are here, and it's a little earlier in the evening, so we have plenty of time to look at everything before you have to go home." He is silent and quizzical. "Does that make sense?"

"But . . . why?"

"Well, I haven't figured that out yet. I'll let you know when I do. In the meantime, we should be moving along. Cookie?"

He takes one and we walk slowly down the corridor. I decide to experiment. "Let's try this one." I slide the bookmark along a door marked *306* and open it. When I flick on the lights there are pumpkin-sized rocks all over the floor, whole and halved, craggy on the outside and streaked with veins of metal inside. "Ooh, look, Henry. Meteorites."

"What's meterites?"

"Rocks that fall from outer space." He looks at me as though I'm from outer space. "Shall we try another door?" He nods. I close the meteorite room and try the door across the corridor. This room is full of birds. Birds in simulated flight, birds perched eternally on branches, bird heads, bird skins. I open one of the hundreds of drawers; it contains a dozen glass tubes, each holding a tiny gold and black bird with its name wrapped around a foot. Henry's eyes are the size of saucers. "Do you want to touch one?"

"Uh-huh."

I remove the cotton wadding from the mouth of a tube and

shake a goldfinch onto my palm. It remains tube-shaped. Henry strokes its small head, lovingly. "It's sleeping?"

"More or less." He looks at me sharply, distrusting my equivocation. I insert the finch gently back into the tube, replace the cotton, replace the tube, shut the drawer. I am so tired. Even the word sleep is a lure, a seduction. I lead the way out into the hall, and suddenly I recollect what it was I loved about this night when I was little.

"Hey, Henry. Let's go to the library." He shrugs. I walk, quickly now, and he runs to keep up. The library is on the third floor, at the east end of the building. When we get there, I stand for a minute, contemplating the locks. Henry looks at me, as though to say, Well, that's that. I feel in my pockets, and find the letter opener. I wiggle the wooden handle off, and lo, there's a nice long thin metal prong in there. I stick one half of it into the lock and feel around. I can hear the tumblers springing, and when I'm all the way back I stick in the other half, use my bookmark on the other lock and presto, Open Sesame!

At last, my companion is suitably impressed. "How'd you do that?"

"It's not that hard. I'll teach you another time. *Entrez!*" I hold open the door and he walks in. I flip on the lights and the Reading Room springs into being; heavy wooden tables and chairs, maroon carpet, forbidding enormous Reference Desk. The Field Museum's Library is not designed to appeal to five-year-olds. It's a closed-stacks library, used by scientists and scholars. There are bookcases lining the room, but they hold mostly leather-bound Victorian science periodicals. The book I'm after is in a huge glass and oak case by itself in the center of the room. I spring the lock with my bobby pin and open the glass door. Really, the Field ought to get more serious about security. I don't feel too terrible about doing this; after all, I'm a bona fide librarian, I do Show and Tells at the Newberry all the time. I walk behind the Reference Desk and find a piece of felt and some support pads, and lay them out on the nearest table. Then I close and carefully lift the book out of its case and onto the felt. I pull out a chair. "Here, stand on this so you can see better." He climbs up, and I open the book.

It's Audubon's *Birds of America,* the deluxe, wonderful double-elephant folio that's almost as tall as my young self. This copy is the finest in existence, and I have spent many rainy afternoons admiring it. I open it to the first plate, and Henry smiles, and looks at me. "'*Common Loon,*'" he reads. "It looks like a duck."

"Yeah, it does. I bet I can guess your favorite bird."

He shakes his head and smiles.

"What'll you bet?"

He looks down at himself in the T-rex T-shirt and shrugs. I know the feeling.

"How about this: if I guess you get to eat a cookie, and if I can't guess you get to eat a cookie?"

He thinks it over and decides this would be a safe bet. I open the book to *Flamingo.* Henry laughs.

"Am I right?"

"Yes!"

It's easy to be omniscient when you've done it all before. "Okay, here's your cookie. And I get one for being right. But we have to save them 'til we're done looking at the book; we wouldn't want to get crumbs all over the bluebirds, right?"

"Right!" He sets the Oreo on the arm of the chair and we begin again at the beginning and page slowly through the birds, so much more alive than the real thing in glass tubes down the hall.

"Here's a great blue heron. He's really big, bigger than a flamingo. Have you ever seen a hummingbird?"

"I saw some today!"

"Here in the museum?"

"Uh-huh."

"Wait 'til you see one outside—they're like tiny helicopters, their wings go so fast you just see a blur. . . ." Turning each page is like making a bed, an enormous expanse of paper slowly rises up and over. Henry stands attentively, waits each time for the new wonder, emits small noises of pleasure for each sandhill crane, American coot, great auk, pileated woodpecker. When we come to the last plate, *Snow Bunting*, he leans down and touches the page, delicately stroking the engraving. I look at him, look at the book, remember, this book, this moment, the first book I loved, remember wanting to crawl into it and sleep.

"You tired?"

"Uh-huh."

"Should we go?"

"Okay."

I close *Birds of America*, return it to its glass home, open it to *Flamingo*, shut the case, lock it. Henry jumps off the chair and eats his Oreo. I return the felt to the desk and push the chair in. Henry turns out the light, and we leave the library.

We wander, chattering amiably of things that fly and things that slither, and eating our Oreos. Henry tells me about Mom and Dad and Mrs. Kim, who is teaching him to make lasagna, and Brenda, whom I had forgotten about, my best pal when I was little until her family moved to Tampa, Florida, about three months from now. We are standing in front of Bushman, the legendary silverback gorilla, whose stuffed magnificence glowers at us from his little marble stand in a first floor hallway, when Henry cries out, and staggers forward, reaching urgently for me, and I grab him, and he's gone. The T-shirt is warm empty cloth in my hands. I sigh, and walk upstairs to ponder the mummies for a while by myself. My young self will be home now, climbing into bed. I remember, I remember. I woke up in the morning and it was all a wonderful dream. Mom laughed and said that time travel sounded fun, and she wanted to try it, too.

That was the first time.

FIRST DATE, TWO

•••••••••••••••••••••••••••••••

Friday, September 23, 1977 (Henry is 36, Clare is 6)

HENRY: I'm in the Meadow, waiting. I wait slightly outside the clearing, naked, because the clothes Clare keeps for me in a box under a stone are not there; the box isn't there either, so I am thankful that the afternoon is fine, early September, perhaps, in some unidentified year. I hunker down in the tall grass. I consider. The fact that there is no box full of clothes means that I have arrived in a time before Clare and I have met. Perhaps Clare isn't even born yet. This has happened before, and it's a pain; I miss Clare and I spend the time hiding naked in the Meadow, not daring to show myself in the neighborhood of Clare's family. I think longingly of the apple trees at the western edge of the Meadow. At this time of year there ought to be apples, small and sour and munched by deer, but edible. I hear the screen door slam and I peer above the grass. A child is running, pell mell, and as it comes down the path through the waving grass my heart twists and Clare bursts into the clearing.

She is very young. She is oblivious; she is alone. She is still wearing her school uniform, a hunter green jumper with a white blouse and knee socks with penny loafers, and she is carrying a Marshall

Field's shopping bag and a beach towel. Clare spreads the towel on the ground and dumps out the contents of the bag: every imaginable kind of writing implement. Old ballpoint pens, little stubby pencils from the library, crayons, smelly Magic Markers, a fountain pen. She also has a bunch of her dad's office stationery. She arranges the implements and gives the stack of paper a smart shake, and then proceeds to try each pen and pencil in turn, making careful lines and swirls, humming to herself. After listening carefully for a while I identify her humming as the theme song of *The Dick Van Dyke Show.*

I hesitate. Clare is content, absorbed. She must be about six; if it's September she has probably just entered first grade. She's obviously not waiting for me, I'm a stranger, and I'm sure that the first thing you learn in first grade is not to have any truck with strangers who show up naked in your favorite secret spot and know your name and tell you not to tell your mom and dad. I wonder if today is the day we are supposed to meet for the first time or if it's some other day. Maybe I should be very silent and either Clare will go away and I can go munch up those apples and steal some laundry or I will revert to my regularly scheduled programming.

I snap from my reverie to find Clare staring straight at me. I realize, too late, that I have been humming along with her.

"Who's there?" Clare hisses. She looks like a really pissed off goose, all neck and legs. I am thinking fast.

"Greetings, Earthling," I intone, kindly.

"Mark! You nimrod!" Clare is casting around for something to throw, and decides on her shoes, which have heavy, sharp heels. She whips them off and does throw them. I don't think she can see me very well, but she lucks out and one of them catches me in the mouth. My lip starts to bleed.

"Please don't do that." I don't have anything to staunch the blood, so I press my hand to my mouth and my voice comes out muffled. My jaw hurts.

"Who is it?" Now Clare is frightened, and so am I.

"Henry. It's Henry, Clare. I won't hurt you, and I wish you wouldn't throw anything else at me."

"Give me back my shoes. I don't know you. Why are you hiding?" Clare is glowering at me.

I toss her shoes back into the clearing. She picks them up and stands holding them like pistols. "I'm hiding because I lost my clothes and I'm embarrassed. I came a long way and I'm hungry and I don't know anybody and now I'm bleeding."

"Where did you come from? Why do you know my name?"

The whole truth and nothing but the truth. "I came from the future. I am a time traveler. In the future we are friends."

"People only time travel in movies."

"That's what we want you to believe."

"Why?"

"If everybody time traveled it would get too crowded. Like when you went to see your Grandma Abshire last Christmas and you had to go through O'Hare Airport and it was very, very crowded? We time travelers don't want to mess things up for ourselves, so we keep it quiet."

Clare chews on this for a minute. "Come out."

"Loan me your beach towel." She picks it up and all the pens and pencils and papers go flying. She throws it at me, overhand, and I grab it and turn my back as I stand and wrap it around my waist. It is bright pink and orange with a loud geometric pattern. Exactly the sort of thing you'd want to be wearing when you meet your future wife for the first time. I turn around and walk into the clearing; I sit on the rock with as much dignity as possible. Clare stands as far away from me as she can get and remain in the clearing. She is still clutching her shoes.

"You're bleeding."

"Well, yeah. You threw a shoe at me."

"Oh."

Silence. I am trying to look harmless, and nice. Nice looms large in Clare's childhood, because so many people aren't.

"You're making fun of me."

"I would never make fun of you. Why do you think I'm making fun of you?"

Clare is nothing if not stubborn. "Nobody time travels. You're lying."

"Santa time travels."

"What?"

"Sure. How do you think he gets all those presents delivered in one night? He just keeps turning back the clock a few hours until he gets down every one of those chimneys."

"Santa is magic. You're not Santa."

"Meaning I'm not magic? Geez, Louise, you're a tough customer."

"I'm not Louise."

"I know. You're Clare. Clare Anne Abshire, born May 24, 1971. Your parents are Philip and Lucille Abshire, and you live with them and your grandma and your brother, Mark, and your sister, Alicia, in that big house up there."

"Just because you know things doesn't mean you're from the future."

"If you hang around a while you can watch me disappear." I feel I can count on this because Clare once told me it was the thing she found most impressive about our first meeting.

Silence. Clare shifts her weight from foot to foot and waves away a mosquito. "Do you know Santa?"

"Personally? Um, no." I have stopped bleeding, but I must look awful. "Hey, Clare, do you happen to have a Band-Aid? Or some food? Time traveling makes me pretty hungry."

She thinks about this. She digs into her jumper pocket and produces a Hershey bar with one bite out of it. She throws it at me.

"Thank you. I love these." I eat it neatly but very quickly. My blood sugar is low. I put the wrapper in her shopping bag. Clare is delighted.

"You eat like a dog."

"I do not!" I am deeply offended. "I have opposable thumbs, thank you very much."

"What are posable thumbs?"

"Do this." I make the "okay" sign. Clare makes the "okay" sign. "Opposable thumbs means you can do that. It means you can open jars and tie your shoes and other things animals can't do."

Clare is not happy with this. "Sister Carmelita says animals don't have souls."

"Of course animals have souls. Where did she get that idea?"

"She said the Pope says."

"The Pope's an old meanie. Animals have much nicer souls than we do. They never tell lies or blow anybody up."

"They eat each other."

"Well, they have to eat each other; they can't go to Dairy Queen and get a large vanilla cone with sprinkles, can they?" This is Clare's favorite thing to eat in the whole wide world (as a child. As an adult Clare's favorite food is sushi, particularly sushi from Katsu on Peterson Avenue).

"They could eat grass."

"So could we, but we don't. We eat hamburgers."

Clare sits down at the edge of the clearing. "Etta says I shouldn't talk to strangers."

"That's good advice."

Silence.

"When are you going to disappear?"

"When I'm good and ready to. Are you bored with me?" Clare rolls her eyes. "What are you working on?"

"Penmanship."

"May I see?"

Clare gets up carefully and collects a few pieces of stationery while fixing me with her baleful stare. I lean forward slowly and extend my hand as though she is a Rottweiler, and she quickly shoves the papers at me and retreats. I look at them intently, as though she has just handed me a bunch of Bruce Rogers' original drawings for Centaur or the Book of Kells or something. She has printed, over and over, large and larger, "Clare Anne Abshire." All the ascenders and descenders have swirling curlicues and all the counters have smiley faces in them. It's quite beautiful.

"This is lovely."

Clare is pleased, as always when she receives homage for her work. "I could make one for you."

"I would like that. But I'm not allowed to take anything with me when I time travel, so maybe you could keep it for me and I could just enjoy it while I'm here."

"Why can't you take anything?"

"Well, think about it. If we time travelers started to move things around in time, pretty soon the world would be a big mess. Let's say I brought some money with me into the past. I could look up all the winning lottery numbers and football teams and make a ton of money. That doesn't seem very fair, does it? Or if I was really dishonest, I could steal things and bring them to the future where nobody could find me."

"You could be a pirate!" Clare seems so pleased with the idea of me as a pirate that she forgets that I am Stranger Danger. "You could bury the money and make a treasure map and dig it up in the future." This is in fact more or less how Clare and I fund our rock-and-roll lifestyle. As an adult Clare finds this mildly immoral, although it does give us an edge in the stock market.

"That's a great idea. But what I really need isn't money, it's clothing."

Clare looks at me doubtfully.

"Does your dad have any clothes he doesn't need? Even a pair of pants would be great. I mean, I like this towel, don't get me wrong, it's just that where I come from, I usually like to wear pants." Philip Abshire is a tad shorter than me and about thirty pounds heavier. His pants are comical but comfortable on me.

"I don't know. . . ."

"That's okay, you don't need to get them right now. But if you bring some next time I come, it would be very nice."

"Next time?"

I find an unused piece of stationery and a pencil. I print in block letters: THURSDAY, SEPTEMBER 29, 1977 AFTER SUPPER. I hand Clare the paper, and she receives it cautiously. My vision is blurring. I can hear Etta calling Clare. "It's a secret, Clare, okay?"

"Why?"

"Can't tell. I have to go, now. It was nice to meet you. Don't take any wooden nickels." I hold out my hand and Clare takes it, bravely. As we shake hands, I disappear.

Wednesday, February 9, 2000 (Clare is 28, Henry is 36)

CLARE: It's early, about six in the morning and I'm sleeping the thin dreamy sleep of six in the morning when Henry slams me awake and I realize he's been elsewhen. He materializes practically on top of me and I yell, and we scare the shit out of each other and then he starts laughing and rolls over and I roll over and look at him and realize that his mouth is bleeding profusely. I jump up to get a washcloth and Henry is still smiling when I get back and start daubing at his lip.

"How'd that happen?"

"You threw a shoe at me." I don't remember ever throwing anything at Henry.

"Did not."

"Did too. We just met for the very first time, and as soon as you laid eyes on me you said, 'That's the man I'm going to marry,' and you pasted me one. I always said you were an excellent judge of character."

Thursday, September 29, 1977 (Clare is 6, Henry is 35)

CLARE: The calendar on Daddy's desk this morning said the same as the paper the man wrote. Nell was making a soft egg for Alicia and Etta was yelling at Mark cause he didn't do his homework and played Frisbee with Steve. I said *Etta can I have some clothes from the trunks?* meaning the trunks in the attic where we play dress up, and Etta said *What for?* and I said *I want to play dress up with Megan* and Etta got mad and said *It was time to go to school and I could worry about playing when I got home.* So I went to school and we did adding and mealworms and language arts and after lunch French and music and religion. I worried all day about pants for the man cause he seemed like he really wanted pants. So when I got home I went to ask Etta again but she was in town but Nell let me lick both the beaters of cake batter which Etta won't let us because you get salmon. And Mama was writing and I was gonna go away without asking but she said *What is it, Baby?* so I asked and she said

I could go look in the Goodwill bags and have anything I wanted. So I went to the laundry room and looked in the Goodwill bags and found three pairs of Daddy's pants but one had a big cigarette hole. So I took two and I found a white shirt like Daddy wears to work and a tie with fishes on it and a red sweater. And the yellow bathrobe that Daddy had when I was little and it smelled like Daddy. I put the clothes in a bag and put the bag in the mudroom closet. When I was coming out of the mud room Mark saw me and he said *What are you doing, asshole?* And I said *Nothing, asshole* and he pulled my hair and I stepped on his foot really hard and then he started to cry and went to tell. So I went up to my room and played Television with Mr. Bear and Jane where Jane is the movie star and Mr. Bear asks her about how it is being a movie star and she says she really wants to be a veterinarian but she is so incredibly pretty she has to be a movie star and Mr. Bear says maybe she could be a veterinarian when she's old. And Etta knocked and said *Why are you stepping on Mark?* and I said *Because Mark pulled my hair for no reason* and Etta said *You two are getting on my nerves* and went away so that was okay. We ate dinner with just Etta because Daddy and Mama went to a party. It was fried chicken with little peas and chocolate cake and Mark got the biggest piece but I didn't say anything because I licked the beaters. So after dinner I asked Etta if I could go outside and she said did I have homework and I said *Spelling and bring leaves for art class,* and she said *Okay as long as you come in by dark.* So I went and got my blue sweater with the zebras and I got the bag and I went out and went to the clearing. But the man wasn't there and I sat on the rock for a while and then I thought I better get some leaves. So I went back to the garden and found some leaves from Mama's little tree that she told me later was Ginkgo, and some leaves from the Maple and the Oak. So then I went back to the clearing he still wasn't there and I thought *Well, I guess he just made up that he was coming and he didn't want pants so bad after all.* And I thought maybe Ruth was right 'cause I told her about the man and she said I was making it up because people don't disappear in real life only on TV. Or maybe it was a dream like when Buster died and I dreamed he was okay and he was in his cage but I woke up and no Buster and Mama said *Dreams are different than real life but important too.* And it was getting cold and I thought maybe I should just leave the bag and if the man came he could have his pants. So I was walking back up the path and there was this noise and somebody said *Ouch. Dang, that hurt.* And then I was scared.

HENRY: I kind of slam into the rock when I appear and scrape my knees. I am in the clearing and the sun is setting beautifully in a spectacular J. M. W. Turner blowout orange and red over the trees. The clearing is empty except for a shopping bag full of clothes and I rapidly deduce that Clare has left these and this is probably a day shortly after our first meeting. Clare is nowhere in sight and I call her name softly. No response. I dig through the bag of clothes. There's the pair of chinos and the beautiful pair of brown wool trousers, a hideous tie with trout all over it, the Harvard sweater, the oxford-cloth white shirt with ring around the collar and sweat stains under the arms, and the exquisite silk bathrobe with Philip's monogram and a big tear over the pocket. All these clothes are old friends, except for the tie, and I'm happy to see them. I don the chinos and the sweater and bless Clare's apparently hereditary good taste and sense. I feel great; except for the lack of shoes I'm well equipped for my current location in spacetime. "Thanks, Clare, you did a great job," I call softly.

I am surprised when she appears at the entrance to the clearing. It's getting dark quickly and Clare looks tiny and scared in the half light.

THE TIME TRAVELER'S WIFE

"Hi."

"Hi, Clare. Thanks for the clothes. They're perfect, and they'll keep me nice and warm tonight."

"I have to go in soon."

"That's okay, it's almost dark. Is it a school night?"

"Uh-huh."

"What's the date?"

"Thursday, September 29, 1977."

"That's very helpful. Thanks."

"How come you don't know that?"

"Well, I just got here. A few minutes ago it was Monday, March 27, 2000. It was a rainy morning and I was making toast."

"But you wrote it down for me." She takes out a piece of Philip's law office letterhead and holds it out for me. I walk to her and take it, and am interested to see the date written on it in my careful block lettering. I pause and grope for the best way to explain the vagaries of time travel to the small child who is Clare at the moment.

"It's like this. You know how to use a tape recorder?"

"Mmhmm."

"Okay. So you put in a tape and you play it from the beginning to the end, right?"

"Yeah. . . ."

"That's how your life is. You get up in the morning and you eat breakfast and you brush your teeth and you go to school, right? You don't get up and suddenly find yourself at school eating lunch with Helen and Ruth and then all of a sudden you're at home getting dressed, right?"

Clare giggles. "Right."

"Now for me, it's different. Because I am a time traveler, I jump around a lot from one time to another. So it's like if you started the tape and played it for a while but then you said Oh I want to hear that song again, so you played that song and then you went back to where you left off but you wound the tape too far ahead so you rewound it again but you still got it too far ahead. You see?"

"Sort of."

"Well, it's not the greatest analogy in the world. Basically, sometimes I get lost in time and I don't know when I am."

"What's analogy?"

"It's when you try to explain something by saying it's like another thing. For example, at the moment I am as snug as a bug in a rug in this nice sweater, and you are as pretty as a picture, and Etta is going to be as mad as a hatter if you don't go in pretty soon."

"Are you going to sleep here? You could come to our house, we have a guest room."

"Gosh, that's very nice of you. Unfortunately, I am not allowed to meet your family until 1991."

Clare is utterly perplexed. I think part of the problem is that she can't imagine dates beyond the '70s. I remember having the same problem with the '60s when I was her age. "Why not?"

"It's part of the rules. People who time travel aren't supposed to go around talking to regular people while they visit their times, because we might mess things up." Actually, I don't believe this; things happen the way they happened, once and only once. I'm not a proponent of splitting universes.

"But you talk to me."

"You're special. You're brave and smart and good at keeping secrets."

Clare is embarrassed. "I told Ruth, but she didn't believe me."

"Oh. Well, don't worry about it. Very few people ever believe me, either. Especially doctors. Doctors don't believe anything unless you can prove it to them."

"I believe you."

Clare is standing about five feet away from me. Her small pale face catches the last orange light from the west. Her hair is pulled back tightly into a ponytail and she is wearing blue jeans and a dark sweater with zebras running across the chest. Her hands are clenched and she looks fierce and determined. Our daughter, I think sadly, would have looked like this.

"Thank you, Clare."

"I have to go in now."

"Good idea."

"Are you coming back?"

I consult the List, from memory. "I'll be back October 16. It's a Friday. Come here, right after school. Bring that little blue diary Megan gave you for your birthday and a blue ballpoint pen." I repeat the date, looking at Clare to make sure she is remembering.

"Au revoir, Clare."

"Au revoir. . . ."

"Henry."

"*Au revoir, Henri.*" Already her accent is better than mine. Clare turns and runs up the path, into the arms of her lighted and welcoming house, and I turn to the dark and begin to walk across the meadow. Later in the evening I chuck the tie in the dumpster behind Dina's Fish 'n Fry.

Lessons in Survival

....

Thursday, June 7, 1973 (Henry is 27, and 9)

HENRY: I am standing across the street from the Art Institute of Chicago on a sunny June day in 1973 in the company of my nine-year-old self. He is traveling from next Wednesday; I have come from 1990. We have a long afternoon and evening to frivol as we will, and so we have come to one of the great art museums of the world for a little lesson in pickpocketing.

"Can't we just look at the art?" pleads Henry. He's nervous. He's never done this before.

"Nope. You need to know this. How are you going to survive if you can't steal anything?"

"Begging."

"Begging is a drag, and you keep getting carted off by the police. Now, listen: when we get in there, I want you to stay away from me and pretend we don't know each other. But be close enough to watch what I'm doing. If I hand you anything, don't drop it, and put it in your pocket as fast as you can. Okay?"

"I guess. Can we go see St. George?"

"Sure." We cross Michigan Avenue and walk between students

and housewives sunning themselves on the museum steps. Henry pats one of the bronze lions as we go by.

I feel moderately bad about this whole thing. On the one hand, I am providing myself with urgently required survival skills. Other lessons in this series include Shoplifting, Beating People Up, Picking Locks, Climbing Trees, Driving, Housebreaking, Dumpster Diving, and How to Use Oddball Things like Venetian Blinds and Garbage Can Lids as Weapons. On the other hand, I'm corrupting my poor innocent little self. I sigh. Somebody's got to do it.

It's Free Day, so the place is swarming with people. We stand in line, move through the entry, and slowly climb the grandiose central staircase. We enter the European Galleries and make our way backward from the seventeenth-century Netherlands to fifteenth-century Spain. St. George stands poised, as always, ready to transfix his dragon with his delicate spear while the pink and green princess waits demurely in the middleground. My self and I love the yellow-bellied dragon wholeheartedly, and we are always relieved to find that his moment of doom has still not arrived.

Henry and I stand before Bernardo Martorell's painting for five minutes, and then he turns to me. We have the gallery to ourselves at the moment.

"It's not so hard," I say. "Pay attention. Look for someone who is distracted. Figure out where the wallet is. Most men use either their back pocket or the inside pocket of their suit jacket. With women you want the purse behind their back. If you're on the street you can just grab the whole purse, but then you have to be sure you can outrun anybody who might decide to chase you. It's much quieter if you can take it without them noticing."

"I saw a movie where they practiced with a suit of clothes with little bells and if the guy moved the suit while he took the wallet the bells rang."

"Yeah, I remember that movie. You can try that at home. Now follow me." I lead Henry from the fifteenth century to the nineteenth; we arrive suddenly in the midst of French Impressionism. The Art Institute is famous for its Impressionist collection. I can take it or leave it, but as usual these rooms are jam-packed with people craning for a glimpse of *La Grande Jatte* or a Monet Haystack. Henry can't see over the heads of the adults, so the paintings are lost on him, but he's too nervous to look at them anyway. I scan the room. A woman is bending over her toddler as it twists and screams. Must be nap time. I nod at Henry and move toward her. Her purse has a simple clasp and is slung over her shoulder, across her back. She's totally focused on getting her child to stop screeching. She's in front of Toulouse-Lautrec's *At the Moulin Rouge*. I pretend to be looking at it as I walk, bump into her, sending her pitching forward, I catch her arm, "I'm so sorry, forgive me, I wasn't looking, are you all right? It's so crowded in here. . . ." My hand is in her purse, she's flustered, she has dark eyes and long hair, large breasts, she's still trying to lose the weight she gained having the kid. I catch her eye as I find her wallet, still apologizing, the wallet goes up my jacket sleeve, I look her up and down and smile, back away, turn, walk, look over my shoulder. She has picked up her boy and is staring back at me, slightly forlorn. I smile and walk, walk. Henry is following me as I take the stairs down to the Junior Museum. We rendezvous by the men's toilets.

"That was weird," says Henry. "Why'd she look at you like that?"

"She's lonely," I euphemize. "Maybe her husband isn't around very much." We cram ourselves into a stall and I open her wallet. Her name is Denise Radke. She lives in Villa Park, Illinois. She is a member of the museum and an alumna of Roosevelt University.

She is carrying twenty-two dollars in cash, plus change. I show all this to Henry, silently, put the wallet back as it was, and hand it to him. We walk out of the stall, out of the men's room, back toward the entrance to the museum. "Give this to the guard. Say you found it on the floor."

"Why?"

"We don't need it; I was just demonstrating." Henry runs to the guard, an elderly black woman who smiles and gives Henry a sort of half-hug. He comes back slowly, and we walk ten feet apart, with me leading, down the long dark corridor which will someday house Decorative Arts and lead to the as-yet-unthought-of Rice Wing, but which at the moment is full of posters. I'm looking for easy marks, and just ahead of me is a perfect illustration of the pickpocket's dream. Short, portly, sunburnt, he looks as though he's made a wrong turn from Wrigley Field in his baseball cap and polyester trousers with light blue short-sleeved button-down shirt. He's lecturing his mousy girlfriend on Vincent van Gogh.

"So he cuts his ear off and gives it to his girl—hey, how'd you like that for a present, huh? An ear! Huh. So they put him in the loony bin . . ."

I have no qualms about this one. He strolls on, braying, blissfully unaware, with his wallet in his left back pocket. He has a large gut but almost no backside, and his wallet is pretty much aching for me to take it. I amble along behind them. Henry has a clear view as I deftly insert my thumb and forefinger into the mark's pocket and liberate the wallet. I drop back, they walk on, I pass the wallet to Henry and he shoves it into his pants as I walk ahead.

I show Henry some other techniques: how to take a wallet from the inside breast pocket of a suit, how to shield your hand from view while it's inside a woman's purse, six different ways to distract someone while you take their wallet, how to take a wallet out of a backpack, and how to get someone to inadvertently show you where their money is. He's more relaxed now, he's even starting to enjoy this. Finally, I say, "Okay, now you try."

He's instantly petrified. "I can't."

"Sure you can. Look around. Find someone." We are standing in the Japanese Print Room. It's full of old ladies.

"Not here."

"Okay, where?"

He thinks for a minute. "The restaurant?"

We walk quietly to the restaurant. I remember this all vividly. I was totally terrified. I look over at my self and sure enough, his face is white with fear. I'm smiling, because I know what comes next. We stand at the end of the line for the garden restaurant. Henry looks around, thinking.

In front of us in line is a very tall middle-aged man wearing a beautifully cut brown lightweight suit; it's impossible to see where the wallet is. Henry approaches him, with one of the wallets I've lifted earlier proffered on his outstretched hand.

"Sir? Is this yours?" says Henry softly. "It was on the floor."

"Uh? Oh, hmm, no," the man checks his right back pants pocket, finds his wallet safe, leans over Henry to hear him better, takes the wallet from Henry and opens it. "Hmm, my, you should take this to the security guards, hmm, there's quite a bit of cash in here, yes," the man wears thick glasses and peers at Henry through them as he speaks and Henry reaches around under the man's jacket and steals his wallet. Since Henry is wearing a short-sleeved T-shirt I walk behind him and he passes the wallet to me. The tall thin brown-suited man points at the stairs, explaining to Henry how to turn in the wallet. Henry toddles off in the direction the man has indicated, and I follow, overtake Henry and lead him right through the museum to the entrance and out, past the guards, onto Michigan Avenue and south, until we end up, grinning like fiends, at the Artists Cafe, where we treat ourselves to milkshakes and french fries with some of our ill-gotten gains. Afterwards we throw all the wallets in a mailbox, sans cash, and I get us a room at the Palmer House.

"So?" I ask, sitting on the side of the bathtub watching Henry brush his teeth.

"O ot?" returns Henry with a mouth full of toothpaste.

"What do you think?"

He spits. "About what?"

"Pickpocketing."

He looks at me in the mirror. "It's okay." He turns and looks directly at me. "I did it!" He grins, largely.

"You were brilliant!"

"Yeah!" The grin fades. "Henry, I don't like to time travel by myself. It's better with you. Can't you always come with me?"

He is standing with his back to me, and we look at each other in the mirror. Poor small self: at this age my back is thin and my shoulder blades stick out like incipient wings. He turns, waiting for an answer, and I know what I have to tell him—me. I reach out and gently turn him and bring him to stand by me, so we are side by side, heads level, facing the mirror.

"Look." We study our reflections, twinned in the ornate gilt Palmer House bathroom splendor. Our hair is the same brown-black, our eyes slant dark and fatigue-ringed identically, we sport exact replicas of each other's ears. I'm taller and more muscular and shave. He's slender and ungainly and is all knees and elbows. I reach up and pull my hair back from my face, show him the scar from the accident. Unconsciously, he mimics my gesture, touches the same scar on his own forehead.

"It's just like mine," says my self, amazed. "How did you get it?"

"The same as you. It is the same. We are the same."

A translucent moment. I didn't understand, and then I did, just like that. I watch it happen. I want to be both of us at once, feel again the feeling of losing the edges of my self, of seeing the admixture of future and present for the first time. But I'm too accustomed, too comfortable with it, and so I am left on the outside, remembering the wonder of being nine and suddenly seeing, knowing, that my friend, guide, brother was *me*. Me, only me. The loneliness of it.

"You're me."

"When you are older."

"But . . . what about the others?"

"Other time travelers?"

He nods.

"I don't think there are any. I mean, I've never met any others."

A tear gathers at the edge of his left eye. When I was little, I imagined a whole society of time travelers, of which Henry, my teacher, was an emissary, sent to train me for eventual inclusion in this vast camaraderie. I still feel like a castaway, the last member of a once numerous species. It was as though Robinson Crusoe discovered the telltale footprint on the beach and then realized that it was his own. My self, small as a leaf, thin as water, begins to cry. I hold him, hold me, for a long time.

Later, we order hot chocolate from room service, and watch Johnny Carson. Henry falls asleep with the light on. As the show ends I look over at him and he's gone, vanished back to my old room in my dad's apartment, standing sleep-addled beside my old bed, falling into it, gratefully. I turn off the TV and the bedside lamp. 1973 street noises drift in the open window. I want to go home. I lie on the hard hotel bed, desolate, alone. I still don't understand.

Sunday, December 10, 1978 (Henry is 15, and 15)

HENRY: I'm in my bedroom with my self. He's here from next March. We are doing what we often do when we have a little privacy, when it's cold out, when both of us are past puberty and haven't quite gotten around to actual girls yet. I think most people would do this, if they had the sort of opportunities I have. I mean, I'm not gay or anything.

It's late Sunday morning. I can hear the bells ringing at St. Joe's. Dad came home late last night; I think he must have stopped at the Exchequer after the concert; he was so drunk he fell down on the stairs and I had to haul him into the apartment and put him to bed. He coughs and I hear him messing around in the kitchen.

My other self seems distracted; he keeps looking at the door. "What?" I ask him. "Nothing," he says. I get up and check the lock. "*No,*" he says. He seems to be making a huge effort to speak. "Come on," I say.

I hear Dad's heavy step right outside my door. "Henry?" he says, and the knob of the door slowly turns and I abruptly realize that I have inadvertently *unlocked* the door and Henry leaps for it but it's too late: Dad sticks his head in and there we are, *in flagrante delicto.* "Oh," he says. His eyes are wide and he looks completely disgusted. "Jesus, Henry." He shuts the door and I hear him walking back to his room. I throw my self a reproachful glare as I pull on a pair of jeans and a T-shirt. I walk down the hall to Dad's bedroom. His door is shut. I knock. No answer. I wait. "Dad?" Silence. I open the door, stand in the doorway. "Dad?" He's sitting with his back to me, on his bed. He continues to sit, and I stand there for a while, but I can't bring myself to walk into the room. Finally I shut the door, walk back to my own room.

"That was completely and totally your fault," I tell my self severely. He is wearing jeans, sitting on the chair with his head in his hands. "You knew, *you knew* that was going to happen and you didn't say a word. Where is your sense of self preservation? What the *hell* is wrong with you? What use is it knowing the future if you can't at least protect us from humiliating little scenes—"

"Shut up," Henry croaks. "Just shut up."

"I will *not* shut up," I say, my voice rising. "I mean, all you had to do was say—"

"Listen." He looks up at me with resignation. "It was like . . . it was like that day at the ice-skating rink."

"Oh. Shit." A couple years ago, I saw a little girl get hit in the head with a hockey puck at Indian Head Park. It was horrible. I found out later that she died in the hospital. And then I started to time travel back to that day, over and over, and I wanted to warn her mother, and I *couldn't*. It was like being in the audience at a movie. It was like being a ghost. I would scream, *No, take her home, don't let her near the ice, take her away, she's going to get hurt, she's going to die,* and I would realize that the words were only in my head, and everything would go on as before.

Henry says, "You talk about changing the future, but for me this is the past, and as far as I can tell there's nothing I can do about it. I mean, I tried, and it was the trying that made it happen. If I hadn't said something, you wouldn't have gotten up. . . ."

"Then why did you say anything?"

"Because I did. You will, just wait." He shrugs. "It's like with Mom. The accident. *Immer weider.*" Always again, always the same.

"Free will?"

He gets up, walks to the window, stands looking out over the Tatingers' backyard. "I was just talking about that with a self from 1992. He said something interesting: he said that he thinks there is only free will when you are in time, in the present. He says in the past we can only do what we did, and we can only be there if we were there."

"But whenever I am, that's my present. Shouldn't I be able to decide—"

"No. Apparently not."

"What did he say about the future?"

"Well, think. You go to the future, you do something, you come back to the present. Then the thing that you did is part of your past. So that's probably inevitable, too."

I feel a weird combination of freedom and despair. I'm sweating; he opens the window and cold air floods into the room. "But then I'm not responsible for anything I do while I'm not in the present."

He smiles. "Thank God."

"And everything has already happened."

"Sure looks that way." He runs his hand over his face, and I see that he could use a shave. "But he said that you have to *behave* as though you have free will, as though you are responsible for what you do."

"Why? What does it matter?"

"Apparently, if you don't, things are bad. Depressing."

"Did he know that personally?"

"Yes."

"So what happens next?"

"Dad ignores you for three weeks. And this"—he waves his hand at the bed—"we've got to stop meeting like this."

I sigh. "Right, no problem. Anything else?"

"Vivian Teska."

Vivian is this girl in Geometry whom I lust after. I've never said a word to her.

"After class tomorrow, go up to her and ask her out."

"I don't even know her."

"Trust me." He's smirking at me in a way that makes me wonder why on earth I would ever trust him but I want to believe. "Okay."

"I should get going. Money, please." I dole out twenty dollars. "More." I hand him another twenty.

"That's all I've got."

"Okay." He's dressing, pulling clothes from the stash of things I don't mind never seeing again. "How about a coat?" I hand him a Peruvian skiing sweater that I've always hated. He makes a face and puts it on. We walk to the back door of the apartment. The church bells are tolling noon. "Bye," says my self.

"Good luck," I say, oddly moved by the sight of me embarking into the unknown, into a cold Chicago Sunday morning he doesn't belong in. He thumps down the wooden stairs, and I turn to the silent apartment.

Wednesday, November 17/ Tuesday, September 28, 1982 (Henry is 19)

HENRY: I'm in the back of a police car in Zion, Illinois. I am wearing handcuffs and not much else. The interior of this particular police car smells like cigarettes, leather, sweat, and another odor I can't identify that seems endemic to police cars. The odor of freak-outedness, perhaps. My left eye is swelling shut and the front of my body is covered with bruises and cuts and dirt from being tackled by the larger of the two policemen in an empty lot full of broken glass. The policemen are standing outside the car talking to the neighbors, at least one of whom evidently saw me trying to break into the yellow and white Victorian house we are parked in front of. I don't know where I am in time. I've been here for about an hour, and I have fucked up completely. I'm very hungry. I'm very tired. I'm supposed to be in Dr. Quarrie's Shakespeare seminar, but I'm sure I've managed to miss it. Too bad. We're doing *A Midsummer Night's Dream.*

The upside of this police car is: it's warm and I'm not in Chicago. Chicago's Finest hate me because I keep disappearing while I'm in custody, and they can't figure it out. Also I refuse to talk to them, so they still don't know who I am, or where I live. The day they find out, I'm toast because there are several outstanding warrants for my arrest: breaking and entering, shoplifting, resisting arrest, breaking arrest, trespassing, indecent exposure, robbery, *und so weiter.* From this one might deduce that I am a very inept criminal, but really the main problem is that it's so hard to be inconspicuous when you're naked. Stealth and speed are my main assets and so, when I try to burgle houses in broad daylight stark naked, sometimes it doesn't work out. I've been arrested seven times, and so far I've always vanished before they can fingerprint me or take a photo.

The neighbors keep peering in the windows of the police car at me. I don't care. I don't care. This is taking a long time. Fuck, I hate this. I lean back and close my eyes.

A car door opens. Cold air—my eyes fly open—for an instant I see the metal grid that separates the front of the car from the back, the cracked vinyl seats, my hands in the cuffs, my gooseflesh legs, the flat sky through the windshield, the black visored hat on the dashboard, the clipboard in the officer's hand, his red face, tufted graying eyebrows and jowls like drapes—everything shimmers, iridescent, butterfly-wing colors and the policeman says, "Hey, he's having some kinda fit—" and my teeth are chattering hard and before my eyes the police car vanishes and I am lying on my back in my own backyard. Yes. Yes! I fill my lungs with the sweet September night air. I sit up and rub my wrists, still marked where the hand-cuffs were.

I laugh and laugh. I have escaped again! Houdini, Prospero, behold me! for I am a magician, too.

Nausea overcomes me, and I heave bile onto Kimy's mums.

Saturday, May 14, 1983 (Clare is 11 almost 12)

CLARE: It's Mary Christina Heppworth's birthday and all the fifth-grade girls from St. Basil's are sleeping over at her house. We have pizza and Cokes and fruit salad for dinner, and Mrs. Hepp-worth made a big cake shaped like a unicorn's head with *Happy Birthday Mary Christina!* in red icing and we sing and Mary Christina blows out all twelve candles in one blow. I think I know what she wished for; I think she wished not to get any taller. That's what I would wish if I were her, anyway. Mary Christina is the tallest person in our class. She's 5'9". Her mom is a little shorter than her, but her dad is really, really tall. Helen asked Mary Christina once and she said he's 6'7". She's the only girl in her family, and her brothers are all older and shave and they're really tall, too. They make a point of ignoring us and eating a lot of cake and Patty and Ruth especially giggle a lot whenever they come where we are. It's so embarrassing. Mary Christina opens her presents. I got her a green sweater just like my blue one that she liked with the crocheted collar from Laura Ashley. After dinner we watch *The Parent Trap* on video and the Heppworth family kind of hangs around watching us until we all take turns putting on our pajamas in the second floor bathroom and we crowd into Mary Christina's room that is deco-rated totally in pink, even the wall-to-wall carpet. You get the feel-ing Mary Christina's parents were really glad to finally have a girl after all those brothers. We have all brought our sleeping bags, but we pile them against one wall and sit on Mary Christina's bed and on the floor. Nancy has a bottle of Peppermint Schnapps and we all drink some. It tastes awful, and it feels like Vicks VapoRub in my chest. We play Truth or Dare. Ruth dares Wendy to run down the hall without her top on. Wendy asks Francie what size bra Lexi, Francie's seventeen-year-old sister, wears. (Answer: 38D.) Francie asks Gayle what she was doing with Michael Plattner at the Dairy Queen last Saturday. (Answer: eating ice cream. Well, duh.) After a while we all get bored with Truth or Dare, mainly because it's hard to think of good dares that any of us will actually do, and because we all pretty much know whatever there is to know about each other, because we've been going to school together since kinder-garten. Mary Christina says, "Let's do Ouija board," and we all agree, because it's her party and cause Ouija board is cool. She gets it out of her closet. The box is all mashed, and the little plastic thing that shows the letters is missing its plastic window. Henry told me once that he went to a seance and the medium had her appendix burst in the middle of it and they had to call an ambulance. The board is only really big enough for two people to do it at once, so Mary Christina and Helen go first. The rule is you have to ask what you want to know out loud or it won't work. They each put their fingers on the plastic thing. Helen looks at Mary Christina, who hesitates and Nancy says, "Ask about Bobby," so Mary Christina asks, "Does Bobby Duxler like me?" Everybody giggles. The answer is no, but the Ouija says *yes,* with a little pushing by Helen. Mary Christina smiles so hugely I can see her braces, top and bottom. Helen asks if any boys like her. The Ouija circles around for a while, and then stops on D, A, V. "David Hanley?" says Patty, and everybody laughs. Dave is the only black kid in our class. He's real shy and small and he's good at math. "Maybe he'll help you with long division," says Laura, who is also very shy. Helen laughs. She's terrible at math. "Here, Clare. You and Ruth try." We take Helen and Mary Christina's places. Ruth looks at me and I shrug. "I don't know what to ask," I say. Everybody snickers; how many possible questions are there? But there are so many things I want to know. *Is Mama going to be okay? Why was Daddy yelling at Etta this morning? Is Henry a real person? Where did Mark hide my French homework?* Ruth says, "What boys like Clare?" I give her a mean look, but she just smiles. "Don't you want to know?" "No," I say, but I put my fingers on the white plastic anyway. Ruth puts her fingers on too and nothing moves. We are both touching the thing very lightly, we are trying to do it right and not push. Then it starts to move, slow. It goes in circles, and then stops on H. Then it speeds up. E, N, R, Y. "Henry," says Mary Christina, "who's Henry?" Helen says, "I don't know, but you're blushing, Clare. Who *is* Henry?" I just shake my head, like it's a mystery to me, too. "You ask, Ruth." She asks (big surprise) who likes her; the Ouija spells out R, I, C, K. I can feel her pushing. Rick is Mr. Malone, our Science teacher, who has a crush on Miss Engle, the English teacher. Everybody except Patty laughs; Patty has a crush on Mr. Malone, too. Ruth and I get up and Laura and Nancy sit down. Nancy has her back to me, so I can't see her face when she asks, "Who is Henry?" Everybody looks at me and gets real quiet. I watch the board. Nothing. Just as I'm thinking I'm safe, the plastic thing starts to move. H, it says. I think maybe it will just spell Henry again; after all, Nancy and Laura don't know anything about Henry. *I* don't even know that much about Henry. Then it goes on: U, S, B, A, N, D. They all look at me. "Well, I'm not *married;* I'm only *eleven.*" "But who's Henry?" wonders Laura. "I don't know. Maybe he's somebody I haven't met yet." She nods. Everyone is weirded out. I'm very weirded out. Husband? *Husband?*

Thursday, April 12, 1984 (Henry is 36, Clare is 12)

HENRY: Clare and I are playing chess in the fire circle in the woods. It's a beautiful spring day, and the woods are alive with birds courting and birds nesting. We are keeping ourselves out of the way of Clare's family, who are out and about this afternoon. Clare has been stuck on her move for a while; I took her Queen three moves ago and now she is doomed but determined to go down fighting.

She looks up. "Henry, who's your favorite Beatle?"

"John. Of course."

"Why 'of course'?"

"Well, Ringo is okay but kind of a sad sack, you know? And George is a little too New Age for my taste."

"What's 'New Age'?"

"Oddball religions. Sappy boring music. Pathetic attempts to convince oneself of the superiority of anything connected with Indians. Non-Western medicine."

"But you don't like regular medicine."

"That's because doctors are always trying to tell me I'm crazy. If I had a broken arm I would be a big fan of Western medicine."

"What about Paul?"

"Paul is for girls."

Clare smiles, shyly. "I like Paul best."

"Well, you're a girl."

"Why is Paul for girls?"

Tread carefully, I tell myself. "Uh, gee. Paul is, like, the Nice Beatle, you know?"

"Is that bad?"

"No, not at all. But guys are more interested in being cool, and John is the Cool Beatle."

"Oh. But he's dead."

I laugh. "You can still be cool when you're dead. In fact, it's much easier, because you aren't getting old and fat and losing your hair."

Clare hums the beginning of "When I'm 64." She moves her rook forward five spaces. I can checkmate her now, and I point this out to her and she hastily takes back the move.

"So why do you like Paul?" I ask her. I look up in time to see her blushing fervently.

"He's so . . . *beautiful,*" Clare says. There's something about the way she says it that makes me feel strange. I study the board, and it occurs to me that Clare could checkmate me if she took my bishop with her knight. I wonder if I should tell her this. If she was a little younger, I would. Twelve is old enough to fend for yourself. Clare is staring dreamily at the board. It dawns on me that I am jealous. Jesus. I can't believe I'm feeling jealous of a multimillionaire rock star geezer old enough to be Clare's dad.

"Hmpf," I say.

Clare looks up, smiling mischievously. "Who do you like?"

You, I think but don't say. "You mean when I was your age?"

"Um, yeah. When were you my age?"

I weigh the value and potential of this nugget before I dole it out. "I was your age in 1975. I'm eight years older than you."

"So you're twenty?"

"Well, no, I'm thirty-six." Old enough to be your dad.

Clare furrows her brow. Math is not her strongest subject. "But if you were twelve in 1975. . . ."

"Oh, sorry. You're right. I mean, I myself am thirty-six, but somewhere out there"—I wave my hand toward the south—"I'm twenty. In real time."

Clare strives to digest this. "So there are two of you?"

"Not exactly. There's always only one me, but when I'm time traveling sometimes I go somewhere I already am, and yeah, then you could say there are two. Or more."

"How come I never see more than one?"

"You will. When you and I meet in my present that will happen fairly frequently." *More often than I'd like, Clare.*

"So who did you like in 1975?"

"Nobody, really. At twelve I had other stuff to think about. But when I was thirteen I had this huge crush on Patty Hearst."

Clare looks annoyed. "A girl you knew at school?"

I laugh. "No. She was a rich Californian college girl who got kidnapped by these awful left-wing political terrorists, and they made her rob banks. She was on the news every night for months."

"What happened to her? Why did you like her?"

"They eventually let her go, and she got married and had kids and now she's a rich lady in California. Why did I like her? Ah, I don't know. It's irrational, you know? I guess I kind of knew how she felt, being taken away and forced to do stuff she didn't want to do, and then it seemed like she was kind of enjoying it."

"Do you do things you don't want to do?"

"Yeah. All the time." My leg has fallen asleep and I stand up and shake it until it tingles. "I don't always end up safe and sound with you, Clare. A lot of times I go places where I have to get clothes and food by stealing."

"Oh." Her face clouds, and then she sees her move, and makes it, and looks up at me triumphantly. "Checkmate!"

"Hey! Bravo!" I salaam her. "You are the chess queen *du jour.*"

"Yes, I am," Clare says, pink with pride. She starts to set the pieces back in their starting positions. "Again?"

I pretend to consult my nonexistent watch. "Sure." I sit down again. "You hungry?" We've been out here for hours and supplies have run low; all we have left is the dregs of a bag of Doritos.

"Mmhmm." Clare holds the pawns behind her back; I tap her right elbow and she shows me the white pawn. I make my standard opening move, Queen's Pawn to Q4. She makes her standard response to my standard opening move, Queen's Pawn to Q4. We play out the next ten moves fairly rapidly, with only moderate bloodshed, and then Clare sits for a while, pondering the board. She is always experimenting, always attempting the *coup d'éclat.* "Who do you like now?" she asks without looking up.

"You mean at twenty? Or at thirty-six?"

"Both."

I try to remember being twenty. It's just a blur of women, breasts, legs, skin, hair. All their stories have jumbled together, and their faces no longer attach themselves to names. I was busy but miserable at twenty. "Twenty was nothing special. Nobody springs to mind."

"And thirty-six?"

I scrutinize Clare. Is twelve too young? I'm sure twelve is really too young. Better to fantasize about beautiful, unattainable, safe Paul McCartney than to have to contend with Henry the Time Traveling Geezer. Why is she asking this anyway?

"Henry?"

"Yeah?"

"Are you married?"

"Yes," I admit reluctantly.

"To who?"

"A very beautiful, patient, talented, smart woman."

Her faces falls. "Oh." She picks up one of my white bishops, which she captured two moves ago, and spins it on the ground like a top. "Well, that's nice." She seems kind of put out by this news.

"What's wrong?"

"Nothing." Clare moves her queen from Q2 to KN5. "Check."

I move my knight to protect my king.

"Am I married?" Clare inquires.

I meet her eyes. "You're pushing your luck today."

"Why not? You never tell me anything anyway. Come on, Henry, tell me if I'm gonna be an old maid."

"You're a nun," I tease her.

Clare shudders. "Boy, I hope not." She takes one of my pawns with her rook. "How did you meet your wife?"

"Sorry. Top secret information." I take her rook with my queen.

Clare makes a face. "Ouch. Were you time traveling? When you met her?"

"*I* was minding my own business."

Clare sighs. She takes another pawn with her other rook. I'm starting to run low on pawns. I move Queen's Bishop to KB4.

"It's not fair that you know everything about me but you never tell me anything about you."

"True. It's not fair." I try to look regretful, and obliging.

"I mean, Ruth and Helen and Megan and Laura tell me everything and I tell them everything."

"Everything?"

"Yeah. Well, I don't tell them about you."

"Oh? Why's that?"

Clare looks a bit defensive. "You're a secret. They wouldn't believe me, anyway." She traps my bishop with her knight, flashes me a sly smile. I contemplate the board, trying to find a way to take her knight or move my bishop. Things are looking grim for White. "Henry, are you really a person?"

I am a bit taken aback. "Yes. What else would I be?"

"I don't know. A spirit?"

"I'm really a person, Clare."

"Prove it."

"How?"

"I don't know."

"I mean, I don't think you could prove that *you're* a person, Clare."

"Sure I can."

"How?"

"I'm just like a person."

"Well, I'm just like a person, too." It's funny that Clare is bringing this up; back in 1999 Dr. Kendrick and I are engaged in philosophical trench warfare over this very issue. Kendrick is convinced that I am a harbinger of a new species of human, as different from everyday folks as Cro-Magnon Man was from his Neanderthal neighbors. I contend that I'm just a piece of messed-up code, and our inability to have kids proves that I'm not going to be the Missing Link. We've taken to quoting Kierkegaard and Heidegger at each other and glowering. Meanwhile, Clare regards me doubtfully.

"*People* don't appear and disappear the way you do. You're like the Cheshire Cat."

"Are you implying that I'm a fictional character?" I spot my move, finally: King's Rook to QR3. Now she can take my bishop but she'll lose her queen in the process. It takes Clare a moment to realize this and when she does she sticks out her tongue at me. Her tongue is a worrisome shade of orange from all the Doritos she's eaten.

"It makes me kind of wonder about fairy tales. I mean, if you're real, then why shouldn't fairy tales be real, too?" Clare stands up, still pondering the board, and does a little dance, hopping around like her pants are on fire. "I think the ground is getting harder. My butt's asleep."

"Maybe they are real. Or some little thing in them is real and then people just added to it, you know?"

"Like maybe Snow White was in a coma?"

"And Sleeping Beauty, too."

"And Jack the beanstalk guy was just a real terrific gardener."

"And Noah was a weird old man with a houseboat and a lot of cats."

Clare stares at me. "Noah is in the *Bible*. He's not a fairy tale."

"Oh. Right. Sorry." I'm getting very hungry. Any minute now Nell will ring the dinner bell and Clare will have to go in. She sits back down on her side of the board. I can tell she's lost interest in the game when she starts building a little pyramid out of all the conquered pieces.

"You still haven't proved you're real," Clare says.

"Neither have you."

"Do you ever wonder if I'm real?" she asks me, surprised.

"Maybe I'm dreaming you. Maybe you're dreaming me; maybe we only exist in each other's dreams and every morning when we wake up we forget all about each other."

Clare frowns, and makes a motion with her hand as though to bat away this odd idea. "Pinch me," she requests. I lean over and pinch her lightly on the arm. "Harder!" I do it again, hard enough to leave a white and red mark that lingers for some seconds and then vanishes. "Don't you think I would wake up, if I was asleep? Anyway, I don't feel asleep."

"Well, I don't feel like a spirit. Or a fictional character."

"How do you know? I mean, if I was making you up, and I didn't want you to know you were made up, I just wouldn't tell you, right?"

I wiggle my eyebrows at her. "Maybe God just made us up and He's not telling us."

"You shouldn't say things like that," Clare exclaims. "Besides, you don't even believe in God. Do you?"

I shrug, and change the subject. "I'm more real than Paul McCartney."

Clare looks worried. She starts to put all the pieces back in their box, carefully dividing white and black. "Lots of people know about Paul McCartney—I'm the only one who knows about you."

"But you've actually met me, and you've never met him."

"My mom went to a Beatles concert." She closes the lid of the chess set and stretches out on the ground, staring up at the canopy of new leaves. "It was at Comiskey Park, in Chicago, August 8, 1965." I poke her in the stomach and she curls up like a hedgehog, giggling. After an interval of tickling and thrashing around, we lie on the ground with our hands clasped across our middles and Clare asks, "Is your wife a time traveler too?"

"Nope. Thank God."

"Why 'thank God'? I think that would be fun. You could go places together."

"One time traveler per family is more than enough. It's dangerous, Clare."

"Does she worry about you?"

"Yes," I say softly. "She does." I wonder what Clare is doing now, in 1999. Maybe she's still asleep. Maybe she won't know I'm gone.

"Do you love her?"

"Very much," I whisper. We lie silently side by side, watching the swaying trees, the birds, the sky. I hear a muffled sniffling noise and glancing at Clare I am astonished to see that tears are streaming across her face toward her ears. I sit up and lean over her. "What's wrong, Clare?" She just shakes her head back and forth and presses her lips together. I smooth her hair, and pull her into a sitting position, wrap my arms around her. She's a child, and then again she isn't. "What's wrong?"

It comes out so quietly that I have to ask her to repeat it: "It's just that I thought maybe you were married to me."

Wednesday, June 27, 1984 (Clare is 13)

CLARE: I am standing in the Meadow. It's late June, late afternoon; in a few minutes it will be time to wash up for supper. The temperature is dropping. Ten minutes ago the sky was coppery blue and there was a heavy heat over the Meadow, everything felt curved, like being under a vast glass dome, all near noises swallowed up in the heat while an overwhelming chorus of insects droned. I have been sitting on the tiny footbridge watching waterbugs skating on the still small pool, thinking about Henry. Today isn't a Henry day; the next one is twenty-two days away. It is now much cooler. Henry is puzzling to me. All my life I have pretty much just accepted Henry as no big deal; that is, although Henry is a secret and therefore automatically fascinating, Henry is also some kind of miracle and just recently it's started to dawn on me that most girls don't have a Henry or if they do they've all been pretty quiet about it. There's a wind coming; the tall grass is rippling and I close my eyes so it sounds like the sea (which I have never seen except on TV). When I open them the sky is yellow and then green. Henry says he comes from the future. When I was little I didn't see any problem with that; I didn't have any idea what it might mean. Now I wonder if it means that the future is a place, or like a place, that I could go to; that is go to in some way other than just getting older. I wonder if Henry could take me to the future. The woods are black and the trees bend over and whip to the side and bow down. The insect hum is gone and the wind is smoothing everything, the grass is flat and the trees are creaking and groaning. I am afraid of the future; it seems to be a big box waiting for me. Henry says he knows me in the future. Huge black clouds are moving up from behind the trees, they come up so suddenly that I laugh, they are like puppets, and everything is swirling toward me and there is a long low peal of thunder. I am suddenly aware of myself standing thin and upright in a Meadow where everything has flattened itself down and so I lie down hoping to be unnoticed by the storm which rolls up and I am flat on my back looking up when water begins to pour down from the sky. My clothes are soaked in an instant and I suddenly feel that Henry is there, an incredible need for Henry to be there and to put his hands on me even while it seems to me that Henry is the rain and I am alone and wanting him.

Sunday, September 23, 1984 (Henry is 35, Clare is 13)

HENRY: I am in the clearing, in the Meadow. It's very early in the morning, just before dawn. It's late summer, all the flowers and grasses are up to my chest. It's chilly. I am alone. I wade through the plants and locate the clothes box, open it up, and find blue jeans and a white oxford shirt and flip-flops. I've never seen these clothes before, so I have no idea where I am in time. Clare has also left me a snack: there's a peanut butter and jelly sandwich carefully wrapped in aluminum foil, with an apple and a bag of Jay's potato chips. Maybe this is one of Clare's school lunches. My expectations veer in the direction of the late seventies or early eighties. I sit down on the rock and eat the food, and then I feel much better. The sun is rising.

The whole Meadow is blue, and then orange, and pink, the shadows are elongated, and then it is day. There's no sign of Clare. I crawl a few feet into the vegetation, curl up on the ground even though it is wet with dew, and sleep.

When I wake up the sun is higher and Clare is sitting next to me reading a book. She smiles at me and says, "Daylight in the swamp. The birds are singing and the frogs are croaking and it's time to get up!"

I groan and rub my eyes. "Hi, Clare. What's the date?"

"Sunday, September 23, 1984."

Clare is thirteen. A strange and difficult age, but not as difficult as what we are going through in my present. I sit up, and yawn. "Clare, if I asked very nicely, would you go into your house and smuggle out a cup of coffee for me?"

"Coffee?" Clare says this as though she has never heard of the substance. As an adult she is as much of an addict as I am. She considers the logistics.

"Pretty please?"

"Okay, I'll try." She stands up, slowly. This is the year Clare got tall, quickly. In the past year she has grown five inches, and she has not yet become accustomed to her new body. Breasts and legs and hips, all newly minted. I try not to think about it as I watch her walk up the path to the house. I glance at the book she was reading. It's a Dorothy Sayers, one I haven't read. I'm on page thirty-three by the time she gets back. She has brought a Thermos, cups, a blanket, and some doughnuts. A summer's worth of sun has freckled Clare's nose, and I have to resist the urge to run my hands through her bleached hair, which falls over her arms as she spreads out the blanket.

"Bless you." I receive the Thermos as though it contains a sacrament. We settle ourselves on the blanket. I kick off the flip-flops, pour out a cup of coffee, and take a sip. It's incredibly strong and bitter. "Yowza! This is rocket fuel, Clare."

"Too strong?" She looks a little depressed, and I hasten to compliment her.

"Well, there's probably no such thing as too strong, but it's pretty strong. I like it, though. Did you make it?"

"Uh-huh. I never made coffee before, and Mark came in and was kind of bugging me, so maybe I did it wrong."

"No, it's fine." I blow on the coffee, and gulp it down. I feel better immediately. I pour another cup.

Clare takes the Thermos from me. She pours herself half an inch of coffee and takes a cautious sip. "Ugh," she says. "This is disgusting. Is it supposed to taste like this?"

"Well, it's usually a little less ferocious. You like yours with lots of cream and sugar."

Clare pours the rest of her coffee into the Meadow and takes a doughnut. Then she says, "You're making me into a freak."

I don't have a ready reply for this, since the idea has never occurred to me. "Uh, no I'm not."

"You are so."

"Am not." I pause. "What do you mean, I'm making you into a freak? I'm not making you into anything."

"You know, like telling me that I like coffee with cream and sugar before I hardly even taste it. I mean, how am I going to figure out if that's what I like or if I just like it because you tell me I like it?"

"But Clare, it's just personal taste. You should be able to figure out how you like coffee whether I say anything or not. Besides, you're the one who's always bugging me to tell you about the future."

"Knowing the future is different from being told what I like," Clare says.

"Why? It's all got to do with free will."

Clare takes off her shoes and socks. She pushes the socks into the shoes and places them neatly at the edge of the blanket. Then she takes my cast-off flip-flops and aligns them with her shoes, as though the blanket is a tatami mat. "I thought free will had to do with sin."

I think about this. "No," I say, "why should free will be limited to right and wrong? I mean, you just decided, of your own free will, to take off your shoes. It doesn't matter, nobody cares if you wear shoes or not, and it's not sinful, or virtuous, and it doesn't affect the future, but you've exercised your free will."

Clare shrugs. "But sometimes you tell me something and I feel like the future is already there, you know? Like my future has happened in the past and I can't do anything about it."

"That's called determinism," I tell her. "It haunts my dreams."

Clare is intrigued. "Why?"

"Well, if *you* are feeling boxed in by the idea that your future is unalterable, imagine how *I* feel. I'm constantly running up against the fact that I can't change anything, even though I am right there, watching it."

"But Henry, you do change things! I mean, you wrote down that stuff that I'm supposed to give you in 1991 about the baby with Down Syndrome. And the List, if I didn't have the List I would never know when to come meet you. You change things all the time."

I smile. "I can only do things that work toward what has already happened. I can't, for example, undo the fact that you just took off your shoes."

Clare laughs. "Why would you care if I take them off or not?"

"I don't. But even if I did, it's now an unalterable part of the history of the universe and I can't do a thing about it." I help myself to a doughnut. It's a Bismarck, my favorite. The frosting is melting in the sun a little, and it sticks to my fingers.

Clare finishes her doughnut, rolls up the cuffs of her jeans and sits cross-legged. She scratches her neck and looks at me with annoyance. "Now you're making me self-conscious. I feel like every time I blow my nose it's a historic event."

"Well, it is."

She rolls her eyes. "What's the opposite of determinism?"

"Chaos."

"Oh. I don't think I like that. Do you like that?"

I take a big bite out of the Bismarck and consider chaos. "Well, I do and I don't. Chaos is more freedom; in fact, total freedom. But no meaning. I want to be free to act, and I also want my actions to mean something."

"But, Henry, you're forgetting about God—why can't there be a God who makes it mean something?" Clare frowns earnestly, and looks away across the Meadow as she speaks.

I pop the last of the Bismarck into my mouth and chew slowly to gain time. Whenever Clare mentions God my palms start to sweat and I have an urge to hide or run or vanish.

"I don't know, Clare. I mean, to me things seem too random and meaningless for there to be a God."

Clare clasps her arms around her knees. "But you just said before that everything seems like it's all planned out beforehand."

"Hpmf," I say. I grab Clare's ankles, pull her feet onto my lap, and hold on. Clare laughs, and leans back on her elbows. Clare's feet are cold in my hands; they are very pink and very clean. "Okay," I say, "let's see. The choices we're working with here are a block universe, where past, present and future all coexist simultaneously and everything has already happened; chaos, where anything can happen and nothing can be predicted because we can't know all the variables; and a Christian universe in which God made everything and it's all here for a purpose but we have free will anyway. Right?"

Clare wiggles her toes at me. "I guess."

"And what do you vote for?"

Clare is silent. Her pragmatism and her romantic feelings about Jesus and Mary are, at thirteen, almost equally balanced. A year ago she would have said God without hesitation. In ten years she will vote for determinism, and ten years after that Clare will believe that the universe is arbitrary, that if God exists he does not hear our prayers, that cause and effect are inescapable and brutal, but meaningless. And after that? I don't know. But right now Clare sits on the threshold of adolescence with her faith in one hand and her growing skepticism in the other, and all she can do is try to juggle them, or squeeze them together until they fuse. She shakes her head. "I don't know. I *want* God. Is that okay?"

I feel like an asshole. "Of course it's okay. That's what you believe."

"But I don't want to just believe it, I want it to be true."

I run my thumbs across Clare's arches, and she closes her eyes. "You and St. Thomas Aquinas both," I say.

"I've heard of him," Clare says, as though she's speaking of a long-lost favorite uncle, or the host of a TV show she used to watch when she was little.

"He wanted order and reason, and God, too. He lived in the thirteenth century and taught at the University of Paris. Aquinas believed in both Aristotle and angels."

"I love angels," says Clare. "They're so beautiful. I wish I could have wings and fly around and sit on clouds."

"'*Ein jeder Engel ist schrecklich.*'"

Clare sighs, a little soft sigh that means *I don't speak German, remember?* "Huh?"

"'Every angel is terrifying.' It's part of a series of poems called *The Duino Elegies,* by a poet named Rilke. He's one of our favorite poets."

Clare laughs. "You're doing it again!"

"What?"

"Telling me what I like." Clare burrows into my lap with her feet. Without thinking I put her feet on my shoulders, but then that seems too sexual, somehow, and I quickly take Clare's feet in my hands again and hold them together with one hand in the air as she lies on her back, innocent and angelic with her hair spread nimbus-like around her on the blanket. I tickle her feet. Clare giggles and twists out of my hands like a fish, jumps up and does a cartwheel across the clearing, grinning at me as if to dare me to come and get her. I just grin back, and she returns to the blanket and sits down next to me.

"Henry?"

"Yeah?"

"You are making me different."

"I know."

I turn to look at Clare and just for a moment I forget that she is young, and that this is long ago; I see Clare, my wife, superimposed on the face of this young girl, and I don't know what to say to this Clare who is old and young and different from other girls, who knows that different might be hard. But Clare doesn't seem to expect an answer. She leans against my arm, and I put my arm around her shoulders.

"*Clare!*" Across the quiet of the Meadow Clare's dad is bellowing her name. Clare jumps up and grabs her shoes and socks.

"It's time for church," she says, suddenly nervous.

"Okay," I say. "Um, bye." I wave at her, and she smiles and mumbles *goodbye* and is running up the path, and is gone. I lie in the sun for a while, wondering about God, reading Dorothy Sayers. After an hour or so has passed I too am gone and there is only a blanket and a book, coffee cups, and clothing, to show that we were there at all.

After the End

••••••••••••••••••••••••••••••••

Saturday, October 27, 1984 (Clare is 13, Henry is 43)

CLARE: I wake up suddenly. There was a noise: someone called my name. It sounded like Henry. I sit up in bed, listening. I hear the wind, and crows calling. But what if it was Henry? I jump out of bed and I run, with no shoes I run downstairs, out the back door, into the Meadow. It's cold, the wind cuts right through my night-gown. Where is he? I stop and look and there, by the orchard, there's Daddy and Mark, in their bright orange hunting clothes, and there's a man with them, they are all standing and looking at some-thing but then they hear me and they turn and I see that the man is Henry. What is Henry doing with Daddy and Mark? I run to them, my feet cut by the dead grasses, and Daddy walks to meet me. "Sweetheart," he says, "what are you doing out here so early?"

"I heard my name," I say. He smiles at me. *Silly girl*, his smile says, and I look at Henry, to see if he will explain. *Why did you call me, Henry?* but he shakes his head and puts his finger to his lips, *Shhh, don't tell, Clare.* He walks into the orchard and I want to see what they were looking at but there's nothing there and Daddy says, "Go back to bed, Clare, it was just a dream." He puts his arm around me and begins to walk back toward the house with me and I look back at Henry and he waves, he's smiling, *It's okay, Clare, I'll explain later* (although knowing Henry he probably won't explain, he'll make me figure it out or it will explain itself one of these days). I wave back at him, and then I check to see if Mark saw that but Mark has his back to us, he's irritated and is waiting for me to go away so he and Daddy can go back to hunting, but what is Henry doing here, what did they say to each other? I look back again but I don't see Henry and Daddy says, "Go on, now, Clare, go back to bed," and he kisses my forehead. He seems upset and so I run, run back to the house, and then softly up the stairs and then I am sitting on my bed, shivering, and I still don't know what just happened, but I know it was bad, it was very, very bad.

Monday, February 2, 1987 (Clare is 15, Henry is 38)

CLARE: When I get home from school Henry is waiting for me in the Reading Room. I have fixed a little room for him next to the furnace room; it's on the opposite side from where all the bicycles are. I have allowed it to be known in my household that I like to spend time in the basement reading, and I do in fact spend a lot of time in here, so that it doesn't seem unusual. Henry has a chair wedged under the doorknob. I knock four knocks and he lets me in. He has made a sort of nest out of pillows and chair cushions and blankets, he has been reading old magazines under my desk lamp. He is wearing Dad's old jeans and a plaid flannel shirt, and he looks tired and unshaven. I left the back door unlocked for him this morning and here he is.

I set the tray of food I have brought on the floor. "I could bring down some books."

"Actually, these are great." He's been reading *Mad* magazines from the '60s. "And this is indispensable for time travelers who need to know all sorts of factoids at a moment's notice," he says, holding up the 1968 *World Almanac.*

I sit down next to him on the blankets, and look over at him to see if he's going to make me move. I can see he's thinking about it, so I hold up my hands for him to see and then I sit on them. He smiles. "Make yourself at home," he says.

"When are you coming from?"

"2001. October."

"You look tired." I can see that he's debating about telling me why he's tired, and decides against it. "What are we up to in 2001?"

"Big things. Exhausting things." Henry starts to eat the roast beef sandwich I have brought him. "Hey, this is good."

"Nell made it."

He laughs. "I'll never understand why it is that you can build huge sculptures that withstand gale force winds, deal with dye recipes, cook kozo, and all that, and you can't do anything whatsoever with food. It's amazing."

"It's a mental block. A phobia."

"It's weird."

"I walk into the kitchen and I hear this little voice saying, 'Go away.' So I do."

"Are you eating enough? You look thin."

I feel fat. "I'm eating." I have a dismal thought. "Am I very fat in 2001? Maybe that's why you think I'm too thin."

Henry smiles at some joke I don't get. "Well, you're kind of plump at the moment, in my present, but it will pass."

"Ugh."

"Plump is good. It will look very good on you."

"No thanks." Henry looks at me, worrying. "You know, I'm not anorexic or anything. I mean, you don't have to worry about it."

"Well, it's just that your mom was always bugging you about it."

" 'Was'?"

"Is."

"Why did you say was?"

"No reason. Lucille is fine. Don't worry." He's lying. My stomach tightens and I wrap my arms around my knees and put my head down.

HENRY: I cannot believe that I have made a slip of the tongue of this magnitude. I stroke Clare's hair, and I wish fervently that I could go back to my present for just a minute, long enough to consult Clare, to find out what I should say to her, at fifteen, about her mother's death. It's because I'm not getting any sleep. If I was getting some sleep I would have been thinking faster, or at least covering better for my lapse. But Clare, who is the most truthful person I know, is acutely sensitive to even small lies, and now the only alternatives are to refuse to say anything, which will make her frantic, or to lie, which she won't accept, or to tell the truth, which will upset her and do strange things to her relationship with her mother. Clare looks at me. "Tell me," she says.

CLARE: Henry looks miserable. "I can't, Clare."

"Why not?"

"It's not good to know things ahead. It screws up your life."

"Yes. But you can't half tell me."

"There's nothing to tell."

I'm really beginning to panic. "She killed herself." I am flooded with certainty. It is the thing I have always feared most.

"*No.* No. Absolutely not."

I stare at him. Henry just looks very unhappy. I cannot tell if he is telling the truth. If I could only read his mind, how much easier life would be. Mama. Oh, Mama.

HENRY: This is dreadful. I can't leave Clare with this "Ovarian cancer," I say, very quietly.

"Thank God," she says, and begins to cry.

Friday, June 5, 1987 (Clare is 16, Henry is 32)

CLARE: I've been waiting all day for Henry. I'm so excited. I got my driver's license yesterday, and Daddy said I could take the Fiat to Ruth's party tonight. Mama doesn't like this at all, but since Daddy has already said yes she can't do much about it. I can hear them arguing in the library after dinner.

"You could have asked me—"

"It seemed harmless, Lucy. . . ."

I take my book and walk out to the Meadow. I lie down in the grass. The sun is beginning to set. It's cool out here, and the grass is full of little white moths. The sky is pink and orange over the trees in the west, and an arc of deepening blue over me. I am thinking about going back to the house and getting a sweater when I hear someone walking through the grass. Sure enough, it's Henry. He enters the clearing and sits down on the rock. I spy on him from the grass. He looks fairly young, early thirties maybe. He's wearing the plain black T-shirt and jeans and hi-tops. He's just sitting quietly, waiting. I can't wait a minute longer, myself, and I jump up and startle him.

"Jesus, Clare, don't give the geezer a heart attack."

"You're not a geezer."

Henry smiles. He's funny about being old.

"Kiss," I demand, and he kisses me.

"What was that for?" he asks.

"I got my driver's license!"

Henry looks alarmed. "Oh, no. I mean, congratulations."

I smile at him; nothing he says can ruin my mood. "You're just jealous."

"I am, in fact. I love to drive, and I never do."

"How come?"

"Too dangerous."

"Chicken."

"I mean for other people. Imagine what would happen if I was driving and I disappeared? The car would still be moving and *kaboom!* lots of dead people and blood. Not pretty."

I sit down on the rock next to Henry. He moves away. I ignore this. "I'm going to a party at Ruth's tonight. Want to come?"

He raises one eyebrow. This usually means he's going to quote from a book I've never heard of or lecture me about something. Instead he only says, "But Clare, that would involve meeting a whole bunch of your friends."

"Why not? I'm tired of being all secretive about this."

"Let's see. You're sixteen. I'm thirty-two right now, only twice your age. I'm sure no one would even notice, and your parents would never hear about it."

I sigh. "Well, I have to go to this party. Come with and sit in the car and I won't stay in very long and then we can go somewhere."

HENRY: We park about a block away from Ruth's house. I can hear the music all the way down here; it's Talking Heads' "Once In a Lifetime." I actually kind of wish I could go with Clare, but it would be unwise. She hops out of the car and says, "Stay!" as though I am a large, disobedient dog, and totters off in her heels and short skirt toward Ruth's. I slump down and wait.

CLARE: As soon as I walk in the door I know this party is a mistake. Ruth's parents are in San Francisco for a week, so at least she will have some time to repair, clean, and explain, but I'm glad it's not my house all the same. Ruth's older brother, Jake, has also invited his friends, and altogether there are about a hundred people here and all of them are drunk. There are more guys than girls and I wish I had worn pants and flats, but it's too late to do anything about it. As I walk into the kitchen to get a drink someone behind me says, "Check out Miss Look-But-Don't-Touch!" and makes an obscene slurping sound. I spin around and see the guy we call Lizardface (because of his acne) leering at me. "Nice dress, Clare."

"Thanks, but it's not for your benefit, Lizardface."

He follows me into the kitchen. "Now, that's not a very nice thing to say, young lady. After all, I'm just trying to express my appreciation of your extremely comely attire, and all you can do is insult me. . . ." He won't shut up. I finally escape by grabbing Helen and using her as a human shield to get out of the kitchen.

"This sucks," says Helen. "Where's Ruth?"

Ruth is hiding upstairs in her bedroom with Laura. They are smoking a joint in the dark and watching out the window as a bunch of Jake's friends skinny dip in the pool. Soon we are all sitting in the window seat gawking.

"Mmm," says Helen. "I'd like some of that."

"Which one?" Ruth asks.

"The guy on the diving board."

"Ooh."

"Look at Ron," says Laura.

"That's Ron?" Ruth giggles.

"Wow. Well, I guess anyone would look better without the Metallica T-shirt and the skanky leather vest," Helen says. "Hey, Clare, you're awfully quiet."

"Um? Yeah, I guess," I say weakly.

"Look at you," says Helen. "You are, like, cross-eyed with lust. I am ashamed of you. How could you let yourself get into such a state?" She laughs. "Seriously, Clare, why don't you just get it over with?"

"I can't," I say miserably.

"Sure you can. Just walk downstairs and yell 'Fuck me!' and about fifty guys would be yelling 'Me! Me!'"

"You don't understand. I don't want—it's not that—"

"She wants somebody in particular," Ruth says, without taking her eyes off the pool.

"Who?" Helen asks.

I shrug my shoulders.

"Come on, Clare, spit it out."

"Leave her alone," Laura says. "If Clare doesn't want to say, she doesn't have to." I am sitting next to Laura, and I lean my head on her shoulder.

Helen bounces up. "I'll be right back."

"Where you going?"

"I brought some champagne and pear juice to make Bellinis, but I left it in the car." She dashes out the door. A tall guy with shoulder-length hair does a backwards somersault off the diving board.

"Ooh la la," say Ruth and Laura in unison.

HENRY: A long time has passed, maybe an hour or so. I eat half the potato chips and drink the warm Coke Clare has brought along.

I nap a bit. She's gone for so long that I'm starting to consider going for a walk. Also I need to take a leak.

I hear heels tapping toward me. I look out the window, but it's not Clare, it's this bombshell blond girl in a tight red dress. I blink, and realize that this is Clare's friend Helen Powell. Uh oh.

She clicks over to my side of the car, leans over and peers at me. I can see right down her dress to Tokyo. I feel slightly woozy.

"Hi, Clare's boyfriend. I'm Helen."

"Wrong number, Helen. But pleased to meet you." Her breath is highly alcoholic.

"Aren't you going to get out of the car and be properly introduced?"

"Oh, I'm pretty comfortable where I am, thanks."

"Well, I'll just join you in there, then." She moves uncertainly around the front of the car, opens the door, and plops herself into the driver's seat.

"I've been wanting to meet you for the longest time," Helen confides.

"You have? Why?" I desperately wish Clare would come and rescue me, but then that would give the game away, wouldn't it?

Helen leans toward me and says, *sotto voce*, "I deduced your existence. My vast powers of observation have led me to the conclusion that whatever remains when you have eliminated the impossible, is the truth, no matter how impossible. Hence," Helen pauses to burp. "How unladylike. Excuse me. Hence, I have concluded that Clare must have a boyfriend, because otherwise, she would not be refusing to fuck all these very nice boys who are very much distressed about it. And here you are. Ta da!"

I've always liked Helen, and I am sad to have to mislead her. This does explain something she said to me at our wedding, though. I love it when little puzzle pieces drop into place like this.

"That's very compelling reasoning, Helen, but I'm not Clare's boyfriend."

"Then why are you sitting in her car?"

I have a brainstorm. Clare is going to kill me for this. "I'm a friend of Clare's parents. They were worried about her taking the car to a party where there might be alcohol, so they asked me to go along and play chauffeur in case she got too pickled to drive."

Helen pouts. "That's extremely not necessary. Our little Clare hardly drinks enough to fill a tiny, tiny thimble—"

"I never said she did. Her parents were just being paranoid."

High heels click down the sidewalk. This time it is Clare. She freezes when she sees that I have company.

Helen jumps out of the car and says, "Clare! This naughty man says he is not your boyfriend."

Clare and I exchange glances. "Well, he's not," says Clare curtly.

"Oh," says Helen. "Are you leaving?"

"It's almost midnight. I'm about to turn into a pumpkin." Clare walks around the car and opens her door. "Come on, Henry, let's go." She starts the car and flips on the lights.

Helen stands stock still in the headlights. Then she walks over to my side of the car. "Not her boyfriend, huh, *Henry?* You had me going there for a minute, yes you did. Bye bye, Clare." She laughs, and Clare pulls out of the parking space awkwardly and drives away. Ruth lives on Conger. As we turn onto Broadway, I see that all the street lights are off. Broadway is a two-lane highway. It's ruler-straight, but without the streetlights it's like driving into an inkwell.

"Better turn on your brights, Clare," I say. She reaches forward and turns the headlights off completely.

"Clare—!"

"Don't tell me what to do!" I shut up. All I can see are the illuminated numbers of the clock radio. It's 11:36. I hear the air rushing past the car, the engine of the car; I feel the wheels passing over the asphalt, but somehow we seem to be motionless, and the world moves around us at forty-five miles per hour. I close my eyes. It makes no difference. I open them. My heart is pounding.

Headlights appear in the distance. Clare turns her lights on and we are rushing along again, perfectly aligned between the yellow stripes in the middle of the road and the edge of the highway. It's 11:38.

Clare is expressionless in the reflected dashboard lights. "Why did you do that?" I ask her, my voice shaking.

"Why not?" Clare's voice is calm as a summer pond.

"Because we could have both died in a fiery wreck?"

Clare slows and turns onto Blue Star Highway. "But that's not what happens," she says. "I grow up and meet you and we get married and here you are."

"For all you know you crashed the car just then and we both spent a year in traction."

"But then you would have warned me not to do it," says Clare.

"I tried, but you yelled at me—"

"I mean, an older you would have told a younger me not to crash the car."

"Well, by then it would have already happened."

We have reached Meagram Lane, and Clare turns onto it. This is the private road that leads to her house. "Pull over, Clare, okay? Please?" Clare drives onto the grass, stops, cuts the engine and the lights. It's completely dark again, and I can hear a million cicadas singing. I reach over and pull Clare close to me, put my arm around her. She is tense and unpliant.

"Promise me something."

"What?" Clare asks.

"Promise you won't do anything like that again. I mean not just with the car, but anything dangerous. Because you don't know. The future is weird, and you can't go around behaving like you're invincible. . . ."

"But if you've seen me in the future—"

"Trust me. Just trust me."

Clare laughs. "Why would I want to do that?"

"I dunno. Because I love you?"

Clare turns her head so quickly that she hits me in the jaw.

"Ouch."

"Sorry." I can barely see the outline of her profile. "You love me?" she asks.

"Yes."

"Right now?"

"Yes."

"But you're not my boyfriend."

Oh. *That's* what's bugging her. "Well, technically speaking, I'm your husband. Since you haven't actually gotten married yet, I suppose we would have to say that you are my girlfriend."

Clare puts her hand someplace it probably shouldn't be. "I'd rather be your mistress."

"You're sixteen, Clare." I gently remove her hand, and stroke her face.

"That's old enough. Ugh, your hands are all wet." Clare turns on the overhead light and I am startled to see that her face and dress are streaked with blood. I look at my palms and they are sticky and red. "Henry! What's wrong?"

"I don't know." I lick my right palm and four deep crescent-shaped cuts appear in a row. I laugh. "It's from my fingernails. When you were driving without the headlights."

Clare snaps off the overhead light and we are sitting in the dark again. The cicadas sing with all their might. "I didn't mean to scare you."

"Yeah, you did. But usually I feel safe when you're driving. It's just—"

"What?"

"I was in a car accident when I was a kid, and I don't like to ride in cars."

"Oh—I'm sorry."

"'S okay. Hey, what time is it?"

"Oh my God." Clare flips the light on. 12:12. "I'm late. And how can I walk in all bloody like this?" She looks so distraught that I want to laugh.

"Here." I rub my left palm across her upper lip and under her nose. "You have a nosebleed."

"Okay." She starts the car, flips on the headlights, and eases back onto the road. "Etta's going to freak when she sees me."

"Etta? What about your parents?"

"Mama's probably asleep by now, and it's Daddy's poker night." Clare opens the gate and we pass through.

"If my kid was out with the car the day after she got her license I would be sitting next to the front door with a stopwatch." Clare stops the car out of sight of the house.

"Do we have kids?"

"Sorry, that's classified."

"I'm gonna apply for that one under the Freedom of Information Act."

"Be my guest." I kiss her carefully, so as not to disturb the faux nosebleed. "Let me know what you find out." I open the car door. "Good luck with Etta."

"Good night."

"'Night." I get out and close the door as quietly as possible. The car glides down the drive, around the bend and into the night. I walk after it toward a bed in the Meadow under the stars.

Sunday, September 27, 1987 (Henry is 32, Clare is 16)

H E N R Y : I materialize in the Meadow, about fifteen feet west of the clearing. I feel dreadful, dizzy and nauseated, so I sit for a few minutes to pull myself together. It's chilly and gray, and I am submerged in the tall brown grass, which cuts into my skin. After a while I feel a little better, and it's quiet, so I stand up and walk into the clearing.

Clare is sitting on the ground, next to the rock, leaning against it. She doesn't say anything, just looks at me with what I can only describe as anger. *Uh oh,* I think. *What have I done?* She's in her Grace Kelly phase; she's wearing her blue wool coat and a red skirt. I'm shivering, and I hunt for the clothes box. I find it, and don black jeans, a black sweater, black wool socks, a black overcoat, black boots, and black leather gloves. I look like I'm about to star in a Wim Wenders film. I sit down next to Clare.

"Hi, Clare. Are you okay?"

"Hi, Henry. Here." She hands me a Thermos and two sandwiches.

"Thanks. I feel kind of sick, so I'll wait a little." I set the food on the rock. The Thermos contains coffee; I inhale deeply. Just the smell makes me feel better. "Are you all right?" She's not looking at me. As I scrutinize Clare, I realize that she's been crying.

"Henry. Would you beat someone up for me?"

"What?"

"I want to hurt someone, and I'm not big enough, and I don't know how to fight. Will you do it for me?"

"Whoa. What are you talking about? Who? Why?"

Clare stares at her lap. "I don't want to talk about it. Couldn't you just take my word that he totally deserves it?"

I think I know what's going on; I think I've heard this story before. I sigh, and move closer to Clare, and put my arm around her. She leans her head on my shoulder.

"This is about some guy you went on a date with, right?"

"Yeah."

"And he was a jerk, and now you want me to pulverize him?"

"Yeah."

"Clare, lots of guys are jerks. *I* used to be a jerk—"

Clare laughs. "I bet you weren't as big of a jerk as Jason Everleigh."

"He's a football player or something, right?"

"Yes."

"Clare, what makes you think I can take on some huge jock half my age? Why were you even going out with someone like that?"

She shrugs. "At school, everybody's been bugging me 'cause I never date anyone. Ruth and Meg and Nancy—I mean, there are all these rumors going around that I'm a lesbian. Even Mama is asking me why I don't go out with boys. Guys ask me out, and I turn them down. And then Beatrice Dilford, who *is* a dyke, asked me if *I* was, and I told her no, and she said that she wasn't surprised, but that's what everybody was saying. So then I thought, well, maybe I'd better go out with a few guys. So the next one who asked was Jason. He's, like, this jock, and he's really good looking, and I knew that if I went out with him everyone would know, and I thought maybe they would shut up."

"So this was the first time you went out on a date?"

"Yeah. We went to this Italian restaurant and Laura and Mike were there, and a bunch of people from Theater class, and I offered to go Dutch but he said no, he never did that, and it was okay, I mean, we talked about school and stuff, football. Then we went to see *Friday the 13th, Part VII,* which was really stupid, in case you were thinking of seeing it."

"I've seen it."

"Oh. Why? It doesn't seem like your kind of thing."

"Same reason you did; my date wanted to see it."

"Who was your date?"

"A woman named Alex."

"What was she like?"

"A bank teller with big tits who liked to be spanked." The second this pops out of my mouth I realize that I am talking to Clare the teenager, not Clare my wife, and I mentally smack myself in the head.

"Spanked?" Clare looks at me, smiling, her eyebrows halfway to her hairline.

"Never mind. So you went to a movie, and . . . ?"

"Oh. Well, then he wanted to go to Traver's."

"What is Traver's?"

"It's a farm on the north side." Clare's voice drops, I can hardly hear her. "It's where people go to . . . make out." I don't say anything. "So I told him I was tired, and wanted to go home, and then he got kind of, um, mad." Clare stops talking; for a while we sit, listening to birds, airplanes, wind. Suddenly Clare says, "He was *really* mad."

"What happened then?"

"He wouldn't take me home. I wasn't sure where we were; somewhere out on Route 12, he was just driving around, down little lanes, God, I don't know. He drove down this dirt road, and there was this little cottage. There was a lake nearby, I could hear it. And he had the key to this place."

THE TIME TRAVELER'S WIFE

I'm getting nervous. Clare never told me any of this; just that she once went on a really horrible date with some guy named Jason, who was a football player. Clare has fallen silent again.

"Clare. Did he rape you?"

"No. He said I wasn't . . . good enough. He said—no, he didn't rape me. He just—hurt me. He made me. . . ." She can't say it. I wait. Clare unbuttons her coat, and removes it. She peels her shirt off, and I see that her back is covered with bruises. They are dark and purple against her white skin. Clare turns and there is a cigarette burn on her right breast, blistered and ugly. I asked her once what that scar was, and she wouldn't say. I am going to kill this guy. I am going to cripple him. Clare sits before me, shoulders back, gooseflesh, waiting. I hand her her shirt, and she puts it on.

"All right," I tell her quietly. "Where do I find this guy?"

"I'll drive you," she says.

Clare picks me up in the Fiat at the end of the driveway, out of sight of the house. She's wearing sunglasses even though it's a dim afternoon, and lipstick, and her hair is coiled at the back of her head. She looks a lot older than sixteen. She looks like she just walked out of *Rear Window*, though the resemblance would be more perfect if she was blond. We speed through the fall trees, but I don't think either of us notices much color. A tape loop of what happened to Clare in that little cottage has begun to play repeatedly in my head.

"How big is he?"

Clare considers. "A couple inches taller than you. A lot heavier. Fifty pounds?"

"Christ."

"I brought this." Clare digs in her purse and produces a handgun.

"Clare!"

"It's Daddy's."

I think fast. "Clare, that's a bad idea. I mean, I'm mad enough to actually use it, and that would be stupid. Ah, wait." I take it from her, open the chamber, and remove the bullets and put them in her purse. "There. That's better. Brilliant idea, Clare." Clare looks at me, questioning. I stick the gun in my overcoat pocket. "Do you want me to do this anonymously, or do you want him to know it's from you?"

"I want to be there."

"Oh."

She pulls into a private lane and stops. "I want to take him somewhere and I want you to hurt him very badly and I want to watch. I want him scared shitless."

I sigh. "Clare, I don't usually do this kind of thing. I usually fight in self-defense, for one thing."

"Please." It comes out of her mouth absolutely flat.

"Of course." We continue down the drive, and stop in front of a large, new faux Colonial house. There are no cars visible. Van Halen emanates from an open second-floor window. We walk to the front door and I stand to the side while Clare rings the bell. After a moment the music abruptly stops and heavy footsteps clump down stairs. The door opens, and after a pause a deep voice says, "What? You come back for more?" That's all I need to hear. I draw the gun and step to Clare's side. I point it at the guy's chest.

"Hi, Jason," Clare says. "I thought you might like to come out with us."

He does the same thing I would do, drops and rolls out of range, but he doesn't do it fast enough. I'm in the door and I take a flying leap onto his chest and knock the wind out of him. I stand up, put my boot on his chest, point the gun at his head. *C'est mag-*

nifique mais ce n'est pas la guerre. He looks kind of like Tom Cruise, very pretty, all-American. "What position does he play?" I ask Clare.

"Halfback."

"Hmm. Never would of guessed. Get up, hands up where I can see them," I tell him cheerfully. He complies, and I walk him out the door. We are all standing in the driveway. I have an idea. I send Clare back into the house for rope; she comes out a few minutes later with scissors and duct tape.

"Where do you want to do this?"

"The woods."

Jason is panting as we march him into the woods. We walk for about five minutes, and then I see a little clearing with a handy young elm at the edge of it. "How about this, Clare?"

"Yeah."

I look at her. She is completely impassive, cool as a Raymond Chandler murderess. "Call it, Clare."

"Tie him to the tree." I hand her the gun, jerk Jason's hands into position behind the tree, and duct tape them together. There's almost a full roll of duct tape, and I intend to use all of it. Jason is breathing strenuously, wheezing. I step around him and look at Clare. She looks at Jason as though he is a bad piece of conceptual art. "Are you asthmatic?"

He nods. His pupils are contracted into tiny points of black. "I'll get his inhaler," says Clare. She hands the gun back to me and ambles off through the woods along the path we came down. Jason is trying to breathe slowly and carefully. He is trying to talk.

"Who . . . are you?" he asks, hoarsely.

"I'm Clare's boyfriend. I'm here to teach you manners, since you have none." I drop my mocking tone, and walk close to him, and say softly, "How could you do that to her? She's so young. She doesn't know anything, and now you've completely fucked up everything. . . ."

"She's a . . . cock . . . tease."

"She has no idea. It's like torturing a kitten because it bit you."

Jason doesn't answer. His breath comes in long, shivering whinnies. Just as I am becoming concerned, Clare arrives. She holds up the inhaler, looks at me. "Darling, do you know how to use this thing?"

"I think you shake it and then put it in his mouth and press down on the top." She does this, asks him if he wants more. He nods. After four inhalations, we stand and watch him gradually subside into more normal breathing.

"Ready?" I ask Clare.

She holds up the scissors, makes a few cuts in the air. Jason flinches. Clare walks over to him, kneels, and begins to cut off his clothes. "Hey," says Jason.

"Please be quiet," I say. "No one is hurting you. At the moment." Clare finishes cutting off his jeans and starts on his T-shirt. I start to duct tape him to the tree. I begin at his ankles, and wind very neatly up his calves and thighs. "Stop there," Clare says, indicating a point just below Jason's crotch. She snips off his underwear. I start to tape his waist. His skin is clammy and he's very tan everywhere except inside a crisp outline of a Speedo-type bathing suit. He's sweating heavily. I wind all the way up to his shoulders, and stop, because I want him to be able to breathe. We step back and admire our work. Jason is now a duct-tape mummy with a large erection. Clare begins to laugh. Her laugh sounds spooky, echoing through the woods. I look at her sharply. There's something knowing and cruel in Clare's laugh, and it seems to me that this moment is the demarcation, a sort of no-man's-land between Clare's childhood and her life as a woman.

"What next?" I inquire. Part of me wants to turn him into hamburger and part of me doesn't want to beat up somebody who's taped to a tree. Jason is bright red. It contrasts nicely with the gray duct tape.

"Oh," says Clare. "You know, I think that's enough."

I am relieved. So of course I say, "You sure? I mean there are all sorts of things I could do. Break his eardrums? Nose? Oh, wait, he's already broken it once himself. We could cut his Achilles' tendons. He wouldn't be playing football in the near future."

"No!" Jason strains against the tape.

"Apologize, then," I tell him.

Jason hesitates. "Sorry."

"That's pretty pathetic—"

"I know," Clare says. She fishes around in her purse and finds a Magic Marker. She walks up to Jason as though he is a dangerous zoo animal, and begins to write on his duct-taped chest. When she's done, she stands back and caps her marker. She's written an account of their date. She sticks the marker back in her purse and says, "Let's go."

"You know, we can't just leave him. He might have another asthma attack."

"Hmm. Okay, I know. I'll call some people."

"Wait a minute," says Jason.

"What?" says Clare.

"Who are you calling? Call Rob."

Clare laughs. "Uh-uh. I'm going to call every girl I know."

I walk over to Jason and place the muzzle of the gun under his chin. "If you mention my existence to one human and I find out about it I will come back and I will devastate you. You won't be able to walk, talk, eat, or fuck when I'm done. As far as you know, Clare is a nice girl who for some inexplicable reason doesn't date. Right?"

Jason looks at me with hatred. "Right."

"We've dealt with you very leniently, here. If you hassle Clare again in any way you will be sorry."

"Okay."

"Good." I place the gun back in my pocket. "It's been fun."

"Listen, dickface—"

Oh, what the hell. I step back and put my whole weight into a side kick to the groin. Jason screams. I turn and look at Clare, who is white under her makeup. Tears are running down Jason's face. I wonder if he's going to pass out. "Let's go," I say. Clare nods. We walk back to the car, subdued. I can hear Jason yelling at us. We climb in, Clare starts the car, turns, and rockets down the driveway and onto the street.

I watch her drive. It's beginning to rain. There's a satisfied smile playing around the edges of her mouth. "Is that what you wanted?" I ask.

"Yes," says Clare. "That was perfect. Thank you."

"My pleasure." I'm getting dizzy. "I think I'm almost gone."

Clare pulls onto a sidestreet. The rain is drumming on the car. It's like riding through a car wash. "Kiss me," she demands. I do, and then I'm gone.

Monday, September 28, 1987 (Clare is 16)

CLARE: At school on Monday, everybody looks at me but no one will speak to me. I feel like Harriet the Spy after her classmates found her spy notebook. Walking down the hall is like parting the Red Sea. When I walk into English, first period, everyone stops talking. I sit down next to Ruth. She smiles and looks worried. I don't say anything either but then I feel her hand on mine under the table, hot and small. Ruth holds my hand for a moment and then

Mr. Partaki walks in and she takes her hand away and Mr. Partaki notices that everyone is uncharacteristically silent. He says mildly, "Did you all have a nice weekend?" and Sue Wong says, "Oh, *yes,*" and there's a shimmer of nervous laughter around the room. Partaki is puzzled, and there's an awful pause. Then he says, "Well, great, then let's embark on *Billy Budd.* In 1851, Herman Melville published *Moby-Dick, or, The Whale,* which was greeted with resounding indifference by the American public. . . ." It's all lost on me. Even with a cotton undershirt on, my sweater feels abrasive, and my ribs hurt. My classmates arduously fumble their way through a discussion of *Billy Budd.* Finally the bell rings, and they escape. I follow, slowly, and Ruth walks with me.

"Are you okay?" she asks.

"Mostly."

"I did what you said."

"What time?"

"Around six. I was afraid his parents would come home and find him. It was hard to cut him out. The tape ripped off all his chest hair."

"Good. Did a lot of people see him?"

"Yeah, everybody. Well, all the girls. No guys, as far as I know." The halls are almost empty. I'm standing in front of my French classroom. "Clare, I understand *why* you did it, but what I don't get is *how* you did it."

"I had some help."

The passing bell rings and Ruth jumps. "Oh my god. I've been late to gym five times in a row!" She moves away as though repelled by a strong magnetic field. "Tell me at lunch," Ruth calls as I turn and walk into Madame Simone's room.

"*Ah, Mademoiselle Abshire, asseyez-vous, s'il vous plaît.*" I sit between Laura and Helen. Helen writes me a note: *Good for you.* The class is translating Montaigne. We work quietly, and Madame walks around the room, correcting. I'm having trouble concentrating. The look on Henry's face after he kicked Jason: utterly indifferent, as though he had just shaken his hand, as though he was thinking about nothing in particular, and then he was worried because he didn't know how I would react, and I realized that Henry enjoyed hurting Jason, and is that the same as Jason enjoying hurting me? But Henry is good. Does that make it okay? Is it okay that I wanted him to do it?

"*Clare, attendez,*" Madame says, at my elbow.

After the bell once again everyone bolts out. I walk with Helen. Laura hugs me apologetically and runs off to her music class at the other end of the building. Helen and I both have third-period gym.

Helen laughs. "Well, dang, girl. I couldn't believe my eyes. How'd you get him taped to that tree?"

I can tell I'm going to get tired of that question. "I have a friend who does things like that. He helped me out."

"Who is 'he'?"

"A client of my dad's," I lie.

Helen shakes her head. "You're such a bad liar." I smile, and say nothing.

"It's Henry, right?"

I shake my head, and put my finger to my lips. We have arrived at the girls' gym. We walk into the locker room and *abracadabra!* all the girls stop talking. Then there's a low ripple of talk that fills the silence. Helen and I have our lockers in the same bay. I open mine and take out my gym suit and shoes. I have thought about what I am going to do. I take off my shoes and stockings, strip down to my undershirt and panties. I'm not wearing a bra because it hurt too much.

"Hey, Helen," I say. I peel off my shirt, and Helen turns.

"Jesus Christ, Clare!" The bruises look even worse than they did yesterday. Some of them are greenish. There are welts on my thighs from Jason's belt. "Oh, Clare." Helen walks to me, and puts her arms around me, carefully. The room is silent, and I look over Helen's shoulder and see that all the girls have gathered around us, and they are all looking. Helen straightens up, and looks back at them, and says, "Well?" and someone in the back starts to clap, and they are all clapping, and laughing, and talking, and cheering, and I feel light, light as air.

Wednesday, July 12, 1995 (Clare is 24, Henry is 32)

CLARE: I'm lying in bed, almost asleep, when I feel Henry's hand brushing over my stomach and realize he's back. I open my eyes and he bends down and kisses the little cigarette burn scar, and in the dim night light I touch his face. "Thank you," I say, and he says, "It was my pleasure," and that is the only time we ever speak of it.

Sunday, September 11, 1988 (Henry is 36, Clare is 17)

HENRY: Clare and I are in the Orchard on a warm September afternoon. Insects drone in the Meadow under golden sun. Everything is still, and as I look across the dry grasses the air shimmers with warmth. We are under an apple tree. Clare leans against its trunk with a pillow under her to cushion the tree roots. I am lying stretched out with my head in her lap. We have eaten, and the remains of our lunch lie scattered around us, with fallen apples interspersed. I am sleepy and content. It is January in my present, and Clare and I are struggling. This summer interlude is idyllic.

Clare says, "I'd like to draw you, just like that."

"Upside down and asleep?"

"Relaxed. You look so peaceful."

Why not? "Go ahead." We are out here in the first place because Clare is supposed to be drawing trees for her art class. She picks up her sketchbook and retrieves the charcoal. She balances the book on her knee. "Do you want me to move?" I ask her.

"No, that would change it too much. As you were, please." I resume staring idly at the patterns the branches make against the sky.

Stillness is a discipline. I can hold quite still for long stretches of time when I'm reading, but sitting for Clare is always surprisingly difficult. Even a pose that seems very comfortable at first becomes torture after fifteen minutes or so. Without moving anything but my eyes, I look at Clare. She is deep in her drawing. When Clare draws she looks as though the world has fallen away, leaving only her and the object of her scrutiny. This is why I love to be drawn by Clare: when she looks at me with that kind of attention, I feel that I am everything to her. It's the same look she gives me when we're making love. Just at this moment she looks into my eyes and smiles.

"I forgot to ask you: when are you coming from?"

"January, 2000."

Her face falls. "Really? I thought maybe a little later."

"Why? Do I look so old?"

Clare strokes my nose. Her fingers travel across the bridge and over my brows. "No, you don't. But you seem happy and calm, and usually when you come from 1998, or '99 or 2000, you're upset, or freaked out, and you won't tell me why. And then in 2001 you're okay again."

I laugh. "You sound like a fortune teller. I never realized you were tracking my moods so closely."

"What else have I got to go on?"

"Remember, it's stress that usually sends me in your direction, here. So you shouldn't get the idea that those years are unremittingly horrible. There are lots of nice things in those years, too."

Clare goes back to her drawing. She has given up asking me about our future. Instead she asks, "Henry, what are you afraid of?"

The question surprises me and I have to think about it. "Cold," I say. "I am afraid of winter. I am afraid of police. I am afraid of traveling to the wrong place and time and getting hit by a car or beat up. Or getting stranded in time, and not being able to come back. I am afraid of losing you."

Clare smiles. "How could you lose me? I'm not going anywhere."

"I worry that you will get tired of putting up with my undependableness and you will leave me."

Clare puts her sketchbook aside. I sit up. "I won't ever leave you," she says. "Even though you're always leaving me."

"But I never want to leave you."

Clare shows me the drawing. I've seen it before; it hangs next to Clare's drawing table in her studio at home. In the drawing I do look peaceful. Clare signs it and begins to write the date. "Don't," I say. "It's not dated."

"It's not?"

"I've seen it before. There's no date on it."

"Okay." Clare erases the date and writes MEADOWLARK on it instead. "Done." She looks at me, puzzled. "Do you ever find that you go back to your present and something has changed? I mean, what if I wrote the date on this drawing right now? What would happen?"

"I don't know. Try it," I say, curious. Clare erases the word MEADOWLARK and writes SEPTEMBER 11, 1988.

"There," she says, "that was easy." We look at each other, bemused. Clare laughs. "If I've violated the space-time continuum it isn't very obvious."

"I'll let you know if you've just caused World War III." I'm starting to feel shaky. "I think I'm going, Clare." She kisses me, and I'm gone.

Thursday, January 13, 2000 (Henry is 36, Clare is 28)

HENRY: After dinner I'm still thinking about Clare's drawing, so I walk out to her studio to look at it. Clare is making a huge sculpture out of tiny wisps of purple paper; it looks like a cross between a Muppet and a bird's nest. I walk around it carefully and stand in front of her table. The drawing is not there.

Clare comes in carrying an armful of abaca fiber. "Hey." She throws it on the floor and walks over to me. "What's up?"

"Where's that drawing that used to hang right there? The one of me?"

"Huh? Oh, I don't know. Maybe it fell down." Clare dives under the table and says, "I don't see it. Oh, wait here it is." She emerges holding the drawing between two fingers. "Ugh, it's all cobwebby." She brushes it off and hands it to me. I look it over. There's still no date on it.

"What happened to the date?"

"What date?"

"You wrote the date at the bottom, here. Under your name. It looks like it's been trimmed off."

Clare laughs. "Okay. I confess. I trimmed it."

"Why?"

"I got all freaked by your World War III comment. I started

thinking, what if we never meet in the future because I insisted on testing this out?"

"I'm glad you did."

"Why?"

"I don't know. I just am." We stare at each other, and then Clare smiles, and I shrug, and that's that. But why does it seem as though something impossible almost happened? Why do I feel so relieved?

CHRISTMAS EVE, ONE
(ALWAYS CRASHING
IN THE SAME CAR)

••••••••••••••••••••••••••••••

Saturday, December 24, 1988 (Henry is 40, Clare is 17)

HENRY: It's a dark winter afternoon. I'm in the basement in Meadowlark House in the Reading Room. Clare has left me some food: roast beef and cheese on whole wheat with mustard, an apple, a quart of milk, and an entire plastic tub of Christmas cookies, snowballs, cinnamon-nut diamonds, and peanut cookies with Hershey's Kisses stuck into them. I am wearing my favorite jeans and a Sex Pistols T-shirt. I ought to be a happy camper, but I'm not: Clare has also left me today's *South Haven Daily;* it's dated December 24, 1988. Christmas Eve. This evening, in the Get Me High Lounge, in Chicago, my twenty-five-year-old self will drink until I quietly slide off the bar stool and onto the floor and end up having my stomach pumped at Mercy Hospital. It's the nineteenth anniversary of my mother's death.

I sit quietly and think about my mom. It's funny how memory erodes. If all I had to work from were my childhood memories, my knowledge of my mother would be faded and soft, with a few sharp moments standing out. When I was five I heard her sing Lulu at the Lyric Opera. I remember Dad, sitting next to me, smiling up at

Mom at the end of the first act with utter exhilaration. I remember sitting with Mom at Orchestra Hall, watching Dad play Beethoven under Boulez. I remember being allowed to come into the living room during a party my parents were giving and reciting Blake's *Tyger, Tyger burning bright* to the guests, complete with growling noises; I was four, and when I was done my mother swept me up and kissed me and everyone applauded. She was wearing dark lipstick and I insisted on going to bed with her lip prints on my cheek. I remember her sitting on a bench in Warren Park while my dad pushed me on a swing, and she bobbed close and far, close and far.

One of the best and most painful things about time traveling has been the opportunity to see my mother alive. I have even spoken to her a few times; little things like "Lousy weather today, isn't it?" I give her my seat on the El, follow her in the supermarket, watch her sing. I hang around outside the apartment my father still lives in, and watch the two of them, sometimes with my infant self, take walks, eat in restaurants, go to the movies. It's the '60s, and they are elegant, young, brilliant musicians with all the world before them. They are happy as larks, they shine with their luck, their joy. When we run across each other they wave; they think I am someone who lives in the neighborhood, someone who takes a lot of walks, someone who gets his hair cut oddly and seems to mysteriously ebb and flow in age. I once heard my father wonder if I was a cancer patient. It still amazes me that Dad has never realized that this man lurking around the early years of their marriage was his son.

I see how my mother is with me. Now she is pregnant, now they bring me home from the hospital, now she takes me to the park in a baby carriage and sits memorizing scores, singing softly with small hand gestures to me, making faces and shaking toys at me. Now we walk hand in hand and admire the squirrels, the cars, the pigeons, anything that moves. She wears cloth coats and loafers with capri pants. She is dark-haired with a dramatic face, a full mouth, wide eyes, short hair; she looks Italian but actually she's Jewish. My mom wears lipstick, eye liner, mascara, blush, and eyebrow pencil to go to the dry cleaner's. Dad is much as he always is, tall, spare, a quiet dresser, a wearer of hats. The difference is his face. He is deeply content. They touch each other often, hold hands, walk in unison. At the beach the three of us wear matching sunglasses and I have a ridiculous blue hat. We all lie in the sun slathered in baby oil. We drink rum and Coke, and Hawaiian Punch.

My mother's star is rising. She studies with Jehan Meck, with Mary Delacroix, and they carefully guide her along the paths of fame; she sings a number of small but gemlike roles, attracting the ears of Louis Behaire at the Lyric. She understudies Linea Waverleigh's Aïda. Then she is chosen to sing Carmen. Other companies take notice, and soon we are traveling around the world. She records Schubert for Decca, Verdi and Weill for EMI, and we go to London, to Paris, to Berlin, to New York. I remember only an endless series of hotel rooms and airplanes. Her performance at Lincoln Center is on television; I watch it with Gram and Gramps in Muncie. I am six years old and I hardly believe that it's my mom, there in black and white on the small screen. She is singing Madama Butterfly.

They make plans to move to Vienna after the end of the Lyric's '69–'70 season. Dad auditions at the Philharmonic. Whenever the phone rings it's Uncle Ish, Mom's manager, or someone from a record label.

I hear the door at the top of the stairs open and clap shut and then slowly descending footsteps. Clare knocks quietly four times and I remove the straight-backed chair from under the doorknob. There's still snow in her hair and her cheeks are red. She is seventeen years old. Clare throws her arms around me and hugs me excitedly. "Merry Christmas, Henry!" she says. "It's so great you're here!" I kiss her on the cheek; her cheer and bustle have scattered my thoughts but my sense of sadness and loss remains. I run my hands over her hair and come away with a small handful of snow that melts immediately.

"What's wrong?" Clare takes in the untouched food, my uncheerful demeanor. "You're sulking because there's no mayo?"

"Hey. Hush." I sit down on the broken old La-Z-Boy and Clare squeezes in beside me. I put my arm around her shoulders. She puts her hand on my inner thigh. I remove it, and hold it. Her hand is cold. "Have I ever told you about my mom?"

"No." Clare is all ears; she's always eager for any bits of autobiography I let drop. As the dates on the List grow few and our two years of separation loom large, Clare is secretly convinced she can find me in real time if I would only dole out a few facts. Of course, she can't, because I won't, and she doesn't.

We each eat a cookie. "Okay. Once upon a time, I had a mom. I had a dad, too, and they were very deeply in love. And they had me. And we were all pretty happy. And both of them were really terrific at their jobs, and my mother, especially, was great at what she did, and we used to travel all over, seeing the hotel rooms of the world. So it was almost Christmas—"

"What year?"

"The year I was six. It was the morning of Christmas Eve, and my dad was in Vienna because we were going to move there soon and he was finding us an apartment. So the idea was that Dad would fly into the airport and Mom and I would drive out and pick him up and we would all continue on to Grandma's house for the holidays.

"It was a gray, snowy morning and the streets were covered in sheets of ice that hadn't been salted yet. Mom was a nervous driver.

She hated expressways, hated driving to the airport, and had only agreed to do this because it made a lot of sense. We got up early, and she packed the car. I was wearing a winter coat, a knit hat, boots, jeans, a pullover sweater, underwear, wool socks that were kind of tight, and mittens. She was dressed entirely in black, which was more unusual then than it is now."

Clare drinks some of the milk directly from the carton. She leaves a cinnamon-colored lipstick print. "What kind of car?"

"It was a white '62 Ford Fairlane."

"What's that?"

"Look it up. It was built like a tank. It had fins. My parents loved it—it had a lot of history for them.

"So we got in the car. I sat in the front passenger seat, we both wore our seatbelts. And we drove. The weather was absolutely awful. It was hard to see, and the defrost in that car wasn't the greatest. We went through this maze of residential streets, and then we got on the expressway. It was after rush hour, but traffic was a mess because of the weather and the holiday. So we were moving maybe fifteen, twenty miles an hour. My mother stayed in the right-hand lane, probably because she didn't want to change lanes without being able to see very well and because we weren't going to be on the expressway very long before we exited for the airport.

"We were behind a truck, well behind it, giving it plenty of room up there. As we passed an entrance a small car, a red Corvette, actually, got on behind us. The Corvette, which was being driven by a dentist who was only slightly inebriated, at 10:30 a.m., got on just a bit too quickly, and was unable to slow down soon enough because of the ice on the road, and hit our car. And in ordinary weather conditions, the Corvette would have been mangled and the indestructible Ford Fairlane would have had a bent fender and it wouldn't have been that big of a deal.

"But the weather was bad, the roads were slick, so the shove from the Corvette sent our car accelerating forward just as traffic slowed down. The truck ahead of us was barely moving. My mother was pumping the brakes but nothing was happening.

"We hit the truck practically in slow motion, or so it seemed to me. In actuality we were going about forty. The truck was an open pickup truck full of scrap metal. When we hit it, a large sheet of steel flew off the back of the truck, came through our windshield, and decapitated my mother."

Clare has her eyes closed. "No."

"It's true."

"But you were right there—you were too short!"

"No, that wasn't it, the steel embedded in my seat right where my forehead should have been. I have a scar where it started to cut my forehead." I show Clare. "It got my hat. The police couldn't figure it out. All my clothes were in the car, on the seat and the floor, and I was found stark naked by the side of the road."

"You time traveled."

"Yes. I time traveled." We are silent for a moment. "It was only the second time it ever happened to me. I had no idea what was going on. I was watching us plow into this truck, and then I was in the hospital. In fact, I was pretty much unhurt, just in shock."

"How . . . why do you think it happened?"

"Stress—pure fear. I think my body did the only trick it could."

Clare turns her face to mine, sad and excited. "So. . . ."

"So. Mom died, and I didn't. The front end of the Ford crumpled up, the steering column went through Mom's chest, her head went through the now empty windshield and into the back of the truck, there was an *unbelievable* amount of blood. The guy in the Corvette was unscathed. The truck driver got out of his truck to see what hit him, saw Mom, fainted on the road and was run over by a schoolbus driver who didn't see him and was gawking at the accident. The truck driver had two broken legs. Meanwhile, I was completely absent from the scene for ten minutes and forty-seven seconds. I don't remember where I went; maybe it was only a second or two for me. Traffic came to a complete halt. Ambulances were trying to come from three different directions and couldn't get near us for half an hour. Paramedics came running on foot. I appeared on the shoulder. The only person who saw me appear was a little girl; she was in the back seat of a green Chevrolet station wagon. Her mouth opened, and she just stared and stared."

"But—Henry, you were—you said you don't remember. And how could you know this anyway? Ten minutes and forty-seven seconds? Exactly?"

I am quiet for a while, searching for the best way to explain. "You know about gravity, right? The larger something is, the more mass it has, the more gravitational pull it exerts? It pulls smaller things to it, and they orbit around and around?"

"Yes. . . ."

"My mother dying . . . it's the pivotal thing . . . everything else goes around and around it . . . I dream about it, and I also—time travel to it. Over and over. If you could be there, and could hover over the scene of the accident, and you could see every detail of it, all the people, cars, trees, snowdrifts—if you had enough time to really look at everything, you would see me. I am in cars, behind bushes, on the bridge, in a tree. I have seen it from every angle, I am even a participant in the aftermath: I called the airport from a nearby gas station to page my father with the message to come immediately to the hospital. I sat in the hospital waiting room and watched my father walk through on his way to find me. He looks gray and ravaged. I walked along the shoulder of the road, waiting for my young self to appear, and I put a blanket around my thin child's shoulders. I looked into my small uncomprehending face, and I thought . . . I thought. . . ." I am weeping now. Clare wraps her arms around me and I cry soundlessly into her mohair-sweatered breasts.

"What? What, Henry?"

"I thought, *I should have died, too.*"

We hold each other. I gradually get hold of myself. I have made a mess of Clare's sweater. She goes to the laundry room and comes back wearing one of Alicia's white polyester chamber music–playing shirts. Alicia is only fourteen, but she's already taller and bigger than Clare. I stare at Clare, standing before me, and I am sorry to be here, sorry to ruin her Christmas.

"I'm sorry, Clare. I didn't mean to put all this sadness on you. I just find Christmas . . . difficult."

"Oh, Henry! I'm so glad you're here, and, you know, I'd rather know—I mean, you just come out of nowhere, and disappear, and if I know things, about your life, you seem more . . . real. Even terrible things . . . I need to know as much as you can say." Alicia is calling down the stairs for Clare. It is time for Clare to join her family, to celebrate Christmas. I stand, and we kiss, cautiously, and Clare says "Coming!" and gives me a smile and then she's running up the stairs. I prop the chair under the door again and settle in for a long night.

CHRISTMAS EVE, TWO

••••••••••••••••••••••••••••••••

Saturday, December 24, 1988 (Henry is 25)

HENRY: I call Dad and ask if he wants me to come over for dinner after the Christmas matinée concert. He makes a half-hearted attempt at inviting me but I back out, to his relief. The Official De-Tamble Day of Mourning will be conducted in multiple locations this year. Mrs. Kim has gone to Korea to visit her sisters; I've been watering her plants and taking in her mail. I call Ingrid Carmichel and ask her to come out with me and she reminds me, crisply, that it's Christmas Eve and some people have families to kowtow to. I run through my address book. Everyone is out of town, or in town with their visiting relatives. I should have gone to see Gram and Gramps. Then I remember they're in Florida. It's 2:53 in the afternoon and stores are closing down. I buy a bottle of schnapps at Al's and stow it in my overcoat pocket. Then I hop on the El at Belmont and ride downtown. It's a gray day, and cold. The train is half full, mostly people with their kids going down to see Marshall Field's Christmas windows and do last-minute shopping at Water Tower Place. I get off at Randolph and walk east to Grant Park. I stand on the IC overpass for a while, drinking, and then I walk down to the skating rink. A few couples and little kids are skating. The kids chase each other and skate backward and do figure eights. I rent a pair of more-or-less-my-size skates, lace them on, and walk onto the ice. I skate the perimeter of the rink, smoothly and without thinking too much. Repetition, movement, balance, cold air. It's nice. The sun is setting. I skate for an hour or so, then return the skates, pull on my boots, and walk.

I walk west on Randolph, and south on Michigan Avenue, past the Art Institute. The lions are decked out in Christmas wreaths. I walk down Columbus Drive. Grant Park is empty, except for the crows, which strut and circle over the evening-blue snow. The streetlights tint the sky orange above me; it's a deep cerulean blue over the lake. At Buckingham Fountain I stand until the cold becomes unbearable watching seagulls wheeling and diving, fighting over a loaf of bread somebody has left for them. A mounted policeman rides slowly around the fountain once and then sedately continues south.

I walk. My boots are not quite waterproof, and despite my several sweaters my overcoat is a bit thin for the dropping temperature. Not enough body fat; I'm always cold from November to April. I walk along Harrison, over to State Street. I pass the Pacific Garden Mission, where the homeless have gathered for shelter and dinner. I wonder what they're having; I wonder if there's any festivity, there, in the shelter. There are few cars. I don't have a watch, but I guess that it's about seven. I've noticed lately that my sense of time passing is different; it seems to run slower than other people's. An afternoon can be like a day to me; an El ride can be an epic journey. Today is interminable. I have managed to get through most of the day without thinking, too much, about Mom, about the accident, about all of it . . . but now, in the evening, walking, it is catching up with me. I realize I'm hungry. The alcohol has worn off. I'm almost at Adams, and I mentally review the amount of cash I have on me and decide to splurge on dinner at the Berghoff, a venerable German restaurant famous for its brewery.

The Berghoff is warm, and noisy. There are quite a few people, eating and standing around. The legendary Berghoff waiters are bustling importantly from kitchen to table. I stand in line, thawing out, amidst chattering families and couples. Eventually I am led to a small table in the main dining room, toward the back. I order a dark beer and a plate of duck wursts with spaetzle. When the food comes, I eat slowly. I polish off all the bread, too, and realize that I can't remember eating lunch. This is good, I'm taking care of myself, I'm not being an idiot, I'm remembering to eat dinner. I lean back in my chair and survey the room. Under the high ceilings, dark paneling, and murals of boats, middle-aged couples eat their dinners. They have spent the afternoon shopping, or at the symphony, and they talk pleasantly of the presents they have bought, their grandchildren, plane tickets and arrival times, Mozart. I have an urge to go to the symphony, now, but there's no evening program. Dad is probably on his way home from Orchestra Hall. I would sit in the upper reaches of the uppermost balcony (the best place to sit, acoustically) and listen to *Das Lied von der Erde,* or Beethoven, or something similarly un-Christmasy. Oh well. Maybe next year. I have a sudden glimpse of all the Christmases of my life lined up one after another, waiting to be gotten through, and despair floods me. No. I wish for a moment that Time would lift me out of this day, and into some more benign one. But then I feel guilty for wanting to avoid the sadness; dead people need us to remember them, even if it eats us, even if all we can do is say *I'm sorry* until it is as meaningless as air. I don't want to burden this warm festive restaurant with grief that I would have to recall the next time I'm here with Gram and Gramps, so I pay and leave.

Back on the street, I stand pondering. I don't want to go home. I want to be with people, I want to be distracted. I suddenly think of the Get Me High Lounge, a place where anything can happen, a haven for eccentricity. Perfect. I walk over to Water Tower Place and catch the #66 Chicago Avenue bus, get off at Damen, and take the #50 bus north. The bus smells of vomit, and I'm the only passenger. The driver is singing "Silent Night" in a smooth church tenor, and I wish him a Merry Christmas as I step off the bus at Wabansia. As I walk past the Fix-It shop snow begins to fall, and I catch the big wet flakes on the tips of my fingers. I can hear music leaking out of the bar. The abandoned ghost train track looms over the street in the sodium vapor glare and as I open the door someone starts to blow a trumpet and hot jazz smacks me in the chest. I walk into it like a drowning man, which is what I have come here to be.

There are about ten people in the place, counting Mia, the bartender. Three musicians, trumpet, standing bass, and clarinet, occupy the tiny stage, and the customers are all sitting at the bar. The musicians are playing furiously, swinging at maximum volume like sonic dervishes and as I sit and listen I make out the melody line of "White Christmas." Mia comes over and stares at me and I shout "Whiskey and water!" at the top of my voice and she bawls "House?" and I yell "Okay!" and she turns to mix it. There is an abrupt halt to the music. The phone rings, and Mia snatches it up and says, "Get Me Hiiiiiiiigh!" She sets my drink in front of me and I lay a twenty on the bar. "No," she says into the phone. "Well, daaaang. Well, fuck you, too." She whomps the receiver back into its cradle like she's dunking a basketball. Mia stands looking pissed off for a few moments, then lights a Pall Mall and blows a huge cloud of smoke at me. "Oh, sorry." The musicians troop over to the bar and she serves them beers. The restroom door is on the stage, so I take advantage of the break between sets to take a leak. When I get back to the bar

Mia has set another drink in front of my bar stool. "You're psychic," I say.

"You're easy." She plunks her ashtray down and leans against the inside of the bar, pondering. "What are you doing, later?"

I review my options. I've been known to go home with Mia a time or two, and she's good fun and all that, but I'm really not in the mood for casual frivolity at the moment. On the other hand, a warm body is not a bad thing when you're down. "I'm planning to get extremely drunk. What did you have in mind?"

"Well, if you're not too drunk you could come over, and if you're not dead when you wake up you could do me a huge favor and come to Christmas dinner at my parents' place in Glencoe and answer to the name Rafe."

"Oh, God, Mia. I'm suicidal just thinking about it. Sorry."

She leans over the bar and speaks emphatically. "C'mon, Henry. Help me out. You're a presentable young person of the male gender. Hell, you're a *librarian*. You won't freak when my parents start asking who your parents are and what college you went to."

"Actually, I will. I will run straight to the powder room and slit my throat. Anyway, what's the point? Even if they love me it just means they'll torture you for years with 'What ever happened to that nice young librarian you were dating?' And what happens when they meet the real Rafe?"

"I don't think I'll have to worry about that. C'mon. I'll perform Triple X sex acts on you that you've never even heard of."

I have been refusing to meet Ingrid's parents for months. I have refused to go to Christmas dinner at their house tomorrow. There's no way I'm going to do this for Mia, whom I hardly know. "Mia. Any other night of the year—look, my goal tonight is to achieve a level of inebriation at which I can barely stand up, much less get it up. Just call your parents and tell them Rafe is having a tonsillectomy or something."

She goes to the other end of the bar to take care of three suspiciously young male college types. Then she messes around with bottles for a while, making something elaborate. She sets the tall glass in front of me. "Here. It's on the house." The drink is the color of strawberry Kool-Aid.

"What is it?" I take a sip. It tastes like 7-Up.

Mia smiles an evil little smile. "It's something I invented. You want to get smashed, this is the express train."

"Oh. Well, thank you." I toast her, and drink up. A sensation of heat and total well-being floods me. "Heavens. Mia, you ought to patent this. You could have little lemonade stands all over Chicago and sell it in Dixie cups. You'd be a millionaire."

"Another?"

"Sure."

As a promising junior partner in DeTamble & DeTamble, Alcoholics at Large, I have not yet found the outer limit in my ability to consume liquor. A few drinks later, Mia is peering at me across the bar with concern.

"Henry?"

"Yeah?"

"I'm cutting you off." This is probably a good idea. I try to nod my agreement with Mia, but it's too much effort. Instead, I slide slowly, almost gracefully, to the floor.

I wake up much later at Mercy Hospital. Mia is sitting next to my bed. Her mascara has run all over her face. I'm hooked up to an IV and I feel bad. Very bad. In fact, every kind of bad. I turn my head and retch into a basin. Mia reaches over and wipes my mouth.

"Henry—" Mia is whispering.

"Hey. What the hell."

"Henry, I'm so sorry—"

"Not your fault. What happened?"

"You passed out and I did the math—how much do you weigh?"

"175."

"Jesus. Did you eat dinner?"

I think about it. "Yeah."

"Well, anyway, the stuff you were drinking was about forty proof. And you had two whiskeys . . . but you seemed perfectly fine and then all of a sudden you looked awful, and then you passed out, and I thought about it and realized you had a lot of booze in you. So I called 911 and here you are."

"Thanks. I think."

"Henry, do you have some kind of death wish?"

I consider. "Yes." I turn to the wall, and pretend to sleep.

Saturday, April 8, 1989 (Clare is 17, Henry is 40)

CLARE: I'm sitting in Grandma Meagram's room, doing the *New York Times* crossword puzzle with her. It's a bright cool April morning and I can see red tulips whipping in the wind in the garden. Mama is down there planting something small and white over by the forsythia. Her hat is almost blowing off and she keeps clapping her hand to her head and finally takes the hat off and sets her work basket on it.

I haven't seen Henry in almost two months; the next date on the List is three weeks away. We are approaching the time when I won't see him for more than two years. I used to be so casual about Henry, when I was little; seeing Henry wasn't anything too unusual. But now every time he's here is one less time he's going to be here. And things are different with us. I want something . . . I want Henry to say something, do something that proves this hasn't all been some kind of elaborate joke. I want. That's all. I am wanting.

Grandma Meagram is sitting in her blue wing chair by the window. I sit in the window seat, with the newspaper in my lap. We are about halfway through the crossword. My attention has drifted.

"Read that one again, child," says Grandma.

"Twenty down. 'Monkish monkey.' Eight letters, second letter 'a,' last letter 'n.'"

"*Capuchin.*" She smiles, her unseeing eyes turn in my direction. To Grandma I am a dark shadow against a somewhat lighter background. "That's pretty good, eh?"

"Yeah, that's great. Geez, try this one: nineteen across, 'Don't stick your elbow out so far.' Ten letters, second letter 'u.'"

"*Burma Shave.* Before your time."

"Arrgh. I'll never get this." I stand up and stretch. I desperately need to go for a walk. My grandmother's room is comforting but claustrophobic. The ceiling is low, the wallpaper is dainty blue flowers, the bedspread is blue chintz, the carpet is white, and it smells of powder and dentures and old skin. Grandma Meagram sits trim and straight. Her hair is beautiful, white but still slightly tinged with the red I have inherited from her, and perfectly coiled and pinned into a chignon. Grandma's eyes are like blue clouds. She has been blind for nine years, and she has adapted well; as long as she is in the house she can get around. She's been trying to teach me the art of crossword solving, but I have trouble caring enough to see one through by myself. Grandma used to do them in ink. Henry loves crossword puzzles.

"It's a beautiful day, isn't it," says Grandma, leaning back in her chair and rubbing her knuckles.

I nod, and then say, "Yes, but it's kind of windy. Mama's down there gardening, and everything keeps blowing away on her."

"How typical of Lucille," says her mother. "Do you know, child, I'd like to go for a walk."

"I was just thinking that same thing," I say. She smiles, and holds out her hands, and I gently pull her out of her chair. I fetch our coats, and tie a scarf around Grandma's hair to stop it from getting messed up by the wind. Then we make our way slowly down the stairs and out the front door. We stand on the drive, and I turn to Grandma and say, "Where do you want to go?"

"Let's go to the Orchard," she says.

"That's pretty far. Oh, Mama's waving; wave back." We wave at Mama, who is all the way down by the fountain now. Peter, our gardener, is with her. He has stopped talking to her and is looking at us, waiting for us to go on so he and Mama can finish the argument they are having, probably about daffodils, or peonies. Peter loves to argue with Mama, but she always gets her way in the end. "It's almost a mile to the Orchard, Grandma."

"Well, Clare, there's nothing wrong with my legs."

"Okay, then, we'll go to the Orchard." I take her arm, and away we go. When we get to the edge of the Meadow I say, "Shade or sun?" and she answers, "Oh, sun, to be sure," and so we take the path that cuts through the middle of the Meadow, that leads to the clearing. As we walk, I describe.

"We're passing the bonfire pile. There's a bunch of birds in it— oh, there they go!"

"Crows. Starlings. Doves, too," she says.

"Yes . . . we're at the gate, now. Watch out, the path is a little muddy. I can see dog tracks, a pretty big dog, maybe Joey from Allinghams'. Everything is greening up pretty good. Here is that wild rose."

"How high is the Meadow?" asks Grandma.

"Only about a foot. It's a real pale green. Here are the little oaks."

She turns her face toward me, smiling. "Let's go and say hello." I lead her to the oaks that grow just a few feet from the path. My grandfather planted these three oak trees in the forties as a memorial to my Great Uncle Teddy, Grandma's brother who was killed in the Second World War. The oak trees still aren't very big, only about fifteen feet tall. Grandma puts her hand on the trunk of the middle one and says, "Hello." I don't know if she's addressing the tree or her brother.

We walk on. As we walk over the rise I see the Meadow laid out before us, and Henry is standing in the clearing. I halt. "What is it?" Grandma asks. "Nothing," I tell her. I lead her along the path. "What do you see?" she asks me. "There's a hawk circling over the woods," I say. "What time is it?" I look at my watch. "Almost noon."

We enter the clearing. Henry stands very still. He smiles at me. He looks tired. His hair is graying. He is wearing his black overcoat, he stands out dark against the bright Meadow. "Where is the rock?" Grandma says. "I want to sit down." I guide her to the rock, help her to sit. She turns her face in Henry's direction and stiffens. "Who's there?" she asks me, urgency in her voice. "No one," I lie.

"There's a man, there," she says, nodding toward Henry. He looks at me with an expression that seems to mean *Go ahead. Tell her.* A dog is barking in the woods. I hesitate.

"Clare," Grandma says. She sounds scared.

"Introduce us," Henry says, quietly.

Grandma is still, waiting. I put my arm around her shoulders. "It's okay, Grandma," I say. "This is my friend Henry. He's the one I told you about." Henry walks over to us and holds out his hand. I place Grandma's hand in his. "Elizabeth Meagram," I say to Henry.

"So you're the one," Grandma says.

"Yes," Henry replies, and this *Yes* falls into my ears like balm. Yes.

"May I?" She gestures with her hands toward Henry.

"Shall I sit next to you?" Henry sits on the rock. I guide Grandma's hand to his face. He watches my face as she touches his. "That tickles," Henry says to Grandma.

"Sandpaper," she says as she runs her fingertips across his unshaven chin. "You're not a boy," she says.

"No."

"How old are you?"

"I'm eight years older than Clare."

She looks puzzled. "Twenty-five?" I look at Henry's salt-and-pepper hair, at the creases around his eyes. He looks about forty, maybe older.

"Twenty-five," he says firmly. Somewhere out there, it's true.

"Clare tells me she's going to marry you," my grandmother says to Henry.

He smiles at me. "Yes, we're going to get married. In a few years, when Clare is out of school."

"In my day, gentlemen came to dinner and met the family."

"Our situation is . . . unorthodox. That hasn't been possible."

"I don't see why not. If you're going to cavort around in meadows with my granddaughter you can certainly come up to the house and be inspected by her parents."

"I'd be delighted to," Henry says, standing up, "but I'm afraid right now I have a train to catch."

"Just a moment, young man—" Grandma begins, as Henry says, "Goodbye, Mrs. Meagram. It was great to finally meet you. Clare, I'm sorry I can't stay longer—" I reach out to Henry but there's the noise like all the sound is being sucked out of the world and he's already gone. I turn to Grandma. She's sitting on the rock with her hands stretched out, an expression of utter bewilderment on her face.

"What happened?" she asks me, and I begin to explain. When I am finished she sits with her head bowed, twisting her arthritic fingers into strange shapes. Finally she raises her face toward me. "But Clare," says my grandmother, "he must be a demon." She says it matter-of-factly, as though she's telling me that my coat's buttoned up wrong, or that it's time for lunch.

What can I say? "I've thought of that," I tell her. I take her hands to stop her from rubbing them red. "But Henry is good. He doesn't *feel* like a demon."

Grandma smiles. "You talk as though you've met a peck of them."

"Don't you think a real demon would be sort of—demonic?"

"I think he would be nice as pie if he wanted to be."

I choose my words carefully. "Henry told me once that his doctor thinks he's a new kind of human. You know, sort of the next step in evolution."

Grandma shakes her head. "That is just as bad as being a demon. Goodness, Clare, why in the world would you want to marry such a person? Think of the children you would have! Popping into next week and back before breakfast!"

I laugh. "But it will be exciting! Like Mary Poppins, or Peter Pan."

She squeezes my hands just a little. "Think for a minute, darling: in fairy tales it's always the children who have the fine adventures. The mothers have to stay at home and wait for the children to fly in the window."

I look at the pile of clothes lying crumpled on the ground where Henry has left them. I pick them up and fold them. "Just a minute," I say, and I find the clothes box and put Henry's clothes in it. "Let's go back to the house. It's past lunchtime." I help her off the rock. The wind is roaring in the grass, and we bend into it and make our way toward the house. When we come to the rise I turn and look back over the clearing. It's empty.

A few nights later, I am sitting by Grandma's bed, reading *Mrs. Dalloway* to her. It's evening. I look up; Grandma seems to be asleep. I stop reading, and close the book. Her eyes open.

"Hello," I say.

"Do you ever miss him?" she asks me.

"Every day. Every minute."

"Every minute," she says. "Yes. It's that way, isn't it?" She turns on her side and burrows into the pillow.

"Good night," I say, turning out the lamp. As I stand in the dark looking down at Grandma in her bed, self-pity floods me as though I have been injected with it. *It's that way, isn't it?* Isn't it.

EAT OR BE EATEN

••••••••••••••••••••••••••••••••

Saturday, November 30, 1991 (Henry is 28, Clare is 20)

HENRY: Clare has invited me to dinner at her apartment. Charisse, Clare's roommate, and Gomez, Charisse's boyfriend, will also be dining. At 6:59 p.m. Central Standard Time, I stand in my Sunday best in Clare's vestibule with my finger on her buzzer, fragrant yellow freesia and an Australian Cabernet in my other arm, and my heart in my mouth. I have not been to Clare's before, nor have I met any of her friends. I have no idea what to expect.

The buzzer makes a horrible sound and I open the door. "All the way up!" hollers a deep male voice. I plod up four flights of stairs. The person attached to the voice is tall and blond, sports the world's most immaculate pompadour and a cigarette and is wearing a Solidarnosc T-shirt. He seems familiar, but I can't place him. For a person named Gomez he looks very . . . Polish. I find out later that his real name is Jan Gomolinski.

"Welcome, Library Boy!" Gomez booms.

"Comrade!" I reply, and hand him the flowers and the wine. We eyeball each other, achieve détente, and with a flourish Gomez ushers me into the apartment.

It's one of those wonderful endless railroad apartments from the twenties—a long hallway with rooms attached almost as after-thoughts. There are two aesthetics at work here, funky and Victorian. This plays out in the spectacle of antique petit point chairs with heavy carved legs next to velvet Elvis paintings. I can hear Duke Ellington's "I Got It Bad and That Ain't Good" playing at the end of the hall, and Gomez leads me in that direction.

Clare and Charisse are in the kitchen. "My kittens, I have brought you a new toy," Gomez intones. "It answers to the name of Henry, but you can call it Library Boy." I meet Clare's eyes. She shrugs her shoulders and holds her face out to be kissed; I oblige with a chaste peck and turn to shake hands with Charisse, who is short and round in a very pleasing way, all curves and long black hair. She has such a kind face that I have an urge to confide something, anything, to her, just to see her reaction. She's a small Filipino Madonna. In a sweet, Don't Fuck With Me voice she says, "Oh, Gomez, do shut up. Hello, Henry. I'm Charisse Bonavant. Please ignore Gomez, I just keep him around to lift heavy objects."

"And sex. Don't forget the sex," Gomez reminds her. He looks at me. "Beer?"

"Sure." He delves into the fridge and hands me a Blatz. I pry off the cap and take a long pull. The kitchen looks as though a Pillsbury dough factory has exploded in it. Clare sees the direction of my gaze. I suddenly recollect that she doesn't know how to cook.

"It's a work in progress," says Clare.

"It's an installation piece," says Charisse.

"Are we going to eat it?" asks Gomez.

I look from one to the other, and we all burst out laughing. "Do any of you know how to cook?"

"No."

"Gomez can make rice."

"Only Rice-A-Roni."

"Clare knows how to order pizza."

"And Thai—I can order Thai, too."

"Charisse knows how to *eat*."

"*Shut up, Gomez,*" say Charisse and Clare in unison.

"Well, uh . . . what was that going to be?" I inquire, nodding at the disaster on the counter. Clare hands me a magazine clipping. It's a recipe for Chicken and Shiitake Risotto with Winter Squash and Pine Nut Dressing. It's from *Gourmand,* and there are about twenty ingredients. "Do you have all this stuff?"

Clare nods. "The shopping part I can do. It's the assembly that perplexes."

I examine the chaos more closely. "I could make something out of this."

"You can cook?" I nod.

"It cooks! Dinner is saved! Have another beer!" Gomez exclaims. Charisse looks relieved, and smiles warmly at me. Clare, who has been hanging back almost fearfully, sidles over to me and whispers, "You're not mad?" I kiss her, just a tad longer than is really polite in front of other people. I straighten up, take off my jacket, and roll up my sleeves. "Give me an apron," I demand. "You, Gomez—open that wine. Clare, clean up all that spilled stuff, it's turning to cement. Charisse, would you set the table?"

One hour and forty-three minutes later we are sitting around the dining room table eating Chicken Risotto Stew with Puréed Squash. Everything has lots of butter in it. We are all drunk as skunks.

CLARE: The whole time Henry is making dinner Gomez is standing around the kitchen making jokes and smoking and drinking beer and whenever no one is looking he makes awful faces at me. Finally Charisse catches him and draws her finger across her throat and he stops. We are talking about the most banal stuff: our jobs, and school, and where we grew up, and all the usual things that people talk about when they meet each other for the first time. Gomez tells Henry about his job being a lawyer, representing abused and neglected children who are wards of the state. Charisse regales us with tales of her exploits at Lusus Naturae, a tiny software company that is trying to make computers understand when people talk to them, and her art, which is making pictures that you look at on a computer. Henry tells stories about the Newberry Library and the odd people who come to study the books.

"Does the Newberry really have a book made out of human skin?" Charisse asks Henry.

"Yep. *The Chronicles of Nawat Wuzeer Hyderabed.* It was found in the palace of the King of Delhi in 1857. Come by some time and I'll pull it out for you."

Charisse shudders and grins. Henry is stirring the stew. When he says "Chow time," we all flock to the table. All this time Gomez and Henry have been drinking beer and Charisse and I have been sipping wine and Gomez has been topping up our glasses and we have not been eating much but I do not realize how drunk we all are until I almost miss sitting down on the chair Henry holds for me and Gomez almost sets his own hair on fire while lighting the candles.

Gomez holds up his glass. "The Revolution!"

Charisse and I raise our glasses, and Henry does, too. "The Revolution!" We begin eating, with enthusiasm. The risotto is slippery and mild, the squash is sweet, the chicken is swimming in butter. It makes me want to cry, it's so good.

Henry takes a bite, then points his fork at Gomez. "Which revolution?"

"Pardon?"

"Which revolution are we toasting?" Charisse and I look at each other in alarm, but it is too late.

Gomez smiles and my heart sinks. "The next one."

"The one where the proletariat rises up and the rich get eaten and capitalism is vanquished in favor of a classless society?"

"That very one."

Henry winks at me. "That seems rather hard on Clare. And what are you planning to do with the intelligentsia?"

"Oh," Gomez says, "we will probably eat them, too. But we'll keep you around, as a cook. This is outstanding grub."

Charisse touches Henry's arm, confidentially. "We aren't really going to eat anybody," she says. "We are just going to redistribute their assets."

"That's a relief," Henry replies. "I wasn't looking forward to cooking Clare."

Gomez says, "It's a shame, though. I'm sure Clare would be very tasty."

"I wonder what cannibal cuisine is like?" I say. "Is there a cannibal cookbook?"

The Raw and The Cooked," says Charisse.

Henry objects. "That's not really a how-to. I don't think Lévi-Strauss gives any recipes."

"We could just adapt a recipe," says Gomez, taking another helping of the chicken. "You know, Clare with Porcini Mushrooms and Marinara Sauce over Linguini. Or Breast of Clare à l'Orange. Or—"

"Hey," I say. "What if I don't *want* to be eaten?"

"Sorry, Clare," Gomez says gravely. "I'm afraid you have to be eaten for the greater good."

Henry catches my eye, and smiles. "Don't worry, Clare; come the Revolution I'll hide you at the Newberry. You can live in the stacks and I'll feed you Snickers and Doritos from the Staff Lunchroom. They'll never find you."

I shake my head. "What about 'First, we kill all the lawyers'?"

"No," Gomez says. "You can't do anything without lawyers. The Revolution would get all balled up in ten minutes if lawyers weren't there to keep it in line."

"But my dad's a lawyer," I tell him, "so you can't eat us after all."

"He's the wrong kind of lawyer," Gomez says. "He does estates for rich people. I, on the other hand, represent the poor oppressed children—"

"Oh, shut up, Gomez," says Charisse. "You're hurting Clare's feelings."

"I'm not! Clare wants to be eaten for the Revolution, don't you, Clare?"

"No."

"Oh."

"What about the Categorical Imperative?" asks Henry.

"Say what?"

"You know, the Golden Rule. Don't eat other people unless you are willing to be eaten."

Gomez is cleaning his nails with the tines of his fork. "Don't you think it's really Eat or Be Eaten that makes the world go round?"

"Yeah, mostly. But aren't you yourself a case in point for altruism?" Henry asks.

"Sure, but I am widely considered to be a dangerous nutcase." Gomez says this with feigned indifference, but I can see that he is puzzled by Henry. "Clare," he says, "what about dessert?"

"Ohmigod, I almost forgot," I say, standing up too fast and grabbing the table for support. "I'll get it."

"I'll help you," says Gomez, following me into the kitchen. I'm wearing heels and as I walk into the kitchen I catch the door sill and stagger forward and Gomez grabs me. For a moment we stand pressed together and I feel his hands on my waist, but he lets me go. "You're drunk, Clare," Gomez tells me.

"I know. So are you." I press the button on the coffee maker and coffee begins to drip into the pot. I lean against the counter and carefully take the cellophane off the plate of brownies. Gomez is standing close behind me, and he says very quietly, leaning so that his breath tickles my ear, "He's the same guy."

"What do you mean?"

"That guy I warned you about. Henry, he's the guy—"

Charisse walks into the kitchen and Gomez jumps away from me and opens the fridge. "Hey," she says. "Can I help?"

"Here, take the coffee cups. . . ." We all juggle cups and saucers and plates and brownies and make it safely back to the table. Henry is waiting as though he's at the dentist, with a look of patient dread. I laugh, it's so exactly the look he used to have when I brought him food in the Meadow . . . but he doesn't remember, he hasn't been there yet. "Relax," I say. "It's only brownies. Even I can do brownies." Everyone laughs and sits down. The brownies turn out to be kind of undercooked. "Brownies tartare," says Charisse. "Salmonella fudge," says Gomez. Henry says, "I've always liked dough," and licks his fingers. Gomez rolls a cigarette, lights it, and takes a deep drag.

HENRY: Gomez lights a cigarette and leans back in his chair. There's something about this guy that bugs me. Maybe it's the casual possessiveness toward Clare, or the garden-variety Marxism? I'm sure I've seen him before. Past or future? Let's find out. "You look very familiar," I say to him.

"Mmm? Yeah, I think we've seen each other around."

I've got it. "Iggy Pop at the Riviera Theater?"

He looks startled. "Yeah. You were with that blond girl, Ingrid Carmichel, I always used to see you with." Gomez and I both look at Clare. She is staring intently at Gomez, and he smiles at her. She looks away, but not at me.

Charisse comes to the rescue. "You saw Iggy without me?"

Gomez says, "You were out of town."

Charisse pouts. "I miss everything," she says to me. "I missed Patti Smith and now she's retired. I missed Talking Heads the last time they toured."

"Patti Smith will tour again," I say.

"She will? How do you know?" asks Charisse. Clare and I exchange glances.

"I'm just guessing," I tell her. We begin exploring each other's musical tastes and discover that we are all devoted to punk. Gomez tells us about seeing the New York Dolls in Florida just before Johnny Thunders left the band. I describe a Lene Lovich concert I managed to catch on one of my time travels. Charisse and Clare are excited because the Violent Femmes are playing the Aragon Ballroom in a few weeks and Charisse has scored free tickets. The evening winds down without further ado. Clare walks me downstairs. We stand in the foyer between the outer door and the inner door.

"I'm sorry," she says.

"Oh, not at all. It was fun, I didn't mind cooking."

"No," Clare says, looking at her shoes, "about Gomez."

It's cold in the foyer. I wrap my arms around Clare and she leans against me. "What about Gomez?" I ask her. Something's on her mind. But then she shrugs. "It'll be okay," she says, and I take her word for it. We kiss. I open the outer door, and Clare opens the inner door; I walk down the sidewalk and look back. Clare is still standing there in the half-open doorway watching me. I stand, wanting to go back and hold her, wanting to go back upstairs with her. She turns and begins to walk upstairs, and I watch until she is out of sight.

Saturday, December 14, 1991/ Tuesday, May 9, 2000 (Henry is 36)

HENRY: I'm stomping the living shit out of a large drunk sub-urban guy who had the effrontery to call me a faggot and then tried to beat me up to prove his point. We are in the alley next to the Vic Theater. I can hear the Smoking Popes' bass leaking out of the the-ater's side exits as I systematically smash this idiot's nose and go to work on his ribs. I'm having a rotten evening, and this fool is taking the brunt of my frustration.

"Hey, Library Boy." I turn from my groaning homophobic yup-pie to find Gomez leaning against a dumpster, looking grim.

"Comrade." I step back from the guy I've been bashing, who slides gratefully to the pavement, doubled up. "How goes it?" I'm very relieved to see Gomez: delighted, actually. But he doesn't seem to share my pleasure.

"Gee, ah, I don't want to *disturb* you or anything, but that's a friend of mine you're dismembering, there."

Oh, surely not. "Well, he requested it. Just walked right up to me and said, 'Sir, I urgently need to be firmly macerated.'"

"Oh. Well, hey, well done. Fucking artistic, actually."

"Thank you."

"Do you mind if I just scoop up ol' Nick here and take him to the hospital?"

"Be my guest." Damn. I was planning to appropriate Nick's clothing, especially his shoes, brand-new Doc Martens, deep red, barely worn. "Gomez."

"Yeah?" He stoops to lift his friend, who spits a tooth into his own lap.

"What's the date?"

"December 14."

"What year?"

He looks up at me like a man who has better things to do than humor lunatics and lifts Nick in a fireman's carry that must be excruciating. Nick begins to whimper. "1991. You must be drunker than you look." He walks up the alley and disappears in the direction of the theater entrance. I calculate rapidly. Today is not that long after Clare and I started dating, therefore Gomez and I hardly know each other. No wonder he was giving me the hairy eyeball.

He reappears unencumbered. "I made Trent deal with it. Nick's his brother. He wasn't best pleased." We start walking east, down the alley. "Forgive me for asking, dear Library Boy, but why on earth are you dressed like that?"

I'm wearing blue jeans, a baby blue sweater with little yellow ducks all over it, and a neon red down vest with pink tennis shoes. Really, it's not surprising that someone would feel they needed to hit me.

"It was the best I could do at the time." I hope the guy I took these off of was close to home. It's about twenty degrees out here. "Why are you consorting with frat boys?"

"Oh, we went to law school together." We are walking by the back door of the Army-Navy surplus store and I experience a deep desire to be wearing normal clothing. I decide to risk appalling Gomez; I know he'll get over it. I stop. "Comrade. This will only take a moment; I just need to take care of something. Could you wait at the end of the alley?"

"What are you doing?"

"Nothing. Breaking and entering. Pay no attention to the man behind the curtain."

"Mind if I come along?"

"Yes." He looks crestfallen. "All right. If you must." I step into the niche which shelters the back door. This is the third time I've broken into this place, although the other two occasions are both in the future at the moment. I've got it down to a science. First I open the insignificant combination lock that secures the security grate, slide the grate back, pick the Yale lock with the inside of an old pen and a safety pin found earlier on Belmont Avenue, and use a piece of aluminum between the double doors to lift the inside bolt. *Voilà.* Altogether, it takes about three minutes. Gomez regards me with almost religious awe.

"*Where* did you learn to do that?"

"It's a knack," I reply modestly. We step inside. There is a panel of blinking red lights trying to look like a burglar alarm system, but I know better. It's very dark in here. I mentally review the layout and the merchandise. "Don't touch anything, Gomez." I want to be warm, and inconspicuous. I step carefully through the aisles, and my eyes adjust to the dark. I start with pants: black Levi's. I select a dark blue flannel shirt, a heavy black wool overcoat with an industrial-strength lining, wool socks, boxers, heavy mountain-climbing gloves, and a hat with ear flaps. In the shoe department I find, to my great satisfaction, Docs exactly like the ones my buddy Nick was wearing. I am ready for action.

Gomez, meanwhile, is poking around behind the counter. "Don't bother," I tell him. "This place doesn't leave cash in the register at night. Let's go." We leave the way we came. I close the door gently and pull the grate across. I have my previous set of clothing in a shopping bag. Later I will try to find a Salvation Army collection bin. Gomez looks at me expectantly, like a large dog who's waiting to see if I have any more lunch meat.

Which reminds me. "I'm ravenous. Let's go to Ann Sather's."

"Ann Sather's? I was expecting you to propose bank robbery, or manslaughter, at the very least. You're on a roll, man, don't stop now!"

"I must pause in my labors to refuel. Come on." We cross from the alley to Ann Sather's Swedish Restaurant's parking lot. The attendant mutely regards us as we traverse his kingdom. We cut over to Belmont. It's only nine o'clock, and the street is teeming with its usual mix of runaways, homeless mental cases, clubbers, and suburban thrill seekers. Ann Sather's stands out as an island of normalcy amid the tattoo parlors and condom boutiques. We enter, and wait by the bakery to be seated. My stomach gurgles. The Swedish decor is comforting, all wood paneling and swirling red marbling. We are seated in the smoking section, right in front of the fireplace. Things are looking up. We remove our coats, settle in, read the menus, even though, as lifelong Chicagoans, we could probably sing them from memory in two-part harmony. Gomez lays all his smoking paraphernalia next to his silverware.

"Do you mind?"

"Yes. But go ahead." The price of Gomez's company is marinating in the constant stream of cigarette smoke that flows from his nostrils. His fingers are a deep ochre color; they flutter delicately over the thin papers as he rolls Drum tobacco into a thick cylinder, licks the paper, twists it, sticks it between his lips, and lights it. "Ahh." For Gomez, a half hour without a smoke is an anomaly. I always enjoy watching people satisfy their appetites, even if I don't happen to share them.

"You don't smoke? Anything?"

"I run."

"Oh. Yeah, shit, you're in great shape. I thought you had about killed Nick, and you weren't even winded."

"He was too drunk to fight. Just a big sodden punching bag."

"Why'd you lay into him like that?"

"It was just stupidity." The waiter arrives, tells us his name is Lance and the specials are salmon and creamed peas. He takes our drink orders and speeds away. I toy with the cream dispenser. "He saw how I was dressed, concluded that I was easy meat, got obnoxious, wanted to beat me up, wouldn't take no for an answer, and got a surprise. I was minding my own business, really I was."

Gomez looks thoughtful. "Which is what, exactly?"

"Pardon?"

"Henry. I may look like a chump, but in fact your old Uncle Gomez is not completely *sans* clues. I have been paying attention to you for some time: before our little Clare brought you home, as a matter of fact. I mean, I don't know if you are aware of it, but you are moderately notorious in certain circles. I know a lot of people who know you. People; well, women. Women who know you." He squints at me through the haze of his smoke. "They say some pretty strange things." Lance arrives with my coffee and Gomez's milk. We order: a cheeseburger and fries for Gomez, split pea soup, the salmon, sweet potatoes, and mixed fruit for me. I feel like I'm going to keel over right this minute if I don't get a lot of calories fast. Lance departs swiftly. I'm having trouble caring very much about the misdeeds of my earlier self, much less justifying them to Gomez. None of his business, anyway. But he's waiting for my answer. I stir cream into my coffee, watching the slight white scum on the top dissipate in swirls. I throw caution to the winds. It doesn't matter, after all.

"What would you like to know, comrade?"

"Everything. I want to know why a seemingly mild-mannered librarian beats a guy into a coma over nothing while wearing kindergarten-teacher clothing. I want to know why Ingrid Carmichel tried to kill herself eight days ago. I want to know why you look ten years older right now than you did the last time I saw you. Your hair's going gray. I want to know why you can pick a Yale lock. I

AUDREY NIFFENEGGER

want to know why Clare had a photograph of you before she actually met you."

Clare had a photo of me before 1991? I didn't know that. Oops. "What did the photo look like?"

Gomez regards me. "More like you look at the moment, not like you looked a couple weeks ago when you came over for dinner." That was two weeks ago? Lord, this is only the second time Gomez and I have met. "It was taken outdoors. You're smiling. The date on the back is June 1988." The food arrives, and we pause to arrange it on our little table. I start eating as though there's no tomorrow.

Gomez sits, watching me eating, his food untouched. I've seen Gomez do his thing in court with hostile witnesses, just like this. He simply wills them to spill the beans. I don't mind telling all, I just want to eat first. In fact, I need Gomez to know the truth, because he's going to save my ass repeatedly in the years to come.

I'm halfway through the salmon and he's still sitting. "Eat, eat," I say in my best imitation of Mrs. Kim. He dips a fry in ketchup and munches it. "Don't worry, I'll confess. Just let me have my last meal in peace." He capitulates, and starts to eat his burger. Neither of us says a word until I've finished consuming my fruit. Lance brings me more coffee. I doctor it, stir it. Gomez is looking at me as though he wants to shake me. I resolve to amuse myself at his expense.

"Okay. Here it is: time travel."

Gomez rolls his eyes and grimaces, but says nothing.

"I am a time traveler. At the moment I am thirty-six years old. This afternoon was May 9, 2000. It was a Tuesday. I was at work, I had just finished a Show and Tell for a bunch of Caxton Club members and I had gone back to the stacks to reshelve the books when I suddenly found myself on School Street, in 1991. I had the usual problem of getting something to wear. I hid under somebody's

142

porch for a while. I was cold, and nobody was coming along, and finally this young guy, dressed—well, you saw how I was dressed. I mugged him, took his cash and everything he was wearing except his underwear. Scared him silly; I think he thought I was going to rape him or something. Anyway, I had clothes. Okay. But in this neighborhood you can't dress like that without having certain misunderstandings arise. So I've been taking shit all evening from various people, and your friend just happened to be the last straw. I'm sorry if he's very damaged. I very much wanted his clothes, especially his shoes." Gomez glances under the table at my feet. "I find myself in situations like that all the time. No pun intended. There's something wrong with me. I get dislocated in time, for no reason. I can't control it, I never know when it's going to happen, or where and when I'll end up. So in order to cope, I pick locks, shoplift, pick pockets, mug people, panhandle, break and enter, steal cars, lie, fold, spindle, and mutilate. You name it, I've done it."

"Murder."

"Well, not that I know of. I've never raped anybody, either." I look at him as I speak. He's poker-faced. "Ingrid. Do you actually know Ingrid?"

"I know Celia Attley."

"Dear me. You do keep strange company. How did Ingrid try to kill herself?"

"An overdose of Valium."

"1991? Yeah, okay. That would be Ingrid's fourth suicide attempt."

"What?"

"Ah, you didn't know that? Celia is only selectively informative. Ingrid actually succeeded in doing herself in on January 2, 1994. She shot herself in the chest."

"Henry—"

"You know, it happened six years ago, and I'm still angry at her. What a waste. But she was severely depressed, for a long time, and she just sunk down into it. I couldn't do anything for her. It was one of the things we used to fight about."

"This is a pretty sick joke, Library Boy."

"You want proof."

He just smiles.

"How about that photo? The one you said Clare has?"

The smile vanishes. "Okay. I admit that I am a wee bit befuddled by that."

"I met Clare for the first time in October, 1991. She met me for the first time in September, 1977; she was six, I will be thirty-eight. She's known me all her life. In 1991 I'm just getting to know her. By the way, you should ask Clare all this stuff. She'll tell you."

"I already did. She told me."

"Well, hell, Gomez. You're taking up valuable time here, making me tell you all over again. You didn't believe her?"

"No. Would you?"

"Sure. Clare is very truthful. It's that Catholic upbringing that does it." Lance comes by with more coffee. I'm already highly caffeinated, but more can't hurt. "So? What kind of proof are you looking for?"

"Clare said you disappear."

"Yeah, it's one of my more dramatic parlor tricks. Stick to me like glue, and sooner or later, I vanish. It may take minutes, hours, or days, but I'm very reliable that way."

"Do we know each other in 2000?"

"Yeah." I grin at him. "We're good friends."

"Tell me my future."

Oh, no. Bad idea. "Nope."

"Why not?"

"Gomez. Things happen. Knowing about them in advance makes everything . . . weird. You can't change anything, anyway."

"Why?"

"Causation only runs forward. Things happen once, only once. If you know things . . . I feel trapped, most of the time. If you are in time, not knowing . . . you're free. Trust me." He looks frustrated. "You'll be the best man at our wedding. I'll be yours. You have a great life, Gomez. But I'm not going to tell you the particulars."

"Stock tips?"

Yeah, why not. In 2000 the stock market is insane, but there are amazing fortunes to be made, and Gomez will be one of the lucky ones. "Ever heard of the Internet?"

"No."

"It's a computer thing. A vast, worldwide network with regular people all plugged in, communicating by phone lines with computers. You want to buy technology stocks. Netscape, America Online, Sun Microsystems, Yahoo!, Microsoft, Amazon.com." He's taking notes.

"Dotcom?"

"Don't worry about it. Just buy it at the IPO." I smile. "Clap your hands if you believe in fairies."

"I thought you were pole-axing anyone who insinuated anything about fairies this evening?"

"It's from *Peter Pan*, you illiterate." I suddenly feel nauseous. I don't want to cause a scene here, now. I jump up. "Follow me," I say, running for the men's room, Gomez close behind me. I burst into the miraculously empty john. Sweat is streaming down my face. I throw up into the sink. "Jesus H. Christ," says Gomez. "Damn it, Library—" but I lose the rest of whatever he's about to say, because I'm lying on my side, naked, on a cold linoleum floor, in pitch blackness. I'm dizzy, so I lie there for a while. I reach out my hand

and touch the spines of books. I'm in the stacks, at the Newberry. I get up and stagger to the end of the aisle and flip the switch; light floods the row I'm standing in, blinding me. My clothes, and the cart of books I was shelving, are in the next aisle over. I get dressed, shelve the books, and gingerly open the security door to the stacks. I don't know what time it is; the alarms could be on. But no, everything is as it was. Isabelle is instructing a new patron in the ways of the Reading Room; Matt walks by and waves. The sun pours in the windows, and the hands of the Reading Room clock point to 4:15. I've been gone less than fifteen minutes. Amelia sees me and points to the door. "I'm going out to Starbucks. You want java?"

"Um, no, I don't think so. But thanks." I have a horrible headache. I stick my face into Roberto's office and tell him I don't feel well. He nods sympathetically, gestures at the phone, which is spewing lightspeed Italian into his ear. I grab my stuff and leave.

Just another routine day at the office for Library Boy.

Sunday, December 15, 1991 (Clare is 20)

CLARE: It's a beautiful sunny Sunday morning, and I'm on my way home from Henry's apartment. The streets are icy and there's a couple inches of fresh snow. Everything is blindingly white and clean. I am singing along with Aretha Franklin, "R-E-S-P-E-C-T!" as I turn off Addison onto Hoyne, and lo and behold, there's a parking space right in front. It's my lucky day. I park and negotiate the slick sidewalk, let myself into the vestibule, still humming. I have that dreamy rubber spine feeling that I'm beginning to associate with sex, with waking up in Henry's bed, with getting home at all hours of the morning. I float up the stairs. Charisse will be at church. I'm looking forward to a long bath and the *New York Times*.

As soon as I open our door, I know I'm not alone. Gomez is sitting in the living room in a cloud of smoke with the blinds closed. What with the red flocked wallpaper and the red velvet furniture and all the smoke, he looks like a blond Polish Elvis Satan. He just sits there, so I start walking back to my room without speaking. I'm still mad at him.

"Clare."

I turn. "What?"

"I'm sorry. I was wrong." I've never heard Gomez admit to anything less than papal infallibility. His voice is a deep croak.

I walk into the living room and open the blinds. The sunlight is having trouble getting through the smoke, so I crack a window. "I don't see how you can smoke this much without setting off the smoke detector."

Gomez holds up a nine-volt battery. "I'll put it back before I leave."

I sit down on the chesterfield. I wait for Gomez to tell me why he's changed his mind. He's rolling another cigarette. Finally he lights it, and looks at me.

"I spent last night with your friend Henry."

"So did I."

"Yeah. What did you do?"

"Went to Facets, saw a Peter Greenaway film, ate Moroccan, went to his place."

"And you just left."

"That's right."

"Well. My evening was less cultural, but more eventful. I came upon your beamish boy in the alley by the Vic, smashing Nick to a pulp. Trent told me this morning that Nick has a broken nose, three broken ribs, five broken bones in his hand, soft-tissue damage, and forty-six stitches. And he's gonna need a new front tooth." I am un-moved. Nick is a big bully. "You should have seen it, Clare. Your boyfriend dealt with Nick like he was an inanimate object. Like Nick was a sculpture he was carving. Real scientific-like. Just considered where to land it for maximum effect, *wham*. I would have totally admired it, if it hadn't been Nick."

"Why was Henry beating up Nick?"

Gomez looks uncomfortable. "It sounded like it might have been Nick's fault. He likes to pick on . . . gays, and Henry was dressed like Little Miss Muffet." I can imagine. Poor Henry.

"And then?"

"Then we burglarized the Army-Navy surplus store." So far so good.

"And?"

"And then we went to Ann Sather's for dinner."

I burst out laughing. Gomez smiles. "And he told me the same whacko story that you told me."

"So why did you believe him?"

"Well, he's so fucking nonchalant. I could tell that he absolutely knew me, through and through. He had my number, and he didn't care. And then he—vanished, and I was standing there, and I just . . . had to. Believe."

I nod, sympathetically. "The disappearing is pretty impressive. I remember that from the very first time I saw him, when I was little. He was shaking my hand, and *poof!* he was gone. Hey, when was he coming from?"

"2000. He looked a lot older."

"He goes through a lot." It's kind of nice to sit here and talk about Henry with someone who knows. I feel a surge of gratitude toward Gomez which evaporates as he leans forward and says, quite gravely, "Don't marry him, Clare."

"He hasn't asked me, yet."

"You know what I mean."

I sit very still, looking at my hands quietly clasped in my lap. I'm cold and furious. I look up. Gomez regards me anxiously.

"I love him. He's my life. I've been waiting for him, my whole life, and now, he's here." I don't know how to explain. "With Henry, I can see everything laid out, like a map, past and future, everything at once, like an angel. . . ." I shake my head. I can't put it into words. "I can reach into him and touch time . . . he loves me. We're married because . . . we're part of each other. . . ." I falter. "It's happened already. All at once." I peer at Gomez to see if I've made any sense.

"Clare. I *like* him, very much. He's fascinating. But he's dangerous. All the women he's been with fall apart. I just don't want you blithely waltzing into the arms of this charming sociopath. . . ."

"Don't you see that you're too late? You're talking about somebody I've known since I was six. I *know* him. You've met him twice and you're trying to tell me to jump off the train. Well, I can't. I've seen my future; I can't change it, and I wouldn't if I could."

Gomez looks thoughtful. "He wouldn't tell me anything about my future."

"Henry cares about you; he wouldn't do that to you."

"He did it to you."

"It couldn't be helped; our lives are all tangled together. My whole childhood was different because of him, and there was nothing he could do. He did the best he could." I hear Charisse's key turning in the lock.

"Clare, don't be mad—I'm just trying to help you."

I smile at him. "You can help us. You'll see."

Charisse comes in coughing. "Oh, sweetie. You've been waiting a long time."

"I've been chatting with Clare. About Henry."

"I'm sure you've been telling her how much you adore him," Charisse says with a note of warning in her voice.

"I've been telling her to run as fast as possible in the opposite direction."

"Oh, Gomez. Clare, don't listen to him. He has terrible taste in men." Charisse sits down primly a foot away from Gomez and he reaches over and pulls her onto his lap. She gives him a look.

"She's always like this after church."

"I want breakfast."

"Of course you do, my dove." They get up and scamper down the hall to the kitchen. Soon Charisse is emitting high-pitched giggles and Gomez is trying to spank her with the *Times Magazine*. I sigh and go to my room. The sun is still shining. In the bathroom I run hot hot water into the huge old tub and strip off last night's clothes. As I climb in I catch sight of myself in the mirror. I look almost plump. This cheers me no end, and I sink down into the water feeling like an Ingres odalisque. *Henry loves me. Henry is here, finally, now, finally. And I love him.* I run my hands over my breasts and a thin film of saliva is reaquified by the water and disperses. *Why does everything have to be complicated? Isn't the complicated part behind us now?* I submerge my hair, watch it float around me, dark and net-like. *I never chose Henry, and he never chose me. So how could it be a mistake?* Again I am faced with the fact that we can't know. I lie in the tub, staring at the tile above my feet, until the water is almost cool. Charisse knocks on the door, asking if I've died in here and can she please brush her teeth? As I wrap my hair in a towel I see myself blurred in the mirror by steam and time seems to fold over onto itself and I see myself as a layering of all my previous days and years and all the time that is coming and suddenly I feel as though I've become invisible. But then the feeling is gone as fast as it came and I stand still for a minute and then I pull on my bathrobe and open the door and go on.

Saturday, December 22, 1991 (Henry is 28, and 33)

HENRY: At 5:25 a.m. the doorbell rings, always an evil omen. I stagger to the intercom and push the button.

"Yeah?"

"Hey. Let me in." I press the button again and the horrible buzzing noise that signifies Welcome to My Hearth and Home is transmitted over the line. Forty-five seconds later the elevator clunks and starts to ratchet its way up. I pull on my robe, I go out and stand in the hall and watch the elevator cables moving through the little safety-glass window. The cage hovers into sight and stops, and sure enough, it's me.

He slides open the cage door and steps into the corridor, naked, unshaven, and sporting really short hair. We quickly cross the empty hall and duck into the apartment. I close the door and we stand for a moment looking ourselves over.

"Well," I say, just for something to say. "How goes it?"

"So-so. What's the date?"

"December 22, 1991. Saturday."

"Oh—Violent Femmes at the Aragon tonight?"

"Yep."

He laughs. "Shit. What an abysmal evening *that* was." He walks over to the bed—*my* bed—and climbs in, pulls the covers over his head. I plop down beside him.

"Hey." No response. "When are you from?"

"November 13, 1996. I was on my way to bed. So let me get some sleep, or you will be sincerely sorry in five years."

AUDREY NIFFENEGGER

This seems reasonable enough. I take off my robe and get back into bed. Now I'm on the wrong side of the bed, Clare's side, as I think of it these days, because my doppelgänger has commandeered my side. Everything is subtly different on this side of the bed. It's like when you close one eye and look at something close up for a while, and then look at it from the other eye. I lie there doing this, looking at the armchair with my clothes scattered over it, a peach pit at the bottom of a wine glass on the windowsill, the back of my right hand. My nails need cutting and the apartment could probably qualify for Federal Disaster Relief funds. Maybe my extra self will be willing to pitch in, help out around the house a little, earn his keep. I run my mind over the contents of the refrigerator and pantry and conclude that we are well provisioned. I am planning to bring Clare home with me tonight and I'm not sure what to do with my superfluous body. It occurs to me that Clare might prefer to be with this later edition of me, since after all they do know each other better. For some reason this plunges me into a funk. I try to remember that anything subtracted now will be added later, but I still feel fretful and wish that one of us would just go away.

I ponder my double. He's curled up, hedgehog style, facing away from me, evidently asleep. I envy him. He is me, but I'm not him, yet. He has been through five years of a life that's still mysterious to me, still coiled tightly waiting to spring out and bite. Of course, whatever pleasures are to be had, he's had them; for me they wait like a box of unpoked chocolates.

I try to consider him with Clare's eyes. Why the short hair? I've always been fond of my black, wavy, shoulder-length hair; I've been wearing it this way since high school. But sooner or later, I'm going to chop it off. It occurs to me that the hair is one of many things that must remind Clare I'm not exactly the man she's known from earliest childhood. I'm a close approximation she is guiding surreptitiously toward a me that exists in her mind's eye. What would I be without her?

Not the man who breathes, slowly, deeply, across the bed from me. His neck and back undulate with vertebrae, ribs. His skin is smooth, hardly haired, tightly tacked onto muscles and bones. He is exhausted, and yet sleeps as though at any moment he may jump up and run. Do I radiate this much tension? I guess so. Clare complains that I don't relax until I'm dead tired, but actually I am often relaxed when I'm with her. This older self seems leaner and more weary, more solid and secure. But with me he can afford to show off: he's got my number so completely that I can only acquiesce to him, in my own best interests.

It's 7:14 and it's obvious that I'm not going back to sleep. I get out of bed and turn on the coffee. I pull on underwear and sweat-pants and stretch out. Lately my knees have been sore, so I wrap supports onto them. I pull on socks and lace up my beater running shoes, probably the cause of the funky knees, and vow to go buy new shoes tomorrow. I should have asked my guest what the weather was like out there. Oh, well, December in Chicago: dreadful weather is *de rigueur.* I don my ancient Chicago Film Festival T-shirt, a black sweatshirt, and a heavy orange sweatshirt with a hood that has big Xs on the front and back made of reflective tape. I grab my gloves and keys and out I go, into the day.

It's not a bad day, as early winter days go. There's very little snow on the ground, and the wind is toying with it, pushing it here and there. Traffic is backed up on Dearborn, making a concert of engine noises, and the sky is gray, slowly lightening into gray.

I lace my keys onto my shoe and decide to run along the lake. I run slowly east on Delaware to Michigan Avenue, cross the overpass, and begin jogging beside the bike path, heading north along Oak Street Beach. Only hard-core runners and cyclists are out today. Lake Michigan is a deep slate color and the tide is out, revealing a dark brown strip of sand. Seagulls wheel above my head and far out over the water. I am moving stiffly; cold is unkind to joints, and I'm slowly realizing that it is pretty cold out here by the lake, probably in the low twenties. So I run a little slower than usual, warming up, reminding my poor knees and ankles that their life's work is to carry me far and fast on demand. I can feel the cold dry air in my lungs, feel my heart serenely pounding, and as I reach North Avenue I am feeling good and I start to speed up. Running is many things to me: survival, calmness, euphoria, solitude. It is proof of my corporeal existence, my ability to control my movement through space if not time, and the obedience, however temporary, of my body to my will. As I run I displace air, and things come and go around me, and the path moves like a filmstrip beneath my feet. I remember, as a child, long before video games and the Web, threading filmstrips into the dinky projector in the school library and peering into them, turning the knob that advanced the frame at the sound of a beep. I don't remember anymore what they looked like, what they were about, but I remember the smell of the library, and the way the beep made me jump every time. I'm flying now, that golden feeling, as if I could run right into the air, and I'm invincible, nothing can stop me, nothing can stop me, nothing, nothing, nothing, nothing—.

Evening, the same day: (Henry is 28 and 33, Clare is 20)

CLARE: We're on our way to the Violent Femmes concert at the Aragon Ballroom. After some reluctance on Henry's part, which I don't understand because he loves *les Femmes,* we are cruising Uptown in search of parking. I loop around and around, past the Green Mill, the bars, the dimly lit apartment buildings and the laundromats that look like stage sets. I finally park on Argyle and we walk shivering down the glassy broken sidewalks. Henry walks fast and I am always a little out of breath when we walk together. I've noticed that he makes an effort to match my pace, now. I pull off my glove and put my hand in his coat pocket, and he puts his arm around my shoulder. I'm excited because Henry and I have never gone dancing before, and I love the Aragon, in all its decaying faux Spanish splendor. My Grandma Meagram used to tell me about dancing to the big bands here in the thirties, when everything was new and lovely and there weren't people shooting up in the balconies and lakes of piss in the men's room. But *c'est la vie*, times change, and we are here.

We stand in line for a few minutes. Henry seems tense, on guard. He holds my hand, but stares out over the crowd. I take the opportunity to look at him. Henry is beautiful. His hair is shoulder-length, combed back, black and sleek. He's cat-like, thin, exuding restlessness and physicality. He looks like he might bite. Henry is wearing a black overcoat and a white cotton shirt with French cuffs which dangle undone below his coat sleeves, a lovely acid-green silk tie which he has loosened just enough so that I can see the muscles in his neck, black jeans and black high-top sneakers. Henry gathers my hair together and wraps it around his wrist. For a moment I am his prisoner, and then the line moves forward and he lets me go.

We are ticketed and flow with masses of people into the building. The Aragon has numerous long hallways and alcoves and balconies that wrap around the main hall and are ideal for getting lost and for hiding. Henry and I go up to a balcony close to the stage and sit at a tiny table. We take off our coats. Henry is staring at me.

"You look lovely. That's a great dress; I can't believe you can dance in it."

My dress is skin-tight lilac blue silk, but it stretches enough to move in. I tried it out this afternoon in front of a mirror and it was fine. The thing that worries me is my hair; because of the dry winter air there seems to be twice as much of it as usual. I start to braid it and Henry stops me.

"Don't, please—I want to look at you with it down."

The opening act begins its set. We listen patiently. Everyone is milling around, talking, smoking. There are no seats on the main floor. The noise is phenomenal.

Henry leans over and yells in my ear. "Do you want something to drink?"

"Just a Coke."

He goes off to the bar. I rest my arms on the railing of the balcony and watch the crowd. Girls in vintage dresses, girls in combat gear, boys with Mohawks, boys in flannel shirts. People of both sexes in T-shirts and jeans. College kids and twenty-somethings, with a few old folks scattered in.

Henry is gone for a long time. The warm-up band finishes, to scattered applause, and roadies begin removing the band's equipment and bringing on a more or less identical bunch of instruments. Eventually I get tired of waiting, and, abandoning our table and coats, I force my way through the dense pack of people on the balcony down the stairs and into the long dim hallway where the bar is. Henry's not there. I move slowly through the halls and alcoves, looking but trying not to look like I'm looking.

I spot him at the end of a hallway. He is standing so close to the woman that at first I think they are embracing; she has her back to the wall and Henry leans over her with his hand braced against the wall above her shoulder. The intimacy of their pose takes my breath. She is blond, and beautiful in a very German way, tall and dramatic.

As I get closer, I realize that they aren't kissing; they are fighting. Henry is using his free hand to emphasize whatever it is he is yelling at this woman. Suddenly her impassive face breaks into anger, almost tears. She screams something back at him. Henry steps back and throws up his hands. I hear the last of it as he walks away:

"I can't, Ingrid, I just can't! I'm *sorry*—"

"Henry!" She is running after him when they both see me, standing quite still in the middle of the corridor. Henry is grim as he takes my arm and we walk quickly to the stairs. Three steps up I turn and see her standing, watching us, her arms at her sides, helpless and intense. Henry glances back, and we turn and continue up the stairs.

We find our table, which miraculously is still free and still boasts our coats. The lights are going down and Henry raises his voice over the noise of the crowd. "I'm sorry. I never made it as far as the bar, and I ran into Ingrid—"

Who is Ingrid? I think of myself standing in Henry's bathroom with a lipstick in my hand and I need to know but blackness descends and the Violent Femmes take the stage.

Gordon Gano stands at the microphone glaring at us all and menacing chords ring out and he leans forward and intones the opening lines of "Blister in the Sun" and we're off and running. Henry and I sit and listen and then he leans over to me and shouts, "Do you want to leave?" The dance floor is a roiling mass of slamming humanity.

"I want to dance!"

Henry looks relieved. "Great! Yes! Come on!" He strips off his tie and shoves it in his overcoat pocket. We wend our way back downstairs and enter the main hall. I see Charisse and Gomez dancing more or less together. Charisse is oblivious and frenzied, Gomez is barely moving, a cigarette absolutely level between his lips. He sees me and gives me a little wave. Moving into the crowd is like

wading in Lake Michigan; we are taken in and buoyed along, floating toward the stage. The crowd is roaring *Add it up! Add it up!* and
the Femmes respond by attacking their instruments with insane
vigor.

Henry is moving, vibrating with the bass line. We are just outside the mosh pit, dancers slamming against each other at high velocity on one side and on the other side dancers shaking their hips,
flailing their arms, stepping to the music.

We dance. The music runs through me, waves of sound that
grab me by the spine, that move my feet my hips my shoulders
without consulting my brain. *(Beautiful girl, love your dress, high
school smile, oh yes, where she is now, I can only guess.)* I open my eyes
and see Henry watching me while he dances. When I raise my arms
he grasps me around the waist and I leap up. I have a panoramic
view of the dance floor for a mighty eternity. Someone waves at me
but before I can see who it is Henry sets me down again. We dance
touching, we dance apart. *(How can I explain personal pain?)* Sweat
is streaming down me. Henry shakes his head and his hair makes a
black blur and his sweat is all over me. The music is goading, mocking *(I ain't had much to live for I ain't had much to live for I ain't had
much to live for)*. We throw ourselves at it. My body is elastic, my
legs are numb, and a sensation of white heat travels from my crotch
to the top of my head. My hair is damp ropes that cling to my arms
and neck and face and back. The music crashes into a wall and
stops. My heart is pounding. I place my hand on Henry's chest and
am surprised that his seems only slightly quickened.

Slightly later, I walk into the ladies' room and see Ingrid sitting on a
sink, crying. A small black woman with beautiful long dreads is
standing in front of her speaking softly and stroking her hair. The
sound of Ingrid's sobs echoes off the dank yellow tile. I start to back

out of the room and my movement attracts their attention. They look at me. Ingrid is a mess. All her Teutonic cool is gone, her face is red and puffy, her makeup is in streaks. She stares at me, bleak and drained. The black woman walks over to me. She is fine and delicate and dark and sad. She stands close and speaks quietly.

"Sister," she says, "what's your name?"

I hesitate. "Clare," I finally say.

She looks back at Ingrid. "Clare. A word to the wise. You are mixing in where you're not wanted. Henry, he's bad news, but he's Ingrid's bad news, and you be a fool to mess with him. You hear what I'm saying?"

I don't want to know but I can't help myself. "What are you talking about?"

"They were going to get married. Then Henry, he breaks it off, tells Ingrid he's sorry, *never* mind, just forget it. I say she's better off without him, but she don't listen. He treats her bad, drinks like they ain't making it no more, disappears for days and then comes around like nothing happened, sleeps with anything that stands still long enough. That's Henry. When he makes you moan and cry, don't say nobody never told you." She turns abruptly and walks back to Ingrid, who is still staring at me, who is looking at me with unconditional despair.

I must be gaping at them. "I'm sorry," I say, and I flee.

I wander the halls and finally find an alcove that's empty except for a young Goth girl passed out on a vinyl couch with a burning cigarette between her fingers. I take it from her and stub it out on the filthy tile. I sit on the arm of the couch and the music vibrates through my tailbone up my spine. I can feel it in my teeth. I still need to pee and my head hurts. I want to cry. I don't understand what just happened. That is, I understand but I don't know what I should do about it. I don't know if I should just forget it, or get upset at Henry and demand an explanation, or what. What did I expect? I wish I could send a postcard into the past, to this cad Henry who I don't know: *Do nothing. Wait for me. Wish you were here.*

Henry sticks his head around the corner. "There you are. I thought I'd lost you."

Short hair. Henry has either gotten his hair cut in the last half hour or I'm looking at my favorite chrono-displaced person. I jump up and fling myself at him.

"Oompf—hey, glad to see you, *too.* . . ."

"I've *missed* you—" now I *am* crying.

"You've been with me almost nonstop for weeks."

"I know but—you're not *you,* yet—I mean, you're different. Damn." I lean against the wall and Henry presses against me. We kiss, and then Henry starts licking my face like a mama cat. I try to purr and start laughing. "You asshole. You're trying to distract me from your *infamous* behavior—"

"What behavior? I didn't know you existed. I was unhappily dating Ingrid. I met you. I broke up with Ingrid less than twenty-four hours later. I mean, infidelity isn't retroactive, you know?"

"She said—"

"Who said?"

"The black woman." I mime long hair. "Short, big eyes, dreads—"

"Oh Lord. That's Celia Attley. She despises me. She's in love with Ingrid."

"She said you were going to marry Ingrid. That you drink all the time, fuck around, and are basically a bad person and I should run. That's what she said."

Henry is torn between mirth and incredulity. "Well, some of

that is actually true. I did fuck around, a lot, and I certainly have been known to drink rather prodigiously. But we weren't *engaged*. I would never have been insane enough to *marry* Ingrid. We were royally miserable together."

"But then why—"

"Clare, very few people meet their soulmates at age six. So you gotta pass the time somehow. And Ingrid was very—patient. Overly patient. Willing to put up with odd behavior, in the hope that someday I would shape up and marry her martyred ass. And when somebody is that patient, you have to feel grateful, and then you want to hurt them. Does that make any sense?"

"I guess. I mean, no, not to me, but I don't think that way."

Henry sighs. "It's very charming of you to be ignorant of the twisted logic of most relationships. Trust me. When we met I was wrecked, blasted, and damned, and I am slowly pulling myself together because I can see that you are a human being and I would like to be one, too. And I have been trying to do it without you noticing, because I still haven't figured out that all pretense is useless between us. But it's a long way from the me you're dealing with in 1991 to me, talking to you right now from 1996. You have to work at me; I can't get there alone."

"Yes, but it's hard. I'm not used to being the teacher."

"Well, whenever you feel discouraged, think of all the hours I spent, am spending, with your tiny self. New math and botany, spelling and American history. I mean, you can say nasty things to me in French because I sat there and drilled you on them."

"Too true. *Il a les défauts de ses qualités.* But I bet it's easier to teach all that than to teach how to be—happy."

"But you make me happy. It's living up to being happy that's the difficult part." Henry is playing with my hair, twirling it into little knots. "Listen, Clare, I'm going to return you to the poor *imbécile* you came in with. I'm sitting upstairs feeling depressed and wondering where you are."

I realize that I have forgotten my present Henry in my joy at seeing my once and future Henry, and I am ashamed. I feel an almost maternal longing to go solace the strange boy who is becoming the man before me, the one who kisses me and leaves me with an admonition to be nice. As I walk up the stairs I see the Henry of my future fling himself into the midst of the slam dancers, and I move as in a dream to find the Henry who is my here and now.

CHRISTMAS EVE, THREE

....

Tuesday, Wednesday, Thursday, December 24, 25, 26, 1991
(Clare is 20, Henry is 28)

CLARE: It's 8:32 a.m. on the twenty-fourth of December and Henry and I are on our way to Meadowlark House for Christmas. It's a beautiful clear day, no snow here in Chicago, but six inches on the ground in South Haven. Before we left, Henry spent time repacking the car, checking the tires, looking under the hood. I don't think he had the slightest idea what he was looking at. My car is a very cute 1990 white Honda Civic, and I love it, but Henry really hates riding in cars, especially small cars. He's a horrible passenger, holding onto the armrest and braking the whole time we're in transit. He would probably be less afraid if he could be the driver, but for obvious reasons Henry doesn't have a driver's license. So we are sailing along the Indiana Toll Road on this fine winter day; I'm calm and looking forward to seeing my family and Henry is a basket case. It doesn't help that he didn't run this morning; I've noticed that Henry needs an incredible amount of physical activity all the time in order to be happy. It's like hanging out with a greyhound. It's different being with Henry in real time. When I was growing up Henry came and went, and our encounters were concentrated and dramatic and unsettling. Henry had a lot of stuff he wasn't going to tell me, and most of the time he wouldn't let me get anywhere near him, so I always had this intense, unsatisfied feeling. When I finally found him in the present, I thought it would be like that. But in fact it's so much better, in many ways. First and foremost, instead of refusing to touch me at all, Henry is constantly touching me, kissing me, making love to me. I feel as though I have become a different person, one who is bathed in a warm pool of desire. And he tells me things! Anything I ask him about himself, his life, his family—he tells me, with names, places, dates. Things that seemed utterly mysterious to me as a child are revealed as perfectly logical. But the best thing of all is that I see him for long stretches of time—hours, days. I know where to find him. He goes to work, he comes home. Sometimes I open my address book just to look at the entry: Henry DeTamble, 714 Dearborn, 11e, Chicago, IL 60610, 312-431-8313. A last name, an address, a phone number. *I can call him on the phone.* It's a miracle. I feel like Dorothy, when her house crash-landed in Oz and the world turned from black and white to color. We're not in Kansas anymore.

In fact, we're about to cross into Michigan, and there's a rest stop. I pull into the parking lot, and we get out and stretch our legs. We head into the building, and there's the maps and brochures for the tourists, and the huge bank of vending machines.

"Wow," Henry says. He goes over and inspects all the junk food, and then starts reading the brochures. "Hey, let's go to Frankenmuth! 'Christmas 365 Days a Year!' God, I'd commit *hara-kiri* after about an hour of that. Do you have any change?"

I find a fistful of change in the bottom of my purse and we gleefully spend it on two Cokes, a box of Good & Plenty, and a Hershey bar. We walk back out into the dry cold air, arm in arm. In the car, we open our Cokes and consume sugar. Henry looks at my watch. "Such decadence. It's only 9:15."

"Well, in a couple minutes, it'll be 10:15."

"Oh, right, Michigan's an hour ahead. How surreal."

I look over at him. "Everything is surreal. I can't believe you're actually going to meet my family. I've spent so much time *hiding* you from my family."

"Only because I adore you beyond reason am I doing this. *I* have spent a lot of time avoiding road trips, meeting girls' families, and Christmas. The fact that I am enduring all three at once proves that I love you."

"Henry—" I turn to him; we kiss. The kiss starts to evolve into something more when out of the corner of my eye I see three pre-pubescent boys and a large dog standing a few feet away from us, watching with interest. Henry turns to see what I am looking at and the boys all grin and give us the thumbs up. They amble off to their parents' van.

"By the way—what are the sleeping arrangements at your house?"

"Oh, dear. Etta called me yesterday about that. I'm in my own room and you are in the blue room. We're down the hall from each other, with my parents and Alicia in between."

"And how committed are we to maintaining this?"

I start the car and we get back on the highway. "I don't know because I've never done this before. Mark just brings his girlfriends downstairs to the rec room and boffs them on the couch in the wee hours, and we all pretend not to notice. If things are difficult we can always go down to the Reading Room; I used to hide you down there."

"Hmm. Oh, well." Henry looks out the window for a while. "You know, this isn't too bad."

"What?"

"Riding. In a car. On the highway."

"Golly. Next you'll be getting on planes."

"Never."

"Paris. Cairo. London. Kyoto."

"No way. I am convinced that I would time travel and Lord knows if I would be able to get back to something flying 350 miles an hour. I'd end up falling out of the sky à la Icarus."

"Seriously?"

"I'm not planning to find out for sure."

"Could you get there by time travel?"

"Well. Here's my theory. Now, this is only a Special Theory of Time Travel as Performed by Henry DeTamble, and not a General Theory of Time Travel."

"Okay."

"First of all, I think it's a brain thing. I think it's a lot like epilepsy, because it tends to happen when I'm stressed, and there are physical cues, like flashing light, that can prompt it. And because things like running, and sex, and meditation tend to help me stay put in the present. Secondly, I have absolutely no conscious control over when or where I go, how long I stay, or when I come back. So time travel tours of the Riviera are very unlikely. Having said that, my subconscious seems to exert tremendous control, because I spend a lot of time in my own past, visiting events that are interesting or important, and evidently I will be spending enormous amounts of time visiting you, which I am looking forward to immensely. I tend to go to places I've already been in real time, although I do find myself in other, more random times and places. I tend to go to the past, rather than the future."

"You've been to the future? I didn't know you could do that."

Henry is looking pleased with himself. "So far, my range is

about fifty years in each direction. But I very rarely go to the future, and I don't think I've ever seen much of anything there that I found useful. It's always quite brief. And maybe I just don't know what I'm looking at. It's the past that exerts a lot of pull. In the past I feel much more solid. Maybe the future itself is less substantial? I don't know. I always feel like I'm breathing thin air, out there in the future. That's one of the ways I can tell it *is* the future: it feels different. It's harder to run, there." Henry says this thoughtfully, and I suddenly have a glimpse of the terror of being in a foreign time and place, without clothes, without friends. . . .

"That's why your feet—"

"Are like leather." The soles of Henry's feet have thick calluses, as though they are trying to become shoes. "I am a beast of the hoof. If anything ever happens to my feet you might as well shoot me."

We ride on in silence for a while. The road rises and dips, dead fields of cornstalks flash by. Farmhouses stand washed in the winter sun, each with their vans and horse trailers and American cars lined up in the long driveways. I sigh. Going home is such a mixed experience. I'm dying to see Alicia and Etta, and I'm worried about my mother, and I don't especially feel like dealing with my father and Mark. But I'm curious to see how they deal with Henry, and he with them. I'm proud of the fact that I kept Henry a secret for so long. Fourteen years. When you're a kid fourteen years is forever.

We pass a Wal-Mart, a Dairy Queen, a McDonald's. More cornfields. An orchard. U-Pick-M Strawberries, Blueberries. In the summer this road is a long corridor of fruit, grain, and capitalism. But now the fields are dead and dry and the cars speed along the sunny cold highway ignoring the beckoning parking lots.

I never thought much about South Haven until I moved to Chicago. Our house always seemed like an island, sitting in the unincorporated area to the south, surrounded by the Meadow, orchards, woods, farms, and South Haven was just Town, as in *Let's go to Town and get an ice cream.* Town was groceries and hardware and Mackenzie's Bakery and the sheet music and records at the Music Emporium, Alicia's favorite store. We used to stand in front of Appleyard's Photography Studio making up stories about the brides and toddlers and families smiling their hideous smiles in the window. We didn't think the library was funny-looking in its faux Greek splendor, nor did we find the cuisine limited and bland, or the movies at the Michigan Theater relentlessly American and mindless. These were opinions I came to later, after I became a denizen of a City, an expatriate anxious to distance herself from the bumpkin ways of her youth. I am suddenly consumed by nostalgia for the little girl who was me, who loved the fields and believed in God, who spent winter days home sick from school reading Nancy Drew and sucking menthol cough drops, who could keep a secret. I glance over at Henry and see that he has fallen asleep.

South Haven, fifty miles.

Twenty-six, twelve, three, one.

Phoenix Road.

Blue Star Highway.

And then: Meagram Lane. I reach over to wake Henry but he's already awake. He smiles nervously and looks out the window at the endless tunnel of bare winter trees as we hurtle along, and as the gate comes into view I fumble in the glove compartment for the opener and the gates swing apart and we pass through.

The house appears like a pop-up in a book. Henry gasps, and starts to laugh.

"What?" I say defensively.

"I didn't realize it was so *huge.* How many rooms does this monster have?"

"Twenty-four," I tell him. Etta is waving at us from the hall window as I pull around the drive and stop near the front door. Her hair is grayer than last time I was here, but her face is pink with pleasure. As we climb out of the car she's gingerly picking her way down the icy front steps in no coat and her good navy blue dress with the lace collar, carefully balancing her stout figure over her sensible shoes, and I run over to her to take her arm but she bats me away until she's at the bottom and then she gives me a hug and a kiss (I breathe in Etta's smell of Noxzema and powder so gladly) as Henry stands by, waiting. "And what have we here?" she says as though Henry is a small child I have brought along unannounced. "Etta Milbauer, Henry DeTamble," I introduce. I see a little 'Oh' on Henry's face and I wonder who he thought she was. Etta beams at Henry as we climb the steps. She opens the front door. Henry lowers his voice and asks me, "What about our stuff?" and I tell him that Peter will deal with it. "Where is everyone?" I ask, and Etta says that lunch is in fifteen minutes and we can take off our coats and wash and go right in. She leaves us standing in the hall and retreats to the kitchen. I turn, take off my coat and hang it in the hall closet. When I turn back to Henry he is waving at someone. I peer around him and see Nell sticking her broad, snub-nosed face out of the dining room door, grinning, and I run down the hall and give her a big sloppy kiss and she chuckles at me and says, "Pretty man, monkey girl," and ducks back into the other room before Henry can reach us.

"Nell?" he guesses and I nod. "She's not shy, just busy," I explain. I lead him up the back stairs to the second floor. "You're in here," I tell him, opening the door to the blue bedroom. He glances in and follows me down the hall. "This is my room," I say apprehensively and Henry slips around me and stands in the middle of the rug just looking and when he turns to me I see that he doesn't recognize any-thing; nothing in the room means a thing to him, and the knife of realization sinks in deeper: all the little tokens and souvenirs in this museum of our past are as love letters to an illiterate. Henry picks up a wren's nest (it happens to be the first of all the many bird's nests he gave me over the years) and says, "Nice." I nod, and open my mouth to tell him and he puts it back on the shelf and says, "Does that door lock?" and I flip the lock and we're late for lunch.

HENRY: I'm almost calm as I follow Clare down the stairs, through the dark cold hall and into the dining room. Everyone is al-ready eating. The room is low ceilinged and comfortable in a William Morrisy sort of way; the air is warm from the fire crackling in the small fireplace and the windows are so frosted over that I can't see out. Clare goes over to a thin woman with pale red hair who must be her mother, who tilts her head to receive Clare's kiss, who half rises to shake my hand. Clare introduces her to me as "my mother" and I call her "Mrs. Abshire" and she immediately says "Oh, but you must call me Lucille, everyone does," and smiles in an exhausted but warm sort of way, as though she is a brilliant sun in some other galaxy. We take our seats across the table from each other. Clare is sitting between Mark and an elderly woman who turns out to be her Great Aunt Dulcie; I am sitting between Alicia and a plump pretty blond girl who is introduced as Sharon and who seems to be with Mark. Clare's father sits at the head of the table and my first impression is that he is deeply disturbed by me. Hand-some, truculent Mark seems equally unnerved. They've seen me be-fore. I wonder what I was doing that caused them to notice me, remember me, recoil ever so slightly in aversion when Clare intro-duces me. But Philip Abshire is a lawyer, and master of his features, and within a minute he is affable and smiling, the host, my girlfriend's dad, a balding middle-aged man with aviator glasses and an athletic body gone soft and paunchy but strong hands, tennis-playing hands, gray eyes that continue to regard me warily despite the confidential grin. Mark has a harder time concealing his distress, and every time I catch his eye he looks at his plate. Alicia is not what I expected; she is matter-of-fact and kind, but a little odd, absent. She has Philip's dark hair, like Mark, and Lucille's features, sort of; Alicia looks as though someone had tried to combine Clare and Mark but had given up and thrown in some Eleanor Roosevelt to fill in the gaps. Philip says something and Alicia laughs, and suddenly she is lovely and I turn to her in surprise as she rises from the table.

"I've got to go to St. Basil's," she informs me. "I've got a rehearsal. Are you coming to church?" I dart a look at Clare, who nods slightly, and I tell Alicia "Of course," and as everyone sighs with—what? relief? I remember that Christmas is, after all, a Christian holiday in addition to being my own personal day of atonement. Alicia leaves. I imagine my mother laughing at me, her well-plucked eyebrows raised high at the sight of her half-Jewish son marooned in the midst of Christmas in Goyland, and I mentally shake my finger at her. *You should talk,* I tell her. *You married an Episcopalian.* I look at my plate and it's ham, with peas and an effete little salad. I don't eat pork and I hate peas.

"Clare tells us you're a librarian," Philip assays, and I admit that this is so. We have a chipper little discussion about the Newberry and people who are Newberry trustees and also clients of Philip's firm, which apparently is based in Chicago, in which case I am not clear about why Clare's family lives way up here in Michigan.

"Summer homes," he tells me, and I remember Clare explaining that her father specializes in wills and trusts. I picture elderly rich people reclining on their private beaches, slathering on sunblock and deciding to cut Junior out of the will, reaching for their cell phones to call Philip. I recollect that Avi, who is first chair to my father's second at the CSO, has a house around here somewhere. I mention this and everyone's ears perk.

"Do you know him?" Lucille asks.

"Sure. He and my dad sit right next to each other."

"Sit next to each other?"

"Well, you know. First and second violin."

"Your father is a violinist?"

"Yeah." I look at Clare, who is staring at her mother with a *don't embarrass me* expression on her face.

"And he plays for the Chicago Symphony Orchestra?"

"Yes."

Lucille's face is suffused with pink; now I know where Clare gets her blushes. "Do you think he would listen to Alicia play? If we gave him a tape?"

I grimly hope that Alicia is very, very good. People are constantly bestowing tapes on Dad. Then I have a better idea.

"Alicia is a cellist, isn't she?"

"Yes."

"Is she looking for a teacher?"

Philip interjects: "She studies with Frank Wainwright in Kalamazoo."

"Because I could give the tape to Yoshi Akawa. One of his students just left to take a job in Paris." Yoshi is a great guy and first chair cello. I know he'll at least listen to the tape; my dad, who doesn't teach, will simply pitch it out. Lucille is effusive; even Philip seems pleased. Clare looks relieved. Mark eats. Great Aunt Dulcie, pink-haired and tiny, is oblivious to this whole exchange. Perhaps she's deaf? I glance at Sharon, who is sitting on my left and who hasn't said a word. She looks miserable. Philip and Lucille are discussing which tape they should give me, or perhaps Alicia should

THE TIME TRAVELER'S WIFE

make a new one? I ask Sharon if this is her first time up here and she nods. Just as I'm about to ask her another question Philip asks me what my mother does and I blink; I give Clare a look that says *Didn't you tell them anything?*

"My mother was a singer. She's dead."

Clare says, quietly, "Henry's mother was Annette Lyn Robinson." She might as well have told them my mom was the Virgin Mary; Philip's face lights up. Lucille makes a little fluttering motion with her hands.

"Unbelievable—fantastic! We have all her recordings—" *und so weiter.* But then Lucille says, "I met her when I was young. My father took me to hear *Madama Butterfly,* and he knew someone who took us backstage afterward, and we went to her dressing room, and she was there, and all these flowers! and she had her little boy— why, that was you!"

I nod, trying to find my voice. Clare says, "What did she look like?" Mark says, "Are we going skiing this afternoon?" Philip nods. Lucille smiles, lost in memory. "She was *so* beautiful—she still had the wig on, that long black hair, and she was teasing the little boy with it, tickling him, and he was dancing around. She had such lovely hands, and she was just my height, so slender, and she was Jewish, you know, but I thought she looked more Italian—" Lucille breaks off and her hand flies to her mouth, and her eyes dart to my plate, which is clean except for a few peas.

"Are you Jewish?" Mark asks, pleasantly.

"I suppose I could be, if I wanted, but nobody ever made a point of it. She died when I was six, and my dad's a lapsed Episcopalian."

"You look just like her," Lucille volunteers, and I thank her. Our plates are removed by Etta, who asks Sharon and me if we drink coffee. We both say *Yes* at the same time, so emphatically that Clare's whole family laughs. Etta gives us a motherly smile and minutes later she sets steaming cups of coffee in front of us and I think *That wasn't so bad, after all.* Everyone talks about skiing, and the weather, and we all stand up and Philip and Mark walk into the hall together; I ask Clare if she's going skiing and she shrugs and asks me if I want to and I explain that I don't ski and have no interest in learning. She decides to go anyway after Lucille says that she needs someone to help with her bindings. As we walk up the stairs I hear Mark say, "— incredible resemblance—" and I smile to myself.

Later, after everyone has left and the house is quiet, I venture down from my chilly room in search of warmth and more coffee. I walk through the dining room and into the kitchen and am confronted by an amazing array of glassware, silver, cakes, peeled vegetables, and roasting pans in a kitchen that looks like something you'd see in a four-star restaurant. In the midst of it all stands Nell with her back to me, singing "Rudolph the Red Nosed Reindeer" and waggling her large hips, waving a baster at a young black girl who points at me mutely. Nell turns around and smiles a huge gap-toothed smile and then says, "What are you doin' in my kitchen, Mister Boyfriend?"

"I was wondering if you have any coffee left?"

"Left? What do you think, I let coffee sit around all day gettin' vile? Shoo, son, get out of here and go sit in the living room and pull on the bell and I will make you some fresh coffee. Didn't your mama teach you about coffee?"

"Actually, my mother wasn't much of a cook," I tell her, venturing closer to the center of the vortex. Something smells wonderful. "What are you making?"

"What you're smellin' is a Thompson's Turkey," Nell says. She opens the oven to show me a monstrous turkey that looks like something that's been in the Great Chicago Fire. It's completely black. "Don't look so dubious, boy. Underneath that crust is the best eatin' turkey on Planet Earth."

I am willing to believe her; the smell is perfect. "What is a Thompson's Turkey?" I ask, and Nell discourses on the miraculous properties of the Thompson's Turkey, invented by Morton Thompson, a newspaperman, in the 1930s. Apparently the production of this marvelous beast involves a great deal of stuffing, basting, and turning. Nell allows me to stay in her kitchen while she makes me coffee and wrangles the turkey out of the oven and wrestles it onto its back and then artfully drools cider gravy all over it before shoving it back into the chamber. There are twelve lobsters crawling around in a large plastic tub of water by the sink. "Pets?" I tease her, and she replies, "That's your Christmas dinner, son; you want to pick one out? You're not a vegetarian, are you?" I assure her that I am not, that I am a good boy who eats whatever is put in front of him.

"You'd never know it, you so thin," Nell says. "I'm gonna feed you up."

"That's why Clare brought me."

"Hmm," Nell says, pleased. "Awright, then. Now scat so I can get on, here." I take my large mug of fragrant coffee and wend my way to the living room, where there is a huge Christmas tree and a fire. It looks like an ad for Pottery Barn. I settle myself in an orange wing chair by the fire and am riffing through the pile of newspapers when someone says, "Where'd you get the coffee?" and I look up and see Sharon sitting across from me in a blue armchair that exactly matches her sweater.

"Hi," I say. "I'm sorry—"

"That's okay," Sharon says.

"I went to the kitchen, but I guess we're supposed to use the bell, wherever that is." We scan the room and sure enough, there's a bell pull in the corner.

"This is so weird," Sharon says. "We've been here since yesterday and I've been just kind of creeping around, you know, afraid to use the wrong fork or something. . . ."

"Where are you from?"

"Florida." She laughs. "I never had a white Christmas 'til I got to Harvard. My dad owns a gas station in Jacksonville. I figured after school I'd go back there, you know, 'cause I don't like the cold, but now I guess I'm stuck."

"How come?"

Sharon looks surprised. "Didn't they tell you? Mark and I are getting married."

I wonder if Clare knows this; it seems like something she would have mentioned. Then I notice the diamond on Sharon's finger. "Congratulations."

"I guess. I mean, thank you."

"Um, aren't you sure? About getting married?" Sharon actually looks like she's been crying; she's all puffy around the eyes.

"Well, I'm pregnant. So. . . ."

"Well, it doesn't necessarily follow—"

"Yeah it does. If you're Catholic." Sharon sighs, and slouches into the chair. I actually know several Catholic girls who have had abortions and weren't struck down by lightning, but apparently Sharon's is a less accommodating faith.

"Well, congratulations. Uh, when . . . ?"

"January eleventh." She sees my surprise and says, "Oh, the baby? April." She makes a face. "I hope it's over spring break, because otherwise I don't see how I'll manage—not that it matters so much now. . . ."

"What's your major?"

"Premed. My parents are furious. They're leaning on me to give it up for adoption."

"Don't they like Mark?"

"They've never even met Mark, it's not that, they're just afraid I won't go to medical school and it will all be a big waste." The front door opens and the skiers have returned. A gust of cold air makes it all the way across the living room and blows over us. It feels good, and I realize that I am being roasted like Nell's turkey by the fire here. "What time is dinner?" I ask Sharon.

"Seven, but last night we had drinks in here first. Mark had just told his mom and dad, and they weren't exactly throwing their arms around me. I mean, they were nice, you know, how people can be nice but be mean at the same time? I mean, you'd think I got pregnant all by myself and Mark had nothing to do with it—"

I'm glad when Clare comes in. She's wearing a funny peaked green cap with a big tassel hanging off it and an ugly yellow skiing sweater over blue jeans. She's flushed from the cold and smiling. Her hair is wet and I see as she walks ebulliently across the enormous Persian carpet in her stocking feet toward me that she does belong here, she's not an aberration, she has simply chosen another kind of life, and I'm glad. I stand up and she throws her arms around me and then just as quickly she turns to Sharon and says, "I just heard! Congratulations!" and Clare embraces Sharon, who looks at me over Clare's shoulder, startled but smiling. Later Sharon tells me, "I think you've got the only nice one." I shake my head but I know what she means.

CLARE: There's an hour before dinner and no one will notice if we're gone. "Come on," I tell Henry. "Let's go outside." He groans.

"Must we?"

"I want to show you something."

We put on our coats and boots and hats and gloves and tromp through the house and out the back door. The sky is clear ultramarine blue and the snow over the meadow reflects it back lighter and the two blues meet in the dark line of trees that is the beginning of the woods. It's too early for stars but there's an airplane blinking its way across space. I imagine our house as a tiny dot of light seen from the plane, like a star.

"This way." The path to the clearing is under six inches of snow. I think of all the times I have stomped over bare footprints so no one would see them running down the path toward the house. Now there are deer tracks, and the prints of a large dog.

The stubble of dead plants under snow, wind, the sound of our boots. The clearing is a smooth bowl of blue snow; the rock is an island with a mushroom top. "This is it."

Henry stands with his hands in his coat pockets. He swivels around, looking. "So this is it," he says. I search his face for a trace of recognition. Nothing. "Do you ever have *déja vu?*" I ask him.

Henry sighs. "My whole life is one long *déja vu.*"

We turn and walk over our own tracks, back to the house.

Later:

I have warned Henry that we dress for dinner on Christmas Eve and so when I meet him in the hall he is resplendent in a black suit, white shirt, maroon tie with a mother-of-pearl tie clasp. "Goodness," I say. "You've shined your shoes!"

"I have," he admits. "Pathetic, isn't it?"

"You look perfect; a Nice Young Man."

"When in fact, I am the Punk Librarian Deluxe. Parents, beware."

"They'll adore you."

"I adore you. Come here." Henry and I stand before the full-length mirror at the top of the stairs, admiring ourselves. I am wearing a pale green silk strapless dress which belonged to my grandmother. I have a photograph of her wearing it on New Year's Eve, 1941. She's laughing. Her lips are dark with lipstick and she's holding a cigarette. The man in the photograph is her brother Teddy, who was killed in France six months later. He's laughing, too. Henry puts his hands on my waist and expresses surprise at all the boning and corsetry under the silk. I tell him about Grandma. "She was smaller than me. It only hurts when I sit down; the ends of the steel thingies poke into my hips." Henry is kissing my neck when someone coughs and we spring apart. Mark and Sharon stand in the door of Mark's room, which Mama and Daddy have reluctantly agreed there is no point in their not sharing.

"None of that, now," Mark says in his annoyed schoolmarm voice. "Haven't you learned anything from the painful example of your elders, boys and girls?"

"Yes," replies Henry. "Be prepared." He pats his pants pocket (which is actually empty) with a smile and we sail down the stairs as Sharon giggles.

Everyone's already had a few drinks when we arrive in the living room. Alicia makes our private hand signal: *Watch out for Mama, she's messed up.* Mama is sitting on the couch looking harmless, her hair all piled up into a chignon, wearing her pearls and her peach velvet dress with the lace sleeves. She looks pleased when Mark goes over and sits down next to her, laughs when he makes some little joke for her, and I wonder for a moment if Alicia is mistaken. But then I see how Daddy is watching Mama and I realize that she must have said something awful just before we came in. Daddy is standing by the drinks cart and he turns to me, relieved, and pours me a Coke and hands Mark a beer and a glass. He asks Sharon and Henry what they'll have. Sharon asks for La Croix. Henry, after pondering for a moment, asks for Scotch and water. My father mixes drinks with a heavy hand, and his eyes bug out a little when Henry knocks back the Scotch effortlessly.

"Another?"

"No, thank you." I know by now that Henry would like to simply take the bottle and a glass and curl up in bed with a book, and that he is refusing seconds because he would then feel no compunction about thirds and fourths. Sharon hovers at Henry's elbow and I abandon them, crossing the room to sit by Aunt Dulcie in the window seat.

"Oh, child, how lovely—I haven't seen that dress since Elizabeth wore it to the party the Lichts had at the Planetarium. . . ." Alicia joins us; she is wearing a navy blue turtleneck with a tiny hole where the sleeve is separating from the bodice and an old bedraggled kilt with wool stockings that bag around her ankles like an old lady's. I know she's doing it to bug Daddy, but still.

"What's wrong with Mama?" I ask her.

Alicia shrugs. "She's pissed off about Sharon."

"What's wrong with Sharon?" inquires Dulcie, reading our lips. "She seems very nice. Nicer than Mark, if you ask me."

"She's pregnant," I tell Dulcie. "They're getting married. Mama thinks she's white trash because she's the first person in her family to go to college."

Dulcie looks at me sharply, and sees that I know what she knows. "Lucille, of all people, ought to be a little understanding of that young girl." Alicia is about to ask Dulcie what she means when the dinner bell rings and we rise, Pavlovian, and file toward the dining room. I whisper to Alicia, "Is she drunk?" and Alicia whispers back, "I think she was drinking in her room before dinner." I squeeze Alicia's hand and Henry hangs back and we go into the dining room and find our places, Daddy and Mama at the head and foot of the table, Dulcie and Sharon and Mark on one side with Mark next to Mama, and Alicia and Henry and me, with Alicia next to Daddy. The room is full of candles, and little flowers floating in cut-glass bowls, and Etta has laid out all the silver and china on Grandma's embroidered tablecloth from the nuns in Provence. In short, it is Christmas Eve, exactly like every Christmas Eve I can remember, except that Henry is at my side sheepishly bowing his head as my father says grace.

"Heavenly Father, we give thanks on this holy night for your mercy and for your benevolence, for another year of health and happiness, for the comfort of family, and for new friends. We thank you for sending your Son to guide us and redeem us in the form of a helpless infant, and we thank you for the baby Mark and Sharon will be bringing into our family. We beg to be more perfect in our love and patience with each other. Amen." *Uh-oh,* I think. *Now he's done it.* I dart a glance at Mama and she is seething. You would never know it if you didn't know Mama: she is very still, and she stares at her plate. The kitchen door opens and Etta comes in with the soup and sets a small bowl in front of each of us. I catch Mark's eye and he inclines his head slightly toward Mama and raises his eyebrows and I just nod a tiny nod. He asks her a question about this year's apple harvest, and she answers. Alicia and I relax a little bit. Sharon is watching me and I wink at her. The soup is chestnut and parsnip, which seems like a bad idea until you taste Nell's. "Wow," Henry says, and we all laugh, and eat up our soup. Etta clears away the soup bowls and Nell brings in the turkey. It is golden and steaming and huge, and we all applaud enthusiastically, as we do every year. Nell beams and says, "Well, now," as she does every year. "Oh, Nell, it's *perfect,*" my mother says with tears in her eyes. Nell looks at her sharply and then at Daddy, and says, "Thank you, Miz Lucille." Etta serves us stuffing, glazed carrots, mashed potatoes, and lemon curd, and we pass our plates to Daddy, who heaps them with turkey. I watch Henry as he takes his first bite of Nell's turkey: surprise, then bliss. "I have seen my future," he announces, and I stiffen. "I am going to give up librarianing and come and live in your kitchen and worship at Nell's feet. Or perhaps I will just marry her."

"You're too late," says Mark. "Nell is already married."

"Oh, well. It will have to be her feet, then. Why don't all of you weigh 300 pounds?"

"I'm working on it," my father says, patting his paunch.

"I'm going to weigh 300 pounds when I'm old and I don't have to drag my cello around anymore," Alicia tells Henry. "I'm going to live in Paris and eat nothing but chocolate and I'm going to smoke cigars and shoot heroin and listen to nothing but Jimi Hendrix and the Doors. Right, Mama?"

"I'll join you," Mama says grandly. "But I would rather listen to Johnny Mathis."

"If you shoot heroin you won't want to eat much of anything," Henry informs Alicia, who regards him speculatively. "Try marijuana instead." Daddy frowns. Mark changes the subject: "I heard on the radio that it's supposed to snow eight inches tonight."

"Eight!" we chorus.

"I'm dreaming of a white Christmas . . . ," Sharon ventures without conviction.

"I hope it doesn't all dump on us while we're in church," Alicia says grumpily. "I get so sleepy after Mass." We chatter on about snowstorms we have known. Dulcie tells about being caught in the Big Blizzard of 1967, in Chicago. "I had to leave my car on Lake Shore Drive and walk all the way from Adams to Belmont."

"I got stuck in that one," says Henry. "I almost froze; I ended up in the rectory of the Fourth Presbyterian Church on Michigan Avenue."

"How old were you?" asks Daddy, and Henry hesitates and replies, "Three." He glances at me and I realize he's talking about an experience he had while time traveling and he adds, "I was with my father." It seems transparently obvious to me that he's lying but no one seems to notice. Etta comes in and clears our dishes and sets out dessert plates. After a slight delay Nell comes in with the flaming plum pudding. "Oompa!" says Henry. She sets the pudding down in front of Mama, and the flames turn Mama's pale hair copper red, like mine, for a moment before they die out. Daddy opens the champagne (under a dish towel, so the cork won't put out anybody's eyeball). We all pass our glasses to him and he fills them and we pass them back. Mama cuts thin slices of plum pudding and Etta serves everyone. There are two extra glasses, one for Etta and one for Nell, and we all stand up for the toasts.

My father begins: "To family."

"To Nell and Etta, who are like family, who work so hard and make our home and have so many talents," my mother says, breathless and soft.

"To peace and justice," says Dulcie.

"To family," says Etta.

"To beginnings," says Mark, toasting Sharon.

"To chance," she replies.

It's my turn. I look at Henry. "To happiness. To here and now."

Henry gravely replies, "To world enough and time," and my heart skips and I wonder how he knows, but then I realize that Marvell's one of his favorite poets and he's not referring to anything but the future.

"To snow and Jesus and Mama and Daddy and catgut and sugar and my new red Converse High Tops," says Alicia, and we all laugh.

"To love," says Nell, looking right at me, smiling her vast smile.

"And to Morton Thompson, inventor of the best eatin' turkey on the Planet Earth."

HENRY: All through dinner Lucille has been careening wildly from sadness to elation to despair. Her entire family has been carefully navigating her mood, driving her into neutral territory again and again, buffering her, protecting her. But as we sit down and begin to eat dessert, she breaks down and sobs silently, her shoulders shaking, her head turned away as though she's going to tuck it under her wing like a sleeping bird. At first I am the only person who notices this, and I sit, horrified, unsure what to do. Then Philip sees her, and then the whole table falls quiet. He's on his feet, by her side. "Lucy?" he whispers. "Lucy, what is it?" Clare hurries to her, saying "Come on, Mama, it's okay, Mama. . . ." Lucille is shaking her head, No, no, no, and wringing her hands. Philip backs off; Clare says, "Hush," and Lucille is speaking urgently but not very clearly: I hear a rush of unintelligableness, then "All wrong," and then "Ruin his chances," and finally "I am just utterly disregarded in this family," and "Hypocritical," and then sobs. To my surprise it's Great Aunt Dulcie who breaks the stunned stillness. "Child, if anybody's a hypocrite here it's you. You did the exact same thing and I don't see that it ruined Philip's chances one bit. Improved them, if you ask me." Lucille stops crying and looks at her aunt, shocked into silence. Mark looks at his father, who nods, once, and then at Sharon, who is smiling as though she's won at bingo. I look at Clare, who doesn't seem particularly astonished, and I wonder how she knew if Mark didn't, and I wonder what else she knows that she hasn't mentioned, and then it is borne in on me that Clare knows everything, our future, our past, everything, and I shiver in the warm room. Etta brings coffee. We don't linger over it.

CLARE: Etta and I have put Mama to bed. She kept apologizing, the way she always does, and trying to convince us that she was well enough to go to Mass, but we finally got her to lie down and almost immediately she was asleep. Etta says that she will stay home in case Mama wakes up, and I tell her not to be silly, I'll stay, but Etta is obstinate and so I leave her sitting by the bed, reading St. Matthew. I walk down the hall and peek into Henry's room, but it's dark. When I open my door I find Henry supine on my bed reading *A Wrinkle in Time*. I lock the door and join him on the bed.

"What's wrong with your mom?" he asks as I carefully arrange myself next to him, trying not to get stabbed by my dress.

"She's manic-depressive."

"Has she always been?"

"She was better when I was little. She had a baby that died, when I was seven, and that was bad. She tried to kill herself. I found her." I remember the blood, everywhere, the bathtub full of bloody water, the towels soaked with it. Screaming for help and nobody was home. Henry doesn't say anything, and I crane my neck and he is staring at the ceiling.

"Clare," he finally says.

"What?"

"How come you didn't tell me? I mean, there's kind of a lot of stuff going on with your family that it would have been good to know ahead of time."

"But you knew...." I trail off. He didn't know. How could he know? "I'm sorry. It's just—I told you when it happened, and I forget that now is before then, and so I think you know all about it...."

Henry pauses, and then says, "Well, I've sort of emptied the bag, as far as my family is concerned; all the closets and skeletons have been displayed for your inspection, and I was just surprised . . . I don't know."

"But you haven't introduced me to him." I'm dying to meet Henry's dad, but I've been afraid to bring it up.

"No. I haven't."

"Are you going to?"

"Eventually."

"When?" I expect Henry to tell me I'm pushing my luck, like he always used to when I asked too many questions, but instead he sits up and swings his legs off the side of the bed. The back of his shirt is all wrinkled.

"I don't know, Clare. When I can stand it, I guess."

I hear footsteps outside the door that stop, and the doorknob jiggles back and forth. "Clare?" my father says. "Why is the door locked?" I get up and open the door. Daddy opens his mouth and then sees Henry and beckons me into the hall.

"Clare, you know your mother and I don't approve of you inviting your friend into your bedroom," he says quietly. "There are plenty of rooms in this house—"

"We were just talking—"

"You can talk in the living room."

"I was telling him about Mama and I didn't want to talk about it in the living room, okay?"

"Honey, I really don't think it's necessary to tell him about your mother—"

"After the performance she just gave what am I supposed to do? Henry can see for himself that she's wacko, he isn't stupid—" my voice is rising and Alicia opens her door and puts her finger to her lips.

"Your mother is not 'wacko,' " my father says sternly.

"Yeah, she is," Alicia affirms, joining the fray.

"*You* stay out of this—"

"The hell I will—"

"Alicia!" Daddy's face is dark red and his eyes are protruding and his voice is very loud. Etta opens Mama's door and looks at the three of us with exasperation. "Go downstairs, if you want to yell," she hisses, and closes the door. We look at each other, abashed.

"Later," I tell Daddy. "Give me a hard time later." Henry has been sitting on my bed this whole time, trying to pretend he's not here. "Come on, Henry. Let's go sit in some other room." Henry, docile as a small rebuked boy, stands and follows me downstairs. Alicia galumphs after us. At the bottom of the stairs I look up and see Daddy looking down at us helplessly. He turns and walks over to Mama's door and knocks.

"Hey, let's watch *It's a Wonderful Life*," Alicia says, looking at her watch. "It's on Channel 60 in five minutes."

"Again? Haven't you seen it, like, two hundred times already?" Alicia has a thing for Jimmy Stewart.

"I've never seen it," says Henry.

Alicia affects shock. "Never? How come?"

"I don't have a television."

Now Alicia really is shocked. "Did yours break or something?"

Henry laughs. "No. I just hate them. They give me headaches." They make him time travel. It's the flickering quality of the picture.

Alicia is disappointed. "So you don't want to watch?"

Henry glances at me; I don't mind. "Sure," I say. "For a while. We won't see the end, though; we have to get ready for Mass."

We troop into the TV room, which is off the living room. Alicia turns on the set. A choir is singing "It Came Upon a Midnight Clear." "Ugh," she sneers. "Look at those bad yellow plastic robes. They look like rain ponchos." She plops down on the floor and Henry sits on the couch. I sit down next to him. Ever since we arrived I have been worrying constantly about how to behave in front of my various family members in terms of Henry. How close should I sit? If Alicia weren't here I would lie down on the couch, put my head on Henry's lap. Henry solves my problem by scooting closer and putting his arm around me. It's kind of a self-conscious arm: we would never sit this way in any other context. Of course, we never watch TV together. Maybe this is how we would sit if we ever watched TV. The choir disappears and a slew of commercials comes on. McDonald's, a local Buick dealership, Pillsbury, Red Lobster: they all wish us a Merry Christmas. I look at Henry, who has an expression of blank amazement on his face.

"What?" I ask him softly.

"The speed. They jump cut every couple seconds; I'm going to be ill." Henry rubs his eyes with his fingers. "I think I'll just go read for a while." He gets up and walks out of the room, and in a minute I hear his feet on the stairs. I offer up a quick prayer: Please, God, let Henry not time travel, especially not when we're about to go to church and I won't be able to explain. Alicia scrambles onto the couch as the opening credits appear on the screen.

"He didn't last long," she observes.

"He gets these really bad headaches. The kind where you have to lie in the dark and not move and if anybody says boo your brain explodes."

"Oh." James Stewart is flashing a bunch of travel brochures, but his departure is cut short by the necessity of attending a dance. "He's really cute."

"Jimmy Stewart?"

"Him too. I meant your guy. Henry."

I grin. I am as proud as if I had made Henry myself. "Yeah."

Donna Reed is smiling radiantly at Jimmy Stewart across a crowded room. Now they are dancing, and Jimmy Stewart's rival has turned the switch that causes the dance floor to open over a swimming pool. "Mama really likes him."

"Hallelujah." Donna and Jimmy dance backwards into the pool; soon people in evening clothes are diving in after them as the band continues playing.

"Nell and Etta approve, also."

"Great. Now we just have to get through the next thirty-six hours without ruining the good first impression."

"How hard can that be? Unless—no, you wouldn't be that dumb. . . ." Alicia looks over at me dubiously. "Would you?"

"Of course not."

"Of course not," she echoes. "God, I can't believe Mark. What a stupid fuck." Jimmy and Donna are singing *Buffalo gals, won't you come out tonight* while walking down the streets of Bedford Falls resplendent in football uniform and bathrobe, respectively. "You should have been here yesterday. I thought Daddy was going to have a coronary right in front of the Christmas tree. I was imagining him crashing into it and the tree falling on him and the paramedics having to heave all the ornaments and presents off him before they could do CPR. . . ." Jimmy offers Donna the moon, and Donna accepts.

"I thought you learned CPR in school."

"I would be too busy trying to revive Mama. It was bad, Clare. There was a lot of yelling."

"Was Sharon there?"

Alicia laughs grimly. "Are you kidding? Sharon and I were in here trying to chat politely, you know, and Mark and the parentals were in the living room screaming at each other. After a while we just sat here and listened."

Alicia and I exchange a look that just means *So what else is new?* We have spent our lives listening to our parents yelling, at each other, at us. Sometimes I feel like if I have to watch Mama cry one more time I'm going to leave forever and never come back. Right now I want to grab Henry and drive back to Chicago, where no one can yell, no one can pretend everything is okay and nothing happened. An irate, paunchy man in an undershirt yells at James Stewart to stop talking Donna Reed to death and just kiss her. I couldn't agree more, but he doesn't. Instead he steps on her robe and she walks obliviously out of it, and the next thing you know she's hiding naked in a large hydrangea bush.

A commercial for Pizza Hut comes on and Alicia turns off the sound. "Um, Clare?"

"Yeah?"

"Has Henry ever been here before?"

Uh-oh. "No, I don't think so, why?"

She shifts uneasily and looks away for a second. "You're gonna think I'm nuts."

"What?"

"See, I had this weird thing happen. A long time ago . . . I was, like, about twelve, and I was supposed to be practicing, but then I remembered that I didn't have a clean shirt for this audition or something, and Etta and everybody were out someplace and Mark was supposed to be baby-sitting but he was in his room doing bongs or whatever. . . . Anyway, so I went downstairs, to the laundry room, and I was looking for my shirt, and I heard this noise, you know, like the door at the south end of the basement, the one that goes into the room with all the bicycles, that sort of whoosh noise? So I thought it was Peter, right? So I was standing in the door of the laundry room, sort of listening, and the door to the bicycle room opens and Clare, you won't believe this, it was this totally naked guy who looked just like Henry."

When I start laughing it sounds fake. "Oh, come on."

Alicia grins. "See, I knew you would think it was nuts. But I swear, it really happened. So this guy just looks a little surprised, you know, I mean I'm standing there with my mouth hanging open and wondering if this naked guy is going to, you know, rape me or kill me or something, and he just looks at me and goes, 'Oh, hi, Alicia,' and walks into the Reading Room and shuts the door."

"Huh?"

"So I run upstairs, and I'm banging on Mark's door and he's telling me to buzz off, and so finally I get him to open the door and he's so stoned that it takes a while before he gets what I'm talking about and then, of course, he doesn't believe me but finally I get him to come downstairs and he knocks on the Reading Room door and we are both really scared, it's like Nancy Drew, you know, where you're thinking, 'Those girls are really dumb, they should just call the police,' but nothing happens, and then Mark opens the door and there's nobody there, and he is mad at me, for, like, making it up, but then we think the man went upstairs, so we both go and sit in the kitchen next to the phone with Nell's big carving knife on the counter."

"How come you never told me about this?"

"Well, by the time you all got home I felt kind of stupid, and I knew that Daddy especially would think it was a big deal, and nothing really happened . . . but it wasn't funny, either, and I didn't feel like talking about it." Alicia laughs. "I asked Grandma once if there were any ghosts in the house, but she said there weren't any she knew of."

"And this guy, or ghost, looked like Henry?"

"Yeah! I swear, Clare, I almost died when you guys came in and I saw him, I mean, he's the guy! Even his voice is the same. Well, the one I saw in the basement had shorter hair, and he was older, maybe around forty . . ."

"But if that guy was forty, and it was five years ago—Henry is only twenty-eight, so he would have been twenty-three then, Alicia."

"Oh. Huh. But Clare, it's too weird—does he have a brother?"

"No. His dad doesn't look much like him."

"Maybe it was, you know, astral projection or something."

"Time travel," I offer, smiling.

"Oh, yeah, right. God, how bizarre." The TV screen is dark for a moment, then we are back with Donna in her hydrangea bush and Jimmy Stewart walking around it with her bathrobe draped over one arm. He's teasing her, telling her he's going to sell tickets to see her. The cad, I think, even as I blush remembering worse things I've said and done to Henry vis à vis the issue of clothing/nakedness. But then a car rolls up and Jimmy Stewart throws Donna her bathrobe. "Your father's had a stroke!" says someone in the car, and off he goes with hardly a backward glance, as Donna Reed stands bereft in her foliage. My eyes tear up. "Jeez, Clare, it's okay, he'll be back," Alicia reminds me. I smile, and we settle in to watch Mr. Potter taunting poor Jimmy Stewart into giving up college and running a doomed savings and loan. "Bastard," Alicia says.

"Bastard," I agree.

HENRY: As we walk out of the cold night air into the warmth and light of the church my guts are churning. I've never been to a Catholic Mass. The last time I attended any sort of religious service was my mom's funeral. I am holding on to Clare's arm like a blind man as she leads us up the central aisle, and we file into an empty pew. Clare and her family kneel on the cushioned kneelers and I sit, as Clare has told me to. We are early. Alicia has disappeared, and Nell is sitting behind us with her husband and their son, who is on leave from the Navy. Dulcie sits with a contemporary of hers. Clare, Mark, Sharon, and Philip kneel side by side in varying attitudes: Clare is self-conscious, Mark perfunctory, Sharon calm and absorbed, Philip exhausted. The church is full of poinsettias. It smells like wax and wet coats. There's an elaborate stable scene with Mary and Joseph and their entourage to the right of the altar. People are filing in, choosing seats, greeting each other. Clare slides onto the seat next to me, and Mark and Philip follow suit; Sharon remains on her knees for a few more minutes and then we are all sitting quietly in a row, waiting. A man in a suit walks onto the stage—altar, whatever—and tests the microphones that are attached to the little reading stands, then disappears into the back again. There are many more people now, it's crowded. Alicia and two other women and a man appear stage left, carrying their instruments. The blond woman is a violinist and the mousy brown-haired woman is the viola player; the man, who is so elderly that he stoops and shuffles, is another violinist. They are all wearing black. They sit in their folding chairs, turn on the lights over their music stands, rattle their sheet music, plink at various strings, and look at each other, for consensus. People are suddenly quiet and into this quiet comes a long, slow, low note that fills the space, that connects to no known piece of music but simply exists, sustains. Alicia is bowing as slowly as it is possible for a human to bow, and the sound she is producing seems to emerge from nowhere, seems to originate between my ears, resonates through my skull like fingers stroking my brain. Then she stops. The silence that follows is brief but absolute. Then all four musicians surge into action. After the simplicity of that single note their music is dissonant, modern and jarring and I think

Bartók? but then I resolve what I am hearing and realize that they are playing "Silent Night." I can't figure out why it sounds so weird until I see the blond violinist kick Alicia's chair and after a beat the piece comes into focus. Clare glances over at me and smiles. Everyone in the church relaxes. "Silent Night" gives way to a hymn I don't recognize. Everyone stands. They turn toward the back of the church, and the priest walks up the central aisle with a large retinue of small boys and a few men in suits. They solemnly march to the front of the church and take up their positions. The music abruptly stops. Oh, no, I think, what now? Clare takes my hand, and we stand together, in the crowd, and if there is a God, then God, let me just stand here quietly and inconspicuously, here and now, here and now.

CLARE: Henry looks as though he's about to pass out. Dear God, please don't let him disappear now. Father Compton is welcoming us in his radio announcer voice. I reach into Henry's coat pocket, push my fingers through the hole at the bottom, find his cock, and squeeze. He jumps as though I've administered an electric shock. "The Lord be with you," says Father Compton. "And also with you," we all reply serenely. The same, everything the same. And yet, here we are, at last, for anyone to see. I can feel Helen's eyes boring into my back. Ruth is sitting five rows behind us, with her brother and parents. Nancy, Laura, Mary Christina, Patty, Dave, and Chris, and even Jason Everleigh; it seems like everyone I went to school with is here tonight. I look over at Henry, who is oblivious to all this. He is sweating. He glances at me, raises one eyebrow. The Mass proceeds. The readings, the Kyrie, *Peace be with you: and also with you.* We all stand for the gospel, Luke, Chapter 2. Everyone in the Roman Empire, traveling to their home towns, to be taxed,

Joseph and Mary, *great with child,* the birth, miraculous, humble. The swaddling clothes, the manger. The logic of it has always escaped me, but the beauty of the thing is undeniable. The shepherds, abiding in the field. The angel: *Fear not: for, behold, I bring you good tidings of great joy.* . . . Henry is jiggling his leg in a very distracting way. He has his eyes closed and he is biting his lip. Multitudes of angels. Father Compton intones, *"But Mary kept all these things, and pondered them in her heart."* "Amen," we say, and sit down for the sermon. Henry leans over and whispers, "Where is the restroom?" "Through that door," I tell him, pointing at the door Alicia and Frank and the others came in through. "How do I get there?" "Walk to the back of the church and then down the side aisle." "If I don't come back—" "You have to come back." As Father Compton says, "On this most joyous of nights. . . ." Henry stands and walks quickly away. Father's eyes follow him as he walks back and over and up to the door. I watch as he slips out the door and it swings shut behind him.

HENRY: I'm standing in what appears to be the hallway of an elementary school. Don't panic, I repeat to myself. No one can see you. Hide somewhere. I look around, wildly, and there's a door: BOYS. I open it, and I'm in a miniature men's room, brown tile, all the fixtures tiny and low to the ground, radiator blasting, intensifying the smell of institutional soap. I open the window a few inches and stick my face above the crack. There are evergreen trees blocking any view there might have been, and so the cold air I am sucking in tastes of pine. After a few minutes I feel less tenuous. I lie down on the tile, curled up, knees to chin. Here I am. Solid. Now. Here on this brown tile floor. It seems like such a small thing to ask. Continuity. Surely, if there is a God, he wants us to be good, and it would be unreasonable to expect anyone to be good without incentives, and Clare is very, very good, and she even believes in God, and why would he decide to embarrass her in front of all those people—

I open my eyes. All the tiny porcelain fixtures have iridescent auras, sky blue and green and purple, and I resign myself to going, there's no stopping now, and I am shaking, "No!" but I'm gone.

CLARE: Father finishes his sermon, which is about world peace, and Daddy leans across Sharon and Mark and whispers, "Is your friend sick?" "Yes," I whisper back, "he has a headache, and sometimes they make him nauseous." "Should I go see if I can help?" "No! He'll be okay." Daddy doesn't seem convinced, but he stays in his seat. Father is blessing the host. I try to suppress my urge to run out and find Henry myself. The first pews stand for communion. Alicia is playing Bach's Cello Suite no. 2. It is sad and lovely. Come back, Henry. Come back.

HENRY: I'm in my apartment in Chicago. It's dark, and I'm on my knees in the living room. I stagger up, and whack my elbow on the bookshelves. "Fuck!" I can't believe this. I can't even get through one day with Clare's family and I've been sucked up and spit out into my own fucking apartment like a fucking pinball—

"Hey." I turn and there I am, sleepily sitting up, on the sofa bed.

"What's the date?" I demand.

"December 28, 1991." Four days from now.

I sit down on the bed. "I can't stand it."

"Relax. You'll be back in a few minutes. Nobody will notice. You'll be perfectly okay for the rest of the visit."

"Yeah?"

"Yeah. Stop whining," my self says, imitating Dad perfectly. I want to deck him, but what would be the point? There's music playing softly in the background.

"Is that Bach?"

"Huh? Oh, yeah, it's in your head. It's Alicia."

"That's odd. Oh!" I run for the bathroom, and almost make it.

CLARE: The last few people are receiving communion when Henry walks in the door, a little pale, but walking. He walks back and up the aisle and squeezes in next to me. "The Mass is ended, go in peace," says Father Compton. "Amen," we respond. The altar boys assemble together like a school of fish around Father, and they proceed jauntily up the aisle and we all file out after them. I hear Sharon ask Henry if he's okay, but I don't catch his reply because Helen and Ruth have intercepted us and I am introducing Henry.

Helen simpers. "But we've met before!"

Henry looks at me, alarmed. I shake my head at Helen, who smirks. "Well, maybe not," she says. "Nice to meet you—Henry." Ruth shyly offers Henry her hand. To my surprise he holds it for a moment and then says, "Hello, Ruth," before I have introduced her, but as far as I can tell she doesn't recognize him. Laura joins us just as Alicia comes up bumping her cello case through the crowd. "Come to my house tomorrow," Laura invites. "My parents are leaving for the Bahamas at four." We all agree enthusiastically; every year Laura's parents go someplace tropical the minute all the presents have been opened, and every year we flock over there as soon as their car disappears around the driveway. We part with a chorus of "Merry Christmas!" and as we emerge through the side door of the church into the parking lot Alicia says, "Ugh, I knew it!" There's deep new snow everywhere, the world has been remade white. I stand still and look at the trees and cars and across the street toward the lake, which is crashing, invisible, on the beach far below the church on the bluff. Henry stands with me, waiting. Mark says, "Come on, Clare," and I do.

HENRY: It's about 1:30 in the morning when we walk in the door of Meadowlark House. All the way home Philip scolded Alicia for her "mistake" at the beginning of "Silent Night," and she sat quietly, looking out the window at the dark houses and trees. Now everyone goes upstairs to their rooms after saying "Merry Christmas" about fifty more times except Alicia and Clare, who disappear into a room at the end of the first floor hall. I wonder what to do with myself, and on an impulse I follow them.

"—a total prick," Alicia is saying as I stick my head in the door. The room is dominated by an enormous pool table which is bathed in the brilliant glare of the lamp suspended over it. Clare is racking up the balls as Alicia paces back and forth in the shadows at the edge of the pool of light.

"Well, if you deliberately try to piss him off and he gets pissed off, I don't see why you're upset," Clare says.

"He's just so *smug*," Alicia says, punching the air with her fists. I cough. They both jump and then Clare says, "Oh, Henry, thank God, I thought you were Daddy."

"Wanna play?" Alicia asks me.

"No, I'll just watch." There is a tall stool by the table, and I sit on it.

Clare hands Alicia a cue. Alicia chalks it and then breaks, sharply. Two stripes fall into corner pockets. Alicia sinks two more before missing, just barely, a combo bank shot. "Uh-oh," says Clare. "I'm in trouble." Clare drops an easy solid, the 2 ball, which was poised on the edge of a corner pocket. On her next shot she sends the cue ball into the hole after the 3, and Alicia fishes out both balls and lines up her shot. She runs the stripes without further ado. "Eight ball, side pocket," Alicia calls, and that is that. "Ouch," sighs Clare. "Sure you don't want to play?" She offers me her cue.

"Come on, Henry," say Alicia. "Hey, do either of you want anything to drink?"

"No," Clare says.

"What have you got?" I ask. Alicia snaps on a light and a beautiful old bar appears at the far end of the room. Alicia and I huddle behind it and lo, there is just about everything I can imagine in the way of alcohol. Alicia mixes herself a rum and Coke. I hesitate before such riches, but finally pour myself a stiff whiskey. Clare decides to have something after all, and as she's cracking the miniature tray of ice cubes into a glass for her Kahlua the door opens and we all freeze.

It's Mark. "Where's Sharon?" Clare asks him. "Lock that," commands Alicia.

He turns the lock and walks behind the bar. "Sharon is sleeping," he says, pulling a Heineken out of the tiny fridge. He uncaps it and saunters over to the table. "Who's playing?"

"Alicia and Henry," says Clare.

"Hmm. Has he been warned?"

"Shut up, Mark," Alicia says.

"She's Jackie Gleason in disguise," Mark assures me.

I turn to Alicia. "Let the games begin." Clare racks again. Alicia gets the break. The whiskey has coated all my synapses, and everything is sharp and clear. The balls explode like fireworks and blossom into a new pattern. The 13 teeters on the edge of a corner pocket and then falls. "Stripes again," Alicia says. She sinks the 15, the 12, and the 9 before a bad leave forces her to try an unmakable two-rail shot.

Clare is standing just at the edge of the light, so that her face is in shadow but her body floats out of the blackness, her arms folded across her chest. I turn my attention to the table. It's been a while. I sink the 2, 3, and 6 easily, and then look for something else to work with. The 1 is smack in front of the corner pocket at the opposite end of the table, and I send the cue ball into the 7 which drops the 1. I send the 4 into a side pocket with a bank shot and get the 5 in the back corner with a lucky carom. It's just slop, but Alicia whistles anyway. The 7 goes down without mishap. "Eight in the corner," I indicate with my cue, and in it goes. A sigh escapes around the table.

"Oh, that was beautiful," says Alicia. "Do it again." Clare is smiling in the dark.

"Not your usual," Mark says to Alicia.

"I'm too tired to concentrate. And too pissed off."

"Because of Dad?"

"Yeah."

"Well, if you poke him, he's going to poke back."

Alicia pouts. "Anybody can make an honest mistake."

"It sounded like Terry Riley for a minute there," I tell Alicia.

She smiles. "It *was* Terry Riley. It was from *Salome Dances for Peace*."

Clare laughs. "How did Salome get into 'Silent Night'?"

"Well, you know, John the Baptist, I figured that was enough of a connection, and if you transpose that first violin part down an octave, it sounds pretty good, you know, la la la, LA. . . ."

"But you can't blame him for getting mad," says Mark. "I mean, he knows that you wouldn't play something that sounded like that by accident."

I pour myself a second drink.

"What did Frank say?" Clare asks.

"Oh, he dug it. He was, like, trying to figure out how to make a whole new piece out of it, you know, like 'Silent Night' meets Stravinsky. I mean, Frank is eighty-seven, he doesn't care if I fuck around as long as he's amused. Arabella and Ashley were pretty snitty about it, though."

"Well, it isn't very professional," says Mark.

"Who cares? This is just St. Basil's, you know?" Alicia looks at me. "What do you think?"

I hesitate. "I don't really care," I say finally. "But if my dad heard you do that, he'd be very angry."

"Really? Why?"

"He has this idea that every piece of music should be treated with respect, even if it isn't something he likes much. I mean, he doesn't like Tchaikovsky, or Strauss, but he will play them very seriously. That's why he's great; he plays everything as though he's in love with it."

"Oh." Alicia walks behind the bar, mixes herself another drink, thinks this over. "Well, you're lucky to have a great dad who loves something besides money."

I'm standing behind Clare, running my fingers up her spine in the dark. She puts her hand behind her back and I clasp it. "I don't think you would say that if you knew my family at all. Besides, your dad seems to care about you very much."

"No," she shakes her head. "He just wants me to be perfect in front of his friends. He doesn't care at all." Alicia racks the balls and swivels them into position. "Who wants to play?"

"I'll play," Mark says. "Henry?"

"Sure." Mark and I chalk our cues and face each other across the table.

I break. The 4 and the 15 go down. "Solids," I call, seeing the 2 near the corner. I sink it, and then miss the 3 altogether. I'm getting tired, and my coordination is softening from the whiskies. Mark plays with determination but no flair, and sinks the 10 and the 11. We soldier on, and soon I have sunk all the solids. Mark's 13 is parked on the lip of a corner pocket. "8 ball," I say pointing at it. "You know, you can't drop Mark's ball or you'll lose," says Alicia. "'S okay," I tell her. I launch the cue ball gently across the table, and it kisses the 8 ball lovingly and sends it smooth and easy toward the 13, and it seems to almost detour around the 13 as though on rails, and plops decorously into the hole, and Clare laughs, but then the 13 teeters, and falls.

"Oh, well," I say. "Easy come, easy go."

"Good game," says Mark.

"God, where'd you learn to play like that?" Alicia asks.

"It was one of the things I learned in college." Along with drinking, English and German poetry, and drugs. We put away the cues and pick up the glasses and bottles.

"What was your major?" Mark unlocks the door and we all walk together down the hall toward the kitchen.

"English lit."

"How come not music?" Alicia balances her glass and Clare's in one hand as she pushes open the dining room door.

I laugh. "You wouldn't believe how unmusical I am. My parents were sure they'd brought home the wrong kid from the hospital."

"That must have been a drag," says Mark. "At least Dad's not pushing you to be a lawyer," he says to Alicia. We enter the kitchen and Clare flips on the light.

"He's not pushing you either," she retorts. "You love it."

"Well, that's what I mean. He's not making any of us do something we don't want to do."

"Was it a drag?" Alicia asks me. "I would have been lapping it up."

"Well, before my mom died, everything was great. After that, everything was terrible. If I had been a violin prodigy, maybe . . . I dunno." I look at Clare, and shrug. "Anyway, Dad and I don't get along. At all."

"How come?"

Clare says, "Bedtime." She means, Enough already. Alicia is waiting for an answer.

I turn my face to her. "Have you ever seen a picture of my mom?" She nods. "I look like her."

"So?" Alicia washes the glasses under the tap. Clare dries.

"So, he can't stand to look at me. I mean, that's just one reason among many."

"But—"

"Alicia—" Clare is trying, but Alicia is unstoppable.

"But he's your *dad*."

I smile. "The things you do to annoy your dad are small beer compared with the things my dad and I have done to each other."

"Like what?"

"Like the numerous times he has locked me out of our apartment, in all kinds of weather. Like the time I threw his car keys into the river. That kind of thing."

"Why'dja do that?"

"I didn't want him to smash up the car, and he was drunk."

Alicia, Mark, and Clare all look at me and nod. They understand perfectly.

"Bedtime," says Alicia, and we all leave the kitchen and go to our rooms without another word, except, "Good night."

CLARE: It's 3:14 a.m. according to my alarm clock and I am just getting warm in my cold bed when the door opens and Henry comes in very quietly. I pull back the covers and he hops in. The bed squeaks as we arrange ourselves.

"Hi," I whisper.

"Hi," Henry whispers back.

"This isn't a good idea."

"It was very cold in my room."

"Oh." Henry touches my cheek, and I have to stifle a shriek. His fingers are icy. I rub them between my palms. Henry burrows deeper into the covers. I press against him, trying to get warm again. "Are you wearing socks?" he asks softly.

"Yes." He reaches down and pulls them off my feet. After a few minutes and a lot of squeaking and *Shhh!* we are both naked.

"Where did you go, when you left church?"

"My apartment. For about five minutes, four days from now."

"Why?"

"Tired. Tense, I guess."

"No, why there?"

"Dunno. Sort of a default mechanism. The time travel air traffic controllers thought I would look good there, maybe." Henry buries his hand in my hair.

It's getting lighter outside. "Merry Christmas," I whisper. Henry doesn't answer, and I lie awake in his arms thinking about multitudes of angels, listening to his measured breath, and pondering in my heart.

HENRY: In the early hours of the morning I get up to take a leak and as I stand in Clare's bathroom sleepily urinating by the illumination of the Tinkerbell nightlight I hear a girl's voice say "Clare?" and before I can figure out where this voice is coming from a door that I thought was a closet opens and I find myself standing stark naked in front of Alicia. "Oh," she whispers as I belatedly grab a towel and cover myself. "Oh, hi, Alicia," I whisper, and we both grin. She disappears back into her room as abruptly as she came in.

CLARE: I'm dozing, listening to the house waking up. Nell is down in the kitchen singing and rattling the pans. Someone walks down the hall, past my door. I look over and Henry is still deep in sleep, and I suddenly realize that I have got to get him out of here without anyone seeing.

I extricate myself from Henry and the blankets and climb out of bed carefully. I pick my nightgown up off the floor and I'm just pulling it on over my head when Etta says, "Clare! Rise and shine, it's Christmas!" and sticks her head in the door. I hear Alicia calling Etta and as I poke my head out of the nightgown I see Etta turn away to answer Alicia and I turn to the bed and Henry is not there. His pajama bottoms are lying on the rug and I kick them under the bed. Etta walks into my room in her yellow bathrobe with her braids trailing over her shoulders. I say "Merry Christmas!" and she is telling me something about Mama, but I'm having trouble listening because I'm imagining Henry materializing in front of Etta. "Clare?" Etta is peering at me with concern.

"Huh? Oh, sorry. I'm still asleep, I guess."

"There's coffee downstairs." Etta is making the bed. She looks puzzled.

"I'll do that, Etta. You go on down." Etta walks to the other side of the bed. Mama sticks her head in the door. She looks beautiful, serene after last night's storm. "Merry Christmas, honey."

I walk to her, kiss her cheek lightly. "Merry Christmas, Mama." It's so hard to stay mad at her when she is my familiar, lovely Mama.

"Etta, will you come down with me?" Mama asks. Etta thwaps the pillows with her hands and the twin impressions of our heads vanish. She glances at me, raises her eyebrows, but doesn't say anything.

"Etta?"

"Coming. . . ." Etta bustles out after Mama. I shut the door after them and lean against it, just in time to see Henry roll out from under the bed. He gets up and starts to put his pajamas on. I lock the door.

"Where were you?" I whisper.

"Under the bed," Henry whispers back, as though this should be obvious.

"All the time?"

"Yeah." For some reason this strikes me as hilarious, and I start to giggle. Henry puts his hand over my mouth, and soon we are both shaking with laughter, silently.

HENRY: Christmas Day is strangely calm after the high seas of yesterday. We gather around the tree, self-conscious in our bathrobes and slippers, and presents are opened, and exclaimed over. After effusive thanks on all sides, we eat breakfast. There is a lull and then we eat Christmas dinner, with great praise for Nell and the lobsters. Everyone is smiling, well-mannered, and good-looking. We are a model happy family, an advertisement for the bourgeoisie. We are everything I always longed for when I sat in the Lucky Wok restaurant with Dad and Mrs. and Mr. Kim every Christmas Day and tried to pretend I was enjoying myself while the adults all watched anxiously. But even as we lounge, well-fed, in the living room after dinner, watching football on television and reading the books we have given each other and attempting to operate the presents which require batteries and/or assembly, there is a noticeable strain. It is as though somewhere, in one of the more remote rooms of the house, a cease-fire has been signed, and now all the parties are endeavoring to honor it, at least until tomorrow, at least until a new consignment of ammunition comes in. We are all acting, pretending to be relaxed, impersonating the ideal mother, father, sisters, brother, boyfriend, fiancée. And so it is a relief when Clare looks at her watch, gets up off the couch, and says, "Come on, it's time to go over to Laura's."

CLARE: Laura's party is in full swing by the time we arrive. Henry is tense and pale and heads for the liquor as soon as we get our coats off. I still feel sleepy from the wine we drank at dinner, so I shake my head when he asks me what I want, and he brings me a Coke. He's holding on to his beer as though it's ballast. "Do not, under any circumstances, leave me to fend for myself," Henry demands, looking over my shoulder, and before I can even turn my head Helen is upon us. There is a momentary, embarrassed silence.

"So, Henry," Helen says, "we hear that you are a librarian. But you don't *look* like a librarian."

"Actually, I am a Calvin Klein underwear model. The librarian thing is just a front."

I've never seen Helen nonplussed before. I wish I had a camera. She recovers quickly, though, looks Henry up and down, and smiles. "Okay, Clare, you can keep him," she says.

"That's a relief," I tell her. "I've lost the receipt." Laura, Ruth, and Nancy converge on us, looking determined, and interrogate us: how did we meet, what does Henry do for a living, where did he go to college, blah, blah, blah. I never expected that when Henry and I finally appeared in public together it would be simultaneously so nerve-racking and so boring. I tune in again just as Nancy says, "It's so weird that your name is Henry."

AUDREY NIFFENEGGER

"Oh?" says Henry, "Why's that?"

Nancy tells him about the slumber party at Mary Christina's, the one where the Ouija board said that I was going to marry someone named Henry. Henry looks impressed. "Really?" he asks me.

"Um, yeah." I suddenly have an urgent need to pee. "Excuse me," I say, detaching myself from the group and ignoring Henry's pleading expression. Helen is hot on my heels as I run upstairs. I have to shut the bathroom door in her face to stop her from following me in.

"Open up, Clare," she says, jiggling the door knob. I take my time, pee, wash my hands, put on fresh lipstick. "Clare," Helen grumbles, "I'm gonna go downstairs and tell your boyfriend every single hideous thing you've ever done in your life if you don't open this door immed—" I swing the door open and Helen almost falls into the room.

"All right, Clare Abshire," Helen says menacingly. She closes the door. I sit down on the side of the bathtub and she leans against the sink, looming over me in her pumps. "Fess up. What is really going on with you and this Henry person? I mean, you just stood there and told a big fat stack of lies. You didn't meet this guy three months ago, you've known him for years! What's the big secret?"

I don't really know how to begin. Should I tell Helen the truth? No. Why not? As far as I know, Helen has only seen Henry once, and he didn't look that different from how he looks right now. I love Helen. She's strong, she's crazy, she's hard to fool. But I know she wouldn't believe me if I said, time travel, Helen. You have to see it to believe it.

"Okay," I say, gathering my wits. "Yeah, I've known him for a long time."

"How long?"

"Since I was six."

Helen's eyes bug out like a cartoon character's. I laugh.

"Why . . . how come . . . well, how long have you been *dating* him?"

"I dunno. I mean, there was a period of time when things were sort of on the verge, but nothing was exactly going on, you know; that is, Henry was pretty adamant that he wasn't going to mess around with a little kid, so I was just kind of hopelessly nuts about him. . . ."

"But—how come we never knew about him? I don't see why it all had to be such a hush hush. You could have told me."

"Well, you kind of knew." This is lame, and I know it.

Helen looks hurt. "That's not the same thing as you telling me."

"I know. I'm sorry."

"Hmpf. So what was the deal?"

"Well, he's eight years older than me."

"So what?"

"So when I was twelve and he was twenty, that was a problem." Not to mention when I was six and he was forty.

"I still don't get it. I mean, I can see you not wanting your *parents* to know you were playing Lolita to his Humbert Humbert, but I don't get why you couldn't tell *us*. *We* would have been totally into it. I mean, we spent all this time feeling sorry for you, and worrying about you, and wondering why you were such a *nun*—" Helen shakes her head. "And there you were, screwing Mario the Librarian the whole time—"

I can't help it, I'm blushing. "I was *not* screwing him the whole time."

"Oh, come, on."

"Really! We waited till I was eighteen. We did it on my birthday."

"Even so, Clare," Helen begins, but there's a heavy knock on the bathroom door, and a deep male voice asks, "Are you girls about done in there?"

"To be continued," Helen hisses at me as we exit the bathroom to the applause of five guys standing in line in the hallway.

I find Henry in the kitchen, listening patiently as one of Laura's inexplicable jock friends babbles on about football. I catch the eye of his blond, button-nosed girlfriend, and she hauls him off to get another drink.

Henry says, "Look, Clare—Baby Punks!" I look and he's pointing at Jodie, Laura's fourteen-year-old sister, and her boyfriend, Bobby Hardgrove. Bobby has a green Mohawk and the full ripped T-shirt/safety pin getup, and Jodie is trying to look like Lydia Lunch but instead just looks like a raccoon having a bad hair day. Somehow they seem like they're at a Halloween party instead of a Christmas party. They look stranded and defensive. But Henry is enthusiastic. "Wow. How old are they, about twelve?"

"Fourteen."

"Let's see, fourteen, from ninety-one, that makes them . . . oh my god, they were born in 1977. I feel old. I need another drink." Laura passes through the kitchen holding a tray of Jell-O shots. Henry takes two and downs them both in rapid succession, then makes a face. "Ugh. How revolting." I laugh. "What do you think they listen to?" Henry says.

"Dunno. Why don't you go over and ask them?"

Henry looks alarmed. "Oh, I couldn't. I'd scare them."

"I think you're scared of them."

"Well, you may be right. They look so tender and young and green, like baby peas or something."

"Did you ever dress like that?"

Henry snorts derisively. "What do you think? Of course not.

Those children are emulating British punk. I am an American punk. No, I used to be into more of a Richard Hell kind of look."

"Why don't you go talk to them? They seem lonely."

"You have to come and introduce us and hold my hand." We venture across the kitchen with caution, like Lévi-Strauss approaching a pair of cannibals. Jodie and Bobby have that fight or flight look you see on deer on the Nature Channel.

"Um, hi, Jodie, Bobby."

"Hi, Clare," says Jodie. I've known Jodie her whole life, but she seems shy all of a sudden, and I decide that the neo-punk apparel must be Bobby's idea.

"You guys looked kind of, um, bored, so I brought Henry over to meet you. He likes your, um, outfits."

"Hi," says Henry, acutely embarrassed. "I was just curious— that is, I was wondering, what do you listen to?"

"Listen to?" Bobby repeats.

"You know—music. What music are you into?"

Bobby lights up. "Well, the Sex Pistols," he says, and pauses.

"Of course," says Henry, nodding. "And the Clash?"

"Yeah. And, um, Nirvana. . . ."

"Nirvana's good," says Henry.

"Blondie?" says Jodie, as though her answer might be wrong.

"I like Blondie," I say. "And Henry likes Deborah Harry."

"Ramones?" says Henry. They nod in unison. "How about Patti Smith?"

Jodie and Bobby look blank.

"Iggy Pop?"

Bobby shakes his head. "Pearl Jam," he offers.

I intercede. "We don't have much of a radio station up here," I tell Henry. "There's no way for them to find out about this stuff."

"Oh," Henry says. He pauses. "Look, do you want me to write

some things down for you? To listen to?" Jodie shrugs. Bobby nods, looking serious, and excited. I forage for paper and pen in my purse. Henry sits down at the kitchen table, and Bobby sits across from him. "Okay," says Henry. "You have to go back to the sixties, right? You start with the Velvet Underground, in New York. And then, right over here in Detroit, you've got the MC5, and Iggy Pop and the Stooges. And then back in New York, there were the New York Dolls, and the Heartbreakers—"

"Tom Petty?" says Jodie. "We've heard of him."

"Um, no, this was a totally different band," says Henry. "Most of them died in the eighties."

"Plane crash?" asks Bobby.

"Heroin," Henry corrects. "Anyway, there was Television, and Richard Hell and the Voidoids, and Patti Smith."

"Talking Heads," I add.

"Huh. I dunno. Would you really consider them punk?"

"They were there."

"Okay," Henry adds them to his list, "Talking Heads. So then, things move over to England—"

"I thought punk started in London," says Bobby.

"No. Of course," says Henry, pushing back his chair, "some people, me included, believe that punk is just the most recent manifestation of this, this spirit, this feeling, you know, that things aren't right and that in fact things are so wrong that the only thing we can do is to say Fuck It, over and over again, really loud, until someone stops us."

"*Yes*," Bobby says quietly, his face glowing with an almost religious fervor under his spiked hair. "Yes."

"You're corrupting a minor," I tell Henry.

"Oh, he would get there anyway, without me. Wouldn't you?"

"I've been trying, but it ain't easy, here."

"I can appreciate that," says Henry. He's adding to the list. I look over his shoulder. Sex Pistols, the Clash, Gang of Four, Buzzcocks, Dead Kennedys, X, the Mekons, the Raincoats, the Dead Boys, New Order, the Smiths, Lora Logic, the Au Pairs, Big Black, PiL, the Pixies, the Breeders, Sonic Youth . . .

"Henry, they're not going to be able to get any of that up here." He nods, and jots the phone number and address for Vintage Vinyl at the bottom of the sheet. "You do have a record player, right?"

"My parents have one," Bobby says. Henry winces.

"What do you *really* like?" I ask Jodie. I feel as though she's fallen out of the conversation during the male bonding ritual Henry and Bobby are conducting.

"Prince," she admits. Henry and I let out a big *Whoo!* and I start singing "1999" as loud as I can, and Henry jumps up and we're doing a bump and grind across the kitchen. Laura hears us and runs off to put the actual record on and just like that, it's a dance party.

HENRY: We're driving back to Clare's parents' house from Laura's party. Clare says, "You're awfully quiet."

"I was thinking about those kids. The Baby Punks."

"Oh, yeah. What about them?"

"I was trying to figure out what would cause that kid—"

"Bobby."

"—Bobby, to revert, to latch on to music that was made the year he was born. . . ."

"Well, I was really into the Beatles," Clare points out. "They broke up the year before I was born."

"Yeah, well, what is that about? I mean, you should have been swooning over Depeche Mode, or Sting or somebody. Bobby and his girlfriend ought to be listening to the Cure if they want to dress up. But instead they've stumbled into this thing, punk, that they don't know anything about—"

"I'm sure it's mostly to annoy their parents. Laura was telling me that her dad won't let Jodie leave the house dressed like that. She puts everything in her backpack and changes in the ladies' room at school," says Clare.

"But that's what everybody did, back when. I mean, it's about asserting your individualism, I understand that, but why are they asserting the individualism of 1977? They ought to be wearing plaid flannel."

"Why do you care?" Clare says.

"It depresses me. It's a reminder that the moment I belonged to is dead, and not just dead, but forgotten. None of this stuff ever gets played on the radio, I can't figure out why. It's like it never happened. That's why I get excited when I see little kids pretending to be punks, because I don't want it all to just disappear."

"Well," says Clare, "you can always go back. Most people are glued to the present; you get to be there again and again."

I think about this. "It's just sad, Clare. Even when I get to do something cool, like, say, go to see a concert I missed the first time around, maybe a band that's broken up or somebody that died, it's sad watching them because I know what's going to happen."

"But how is that different from the rest of your life?"

"It isn't." We have reached the private road that leads to Clare's house. She turns in.

"Henry?"

"Yeah?"

"If you could stop, now . . . if you could not time travel any more, and there would be no consequences, would you?"

"If I could stop now and still meet you?"

"You've already met me."

"Yes. I would stop." I glance at Clare, dim in the dark car.

"It would be funny," she says, "I would have all these memories that you would never get to have. It would be like—well, it *is* like being with somebody who has amnesia. I've been feeling that way ever since we got here."

I laugh. "So in the future you can watch me lurch along into each memory, until I've got the complete set. Collect 'em all."

She smiles. "I guess so." Clare pulls into the circular driveway in front of the house. "Home sweet home."

Later, after we have crept upstairs into our separate rooms and I have put on pajamas and brushed my teeth and sneaked into Clare's room and remembered to lock the door this time and we are warm in her narrow bed, she whispers, "I wouldn't want you to miss it."

"Miss what?"

"All the things that happened. When I was a kid. I mean, so far they have only halfway happened, because you aren't there yet. So when they happen to you, then it's real."

"I'm on my way." I run my hand over her belly, and down between her legs. Clare squeals.

"*Shhh.*"

"Your hand is *icy.*"

"Sorry." We fuck carefully, silently. When I finally come it's so intense that I get a horrible headache, and for a minute I'm afraid I'm going to disappear, but I don't. Instead I lie in Clare's arms, cross-eyed with pain. Clare snores, quiet animal snores that feel like bulldozers running through my head. I want my own bed, in my own apartment. Home sweet home. No place like home. Take me home, country roads. Home is where the heart is. But my heart is here. So I must be home. Clare sighs, turns her head, and is quiet. Hi, honey, I'm home. I'm home.

CLARE: It's a clear, cold morning. Breakfast has been eaten. The car is packed. Mark and Sharon have already left with Daddy for the airport in Kalamazoo. Henry is in the hall saying goodbye to Alicia; I run upstairs to Mama's room.

"Oh, is it so late?" she asks when she sees me wearing my coat and boots. "I thought you were staying to lunch." Mama is sitting at her desk, which as always is covered with pieces of paper which are covered with her extravagant handwriting.

"What are you working on?" Whatever it is, it's full of scratched-out words and doodles.

Mama turns the page face down. She's very secretive about her writing. "Nothing. It's a poem about the garden under the snow. It isn't coming out well at all." Mama stands up, walks to the window. "Funny how poems are never as nice as the real garden. My poems, anyway."

I can't really comment on this because Mama has never let me read one of her poems, so I say, "Well, the garden is beautiful," and she waves the compliment away. Praise means nothing to Mama, she doesn't believe it. Only criticism can flush her cheeks and catch her attention. If I were to say something disparaging she would remember it always. There is an awkward pause. I realize that she is waiting for me to leave so she can go back to her writing.

"Bye, Mama," I say. I kiss her cool face, and escape.

HENRY: We've been on the road for about an hour. For miles the highway was bordered by pine trees; now we are in flat land full of barbed-wire fences. Neither of us has spoken in a while. As soon as I notice it the silence is strange, and so I say something.

"That wasn't so bad." My voice is too cheerful, too loud in the small car. Clare doesn't answer, and I look over at her. She's crying; tears are running down her cheeks as she drives, pretending that she's not crying. I've never seen Clare cry before, and something about her silent stoic tears unnerves me. "Clare. Clare, maybe— could you maybe pull over for a minute?" Without looking at me, she slows down and drives onto the shoulder, stops. We are some- where in Indiana. The sky is blue and there are many crows in the field at the side of the road. Clare leans her forehead against the steering wheel and takes a long ragged breath.

"Clare." I'm talking to the back of her head. "Clare, I'm sorry. Was it—did I fuck up somehow? What happened? I—"

"It's not you," she says under her veil of hair. We sit like this for minutes.

"What's wrong, then?" Clare shakes her head, and I sit and stare at her. Finally I gather enough courage to touch her. I stroke her hair, feeling the bones of her neck and spine through the thick shimmering waves. She turns and I'm holding her awkwardly across the divided seats and now Clare is crying hard, shuddering.

Then she's quiet. Then she says, "God damn Mama."

Later we are sitting in a traffic jam on the Dan Ryan Express- way, listening to Irma Thomas. "Henry? Was it—did you mind very much?"

"Mind what?" I ask, thinking about Clare crying.

But she says, "My family? Are they—did they seem—?"

"They were fine, Clare. I really liked them. Especially Alicia."

"Sometimes I just want to push them all into Lake Michigan and watch them sink."

"Um, I know the feeling. Hey, I think your dad and your brother have seen me before. And Alicia said something really strange just as we were leaving."

"I saw you with Dad and Mark once. And Alicia definitely saw you in the basement one day when she was twelve."

"Is that going to be a problem?"

"No, because the explanation is too weird to be believed." We both laugh, and the tension that has ridden with us all the way to Chicago dissipates. Traffic begins to accelerate. Soon Clare stops in front of my apartment building. I take my bag from the trunk, and I watch as Clare pulls away and glides down Dearborn, and my throat closes up. Hours later I identify what I am feeling as loneliness, and Christmas is officially over for another year.

HOME IS ANYWHERE
YOU HANG YOUR HEAD

....

Saturday, May 9, 1992 (Henry is 28)

HENRY: I've decided that the best strategy is to just ask straight out; either he says yes or no. I take the Ravenswood El to Dad's apartment, the home of my youth. I haven't been here much lately; Dad seldom invites me over and I'm not given to showing up unannounced, the way I'm about to do. But if he won't answer his phone, what does he expect? I get off at Western and walk west on Lawrence. The two-flat is on Virginia; the back porch looks over the Chicago River. As I stand in the foyer fumbling for my key Mrs. Kim peeps out of her door and furtively gestures for me to step in. I am alarmed; Kimy is usually very hearty and loud and affectionate, and although she knows everything there is to know about us she never interferes. Well, almost never. Actually, she gets pretty involved in our lives, but we like it. I sense that she is really upset.

"You like a Coke?" She's already marching toward her kitchen.

"Sure." I set my backpack by the front door and follow her. In the kitchen she cracks the metal lever of an old-fashioned ice cube tray. I always marvel at Kimy's strength. She must be seventy and to me she seems exactly the same as when I was little. I spent a lot of time down here, helping her make dinner for Mr. Kim (who died five years ago), reading, doing homework, and watching TV. I sit at the kitchen table and she sets a glass of Coke brimming with ice before me. She has a half-consumed cup of instant coffee in one of the bone china cups with hummingbirds painted around the rim. I remember the first time she allowed me to drink coffee out of one of those cups; I was thirteen. I felt like a grown-up.

"Long time no see, buddy."

Ouch. "I know. I'm sorry . . . time has been moving kind of fast, lately."

She appraises me. Kimy has piercing black eyes, which seem to see the very back of my brain. Her flat Korean face conceals all emotion unless she wants you to see it. She is a fantastic bridge player.

"You been time traveling?"

"No. In fact, I haven't been anywhere for months. It's been great."

"You got a girlfriend?"

I grin.

"Ho ho. Okay, I know all about it. What's her name? How come you don't bring her around?"

"Her name is Clare. I have offered to bring her around several times and he always turns me down."

"You don't offer to *me*. You come here, Richard will come, too. We'll have duck almondine."

As usual I am impressed with my own obtusity. Mrs. Kim knows the perfect way to dissolve all social difficulties. My dad feels no compunction about being a jerk to me, but he will always make an effort for Mrs. Kim, as well he should, since she pretty much raised his child and probably isn't charging him market rent.

"You're a genius."

"Yes, I am. How come I don't get a MacArthur grant? I ask you?"

"Dunno. Maybe you're not getting out of the house enough. I don't think the MacArthur people are hanging out at Bingo World."

"No, they already got enough money. So when you getting married?"

Coke comes up my nose, I'm laughing so hard. Kimy lurches up and starts thumping me on the back. I subside, and she sits back down, grumpily. "What's so funny? I'm just asking. I get to ask, huh?"

"No, that's not it—I mean, I'm not laughing because it's ludicrous, I'm laughing because you are reading my mind. I came over to ask Dad to let me have Mom's rings."

"Ohhhhh. Boy, I don't know. Wow, you're getting married. Hey! That's great! She gonna say yes?"

"I think so. I'm ninety-nine percent sure."

"Well, that's pretty good. I don't know about your mom's rings, though. See, what I want to tell you—" her eyes glance at the ceiling "your dad, he's not doing too good. He's yelling a lot, and throwing stuff, and he's not practicing."

"Oh. Well, that's not totally surprising. But it's not good. You been up there, lately?" Kimy is ordinarily in Dad's apartment a lot. I think she surreptitiously cleans it. I've seen her defiantly ironing Dad's tux shirts, daring me to comment.

"He won't let me in!" She's on the verge of tears. This is very bad. My dad certainly has his problems, but it is monstrous of him to let them affect Kimy.

"But when he's not there?" Usually I pretend not to know that Kimy is in and out of Dad's apartment without his knowledge; she pretends that she would never do such a thing. But actually I'm appreciative, now that I no longer live here. Someone has to keep an eye on him.

She looks guilty, and crafty, and slightly alarmed that I am mentioning this. "Okay. Yeah, I go in *once*, 'cause I worry about him. He's got trash everywhere; we're gonna get bugs if he keep this up. He's got nothing in that fridge but beer and lemons. He's got so much clothes on the bed I don't think he sleeps in it. I don't know what he's doing. I never seen him this bad since when your mom died."

"Oh boy. What do you think?" There's a big crash above our heads, which means Dad has dropped something on the kitchen floor. He's probably just getting up. "I guess I'd better go up there."

"Yeah." Kimy is wistful. "He's such a nice guy, your dad; I don't know why he lets it get like this."

"He's an alcoholic. That's what alcoholics do. It's in their job description: Fall apart, and then keep falling apart."

She levels her devastating gaze at me. "Speaking of jobs. . . ."

"Yes?" Oh shit.

"I don't think he's been working."

"Well, it's the off-season. He doesn't work in May."

"They are touring Europe and he's here. Also, he don't pay rent last two months."

Damn damn damn. "Kimy, why didn't you call me? That's awful. Geez." I am on my feet and down the hall; I grab my backpack and return to the kitchen. I delve around in it and find my checkbook. "How much does he owe you?"

Mrs. Kim is deeply embarrassed. "No, Henry, don't—he'll pay it."

"He can pay me back. C'mon, buddy, it's okay. Cough it out, now, how much?"

She's not looking at me. "$1,200.00," she says in a small voice.

"That's all? What are you doing, buddy, running the Philanthropic Society for the Support of Wayward DeTambles?" I write the check and stick it under her saucer. "You better cash that or I'll come looking for you."

"Well, then I won't cash it and you will have to visit me."

"I'll visit you anyway." I am utterly guilt stricken. "I will bring Clare."

Kimy beams at me. "I hope so. I'm gonna be your maid of honor, right?"

"If Dad doesn't shape up you can give me away. Actually, that's a great idea: you can walk me down the aisle, and Clare will be waiting in her tux, and the organist will be playing *Lohengrin....*"

"I better buy a dress."

"Yow. Don't buy any dresses until I tell you it's a done deal." I sigh. "I guess I better go up there and talk to him." I stand up. In Mrs. Kim's kitchen I feel enormous, suddenly, as though I'm visiting my old grammar school and marveling over the size of the desks. She stands slowly and follows me to the front door. I hug her. For a moment she seems fragile and lost, and I wonder about her life, the telescoping days of cleaning and gardening and bridge playing, but then my own concerns crash back in again. I will come back soon; I can't spend my entire life hiding in bed with Clare. Kimy watches as I open Dad's door.

"Hey, Dad? You home?"

There's a pause, and then, "GO AWAY."

I walk up the stairs and Mrs. Kim shuts her door.

The first thing that hits me is the smell: something is rotting in here. The living room is devastated. Where are all the books? My parents had tons of books, on music, on history, novels, in French, in German, in Italian: where are they? Even the record and CD collection seems smaller. There are papers all over, junk mail, newspapers, scores, covering the floor. My mother's piano is coated with dust and there is a vase of long-dead gladiolas mummifying on the windowsill. I walk down the hall, glancing in the bedrooms. Utter chaos; clothes, garbage, more newspapers. In the bathroom a bottle of Michelob lies under the sink and a glossy dry layer of beer varnishes the tile.

In the kitchen my father sits at the table with his back to me, looking out the window at the river. He doesn't turn around as I enter. He doesn't look at me when I sit down. But he doesn't get up and leave, either, so I take it as a sign that conversation may proceed.

"Hi, Dad."

Silence.

"I saw Mrs. Kim, just now. She says you're not doing too good."

Silence.

"I hear you're not working."

"It's May."

"How come you're not on tour?"

He finally looks at me. Under the stubbornness there is fright. "I'm on sick leave."

"Since when?"

"March."

"Paid sick leave?"

Silence.

"Are you sick? What's wrong?"

I think he's going to ignore me, but then he answers by holding out his hands. They are shaking as though they are in their own tiny earthquake. He's done it, finally. Twenty-three years of determined drinking and he's destroyed his ability to play the violin.

"Oh, Dad. Oh, God. What does Stan say?"

"He says that's it. The nerves are shot, and they aren't coming back."

"Jesus." We look at each other for an unendurable minute. His face is anguished, and I'm beginning to understand: he has nothing. There is nothing left to hold him, to keep him, to be his life. First

Mom, then his music, gone, gone. I never mattered much to begin with, so my belated efforts will be inconsequential. "What happens now?"

Silence. Nothing happens now.

"You can't just stay up here and drink for the next twenty years."

He looks at the table.

"What about your pension? Workers' comp? Medicare? AA?"

He's done nothing, let everything slide. Where have I been?

"I paid your rent."

"Oh." He's confused. "Didn't I pay it?"

"No. You owed for two months. Mrs. Kim was very embarrassed. She didn't want to tell me, and she didn't want me giving her money, but there's no sense making your problems her problems."

"Poor Mrs. Kim." Tears are coursing down my father's cheeks. He is old. There's no other word for it. He's fifty-seven, and he's an old man. I am not angry, now. I'm sorry, and frightened for him.

"Dad." He is looking at me again. "Look. You have to let me do some things for you, okay?" He looks away, out the window again at the infinitely more interesting trees on the other side of the water. "You need to let me see your pension documents and bank statements and all that. You need to let Mrs. Kim and me clean this place. And you need to stop drinking."

"No."

"No, what? Everything or just some of it?"

Silence. I'm starting to lose my patience, so I decide to change the subject. "Dad. I'm going to get married."

Now I have his attention.

"To who? Who would marry you?" He says this, I think, without malice. He's genuinely curious. I take out my wallet and remove a picture of Clare from its plastic pocket. In the picture Clare is looking out serenely over Lighthouse Beach. Her hair floats like a banner in the breeze and in the early morning light she seems to glow against a background of dark trees. Dad takes the picture and studies it carefully.

"Her name is Clare Abshire. She's an artist."

"Well. She's pretty," he says grudgingly. This is as close as I'm going to get to a paternal blessing.

"I would like . . . I would really like to give her Mom's wedding and engagement rings. I think Mom would have liked that."

"How would you know? You probably hardly remember her."

I don't want to discuss it, but I feel suddenly determined to have my way. "I see her on a regular basis. I've seen her hundreds of times since she died. I see her walking around the neighborhood, with you, with me. She goes to the park and learns scores, she shops, she has coffee with Mara at Tia's. I see her with Uncle Ish. I see her at Juilliard. *I hear her sing!*" Dad is gaping at me. I'm destroying him, but I can't seem to stop. "I have spoken to her. Once I stood next to her on a crowded train, touching her." Dad is crying. "It's not always a curse, okay? Sometimes time travel is a great thing. I *needed* to see her, and sometimes I *get* to see her. She would have *loved* Clare, she would have *wanted* me to be happy, and she would *deplore* the way you've fucked everything up just because she died."

He sits at the kitchen table and weeps. He cries, not covering his face, but simply lowering his head and letting the tears stream from him. I watch him for a while, the price of losing my temper. Then I go to the bathroom and return with the roll of toilet paper. He takes some, blindly, and blows his nose. Then we sit there for a few minutes.

"Why didn't you tell me?"

"What do you mean?"

"Why didn't you tell me you could see her? I would've liked . . . to know that."

Why didn't I tell him? Because any normal father would have figured out by now that the stranger haunting their early married life was really his abnormal, time-traveling son. Because I was scared to: because he hated me for surviving. Because I could secretly feel superior to him for something he saw as a defect. Ugly reasons like that.

"Because I thought it would hurt you."

"Oh. No. It doesn't . . . hurt me; I . . . it's good to know she's there, somewhere. I mean . . . the worst thing is that she's gone. So it's good that she's out there. Even if I can't see her."

"She seems happy, usually."

"Yes, she was very happy . . . we were happy."

"Yeah. You were like a different person. I always wondered what it would have been like to grow up with you the way you were, then."

He stands up, slowly. I remain seated, and he walks unsteadily down the hall and into his bedroom. I hear him rummaging around, and then he comes slowly back with a small satin pouch. He reaches into it, and withdraws a dark blue jeweler's box. He opens it, and takes out the two delicate rings. They rest like seeds in his long, shaking hand. Dad puts his left hand over the right hand that holds the rings, and sits like that for a bit, as though the rings are lightning bugs trapped in his two hands. His eyes are closed. Then he opens his eyes, and reaches out his right hand: I cup my hands together, and he turns the rings onto my waiting palms.

The engagement ring is an emerald, and the dim light from the window is refracted green and white in it. The rings are silver, and they need cleaning. They need wearing, and I know just the girl to wear them.

BIRTHDAY

••••••••••••••••••••••••••••••

Sunday, May 24, 1992 (Clare is 21, Henry is 28)

CLARE: It's my twenty-first birthday. It's a perfect summer evening. I'm at Henry's apartment, in Henry's bed, reading *The Moonstone.* Henry is in the tiny kitchenette making dinner. As I don his bathrobe and head for the bathroom I hear him swearing at the blender. I take my time, wash my hair, steam up the mirrors. I think about cutting my hair. How nice it would be to wash it, run a quick comb through it, and presto! all set, ready to rock and roll. I sigh. Henry loves my hair almost as though it is a creature unto itself, as though it has a soul to call its own, as though it could love him back. I know he loves it as part of me, but I also know that he would be deeply upset if I cut it off. And I would miss it, too . . . it's just so much effort, sometimes I want to take it off like a wig and set it aside while I go out and play. I comb it carefully, working out the tangles. My hair is heavy when it's wet. It pulls on my scalp. I prop the bathroom door open to dissipate the steam. Henry is singing something from *Carmina Burana;* it sounds weird and off key. I emerge from the bathroom and he is setting the table.

"Perfect timing; dinner is served."

"Just a minute, let me get dressed."

"You're fine as you are. Really." Henry walks around the table, opens the bathrobe, and runs his hands lightly over my breasts.

"Mmm. Dinner will get cold."

"Dinner *is* cold. I mean, it's supposed to be cold."

"Oh. . . . Well, let's eat." I'm suddenly exhausted, and cranky.

"Okay." Henry releases me without comment. He returns to setting out silverware. I watch him for a minute, then pick up my clothes from their various places on the floor and put them on. I sit down at the table; Henry brings out two bowls of soup, pale and thick. "Vichyssoise. This is my grandmother's recipe." I take a sip. It's perfect, buttery and cool. The next course is salmon, with long pieces of asparagus in an olive oil and rosemary marinade. I open my mouth to say something nice about the food and instead say, "Henry—do other people have sex as much as we do?"

Henry considers. "Most people . . . no, I imagine not. Only people who haven't known each other very long and still can't believe their luck, I would think. Is it too much?"

"I don't know. Maybe." I say this looking at my plate. I can't believe I'm saying this; I spent my entire adolescence begging Henry to fuck me and now I'm telling him it's too much. Henry sits very still.

"Clare, I'm so sorry. I didn't realize; I wasn't thinking."

I look up; Henry looks stricken. I burst out laughing. Henry smiles, a little guilty, but his eyes are twinkling.

"It's just—you know, there are days when I can't sit down."

"Well . . . you just have to say. Say 'Not tonight, dear, we've already done it twenty-three times today and I would rather read *Bleak House*.'"

"And you will meekly cease and desist?"

"I did, just then, didn't I? That was pretty meek."

"Yeah. But then I felt guilty."

Henry laughs. "You can't expect me to help you out there. It may be my only hope: day after day, week after week, I will languish, starving for a kiss, withering away for want of a blow job, and after a while you will look up from your book and realize that I'm actually going to die at your feet if you don't fuck me immediately but I won't say a word. Maybe a few little whimpering noises."

"But—I don't know, I mean, I'm exhausted, and you seem . . . fine. Am I abnormal, or something?"

Henry leans across the table and holds out his hands. I place mine in his.

"Clare."

"Yes?"

"It may be indelicate to mention this, but if you will excuse me for saying so, your sex drive far outstrips that of *almost* all the women I've dated. Most women would have cried Uncle and turned on their answering machines months ago. But I should have thought . . . you always seemed into it. But if it's too much, or you don't feel like it, you have to say so, because otherwise I'll be tiptoeing around, wondering if I'm burdening you with my hideous demands."

"But how much sex is enough?"

"For me? Oh, God. My idea of the perfect life would be if we just stayed in bed all the time. We could make love more or less continuously, and only get up to bring in supplies, you know, fresh water and fruit to prevent scurvy, and make occasional trips to the bathroom to shave before diving back into bed. And once in a while we could change the sheets. And go to the movies to prevent bedsores. And running. I would still have to run every morning." Running is a religion with Henry.

"How come running? Since you'd be getting so much exercise anyway?"

He is suddenly serious. "Because quite frequently my life depends on running faster than whoever's chasing me."

"Oh." Now it's my turn to be abashed, because I already knew that. "But—how do I put this?—you never seem to go anywhere—that is, since I met you here in the present you've hardly time traveled at all. Have you?"

"Well, at Christmas, you saw that. And around Thanksgiving. You were in Michigan, and I didn't mention it because it was depressing."

"You were watching the accident?"

Henry stares at me. "Actually, I was. How did you know?"

"A few years ago you showed up at Meadowlark on Christmas Eve and told me about it. You were really upset."

"Yeah. I remember being unhappy just seeing that date on the List, thinking, gee, an extra Christmas to get through. Plus that was a bad one in regular time; I ended up with alcohol poisoning and had to have my stomach pumped. I hope I didn't ruin yours."

"No . . . I was happy to see you. And you were telling me something that was important, personal, even though you were careful not to tell any names or places. It was still your real life, and I was desperate for anything that helped me believe you were real and not some psychosis of mine. That's also why I was always touching you." I laugh. "I never realized how difficult I was making things for you. I mean, I did everything I could think of, and you were just cool as could be. You must have been *dying*."

"For example?"

"What's for dessert?"

Henry dutifully gets up and brings dessert. It's mango ice cream with raspberries. It has one little candle sticking out of it at an angle; Henry sings "Happy Birthday" and I giggle because he's so off-key; I make a wish and blow out the candle. The ice cream tastes superb; I am very cheerful, and I scan my memory for an especially egregious episode of Henry baiting.

"Okay. This was the worst. When I was sixteen, I was waiting for you late one night. It was about eleven o'clock, and there was a new moon, so it was pretty dark in the clearing. And I was kind of annoyed with you, because you were resolutely treating me like—a child, or a pal, or whatever—and I was just *crazy* to lose my virginity. I suddenly got the idea that I would hide your clothes. . . ."

"Oh, no."

"Yes. So I moved the clothes to a different spot. . . ." I'm a little ashamed of this story, but it's too late now.

"And?"

"And you appeared, and I basically teased you until you couldn't take it."

"And?"

"And you jumped me and pinned me, and for about thirty seconds we both thought 'This is it.' I mean, it wasn't like you would've been raping me, because I was absolutely asking for it. But you got this look on your face, and you said 'No,' and you got up and walked away. You walked right through the Meadow into the trees and I didn't see you again for three weeks."

"Wow. That's a better man than I."

"I was so chastened by the whole thing that I made a huge effort to behave myself for the next two years."

"Thank goodness. I can't imagine having to exercise that much willpower on a regular basis."

"Ah, but you will, that's the amazing part. For a long time I actually thought you were not attracted to me. Of course, if we are going to spend our whole lives in bed, I suppose you can exercise a little restraint on your jaunts into my past."

"Well, you know, I'm not kidding about wanting that much sex.

I mean, I realize that it's not practical. But I've been wanting to tell you: I feel so different. I just . . . feel so connected to you. And I think that it holds me here, in the present. Being physically connected the way that we are, it's kind of rewiring my brain." Henry is stroking my hand with his fingertips. He looks up. "I have something for you. Come and sit over here."

I get up and follow him into the living room. He's turned the bed into the couch and I sit down. The sun is setting and the room is washed in rose and tangerine light. Henry opens his desk, reaches into a pigeonhole, and produces a little satin bag. He sits slightly apart from me; our knees are touching. *He must be able to hear my heart beating,* I think. *It's come to this,* I think. Henry takes my hands and looks at me gravely. *I've waited for this so long and here it is and I'm frightened.*

"Clare?"

"Yes?" My voice is small and scared.

"You know that I love you. Will you marry me?"

"Yes . . . Henry." I have an overwhelming sense of *déja vu.* "But you know, really . . . I already have."

Sunday, May 31, 1992 (Clare is 21, Henry is 28)

CLARE: Henry and I are standing in the vestibule of the apartment building he grew up in. We're a little late already, but we are just standing here; Henry is leaning against the mailboxes and breathing slowly with his eyes closed.

"Don't worry," I say. "It can't be any worse than you meeting Mama."

"Your parents were very nice to me."

"But Mama is . . . unpredictable."

"So's Dad." Henry inserts his key into the front door lock and we walk up one flight of stairs and Henry knocks on the door of an apartment. Immediately it is opened by a tiny old Korean woman: Kimy. She's wearing a blue silk dress and bright red lipstick, and her eyebrows have been drawn on a little lopsided. Her hair is salt-and-pepper gray; it's braided and coiled into two buns at her ears. For some reason she reminds me of Ruth Gordon. She comes up to my shoulder, and she tilts her head back and says, "Ohhh, Henry, she's bee-yoo-tiful!" I can feel myself turn red. Henry says, "Kimy, where are your manners?" and Kimy laughs and says, "Hello, Miss Clare Abshire!" and I say "Hello, Mrs. Kim." We smile at each other, and she says, "Oh, you got to call me Kimy, everybody call me Kimy." I nod and follow her into the living room and there's Henry's dad, sitting in an armchair.

He doesn't say anything, just looks at me. Henry's dad is thin, tall, angular, and tired. He doesn't look much like Henry. He has short gray hair, dark eyes, a long nose, and a thin mouth whose corners turn down a little. He's sitting all bunched up in his chair, and I notice his hands, long elegant hands that lie in his lap like a cat napping.

Henry coughs and says, "Dad, this is Clare Abshire. Clare, this is my father, Richard DeTamble."

Mr. DeTamble slowly extends one of his hands, and I step forward and shake it. It's ice cold. "Hello, Mr. DeTamble. It's nice to meet you," I say.

"Is it? Henry must not have told you very much about me, then." His voice is hoarse and amused. "I will have to capitalize on your optimism. Come and sit down by me. Kimy, may we have something to drink?"

"I was just going to ask everyone—Clare, what would you like? I made sangria, you like that? Henry, how 'bout you? Sangria? Okay. Richard, you like a beer?"

Everyone seems to pause for a moment. Then Mr. DeTamble says, "No, Kimy, I think I'll just have tea, if you don't mind making it." Kimy smiles and disappears into the kitchen, and Mr. DeTamble turns to me and says, "I have a bit of a cold. I've taken some of that cold medicine, but I'm afraid it just makes me drowsy."

Henry is sitting on the couch, watching us. All the furniture is white and looks as though it was bought at a JCPenney around 1945. The upholstery is protected with clear plastic, and there are vinyl runners over the white carpet. There's a fireplace that looks as though it's never used; above it is a beautiful ink painting of bamboo in wind.

"That's a wonderful painting," I say, because no one is saying anything.

Mr. DeTamble seems pleased. "Do you like it? Annette and I brought it back from Japan in 1962. We bought it in Kyoto, but the original is from China. We thought Kimy and Dong would like it. It is a seventeenth-century copy of a much older painting."

"Tell Clare about the poem," Henry says.

"Yes; the poem goes something like this: 'Bamboo without mind, yet sends thoughts soaring among clouds. Standing on the lone mountain, quiet, dignified, it typifies the will of a gentleman. —Painted and written with a light heart, Wu Chen.'"

"That's lovely," I say. Kimy comes in with drinks on a tray, and Henry and I each take a glass of sangria while Mr. DeTamble carefully grasps his tea with both hands; the cup rattles against the saucer as he sets it on the table beside him. Kimy sits in a small armchair by the fireplace and sips her sangria. I taste mine and realize that it's really strong. Henry glances at me and raises his eyebrows.

Kimy says, "Do you like gardens, Clare?"

"Um, yes," I say. "My mother is a gardener."

"You got to come out before dinner and see the backyard. All my peonies are blooming, and we got to show you the river."

"That sounds nice." We all troop out to the yard. I admire the Chicago River, placidly flowing at the foot of a precarious stairway; I admire the peonies. Kimy asks, "What kind of garden does your mom have? Does she grow roses?" Kimy has a tiny but well-ordered rose garden, all hybrid teas as far as I can tell.

"She does have a rose garden. Actually, Mama's real passion is irises."

"Oh. I got irises. They're over there." Kimy points to a clump of iris. "I need to divide them, you think your mom would like some?"

"I don't know. I could ask." Mama has more than two hundred varieties of iris. I catch Henry smiling behind Kimy's back and I frown at him. "I could ask her if she wants to trade you some of hers; she has some that she bred herself, and she likes to give them to friends."

"Your mother breeds iris?" Mr. DeTamble asks.

"Uh-huh. She also breeds tulips, but the irises are her favorites."

"She is a professional gardener?"

"No," I say. "Just an amateur. She has a gardener who does most of the work and there's a bunch of people who come in and mow and weed and all that."

"Must be a big yard," Kimy says. She leads the way back into the apartment. In the kitchen a timer goes off. "Okay," says Kimy. "It's time to eat." I ask if I can help but Kimy waves me into a chair. I sit across from Henry. His dad is on my right and Kimy's empty chair is on my left. I notice that Mr. DeTamble is wearing a sweater, even though it's pretty warm in here. Kimy has very pretty china; there are hummingbirds painted on it. Each of us has a sweating cold glass of water. Kimy pours us white wine. She hesitates at Henry's dad's glass but passes him over when he shakes his head. She brings out salads and sits down. Mr. DeTamble raises his water glass. "To the happy couple," he says. "Happy couple," says Kimy, and we all touch glasses and drink. Kimy says, "So, Clare, Henry say you are an artist. What kind of artist?"

"I make paper. Paper sculptures."

"Ohh. You have to show me sometime 'cause I don't know about that. Like origami?"

"Uh, no."

Henry intercedes. "They're like that German artist we saw down at the Art Institute, you know, Anselm Kiefer. Big dark scary paper sculptures."

Kimy looks puzzled. "Why would a pretty girl like you make ugly things like that?"

Henry laughs. "It's art, Kimy. Besides, they're beautiful."

"I use a lot of flowers," I tell Kimy. "If you give me your dead roses I'll put them in the piece I'm working on now."

"Okay," she says. "What is it?"

"A giant crow made out of roses, hair, and daylily fiber."

"Huh. How come a crow? Crows are bad luck."

"They are? I think they're gorgeous."

Mr. DeTamble raises one eyebrow and for just a second he does look like Henry; he says, "You have peculiar ideas about beauty."

Kimy gets up and clears our salad plates and brings in a bowl of green beans and a steaming plate of "Roast Duck with Raspberry Pink Peppercorn Sauce." It's heavenly. I realize where Henry learned to cook. "What you think?" Kimy demands. "It's delicious, Kimy," says Mr. DeTamble, and I echo his praise. "Maybe cut down on the sugar?" Henry asks. "Yeah, I think so, too," says Kimy. "It's really tender though," Henry says, and Kimy grins. I stretch out my hand to pick up my wine glass. Mr. DeTamble nods at me and says, "Annette's ring looks well on you."

"It's very beautiful. Thank you for letting me have it."

"There's a lot of history in that ring, and the wedding band that goes with it. It was made in Paris in 1823 for my great-great-great-grandmother, whose name was Jeanne. It came to America in 1920 with my grandmother, Yvette, and it's been sitting in a drawer since 1969, when Annette died. It's good to see it back out in the light of day."

I look at the ring, and think, *Henry's mom was wearing this when she died.* I glance at Henry, who seems to be thinking the same thing, and at Mr. DeTamble, who is eating his duck. "Tell me about Annette," I ask Mr. DeTamble.

He puts down his fork and leans his elbows on the table, puts his hands against his forehead. He peers at me from behind his hands. "Well, I'm sure Henry must have told you something."

"Yes. A little. I grew up listening to her records; my parents are fans of hers."

Mr. DeTamble smiles. "Ah. Well then, you know that Annette had the most marvelous voice . . . rich, and pure, such a voice, and such range . . . she could express her soul with that voice, whenever I listened to her I felt my life meant more than mere biology . . . she could really hear, she understood structure and she could analyze exactly what it was about a piece of music that had to be rendered just so . . . she was a very emotional person, Annette. She brought that out in other people. After she died I don't think I ever really felt anything again."

He pauses. I can't look at Mr. DeTamble so I look at Henry. He's staring at his father with an expression of such sadness that I look at my plate.

Mr. DeTamble says, "But you asked about Annette, not about me. She was kind, and she was a great artist; you don't often find that those go together. Annette made people happy; she was happy herself. She enjoyed life. I only saw her cry twice: once when I gave her that ring and the other time when she had Henry."

Another pause. Finally I say, "You were very lucky."

He smiles, still shielding his face in his hands. "Well, we were and we weren't. One minute we had everything we could dream of, and the next minute she was in pieces on the expressway." Henry winces.

"But don't you think," I persist, "that it's better to be extremely happy for a short while, even if you lose it, than to be just okay for your whole life?"

Mr. DeTamble regards me. He takes his hands away from his face and stares. Then he says, "I've often wondered about that. Do you believe that?"

I think about my childhood, all the waiting, and wondering, and the joy of seeing Henry walking through the Meadow after not seeing him for weeks, months, and I think about what it was like not to see him for two years and then to find him standing in the Reading Room at the Newberry Library: the joy of being able to touch him, the luxury of knowing where he is, of knowing he loves me. "Yes," I say. "I do." I meet Henry's eyes and smile.

Mr. DeTamble nods. "Henry has chosen well." Kimy gets up to bring coffee and while she's in the kitchen Mr. DeTamble continues, "He isn't calibrated to bring peace to anyone's life. In fact, he is in many ways the opposite of his mother: unreliable, volatile, and not even especially concerned with anyone but himself. Tell me, Clare: why on earth would a lovely girl like you want to marry Henry?"

Everything in the room seems to hold its breath. Henry stiffens but doesn't say anything. I lean forward and smile at Mr. DeTamble and say, with enthusiasm, as though he has asked me what flavor of ice cream I like best: "Because he's really, *really* good in bed." In the kitchen there's a howl of laughter. Mr. DeTamble glances at Henry, who raises his eyebrows and grins, and finally even Mr. DeTamble smiles, and says "*Touché*, my dear."

Later, after we have drunk our coffee and eaten Kimy's perfect almond torte, after Kimy has shown me photographs of Henry as a baby, a toddler, a high school senior (to his extreme embarrassment); after Kimy has extracted more information about my family ("How many rooms? That many! Hey, buddy, how come you don't tell me she beautiful *and* rich?"), we all stand at the front door and I thank Kimy for dinner and say good night to Mr. DeTamble.

"It was a pleasure, Clare," he says. "But you must call me Richard."

"Thank you . . . Richard." He takes my hand for a moment and for just that moment I see him as Annette must have seen him, years ago—and then it's gone and he nods awkwardly at Henry, who kisses Kimy, and we walk downstairs and into the summer evening. It seems like years have passed since we went inside.

"Whoosh," says Henry. "I died a thousand deaths, just watching that."

"Was I okay?"

"Okay? You were brilliant! He loved you!"

We are walking down the street, holding hands. There's a playground at the end of the block and I run to the swings and climb on, and Henry takes the one next to me, facing the opposite direction, and we swing higher and higher, passing each other, sometimes in synch and sometimes streaming past each other so fast it seems like we're going to collide, and we laugh, and laugh, and nothing can ever be sad, no one can be lost, or dead, or far away: right now we are here, and nothing can mar our perfection, or steal the joy of this perfect moment.

Wednesday, June 10, 1992 (Clare is 21)

CLARE: I'm sitting by myself at a tiny table in the front window of Café Peregolisi, a venerable little rat hole with excellent coffee. I'm supposed to be working on a paper on *Alice in Wonderland* for the History of the Grotesque class I'm taking this summer; instead I'm daydreaming, staring idly at the natives, who are bustling and hustling in the early evening of Halsted Street. I don't often come to Boy's Town. I figure I will get more work done if I'm somewhere that no one I know will think to look for me. Henry has disappeared. He's not home and he wasn't at work today. I am trying not to worry about it. I am trying to cultivate a nonchalant and carefree attitude. Henry can take care of himself. Just because I have no idea where he might be doesn't mean anything is wrong. Who knows? Maybe he's with me.

Someone is standing on the other side of the street, waving. I squint, focus, and realize that it's the short black woman who was with Ingrid that night at the Aragon. Celia. I wave back, and she crosses the street. Suddenly she's standing in front of me. She is so small that her face is level with mine, although I am sitting and she is standing.

"Hi, Clare," Celia says. Her voice is like butter. I want to wrap myself in her voice and go to sleep.

"Hello, Celia. Have a seat." She sits, opposite me, and I realize that all of her shortness is in her legs; sitting down she is much more normal looking.

"I hear tell you got engaged," she says.

I hold up my left hand, show her the ring. The waiter slouches over to us and Celia orders Turkish coffee. She looks at me, and gives me a sly smile. Her teeth are white and long and crooked. Her eyes are large and her eyelids hover halfway closed as though she's falling asleep. Her dreadlocks are piled high and decorated with pink chopsticks that match her shiny pink dress.

"You're either brave or crazy," she says.

"So people tell me."

"Well, by now you ought to know."

I smile, shrug, sip my coffee, which is room temperature and too sweet.

Celia says, "Do you know where Henry is right now?"

"No. Do you know where Ingrid is right now?"

"Uh-huh," Celia says. "She's sitting on a bar stool in Berlin, waiting on me." She checks her watch. "I'm late." The light from the street turns her burnt-umber skin blue and then purple. She looks like a glamorous Martian. She smiles at me. "Henry is running down Broadway in his birthday suit with a pack of skinheads on his tail." Oh, no.

The waiter brings Celia's coffee and I point at my cup. He refills it and I carefully measure a teaspoon of sugar in and stir. Celia stands a demitasse spoon straight up in the tiny cup of Turkish coffee. It is black and dense as molasses. *Once upon a time there were three little sisters . . . and they lived at the bottom of a well. . . . Why did they live at the bottom of a well? . . . It was a treacle well.*

Celia is waiting for me to say something. *Curtsy while you're thinking what to say. It saves time.* "Really?" I say. Oh, brilliant, Clare.

"You don't seem too worried. My man were running around in his altogether like that I would wonder a little bit, myself."

"Yeah, well, Henry's not exactly the most average person."

Celia laughs. "You can say that again, sister." How much does she know? Does Ingrid know? Celia leans toward me, sips her coffee, opens her eyes wide, raises her eyebrows and purses her lips. "You really gonna *marry* him?"

A mad impulse makes me say, "If you don't believe me you can watch me do it. Come to the wedding."

Celia shakes her head. "Me? You know, Henry don't like me at all. Not one bit."

"Well, you don't seem to be a big fan of his, either."

Celia grins. "I am *now*. He dumped Miss Ingrid Carmichel *hard*, and I'm picking up the pieces." She glances at her watch again. "Speaking of whom, I am late for my date." Celia stands up, and says, "Why don't you come along?"

"Oh, no thanks."

"Come on, girl. You and Ingrid ought to get to know each other. You have so much in common. We'll have a little bachelorette party."

"In Berlin?"

Celia laughs. "Not the city. The bar." Her laugh is caramel; it seems to emanate from the body of someone much larger. I don't want her to go, but . . .

"No, I don't think that would be such a good idea." I look Celia in the eye. "It seems mean." Her gaze holds me, and I think of snakes, of cats. *Do cats eat bats? . . . Do bats eat cats?* "Besides, I have to finish this."

Celia flashes a look at my notebook. "What, is that homework? Ohh, it's a school night! Now just listen to your big sister Celia, who knows what's best for little schoolgirls—hey, you old enough to drink?"

"Yes," I tell her proudly. "As of three weeks ago."

Celia leans close to me. She smells like cinnamon. "Come on come on come on. You got to live it up a little before you settle down with Mr. Librarian Man. Come oooooonnnn, Clare. Before you know it you be up to your ears in Librarian babies shitting their Pampers full of that Dewey decimal system."

"I really don't think—"

"Then don't say nothin', just come *on.*" Celia is packing up my books and manages to knock over the little pitcher of milk. I start to mop it up but Celia just marches out of the café holding my books. I rush after her.

"Celia, don't, I need those—" For someone with short legs and five-inch heels she's moving fast.

"Uh-uh, I'm not giving 'em back till you promise you're coming with me."

"Ingrid won't like it." We are walking in step, heading south on Halsted toward Belmont. I don't want to see Ingrid. The first and last time I saw her was the Violent Femmes concert and that's fine with me.

"'Course she will. Ingrid's been very curious about you." We turn onto Belmont, walk past tattoo parlors, Indian restaurants, leather shops and storefront churches. We walk under the El and there's Berlin. It doesn't look too enticing on the outside; the windows are painted black and I can hear disco pulsating from the darkness behind the skinny freckled guy who cards me but not Celia, stamps our hands and suffers us to enter the abyss.

As my eyes adjust I realize that the entire place is full of women. Women are crowded around the tiny stage watching a female stripper strutting in a red sequined G-string and pasties. Women are laughing and flirting at the bar. It's Ladies' Night. Celia is pulling me toward a table. Ingrid is sitting there by herself with a tall glass of sky blue liquid in front of her. She looks up and I can tell that she's not too pleased to see me. Celia kisses Ingrid and waves me to a chair. I remain standing.

"Hey, baby," Celia says to Ingrid.

"You've got to be kidding," says Ingrid. "What did you bring her for?" They both ignore me. Celia still has her arms wrapped around my books.

"It's cool, Ingrid, she's all right. I thought y'all might want to become better acquainted, that's all." Celia seems almost apologetic, but even I can see that she's enjoying Ingrid's discomfort.

Ingrid glares at me. "Why did you come? To gloat?" She leans back in her chair and tilts her chin up. Ingrid looks like a blond vampire, black velvet jacket and blood red lips. She is ravishing. I feel like a small-town school girl. I hold out my hands to Celia and she gives me my books.

"I was coerced. I'm leaving now." I begin to turn away but Ingrid shoots out a hand and grabs my arm.

"Wait a minute—" She wrenches my left hand toward her, and I stumble and my books go flying. I pull my hand back and Ingrid says, "— you're *engaged?*" and I realize that she's looking at Henry's ring.

I say nothing. Ingrid turns to Celia. "You knew, didn't you?" Celia looks down at the table, says nothing. "You brought her here to rub it in, you bitch." Her voice is quiet. I can hardly hear her over the pulsing music.

"No, Ing, I just—"

"Fuck you, Celia." Ingrid stands up. For a moment her face is close to mine and I imagine Henry kissing those red lips. Ingrid stares at me. She says, "You tell Henry he can go to hell. And tell him I'll see him there." She stalks out. Celia is sitting with her face in her hands.

I begin to gather up my books. As I turn to go Celia says, "Wait."

I wait.

Celia says, "I'm sorry, Clare." I shrug. I walk to the door, and when I turn back I see that Celia is sitting alone at the table, sipping Ingrid's blue drink and leaning her face against her hand. She is not looking at me.

Out on the street I walk faster and faster until I am at my car, and then I drive home and I go to my room and I lie on my bed and I dial Henry's number but he's not home and I turn out the light but I don't sleep.

BETTER LIVING
THROUGH CHEMISTRY

••••••••••••••••••••••••••••••••••

Sunday, September 5, 1993 (Clare is 22, Henry is 30)

CLARE: Henry is perusing his dog-eared copy of the *Physicians' Desk Reference.* Not a good sign.

"I never realized you were such a drug fiend."

"I'm not a drug fiend. I'm an alcoholic."

"You're not an alcoholic."

"Sure I am."

I lie down on his couch and put my legs across his lap. Henry puts the book on top of my shins and continues to page through it.

"You don't drink all that much."

"I used to. I slowed down somewhat after I almost killed myself. Also my dad is a sad cautionary tale."

"What are you looking for?"

"Something I can take for the wedding. I don't want to leave you standing at the altar in front of four hundred people."

"Yeah. Good idea." I ponder this scenario and shudder. "Let's elope."

He meets my eyes. "Let's. I'm all for it."

"My parents would disown me."

"Surely not."

"You haven't been paying attention. This is a major Broadway production. We are just an excuse for my dad to entertain lavishly and impress all his lawyer buddies. If we bowed out my parents would have to hire actors to impersonate us."

"Let's go down to City Hall and get married beforehand. Then if anything happens, at least we'll be married."

"Oh, but . . . I wouldn't like that. It would be lying . . . I would feel weird. How about we do that after, if the real wedding gets messed up?"

"Okay. Plan B." He holds out his hand, and I shake it.

"So are you finding anything?"

"Well, ideally I would like a neuroleptic called Risperdal, but it won't be marketed until 1994. The next best thing would be Clozaril, and a possible third choice would be Haldol."

"They all sound like high-tech cough medicine."

"They're antipsychotics."

"Seriously?"

"Yes."

"You're not psychotic."

Henry looks at me and makes a horrible face and claws at the air like a silent movie werewolf. Then he says, quite seriously, "On an EEG, I have the brain of a schizophrenic. More than one doctor has insisted that this little time-travel delusion of mine is due to schizophrenia. These drugs block dopamine receptors."

"Side effects?"

"Well . . . dystonia, akathisia, pseudo-Parkinsonism. That is, involuntary muscle contractions, restlessness, rocking, pacing, insomnia, immobility, lack of facial expression. And then there's tardive dyskinesia, chronic uncontrollable facial muscles, and agranulocytosis, the destruction of the body's ability to make white blood cells.

And then there's the loss of sexual function. And the fact that all the drugs that are currently available are somewhat sedative."

"You're not seriously thinking of taking any of these, are you?"

"Well, I've taken Haldol in the past. And Thorazine."

"And . . . ?"

"Really horrible. I was totally zombified. It felt like my brain was full of Elmer's Glue."

"Isn't there anything else?"

"Valium. Librium. Xanax."

"Mama takes those. Xanax and Valium."

"Yeah, that would make sense." He makes a face and sets the *Physicians' Desk Reference* aside and says, "Move over." We adjust our positions on the couch until we are lying side by side. It's very cozy.

"Don't take anything."

"Why not?"

"You're not sick."

Henry laughs. "That's what I love you for: your inability to perceive all my hideous flaws." He's unbuttoning my shirt and I wrap my hand around his. He looks at me, waiting. I am a little angry.

"I don't understand why you talk like that. You're always saying horrible things about yourself. You aren't like that. You're good."

Henry looks at my hand and disengages his, and draws me closer. "I'm not good," he says softly, in my ear. "But maybe I will be, hmmm?"

"You better be."

"I'm good to you." Too true. "Clare?"

"Hmmm?"

"Do you ever lie awake wondering if I'm some kind of joke God is playing on you?"

"No. I lie awake worrying that you might disappear and never come back. I lie awake brooding about some of the stuff I sort of half know about in the future. But I have total faith in the idea that we are supposed to be together."

"Total faith."

"Don't you?"

Henry kisses me. "*'Nor Time, nor Place, nor Chance, nor Death can bow/my least desires unto the least remove.'*"

"Come again?"

"I don't mind if I do."

"Braggart."

"Now who's saying horrible things about me?"

Monday, September 6, 1993 (Henry is 30)

HENRY: I'm sitting on the stoop of a dingy white aluminum-sided house in Humboldt Park. It's Monday morning, around ten. I'm waiting for Ben to get back from wherever he is. I don't like this neighborhood very much; I feel kind of exposed sitting here at Ben's door, but he's an extremely punctual guy, so I continue to wait with confidence. I watch two young Hispanic women push baby strollers along the pitched and broken sidewalk. As I meditate on the inequity of city services, I hear someone yell "Library Boy!" in the distance. I look in the direction of the voice and sure enough, it's Gomez. I groan inwardly; Gomez has an amazing talent for running into me when I'm up to something particularly nefarious. I will have to get rid of him before Ben shows up.

Gomez comes sailing toward me happily. He's wearing his lawyer outfit, and carrying his briefcase. I sigh.

"*Ça va*, comrade."

"*Ça va.* What are you doing here?"

Good question. "Waiting on a friend. What time is it?"

"Quarter after ten. September 6, 1993," he adds helpfully.

"I know, Gomez. But thanks anyway. You visiting a client?"

"Yeah. Ten-year-old girl. Mom's boyfriend made her drink Drano. I do get tired of humans."

"Yeah. Too many maniacs, not enough Michelangelos."

"You had lunch? Or breakfast, I guess it would be?"

"Yeah. I kind of need to stay here, wait for my friend."

"I didn't know any of your friends lived out this way. All the people I know over here are sadly in need of legal counsel."

"Friend from library school." And here he is. Ben drives up in his '62 silver Mercedes. The inside is a wreck, but from the outside it's a sweet-looking car. Gomez whistles softly.

"Sorry I'm late," Ben says, hurrying up the walk. "Housecall."

Gomez looks at me inquisitively. I ignore him. Ben looks at Gomez, and at me.

"Gomez, Ben. Ben, Gomez. So sorry you have to leave, comrade."

"Actually, I've got a couple hours free—"

Ben takes the situation in hand. "Gomez. Great meeting you. Some other time, yes?" Ben is quite nearsighted, and he peers kindly at Gomez through his thick glasses that magnify his eyes to twice their normal size. Ben's jingling his keys in his hand. It's making me nervous. We both stand quietly, waiting for Gomez to leave.

"Okay. Yeah. Well, bye," says Gomez.

"I'll call you this afternoon," I tell him. He turns without looking at me and walks away. I feel bad, but there are things I don't want Gomez to know, and this is one of them. Ben and I turn to each other, share a look that acknowledges the fact that we know things about each other that are problematic. He opens his front door. I have always itched to try my hand at breaking into Ben's place, because he has a large number and variety of locks and security devices. We enter the dark narrow hall. It always smells like cabbage in here, even though I know for a fact that Ben never cooks much in the way of food, let alone cabbage. We walk to the back stairway, up and into another hallway, through one bedroom and into another, which Ben has set up as a lab. He sets down his bag and hangs up his jacket. I half expect him to put on some tennis shoes, à la Mr. Rogers, but instead he putters around with his coffee maker. I sit down on a folding chair and wait for Ben to finish.

More than anyone else I know, Ben looks like a librarian. And I did in fact meet him at Rosary, but he quit before finishing his MLS. He has gotten thinner since I saw him last, and lost a little more hair. Ben has AIDS, and every time I see him I pay attention, because I never know how it will go, with him.

"You're looking good," I tell him.

"Massive doses of AZT. And vitamins, and yoga, and visual imaging. Speaking of which. What can I do for you?"

"I'm getting married."

Ben is surprised, and then delighted. "Congratulations. To whom?"

"Clare. You met her. The girl with very long red hair."

"Oh—yes." Ben looks grave. "She knows?"

"Yes."

"Well, great." He gives me a look that says that this is all very nice, but what of it?

"So her parents have planned this huge wedding, up in Michigan. Church, bridesmaids, rice, the whole nine yards. And a lavish reception at the Yacht Club, afterward. White tie, no less."

Ben pours out coffee and hands me a mug with Winnie the Pooh on it. I stir powdered creamer into it. It's cold up here, and the coffee smells bitter but kind of good.

"I need to be there. I need to get through about eight hours of huge, mind-boggling stress, without disappearing."

"Ah." Ben has a way of taking in a problem, just accepting it, which I find very soothing.

"I need something that's going to K.O. every dopamine receptor I've got."

"Navane, Haldol, Thorazine, Serentil, Mellaril, Stelazine . . ." Ben polishes his glasses on his sweater. He looks like a large hairless mouse without them.

"I was hoping you could make this for me." I fish around in my jeans for the paper, find it and hand it over. Ben squints at it, reads.

"3-[2-[4-96-fluoro-1,2-benizisoxazol-3-yl) . . . colloidal silicon dioxide, hydroxypropyl methylcellulose . . . propylene glycol . . ." He looks up at me, bewildered. "What is this?"

"It's a new antipsychotic called risperidone, marketed as Risperdal. It will be commercially available in 1998, but I would like to try it now. It belongs to a new class of drugs called benzisoxazole derivatives."

"Where did you get this?"

"PDR. The 2000 edition."

"Who makes it?"

"Janssen."

"Henry, you know you don't tolerate antipsychotics very well. Unless this works in some radically different way?"

"They don't know how it works. 'Selective monoaminergic antagonist with high affinity for serotonin type 2, dopamine type 2, blah blah blah.'"

"Well, same old same old. What makes you think this is going to be any better than Haldol?"

I smile patiently. "It's an educated guess. I don't know for sure. Can you make that?"

Ben hesitates. "I *can*, yes."

"How soon? It takes a while to build up in the system."

"I'll let you know. When's the wedding?"

"October 23."

"Mmm. What's the dosage?"

"Start with 1 milligram and build from there."

Ben stands up, stretches. In the dim light of this cold room he seems old, jaundiced, paper-skinned. Part of Ben likes the challenge (*hey, let's replicate this avant-garde drug that nobody's even invented yet*) and part of him doesn't like the risk. "Henry, you don't even know for sure that dopamine's your problem."

"You've seen the scans."

"Yeah, yeah. Why not just live with it? The cure might be worse than the problem."

"Ben. What if I snapped my fingers right *now*—" I stand up, lean close to him, snap my fingers: "and *right now* you suddenly found yourself standing in Allen's bedroom, in 1986—"

"—I'd kill the fucker."

"But you can't, because you didn't." Ben closes his eyes, shakes his head. "And you can't change anything: he will still get sick, you will still get sick, *und so weiter.* What if you had to watch him die over and over?" Ben sits in the folding chair. He's not looking at me. "That's what it's like, Ben. I mean, yeah, sometimes it's fun. But mostly it's getting lost and stealing and trying to just . . ."

"Cope." Ben sighs. "God, I don't know why I put up with you."

"Novelty? My boyish good looks?"

"Dream on. Hey, am I invited to this wedding?"

I am startled. It never occurred to me that Ben would want to come. "Yeah! Really? You would come?"

"Beats funerals."

"Great! My side of the church is filling up rapidly. You'll be my eighth guest."

Ben laughs. "Invite all your ex-girlfriends. That'll swell the ranks."

"I'd never survive it. Most of them want my head on a stick."

"Mmm." Ben gets up and rummages in one of his desk drawers. He pulls out an empty pill bottle and opens another drawer, takes out a huge bottle of capsules, opens it and places three pills in the small bottle. He tosses it to me.

"What is it?" I ask, opening the bottle and shaking a pill onto my palm.

"It's an endorphin stabilizer combined with an antidepressant. It's—hey, don't—" I have popped the pill into my mouth and swallowed. "It's morphine-based." Ben sighs. "You have the most casually arrogant attitude toward drugs."

"I like opiates."

"I bet. Don't think I'm going to let you have a ton of those, either. Let me know if you think that would do the job for the wedding. In case this other thing doesn't pan out. They last about four hours, so you would need two." Ben nods at the two remaining pills. "Don't gobble those up just for fun, okay?"

"Scout's honor."

Ben snorts. I pay him for the pills and leave. As I walk downstairs I feel the rush grab me and I stop at the bottom of the stairs to luxuriate in it. It's been a while. Whatever Ben has mixed in here, it's fantastic. It's like an orgasm times ten plus cocaine, and it seems to be getting stronger. As I walk out the front door I practically trip over Gomez. He's been waiting for me.

"Care for a ride?"

"Sure." I am deeply moved by his concern. Or his curiosity. Or whatever. We walk to his car, a Chevy Nova with two bashed headlights. I climb into the passenger seat. Gomez gets in and slams his door. He coaxes the little car into starting and we set off.

The city is gray and dingy and it's starting to rain. Fat drops smack the windshield as crack houses and empty lots flow by us.

Gomez turns on NPR and they're playing Charles Mingus who sounds a little slow to me but then again why not? it's a free country. Ashland Avenue is full of brain-jarring potholes but otherwise things are fine, quite fine actually, my head is fluid and mobile, like liquid mercury escaped from a broken thermometer, and it's all I can do to keep myself from moaning with pleasure as the drug laps all my nerve endings with its tiny chemical tongues. We pass ESP Psychic Card Reader, Pedro's Tire Outlet, Burger King, Pizza Hut, and *I am the passenger* runs through my head weaving its way into the Mingus. Gomez says something which I don't catch and then again,

"Henry!"

"Yes?"

"What are you on?"

"I'm not quite sure. A science experiment, of sorts."

"Why?"

"Stellar question. I'll get back to you on that."

We don't say anything else until the car stops in front of Clare and Charisse's apartment. I look at Gomez in confusion.

"You need company," he tells me gently. I don't disagree. Gomez lets us in the front door and we walk upstairs. Clare opens the door and when she sees me she looks upset, relieved, and amused, all at once.

CLARE: I have talked Henry into getting into my bed, and Gomez and I are sitting in the living room drinking tea and eating peanut butter and kiwi jelly sandwiches.

"Learn to cook, woman," intones Gomez. He sounds like Charleton Heston handing down the Ten Commandments.

"One of these days." I stir sugar into my tea. "Thank you for going and getting him."

"Anything for you, kitten." He starts to roll a cigarette. Gomez is the only person I know who smokes during a meal. I refrain from commenting. He lights up. He looks at me, and I brace myself. "So, what was that little episode all about, hmm? Most of the people who go to Compassionate Pharmacopoeia are AIDS victims or cancer patients."

"You know Ben?" I don't know why I'm surprised. Gomez knows everybody.

"I know *of* Ben. My mom used to go to Ben when she was having chemo."

"Oh." I review the situation, searching for things I can safely mention.

"Whatever Ben gave him really put him in the Slow Zone."

"We're trying to find something that will help Henry stay in the present."

"He seems a little too inanimate for daily use."

"Yeah." Maybe a lower dosage?

"Why are you doing this?"

"Doing what?"

"Aiding and abetting Mr. Mayhem. Marrying him, no less."

Henry calls my name. I get up. Gomez reaches out and grabs my hand.

"Clare. Please—"

"Gomez. Let go." I stare him down. After a long, awful moment he drops his eyes and lets me go. I hurry down the hall into my room and shut the door.

Henry is stretched out like a cat, diagonally across the bed face down. I take off my shoes and stretch out beside him.

"How's it going?" I ask him.

Henry rolls over and smiles. "Heaven." He strokes my face. "Care to join me?"

"No."

Henry sighs. "You are so good. I shouldn't be trying to corrupt you."

"I'm not good. I'm afraid." We lie together in silence for a long time. The sun is shining now, and it shows me my bedroom in early afternoon: the curve of the walnut bed frame, the gold and violet Oriental rug, the hairbrush and lipstick and bottle of hand lotion on the bureau. A copy of *Art in America* with Leon Golub on the cover lies on the seat of my old garage-sale armchair partially obscured by *A rebours*. Henry is wearing black socks. His long bony feet hang off the edge of the bed. He seems thin to me. Henry's eyes are closed; perhaps he can feel me staring at him, because he opens his eyes and smiles at me. His hair is falling into his face and I brush it back. Henry takes my hand and kisses the palm. I unbutton his jeans and slide my hand over his cock, but Henry shakes his head and takes my hand and holds it.

"Sorry, Clare," he says softly. "There's something in this stuff that seems to have short-circuited the equipment. Later, maybe."

"That'll be fun on our wedding night."

Henry shakes his head. "I can't take this for the wedding. It's too much fun. I mean, Ben's a genius, but he's used to working with people who are terminally ill. Whatever he's got in here, it plays like a near-death experience." He sighs and sets the pill bottle on my nightstand. "I should mail those to Ingrid. This is her perfect drug." I hear the front door open and then it slams shut; Gomez leaving.

"You want something to eat?" I ask.

"No thanks."

"Is Ben going to make that other drug for you?"

"He's going to try," Henry says.

"What if it's not right?"

"You mean if Ben fucks up?"

"Yeah."

Henry says, "Whatever happens, we both know that I live to be at least forty-three. So don't worry about it."

Forty-three? "What happens after forty-three?"

"I don't know, Clare. Maybe I figure out how to stay in the present." He gathers me in and we are quiet. When I wake up later it is dark and Henry is sleeping beside me. The little bottle of pills shines red in the light of the LED display of the alarm clock. Forty-three?

Monday, September 27, 1993 (Clare is 22, Henry is 30)

CLARE: I let myself into Henry's apartment and turn on the lights. We're going to the opera tonight; it's *The Ghosts of Versailles.* The Lyric Opera won't seat latecomers, so I'm flustered and at first I don't realize that no lights means Henry isn't here. Then I do realize it, and I'm annoyed because he's going to make us late. Then I wonder if he's gone. Then I hear someone breathing.

I stand still. The breathing is coming from the kitchen. I run into the kitchen and turn on the light and Henry is lying on the floor, fully clothed, in a strange, rigid pose, staring straight ahead. As I stand there he makes a low sound, not like a human sound, a groan that clatters in his throat, that tears through his clenched teeth.

"Oh, God, oh, God." I call 911. The operator assures me they'll be here in minutes. And as I sit on the kitchen floor staring at Henry I feel a wave of anger and I find Henry's Rolodex in his desk and I dial the number.

"Hello?" The voice is tiny and distant.

"Is this Ben Matteson?"

"Yes. Who is this?"

"Clare Abshire. Listen, Ben, Henry is lying on the floor totally rigid and can't talk. *What the fuck?*"

"What? Shit! Call 911!"

"I did—"

"The drug is mimicking Parkinson's, he needs dopamine! Tell them—shit, call me from the hospital—"

"They're here—"

"Okay! Call me—" I hang up, and face the paramedics.

Later, after the ambulance ride to Mercy Hospital, after Henry has been admitted, injected, and intubated and is lying in a hospital bed attached to a monitor, relaxed and sleeping, I look up and see a tall gaunt man in the doorway of Henry's room, and I remember that I have forgotten to call Ben. He walks in and stands across from me on the other side of the bed. The room is dark and the light from the hallway silhouettes Ben as he bows his head and says, "I'm so sorry. So sorry."

I reach across the bed, take his hands. "It's okay. He's going to be fine. Really."

Ben shakes his head. "It's completely my fault. I should never have made it for him."

"What happened?"

Ben sighs and sits down in the chair. I sit on the bed. "It could be several things," he says. "It could be just a side effect, could happen to anybody. But it could be that Henry didn't have the recipe quite right. I mean, it's a lot to memorize. And I couldn't check it."

We are both silent. Henry's monitor drips fluid into his arm. An orderly walks by with a cart. Finally I say, "Ben?"

"Yes, Clare?"

"Do something for me?"

"Anything."

"Cut him off. No more drugs. Drugs aren't going to work."

Ben grins at me, relieved. "Just say no."

"Exactly." We laugh. Ben sits with me for a while. When he gets up to leave, he takes my hand and says, "Thank you for being kind about it. He could easily have died."

"But he didn't."

"No, he didn't."

"See you at the wedding."

"Yes." We are standing in the hall. In the glaring fluorescent light Ben looks tired and ill. He ducks his head and turns, and walks down the hall, and I turn back to the dim room where Henry lies sleeping.

TURNING POINT

....

Friday, October 22, 1993 (Henry is 30)

HENRY: I am strolling down Linden Street, in South Haven, at
large for an hour while Clare and her mother do something at the
florist's. The wedding is tomorrow, but as the groom I don't seem to
have too many responsibilities. Be there; that's the main item on my
To Do list. Clare is constantly being whisked away to fittings, con-
sultations, bridal showers. When I do see her she always looks
rather wistful.

It's a clear cold day, and I dawdle. I wish South Haven had a decent bookstore. Even the library consists mainly of Barbara Cart-
land and John Grisham. I have the Penguin edition of Kleist with
me, but I'm not in the mood. I pass an antiques shop, a bakery, a
bank, another antiques shop. As I walk by the barber shop I peer in;
there's an old man being shaved by a dapper little balding barber,
and I know at once what I'm going to do.

Little bells clang against the door as I walk into the shop. It
smells of soap, steam, hair lotion, and elderly flesh. Everything is
pale green. The chair is old and ornate with chrome, and there are
elaborate bottles lining dark wooden shelves, and trays of scissors,

combs, and razors. It's almost medical; it's very Norman Rockwell. The barber glances up at me. "Haircut?" I ask. He nods at the row of empty straight-backed chairs with magazines neatly stacked on a rack at one end of the row. Sinatra is playing on the radio. I sit down and leaf through a copy of *Reader's Digest*. The barber wipes traces of lather from the old man's chin, and applies aftershave. The old man climbs gingerly from the chair and pays up. The barber helps him into his coat and hands him his cane. "See you, George," says the old man as he creeps out. "'Bye, Ed," replies the barber. He turns his attention to me. "What'll it be?" I hop into the chair and he steps me up a few inches and swivels me around to face the mirror. I take a long last look at my hair. I hold my thumb and forefinger about an inch apart. "Cut it all off." He nods his approval and ties a plastic cape around my neck. Soon his scissors are flashing little metal on metal noises around my head, and my hair is falling to the floor. When he is done he brushes me off and removes the cape and *voilà*, I've become the me of my future.

GET ME TO THE CHURCH ON TIME

....

Saturday, October 23, 1993 (Henry is 30, Clare is 22)
(6:00 a.m.)

HENRY: I wake up at 6:00 a.m. and it's raining. I am in a snug little green room under the eaves in a cozy little bed-and-breakfast called Blake's, which is right on the south beach in South Haven. Clare's parents have chosen this place; my dad is sleeping in an equally cozy pink room downstairs, next to Mrs. Kim in a lovely yellow room; Grandpa and Grams are in the *über*-cozy blue master bedroom. I lie in the extra-soft bed under Laura Ashley sheets, and I can hear the wind flinging itself against the house. The rain is pouring down in sheets. I wonder if I can run in this monsoon. I hear it coursing through the gutters and drumming on the roof, which is about two feet above my face. This room is like a garret. It has a delicate little writing desk, in case I need to pen any ladylike missives on my wedding day. There's a china ewer and basin on the bureau; if I actually wanted to use them I'd probably have to break the ice on the water first, because it's quite cold up here. I feel like a pink worm in the core of this green room, as though I have eaten my way in and should be working on becoming a butterfly, or something. I'm not real awake, here, at the moment. I hear some-body coughing. I hear my heart beating and the high-pitched sound which is my nervous system doing its thing. Oh, God, let today be a normal day. Let me be normally befuddled, normally nervous; get me to the church on time, in time. Let me not startle anyone, espe-cially myself. Let me get through our wedding day as best I can, with no special effects. Deliver Clare from unpleasant scenes. Amen.

(7:00 a.m.)

CLARE: I wake up in my bed, the bed of my childhood. As I float on the surface of waking I can't find myself in time; is it Christmas, Thanksgiving? Is it third grade, again? Am I sick? Why is it raining? Outside the yellow curtains the sky is dead and the big elm tree is being stripped of its yellow leaves by the wind. I have been dreaming all night. The dreams merge, now. In one part of this dream I was swimming in the ocean, I was a mermaid. I was sort of new at being a mermaid and one of the other mermaids was trying to teach me; she was giving me mermaid lessons. I was afraid to breathe under water. The water got into my lungs and I couldn't figure out how it was supposed to work, it felt terrible and I kept having to rise up to the surface and breathe and the other mermaid kept saying, *No, Clare, like this* . . . until finally I realized that she had gills in her neck, and I did too, and then it was better. Swim-ming was like flying, all the fish were birds. . . . There was a boat on the surface of the ocean, and we all swam up to see the boat. It was just a little sailboat, and my mother was on it, all by herself. I swam up to her and she was surprised to see me there, she said *Why Clare, I thought you were getting married today,* and I suddenly realized, the way you do in dreams, that I couldn't get married to Henry if I was a mermaid, and I started to cry, and then I woke up and it was the middle of the night. So I lay there for a while in the dark and I made up that I became a regular woman, like the Little Mermaid except I didn't have any of that nonsense about hideous pain in my feet or getting my tongue cut out. Hans Christian Andersen must have been a very strange and sad person. Then I went back to sleep and now I am in bed and Henry and I are getting married today.

(7:16 a.m.)

HENRY: The ceremony is at 2:00 p.m. and it will take me about half an hour to dress and twenty minutes for us to drive over to St. Basil's. It is now 7:16 a.m., which leaves five hours and forty-four minutes to kill. I throw on jeans and a skanky old flannel shirt and high-tops and creep as quietly as possible downstairs seeking coffee. Dad has beat me to it; he's sitting in the breakfast room with his hands wrapped around a dainty cup of steaming black joe. I pour one for myself and sit across from him. Through the lace-curtained windows the weak light gives Dad a ghostly look; he's a colorized version of a black and white movie of himself this morning. His hair is standing up every which way and without thinking I smooth mine down, as though he were a mirror. He does the same, and we smile.

(8:17 a.m.)

CLARE: Alicia is sitting on my bed, poking me. "Come on, Clare," she pokes. "Daylight in the swamp. The birds are singing," (quite untrue) "and the frogs are jumping and it's *time to get up!*" Alicia is tickling me. She throws off the covers and we are wrestling and just as I pin her Etta sticks her head in the door and hisses "Girls! What is all this *bumping.* Your father, he thinks a *tree* fell on the house, but no, it is you sillies trying to *kill* each other. Breakfast is almost ready." With that Etta abruptly withdraws her head and we hear her barging down the stairs as we dissolve into laughter.

(8:32 a.m.)

HENRY: It's still blowing gales out there but I am going running anyway. I study the map of South Haven ("A shining jewel on the Sunset Coast of Lake Michigan!") which Clare has provided me with. Yesterday I ran along the beach, which was pleasant but not something to do this morning. I can see six-foot-tall waves throwing themselves at the shore. I measure out a mile of streets and figure I will run laps; if it's too awful out there I can cut it short. I stretch out. Every joint pops. I can almost hear tension crackling in my nerves like static in a phone line. I get dressed, and out into the world I go.

The rain is a slap in the face. I am drenched immediately. I soldier slowly down Maple Street. It's just going to be a slog; I am fighting the wind and there's no way to get up any speed. I pass a woman standing at the curb with her bulldog and she looks at me with amazement. This isn't mere exercise, I tell her silently. This is desperation.

(8:54 a.m.)

CLARE: We're gathered around the breakfast table. Cold leaks in from all the windows, and I can barely see outside, it's raining so hard. How is Henry going to run in this?

"Perfect weather for a wedding," Mark jokes.

I shrug. "*I* didn't pick it."

"You didn't?"

"*Daddy* picked it."

"Well, I'm paying for it," Daddy says petulantly.

"True." I munch my toast.

My mother eyes my plate critically. "Honey, why don't you have some nice bacon? And some of these eggs?"

The very thought turns my stomach. "I can't. Really. Please."

"Well, at least put some peanut butter on that toast. You need protein." I make eye contact with Etta, who strides into the kitchen and comes back a minute later with a tiny crystal dish full of peanut butter. I thank her and spread some on the toast.

I ask my mother, "Do I have any time before Janice shows up?" Janice is going to do something hideous to my face and hair.

"She's coming at eleven. Why?"

"I need to run into Town, to get something."

"I can get it for you, sweetie." She looks relieved at the thought of getting out of the house.

"I would like to go, myself."

"We can both go."

"By myself." I mutely plead with her. She's puzzled but relents.

"Well, okay. Goodness."

"Great. I'll be right back." I get up to leave. Daddy clears his throat.

"May I be excused?"

"Certainly."

"Thank you." I flee.

(9:35 a.m.)

HENRY: I'm standing in the immense, empty bathtub struggling out of my cold, soaked clothes. My brand-new running shoes have acquired an entirely new shape, reminiscent of marine life. I have left a trail of water from the front door to the tub, which I hope Mrs. Blake won't mind too much.

Someone knocks on my door. "Just a minute," I call. I squoosh over to the door and crack it open. To my complete surprise, it's Clare.

"What's the password?" I say softly.

"Fuck me," replies Clare. I swing the door wide.

Clare walks in, sits on the bed, and starts taking off her shoes. "You're not joking?"

"Come on, O almost-husband mine. I've got to be back by eleven." She looks me up and down. "You went running! I didn't think you'd run in this rain."

"Desperate times call for desperate measures." I peel off my T-shirt and throw it into the tub. It lands with a splat. "Isn't it supposed to be bad luck for the groom to see the bride before the wedding?"

"So close your eyes." Clare trots into the bathroom and grabs a towel. I lean over and she dries my hair. It feels wonderful. I could do with a lifetime of this. Yes, indeed.

"It's really cold up here," says Clare.

"Come and be bedded, almost-wife. It's the only warm spot in the whole place." We climb in.

"We do everything out of order, don't we?"

"You have a problem with that?"

"No. I like it."

"Good. You've come to the right man for all your extrachronological needs."

(11:15 a.m.)

CLARE: I walk in the back door and leave my umbrella in the mud room. In the hall I almost bump into Alicia.

"Where have you been? Janice is here."

"What time is it?"

"Eleven-fifteen. Hey, you've got your shirt on backward and inside out."

"I think that's good luck, isn't it?"

"Maybe, but you'd better change it before you go upstairs." I duck back into the mud room and reverse my shirt. Then I run upstairs. Mama and Janice are standing in the hall outside my room. Janice is carrying a huge bag of cosmetics and other implements of torture.

"There you are. I was getting worried." Mama shepherds me into my room and Janice brings up the rear. "I have to go talk to the caterers." She is almost wringing her hands as she departs.

I turn to Janice, who examines me critically. "Your hair's all wet and tangled. Why don't you comb it out while I set up?" She starts to take a million tubes and bottles from her bag and sets them on my dresser.

"Janice." I hand her the postcard from the Uffizi. "Can you do this?" I have always loved the little Medici princess whose hair is not unlike mine; hers has many tiny braids and pearls all swooped together in a beautiful fall of amber hair. The anonymous artist must have loved her, too. How could he not love her?

Janice considers. "This isn't what your mom thinks we're doing."

"Uh-huh. But it's my wedding. And my hair. And I'll give you a very large tip if you do it my way."

"I won't have time to do your face if we do this; it'll take too long to do all these braids."

Hallelujah. "It's okay. I'll put on my own makeup."

"Well, all right. Just comb it for me and we'll get started." I begin to pick out the tangles. I'm starting to enjoy this. As I surrender to Janice's slender brown hands I wonder what Henry is up to.

(11:36 a.m.)

HENRY: The tux and all its attendant miseries are laid out on the bed. I'm freezing my undernourished ass off in this cold room. I throw all my cold wet clothing out of the tub and into the sink. This bathroom is amazingly as big as the bedroom. It's carpeted, and relentlessly pseudo-Victorian. The tub is an immense claw-footed thing amid various ferns and stacks of towels and a commode and a large framed reproduction of Hunt's *The Awakened Conscience*. The windowsill is six inches from the floor and the curtains are filmy white muslin, so I can see Maple Street in all its dead leafy glory. A beige Lincoln Continental cruises lazily up the street. I run hot water into the tub, which is so large that I get tired of waiting for it to fill and climb in. I amuse myself playing with the European-style shower attachment and taking the caps off the ten or so shampoos, shower gels, and conditioners and sniffing them all; by the fifth one I have a headache. I sing "Yellow Submarine." Everything within a four-foot radius gets wet.

(12:35 p.m.)

CLARE: Janice releases me, and Mama and Etta converge. Etta says, "Oh, Clare, you look beautiful!" Mama says, "That's not the hairstyle we agreed on, Clare." Mama gives Janice a hard time and then pays her and I give Janice her tip when Mama's not looking. I'm supposed to get dressed at the church, so they pack me into the car and we drive over to St. Basil's.

(12:55 p.m.) (Henry is 38)

HENRY: I'm walking along Highway 12, about two miles south of South Haven. It's an unbelievably awful day, weatherwise. It's fall, rain is gusting and pouring down in sheets, and it's cold and windy. I'm wearing nothing but jeans, I'm barefoot, and I am soaked to the skin. I have no idea where I am in time. I'm headed for Meadowlark House, hoping to dry out in the Reading Room and maybe eat something. I have no money, but when I see the pink neon light of the CUT-RATE GAS FOR LESS sign I veer toward it. I enter the gas station and stand for a moment, streaming water onto the linoleum and catching my breath.

"Quite a day to be out in," says the thin elderly gent behind the counter.

"Yep," I reply.

"Car break down?"

"Huh? Um, no." He's taking a good look at me, noting the bare feet, the unseasonable clothing. I pause, feign embarrassment. "Girlfriend threw me out of the house."

He says something but I don't hear it because I am looking at the *South Haven Daily*. Today is Saturday, October 23, 1993. Our wedding day. The clock above the cigarette rack says 1:10.

"Gotta run," I say to the old man, and I do.

(1:42 p.m.)

CLARE: I'm standing in my fourth-grade classroom wearing my wedding dress. It's ivory watered silk with lots of lace and seed pearls. The dress is tightly fitted in the bodice and arms but the skirt is huge, floor-length with a train and twenty yards of fabric. I could hide ten midgets under it. I feel like a parade float, but Mama is making much of me; she's fussing and taking pictures and trying to get me to put on more makeup. Alicia and Charisse and Helen and Ruth are all fluttering around in their matching sage green velvet bridesmaids' outfits. Since Charisse and Ruth are both short and Alicia and

Helen are both tall they look like some oddly assorted Girl Scouts but we've all agreed to be cool about it when Mama's around. They are comparing the dye jobs on their shoes and arguing about who should get to catch the bouquet. Helen says, "Charisse, you're already engaged, you shouldn't even be trying to catch it," and Charisse shrugs and says, "Insurance. With Gomez you never know."

(1:48 p.m.)

HENRY: I'm sitting on a radiator in a musty room full of boxes of prayer books. Gomez is pacing back and forth, smoking. He looks terrific in his tux. I feel like I'm impersonating a game show host. Gomez paces and flicks his ashes into a teacup. He's making me even more nervous than I already am.

"You've got the ring?" I ask for the gazillionth time.

"Yeah. I've got the ring."

He stops pacing for a moment and looks at me. "Want a drink?"

"Yeah." Gomez produces a flask and hands it to me. I uncap it and take a swallow. It's very smooth Scotch. I take another mouthful and hand it back. I can hear people laughing and talking out in the vestibule. I'm sweating, and my head aches. The room is very warm. I stand up and open the window, hang my head out, breathe. It's still raining.

There's a noise in the shrubbery. I open the window farther and look down. There I am, sitting in the dirt, under the window, soaking wet, panting. He grins at me and gives me the thumbs up.

(1:55 p.m.)

CLARE: We're all standing in the vestibule of the church. Daddy says, "Let's get this show on the road," and knocks on the door of the room Henry is dressing in. Gomez sticks his head out and says, "Give us a minute." He throws me a look that makes my stomach clench and pulls his head in and shuts the door. I am walking toward the door when Gomez opens it again, and Henry appears, doing up his cuff links. He's wet, dirty, and unshaven. He looks about forty. But he's *here,* and he gives me a triumphant smile as he walks through the doors of the church and down the aisle.

Sunday, June 13, 1976 (Henry is 30)

HENRY: I am lying on the floor in my old bedroom. I'm alone, and it's a perfect summer night in an unknown year. I lie there swearing and feeling like an idiot for a while. Then I get up and go into the kitchen and help myself to several of Dad's beers.

Saturday, October 23, 1993 (Clare is 22, Henry is 38, and 30)
(2:37 p.m.)

CLARE: We are standing at the altar. Henry turns to me and says, "I, Henry, take you, Clare, to be my wife. I promise to be true to you in good times and in bad, in sickness and in health. I will love you and honor you all the days of my life." I think: *remember this.* I repeat the promise to him. Father Compton smiles at us and says, ". . . What God has joined, men must not divide." I think: *that's not really the problem.* Henry slides the thin silver ring over my finger into place above the engagement ring. I place his plain gold band on his finger, the only time he will ever wear it. The Mass proceeds, and I think *this is all that matters: he's here, I'm here, it doesn't matter how, as long as he's with me.* Father Compton blesses us, and says, "The Mass is ended, go in peace." We walk down the aisle, arm in arm, together.

(6:26 p.m.)

HENRY: The reception is just getting underway. The caterers are rushing back and forth with steel carts and covered trays. People are arriving and checking their coats. The rain has finally stopped. The South Haven Yacht Club is on North Beach, a 1920s building done up in paneling and leather, red carpet, and paintings of ships. It's dark out now, but the lighthouse is blinking away out on the pier. I'm standing at a window, drinking Glenlivet, waiting for Clare, who has been whisked away by her mother for some reason I'm not privy to. I see Gomez and Ben's reflections, heading toward me, and I turn.

Ben looks worried. "How are you?"

"I'm okay. Can you guys do me a favor?" They nod. "Gomez, go back to the church. I'm there, waiting in the vestibule. Pick me up, and bring me here. Smuggle me into the downstairs men's john and leave me there. Ben, keep an eye on me," (I point at my chest) "and when I tell you to, grab my tux and bring it to me in the men's room. Okay?"

Gomez asks, "How much time do we have?"

"Not much."

He nods, and walks away. Charisse approaches, and Gomez kisses her on the forehead and continues on. I turn to Ben, who looks tired. "How are you?" I ask him.

Ben sighs. "Kind of fatigued. Um, Henry?"

"Hmm?"

"When are you coming from?"

"2002."

"Can you . . . Look, I know you don't like this, but. . . ."

"What? It's okay, Ben. Whatever you want. It's a special occasion."

"Tell me: am I still alive?" Ben isn't looking at me; he stares at the band, tuning up in the ballroom.

"Yes. You're doing fine. I just saw you a few days ago; we played pool."

Ben lets his breath out in a rush. "Thank you."

"No problem." Tears are welling up in Ben's eyes. I offer him my handkerchief, and he takes it, but then hands it back unused and goes off in search of the men's room.

(7:04 p.m.)

CLARE: Everyone is sitting down to dinner and no one can find Henry. I ask Gomez if he's seen him, and Gomez just gives me one of his Gomez looks and says that he's sure Henry will be here any minute. Kimy comes up to us, looking very fragile and worried in her rose silk dress.

"Where is Henry?" she asks me.

"I don't know, Kimy."

She pulls me toward her and whispers in my ear, "I saw his young friend Ben carrying a pile of clothing out of the Lounge." Oh, no. If Henry has snapped back to his present it will be hard to explain. Maybe I could say that there was an emergency? Some kind of library emergency that required Henry's immediate attention. But all his co-workers are here. Maybe I could say Henry has amnesia, has wandered away . . .

"There he is," Kimy says. She squeezes my hand. Henry is standing in the doorway scanning the crowd, and sees us. He comes running over.

I kiss him. "Howdy, stranger." He is back in the present, my younger Henry, the one who belongs here. Henry takes my arm, and Kimy's arm, and leads us in to dinner. Kimy chuckles, and says something to Henry that I don't catch. "What'd she say?" I ask as we sit down. "She asked me if we were planning a *ménage à trois* for the wedding night." I turn lobster red. Kimy winks at me.

(7:16 p.m.)

HENRY: I'm hanging out in the club library, eating canapés and reading a sumptuously bound and probably never opened first edition of *Heart of Darkness*. Out of the corner of my eye I see the manager of the club speeding toward me. I close the book and replace it on the shelf.

"I'm sorry, sir, I'm afraid I'll have to ask you to leave." No shirt, no shoes, no service.

"Okay." I stand up, and as the manager turns his back blood rushes to my head and I vanish. I come to on our kitchen floor on March 2, 2002, laughing. I've *always* wanted to do that.

(7:21 p.m.)

CLARE: Gomez is making a speech: "Dear Clare, and Henry, family and friends, members of the jury . . . wait, scratch that. Dearly beloved, we have gathered here this evening on the shores of the Land of Singledom to wave our handkerchiefs at Clare and Henry as they embark together on their voyage on the Good Ship Matrimony. And while we are sad to watch them bid farewell to the joys of single life, we are confident that the much-ballyhooed state of Wedded Bliss will be a more than adequate new address. Some of us may even join them there shortly unless we can think of a way to avoid it. And so, let us have a toast: to Clare Abshire DeTamble, a beautiful artbabe who deserves every happiness that may befall her in her new world. And to Henry DeTamble, a damn fine fellow and a lucky son of a bitch: may the Sea of Life stretch before you like glass, and may you always have the wind at your backs. To the happy couple!" Gomez leans over and kisses me on the mouth, and I catch his eyes for a moment, and then the moment is gone.

(8:48 p.m.)

HENRY: We have cut and eaten the wedding cake. Clare has thrown her bouquet (Charisse caught it) and I have thrown Clare's garter (Ben, of all people, caught that). The band is playing "Take the A Train," and people are dancing. I have danced with Clare, and Kimy, Alicia, and Charisse; now I am dancing with Helen, who is pretty hot stuff, and Clare is dancing with Gomez. As I casually twirl Helen I see Celia Attley cut in on Gomez, who in turn cuts in on me. As he whirls Helen away I join the crowd by the bar and watch Clare dancing with Celia. Ben joins me. He's drinking seltzer. I order vodka and tonic. Ben is wearing Clare's garter around his arm like he's in mourning.

"Who's that?" he asks me.

"Celia Attley. Ingrid's girlfriend."

"That's weird."

"Yep."

"What's with that guy Gomez?"

"What do you mean?"

Ben stares at me and then turns his head. "Never mind."

(10:23 p.m.)

CLARE: It's over. We have kissed and hugged our way out of the club, have driven off in our shaving-cream-and-tin-can-covered car. I pull up in front of the Dew Drop Inn, a tiny, tacky motel on

Silver Lake. Henry is asleep. I get out, check in, get the desk guy to help me walk Henry into our room and dump him on the bed. The guy brings in the luggage, eyeballs my wedding dress and Henry's inert state, and smirks at me. I tip him. He leaves. I remove Henry's shoes, loosen his tie. I take off my dress and lay it over the armchair.

I'm standing in the bathroom, shivering in my slip and brushing my teeth. In the mirror I can see Henry lying on the bed. He's snoring. I spit out the toothpaste and rinse my mouth. Suddenly it comes over me: happiness. And the realization: we're married. Well, *I'm* married, anyway.

When I turn out the light I kiss Henry goodnight. He smells of alcohol sweat and Helen's perfume. Goodnight, goodnight, don't let the bedbugs bite. And I fall asleep, dreamless and happy.

Monday, October 25, 1993 (Henry is 30, Clare is 22)

HENRY: The Monday after the wedding Clare and I are at Chicago City Hall, being married by a judge. Gomez and Charisse are the witnesses. Afterward we all go out for dinner at Charlie Trotter's, a restaurant so expensive that the decor resembles the first-class section of an airplane or a minimalist sculpture. Fortunately, although the food looks like art, it tastes great. Charisse takes photographs of each course as it appears in front of us.

"How's it feel, being married?" asks Charisse.

"I feel *very* married," Clare says.

"You could keep going," says Gomez. "Try out all the different ceremonies, Buddhist, nudist . . ."

"I wonder if I'm a bigamist?" Clare is eating something pistachio-colored that has several large shrimp poised over it as though they are nearsighted old men reading a newspaper.

"I think you're allowed to marry the same person as many times as you want," Charisse says.

"*Are* you the same person?" Gomez asks me. The thing I'm eating is covered with thin slices of raw tuna that melt on my tongue. I take a moment to appreciate them before I answer:

"Yes, but more so."

Gomez is disgruntled and mutters something about Zen koans, but Clare smiles at me and raises her glass. I tap hers with mine: a delicate crystal note rings out and falls away in the hum of the restaurant.

And so, we are married.

II

·····································

A Drop of Blood
in a Bowl of Milk

"What is it? My dear?"

"Ah, how can we bear it?"

"Bear what?"

"This. For so short a time. How can we sleep this time away?"

"We can be quiet together, and pretend—since it is only the beginning—that we have all the time in the world."

"And every day we shall have less. And then none."

"Would you rather, therefore, have had nothing at all?"

"No. This is where I have always been coming to. Since my time began. And when I go away from here, this will be the mid-point, to which everything ran, before, and *from* which everything will run. But now, my love, we are here, we are *now,* and those other times are running elsewhere."

—A. S. Byatt, *Possession*

MARRIED LIFE

••••••••••••••••••••••••••••••••

March 1994 (Clare is 22, Henry is 30)

CLARE: And so we are married. At first we live in a two-bedroom apartment in a two-flat in Ravenswood. It's sunny, with butter-colored hardwood floors and a kitchen full of antique cabinets and antiquated appliances. We buy things, spend Sunday afternoons in Crate & Barrel exchanging wedding presents, order a sofa that can't fit through the doors of the apartment and has to be sent back. The apartment is a laboratory in which we conduct experiments, perform research on each other. We discover that Henry hates it when I absentmindedly click my spoon against my teeth while reading the paper at breakfast. We agree that it is okay for me to listen to Joni Mitchell and it is okay for Henry to listen to the Shaggs as long as the other person isn't around. We figure out that Henry should do all the cooking and I should be in charge of laundry and neither of us is willing to vacuum so we hire a cleaning service.

We fall into a routine. Henry works Tuesdays through Saturdays at the Newberry. He gets up at 7:30 and starts the coffee, then throws on his running clothes and goes for a run. When he gets back he showers and dresses, and I stagger out of bed and chat with him while he fixes breakfast. After we eat, he brushes his teeth and speeds out the door to catch the El, and I go back to bed and doze for an hour or so.

When I get up again the apartment is quiet. I take a bath and comb my hair and put on my work clothes. I pour myself another cup of coffee, and I walk into the back bedroom which is my studio, and I close the door.

I am having a hard time, in my tiny back bedroom studio, in the beginning of my married life. The space that I can call mine, that isn't full of Henry, is so small that my ideas have become small. I am like a caterpillar in a cocoon of paper; all around me are sketches for sculptures, small drawings that seem like moths fluttering against the windows, beating their wings to escape from this tiny space. I make maquettes, tiny sculptures that are rehearsals for huge sculptures. Every day the ideas come more reluctantly, as though they know I will starve them and stunt their growth. At night I dream about color, about submerging my arms into vats of paper fiber. I dream about miniature gardens I can't set foot in because I am a giantess.

The compelling thing about making art—or making anything, I suppose—is the moment when the vaporous, insubstantial idea becomes a solid *there*, a thing, a substance in a world of substances. Circe, Nimbue, Artemis, Athena, all the old sorceresses: they must have known the feeling as they transformed mere men into fabulous creatures, stole the secrets of the magicians, disposed armies: ah, look, there it is, the new thing. Call it a swine, a war, a laurel tree. Call it art. The magic I can make is small magic now, deferred magic. Every day I work, but nothing ever materializes. I feel like Penelope, weaving and unweaving.

And what of Henry, my Odysseus? Henry is an artist of another sort, a disappearing artist. Our life together in this too-small apartment is punctuated by Henry's small absences. Sometimes he disappears unobtrusively; I might be walking from the kitchen into the hall and find a pile of clothing on the floor. I might get out of bed in the morning and find the shower running and no one in it. Sometimes it's frightening. I am working in my studio one afternoon when I hear someone moaning outside my door; when I open it I find Henry on his hands and knees, naked, in the hall, bleeding heavily from his head. He opens his eyes, sees me, and vanishes. Sometimes I wake up in the night and Henry is gone. In the morning he will tell me where he's been, the way other husbands might tell their wives a dream they had: "I was in the Selzer Library in the dark, in 1989." Or: "I was chased by a German Shepherd across somebody's backyard and had to climb a tree." Or: "I was standing in the rain near my parents' apartment, listening to my mother sing." I am waiting for Henry to tell me that he has seen me as a child, but so far this hasn't happened. When I was a child I looked forward to seeing Henry. Every visit was an event. Now every absence is a nonevent, a subtraction, an adventure I will hear about when my adventurer materializes at my feet, bleeding or whistling, smiling or shaking. Now I am afraid when he is gone.

HENRY: When you live with a woman you learn something every day. So far I have learned that long hair will clog up the shower drain before you can say "Liquid-Plumr"; that it is not advisable to clip something out of the newspaper before your wife has read it, even if the newspaper in question is a week old; that I am the only person in our two-person household who can eat the same thing for dinner three nights in a row without pouting; and that headphones were invented to preserve spouses from each other's musical excesses. (How can Clare listen to Cheap Trick? Why does she like the Eagles? I'll never know, because she gets all defensive when I ask her. How can it be that the woman I love doesn't want to listen to *Musique du Garrot et de la Farraille?*) The hardest lesson is Clare's solitude. Sometimes I come home and Clare seems kind of irritated; I've interrupted some train of thought, broken into the dreamy silence of her day. Sometimes I see an expression on Clare's face that is like a closed door. She has gone inside the room of her mind and is sitting there knitting or something. I've discovered that Clare likes to be alone. But when I return from time traveling she is always relieved to see me.

When the woman you live with is an artist, every day is a surprise. Clare has turned the second bedroom into a wonder cabinet, full of small sculptures and drawings pinned up on every inch of wall space. There are coils of wire and rolls of paper tucked into shelves and drawers. The sculptures remind me of kites, or model airplanes. I say this to Clare one evening, standing in the doorway of her studio in my suit and tie, home from work, about to begin making dinner, and she throws one at me; it flies surprisingly well, and soon we are standing at opposite ends of the hall, tossing tiny sculptures at each other, testing their aerodynamics. The next day I come home to find that Clare has created a flock of paper and wire birds, which are hanging from the ceiling in the living room. A week later our bedroom windows are full of abstract blue translucent shapes that the sun throws across the room onto the walls, making a sky for the bird shapes Clare has painted there. It's beautiful.

The next evening I'm standing in the doorway of Clare's studio, watching her finish drawing a thicket of black lines around a little red bird. Suddenly I see Clare, in her small room, closed in by all her stuff, and I realize that she's trying to say something, and I know what I have to do.

Wednesday, April 13, 1994 (Clare is 22, Henry is 30)

CLARE: I hear Henry's key in the front door and I come out of the studio as he walks in. To my surprise he's carrying a television set. We don't own a TV because Henry can't watch it and I can't be bothered to watch by myself. The TV is an old, small, dusty black and white set with a broken antennae.

"Hi, honey, I'm home," says Henry, setting the TV on the dining room table.

"Ugh, it's filthy," I say. "Did you find it in the alley?"

Henry looks offended. "I bought it at the Unique. Ten bucks."

"Why?"

"There's a program on tonight that I thought we should watch."

"But—" I can't imagine what show would make Henry risk time traveling.

"It's okay, I won't sit and stare at it. I want you to see this."

"Oh. What?" I'm so out of touch with what's on television.

"It's a surprise. It's on at eight."

The TV sits on the floor of the dining room while we eat dinner. Henry refuses to answer any questions about it, and makes a point of teasing me by asking what I would do if I had a huge studio.

"What does it matter? I have a closet. Maybe I'll take up origami."

"Come on, seriously."

"I don't know." I twirl linguine onto my fork. "I would make every maquette one hundred times bigger. I'd draw on ten-foot-by-ten-foot pieces of cotton rag paper. I would wear roller skates to get from one end of the studio to the other. I'd set up huge vats, and a Japanese drying system, and a ten-pound Reina beater. . . ." I'm captivated by my mental image of this imaginary studio, but then I remember my real studio, and I shrug. "Oh well. Maybe someday." We get by okay on Henry's salary and the interest on my trust fund, but to afford a real studio I would have to get a job, and then I wouldn't have any time to spend in the studio. It's a Catch-22. All my artist friends are starving for money or time or both. Charisse is designing computer software by day and making art at night. She and Gomez are getting married next month. "What should we get the Gomezes for a wedding present?"

"Huh? Oh, I dunno. Can't we just give them all those espresso machines we got?"

"We traded those in for the microwave and the bread-making machine."

"Oh, yeah. Hey, it's almost eight. Grab your coffee, let's go sit in the living room." Henry pushes back his chair and hoists the television, and I carry both our cups of coffee into the living room. He sets the set on the coffee table and after messing around with an extension cord and fussing with the knobs we sit on the couch watching a waterbed commercial on Channel 9. It looks like it's snowing in the waterbed showroom. "Damn," says Henry, peeking at the screen. "It worked better in the Unique." The logo for the Illinois Lottery flashes on the screen. Henry digs in his pants pocket and hands me a small white piece of paper. "Hold this." It's a lottery ticket.

"My god. You didn't—"

"Shh. Watch." With great fanfare, the Lottery officials, serious men in suits, announce the numbers on the randomly chosen ping pong balls that pop one by one into position on the screen. 43, 2, 26,

51, 10, 11. Of course they match the numbers on the ticket in my hand. The Lottery men congratulate us. We have just won eight million dollars.

Henry clicks off the TV. He smiles. "Neat trick, huh?"

"I don't know what to say." Henry realizes that I am not jumping for joy.

"Say, 'Thank you, darling, for providing the bucks we need to buy a house.' That would work for me."

"But—Henry—it's not real."

"Sure it is. That's a real lottery ticket. If you take it to Katz's Deli, Minnie will give you a big hug and the State of Illinois will write you a real check."

"But you knew."

"Sure. Of course. It was just a matter of looking it up in tomorrow's *Trib*."

"We can't . . . it's cheating."

Henry smacks himself dramatically on the forehead. "How silly of me. I completely forgot that you're supposed to buy tickets without having the slightest idea what the numbers will be. Well, we can fix it." He disappears down the hall into the kitchen and returns with a box of matches. He lights a match and holds the ticket up to it.

"No!"

Henry blows out the match. "It doesn't matter, Clare. We could win the lottery every week for the next year if we felt like it. So if you have a problem with it, it's no big deal." The ticket is a little singed on one corner. Henry sits next to me on the couch. "Tell you what. Why don't you just hang on to this, and if you feel like cashing it we will, and if you decide to give it to the first homeless person you meet you could do that—"

"No fair."

"What's no fair?"

"You can't just leave me with this huge responsibility."

"Well, I'm perfectly happy either way. So if you think we're cheating the State of Illinois out of the money they've scammed from hard-working suckers, then let's just forget about it. I'm sure we can think of some other way to get you a bigger studio."

Oh. A bigger studio. It dawns on me, stupid me, that Henry could win the lottery anytime at all; that he has never bothered to do so because it's not *normal;* that he has decided to set aside his fanatical dedication to living like a *normal* person so I can have a studio big enough to roller-skate across; that I am being an ingrate.

"Clare? Earth to Clare . . ."

"Thank you," I say, too abruptly.

Henry raises his eyebrows. "Does that mean we're going to cash in that ticket?"

"I don't know. It means 'Thank you.'"

"You're welcome." There is an uncomfortable silence. "Hey, I wonder what's on TV?"

"Snow."

Henry laughs, stands up, and pulls me off the couch. "Come on, let's go spend our ill-gotten gains."

"Where are we going?"

"I dunno." Henry opens the hall closet, hands me my jacket. "Hey, let's buy Gomez and Charisse a car for their wedding."

"I think they gave us wine glasses." We are galumphing down the stairs. Outside it's a perfect spring night. We stand on the sidewalk in front of our apartment building, and Henry takes my hand, and I look at him, and I raise our joined hands and Henry twirls me around and soon we're dancing down Belle Plaine Avenue, no music but the sound of cars whooshing by and our own laughter, and the smell of cherry blossoms that fall like snow on the sidewalk as we dance underneath the trees.

Wednesday, May 18, 1994 (Clare is 22, Henry is 30)

CLARE: We are attempting to buy a house. Shopping for houses is amazing. People who would never invite you into their homes under any other circumstances open their doors wide, allow you to peer into their closets, pass judgment on their wallpaper, ask pointed questions about their gutters.

Henry and I have very different ways of looking at houses. I walk through slowly, consider the woodwork, the appliances, ask questions about the furnace, check for water damage in the basement. Henry just walks directly to the back of the house, peers out the back window, and shakes his head at me. Our realtor, Carol, thinks he is a lunatic. I tell her he is a gardening fanatic. After a whole day of this, we are driving home from Carol's office and I decide to inquire about the method in Henry's madness.

"What the hell," I ask, politely, "are you doing?"

Henry looks sheepish. "Well, I wasn't sure if you wanted to know this, but I've been in our home-to-be. I don't know when, but I was—will be—there on a beautiful autumn day, late afternoon. I stood at a window at the back of the house, next to that little marble topped table you got from your grandmother, and looked out over the backyard into the window of a brick building which seemed to be your studio. You were pulling sheets of paper back there. They were blue. You wore a yellow bandanna to keep your hair back, and a green sweater and your usual rubber apron and all that. There's a grape arbor in the yard. I was there for about two minutes. So I'm just trying to duplicate that view, and when I do I figure that's our house."

"Jeez. Why didn't you mention it? Now I feel silly."

"Oh, no. Don't. I just thought you would enjoy doing it the regular way. I mean, you seemed so thorough, and you read all those books about how to do it, and I thought you wanted to, you know, *shop,* and not have it be inevitable."

"*Somebody* has to ask about termites, and asbestos, and dry rot, and sump pumps. . . ."

"Exactly. So let us continue as we are, and surely we will arrive separately at our mutual conclusion."

This does eventually happen, although there are a couple tense moments before then. I find myself entranced with a white elephant in East Rogers Park, a dreadful neighborhood at the northern perimeter of the city. It's a mansion, a Victorian monster big enough for a family of twelve and their servants. I know even before I ask that it's not our house; Henry is appalled by it even before we get in the front door. The backyard is a parking lot for a huge drug store. The inside has the bones of a truly beautiful house; high ceilings, fireplaces with marble mantels, ornate woodwork . . . "Please," I wheedle. "It's so incredible."

"Yeah, incredible is the word. We'd be raped and pillaged once a week in this thing. Plus it needs total rehab, wiring, plumbing, new furnace, probably a new roof. . . . It's just not it." His voice is final, the voice of one who has seen the future, and has no plans to mess with it. I sulk for a couple days after that. Henry takes me out for sushi.

"Tchotchka. Amorta. Heart of my heart. Speak to me."

"I'm not not speaking to you."

"I know. But you're sulking. And I would rather not be sulked at, especially for speaking common sense."

The waitress arrives, and we hurriedly consult our menus. I don't want to bicker in Katsu, my favorite sushi restaurant, a place we eat at a lot. I reflect that Henry is counting on this, in addition to the intrinsic happiness of sushi, to placate me. We order goma-ae, hijiki, futomaki, kappamaki, and an impressive array of raw things on rice rectangles. Kiko, the waitress, disappears with our order.

"I'm not mad at you." This is only sort of true.

Henry raises one eyebrow. "Okay. Good. What's wrong, then?"

"Are you absolutely sure this place you were in is our house? What if you're wrong and we turn down something really great just because it doesn't have the right view of the backyard?"

"It had an awful lot of our stuff in it to be anything but our house. I grant you that it might not be our *first* house—I wasn't close enough to you to see how old you were. I thought you were pretty young, but maybe you were just well-preserved. But I swear to you that it's really nice, and won't it be great to have a studio in the back like that?"

I sigh. "Yeah. It will. God. I wish you could videotape some of your excursions. I would love to see this place. Couldn't you have looked at the address, while you were at it?"

"Sorry. It was just a quickie."

Sometimes I would give anything to open up Henry's brain and look at his memory like a movie. I remember when I first learned to use a computer; I was fourteen and Mark was trying to teach me to draw on his Macintosh. After about ten minutes I wanted to push my hands through the screen and get at the real thing in there, whatever it was. I like to do things directly, touch the textures, see the colors. House shopping with Henry is making me crazy. It's like driving one of those awful toy remote control cars. I always drive them into walls. On purpose.

"Henry. Would you mind if I went house hunting by myself for a while?"

"No, I guess not." He seems a little hurt. "If you really want to."

"Well, we're going to end up in this place anyway, right? I mean, it won't change anything."

"True. Yeah, don't mind me. But try not to fall for any more hellholes, okay?"

I finally find it about a month and twenty or so houses later. It's on Ainslie, in Lincoln Square, a red brick bungalow built in 1926. Carol pops open the key box and wrestles with the lock, and as the door opens I have an overwhelming sensation of something fitting . . . I walk right through to the back window, peer out at the backyard, and there's my future studio, and there's the grape arbor and as I turn around Carol looks at me inquisitively and I say, "We'll buy it."

She is more than a bit surprised. "Don't you want to see the rest of the house? What about your husband?"

"Oh, he's already seen it. But yeah, sure, let's see the house."

Saturday, July 9, 1994 (Henry is 31, Clare is 23)

H E N R Y : Today was Moving Day. All day it was hot; the movers' shirts stuck to them as they walked up the stairs of our apartment this morning, smiling because they figured a two-bedroom apartment would be no big deal and they'd be done before lunch time. Their smiles fell when they stood in our living room and saw Clare's heavy Victorian furniture and my seventy-eight boxes of books. Now it's dark and Clare and I are wandering through the house, touching the walls, running our hands over the cherry windowsills. Our bare feet slap the wood floors. We run water into the claw-footed bathtub, turn the burners of the heavy Universal stove on and off. The windows are naked; we leave the lights off and street light pours over the empty fireplace through dusty glass. Clare moves from room to room, caressing her house, our house. I follow her, watching as she opens closets, windows, cabinets. She stands on tiptoe in the dining room, touches the etched-glass light fixture with a fingertip. Then she takes off her shirt. I run my tongue over her breasts. The house envelops us, watches us, contemplates us as we make love in it for the first time, the first of many times, and afterward, as we lie spent on the bare floor surrounded by boxes, I feel that we have found our home.

Sunday, August 28, 1994 (Clare is 23, Henry is 31)

CLARE: It's a humid sticky hot Sunday afternoon, and Henry, Gomez, and I are at large in Evanston. We spent the morning at Lighthouse Beach, playing in Lake Michigan and roasting ourselves. Gomez wanted to be buried in the sand, so Henry and I obliged. We ate our picnic, and napped. Now we are walking down the shady side of Church Street, licking Orangsicles, groggy with sun.

"Clare, your hair is full of sand," says Henry. I stop and lean over and beat my hair like a carpet with my hand. A whole beach falls out of it.

"My ears are full of sand. And my unmentionables," Gomez says.

"I'll be glad to whack you in the head, but you will have to do the rest yourself," I say. A small breeze blows up and we hold our bodies out to it. I coil my hair onto the top of my head and immediately feel better.

"What shall we do next?" Gomez inquires. Henry and I exchange glances.

"Bookman's Alley," we chant in unison.

Gomez groans. "Oh, God. Not a bookstore. Lord, Lady, have mercy on your humble servant—"

"Bookman's Alley it is, then," Henry says blithely.

"Just promise me we won't spend more than, oh, say, three hours. . . ."

"I think they close at five," I tell him, "and it's already 2:30."

"You could go have a beer," says Henry.

"I thought Evanston was dry."

"No, I think they changed it. If you can prove you're not a member of the YMCA you can have a beer."

"I'll come with you. All for one and one for all." We turn onto Sherman, walk past what used to be Marshall Field's and is now a sneaker outlet store, past what used to be the Varsity Theater and is now a Gap. We turn into the alley that runs between the florist's and the shoe repair shop and lo and behold, it's Bookman's Alley. I push the door open and we troop into the dim cool shop as though we are tumbling into the past.

Roger is sitting behind his little untidy desk chatting with a ruddy white-haired gentleman about something to do with chamber music. He smiles when he sees us. "Clare, I've got something you will like," he says. Henry makes a beeline for the back of the store where all the printing and bibliophilic stuff is. Gomez meanders around looking at the weird little objects that are tucked into the various sections: a saddle in Westerns, a deerstalker's cap in Mysteries. He takes a gumdrop from the immense bowl in the Children's section, not realizing that those gumdrops have been there for years and you can hurt yourself on them. The book Roger has for me is a Dutch catalog of decorative papers with real sample papers tipped in. I can see immediately that it's a find, so I lay it on the table by the desk, to start the pile of things I want. Then I begin to peruse the shelves dreamily, inhaling the deep dusty smell of paper, glue, old carpets and wood. I see Henry sitting on the floor in the Art section with something open on his lap. He's sunburned, and his hair stands up every which way. I'm glad he cut it. He looks more like himself to me now, with the short hair. As I watch him he puts his hand up to twirl a piece of it around his finger, realizes it's too short to do that, and scratches his ear. I want to touch him, run my hands through his funny sticking-up hair, but I turn and burrow into the Travel section instead.

HENRY: Clare is standing in the main room by a huge stack of new arrivals. Roger doesn't really like people fiddling with unpriced stuff, but I've noticed that he'll let Clare do pretty much whatever she wants in his store. She has her head bent over a small red book. Her hair is trying to escape from the coil on her head, and one strap of her sundress is hanging off her shoulder, exposing a bit of her bathing suit. This is so poignant, so powerful, that I urgently need to walk over to her, touch her, possibly, if no one is looking, bite her, but at the same time I don't want this moment to end, and suddenly I notice Gomez, who is standing in the Mystery section looking at Clare with an expression that so exactly mirrors my own feelings that I am forced to see—.

At this moment, Clare looks up at me and says, "Henry, look, it's Pompeii." She holds out the tiny book of picture postcards, and something in her voice says, *See, I have chosen you.* I walk to her, put my arm around her shoulders, straighten the fallen strap. When I look up a second later, Gomez has turned his back on us and is intently surveying the Agatha Christies.

Sunday, January 15, 1995 (Clare is 23, Henry is 31)

CLARE: I am washing dishes and Henry is dicing green peppers. The sun is setting very pinkly over the January snow in our backyard on this early Sunday evening, and we are making chili and singing "Yellow Submarine":

In the town where I was born
Lived a man who sailed to sea . . .

Onions hiss in the pan on the stove. As we sing *And our friends are all on board* I suddenly hear my voice floating alone and I turn and Henry's clothes lie in a heap, the knife is on the kitchen floor. Half of a pepper sways slightly on the cutting board.

I turn off the heat and cover the onions. I sit down next to the pile of clothes and scoop them up, still warm from Henry's body, and sit until all their warmth is from my body, holding them. Then I get up and go into our bedroom, fold the clothes neatly and place them on our bed. Then I continue making dinner as best I can, and eat by myself, waiting and wondering.

Friday, February 3, 1995 (Clare is 23, Henry is 31, and 39)

CLARE: Gomez and Charisse and Henry and I are sitting around our dining room table playing Modern Capitalist Mind-Fuck. It's a game Gomez and Charisse have invented. We play it with a Monopoly set. It involves answering questions, getting points, accumulating money, and exploiting your fellow players. It's Gomez's turn. He shakes the dice, gets a six, and lands on Community Chest. He draws a card.

"Okay, everybody. What modern technological invention would you deep-six for the good of society?"

"Television," I say.

"Fabric softener," says Charisse.

"Motion detectors," says Henry vehemently.

"And I say gunpowder."

"That's hardly modern," I object.

"Okay. The assembly line."

"You don't get two answers," says Henry.

"Sure I do. What kind of a lame-ass answer is 'motion detectors,' anyway?"

"I keep getting ratted on by the motion detectors in the stacks at the Newberry. Twice this week I've ended up in the stacks after hours, and as soon as I show up the guard is upstairs checking it out. It's driving me nuts."

"I don't think the proletariat would be affected much by the de-invention of motion sensors. Clare and I each get ten points for correct answers, Charisse gets five points for creativity, and Henry gets to go backward three spaces for valuing the needs of the individual over the collective good."

"That puts me back on Go. Give me $200, Banker." Charisse gives Henry his money.

"Oops," says Gomez. I smile at him. It's my turn. I roll a four.

"Park Place. I'll buy it." In order to buy anything I must correctly answer a question. Henry draws from the Chance pile.

"Whom would you prefer to have dinner with and why: Adam Smith, Karl Marx, Rosa Luxembourg, Alan Greenspan?"

"Rosa."

"Why?"

"Most interesting death." Henry, Charisse, and Gomez confer and agree that I can buy Park Place. I give Charisse my money and she hands me the deed. Henry shakes and lands on Income Tax. Income Tax has its own special cards. We all tense, in apprehension. He reads the card.

"Great Leap Forward."

"Damn." We all hand Charisse all our real estate, and she puts it back in the Bank's holdings, along with her own.

"Well, so much for Park Place."

"Sorry." Henry moves halfway across the board, which puts him on St. James. "I'll buy it."

"My poor little St. James," laments Charisse. I draw a card from the Free Parking pile.

"What is the exchange rate of the Japanese yen against the dollar today?"

"I have no idea. Where did that question come from?"

"Me." Charisse smiles.

"What's the answer?"

"99.8 yen to the dollar."

"Okay. No St. James. Your turn." Henry hands Charisse the dice. She rolls a four and ends up going to Jail. She picks a card that tells her what her crime is: Insider Trading. We laugh.

"That sounds more like you guys," says Gomez. Henry and I smile modestly. We are making a killing in the stock market these days. To get out of Jail Charisse has to answer three questions.

Gomez picks from the Chance pile. "Question the First: name two famous artists Trotsky knew in Mexico."

"Diego Rivera and Frida Kahlo."

"Good. Question the Second: How much does Nike pay its Vietnamese workers per diem to make those ridiculously expensive sneakers?"

"Oh, God. I don't know . . . $3? Ten cents?"

"What's your answer?" There is an immense crash in the kitchen. We all jump up, and Henry says, "Sit down!" so emphatically that we do. He runs into the kitchen. Charisse and Gomez look at me, startled. I shake my head. "I don't know." But I do. There is a low murmur of voices and a moan. Charisse and Gomez are frozen, listening. I stand up and softly follow Henry.

He is kneeling on the floor, holding a dish cloth against the head of the naked man lying on the linoleum, who is of course Henry. The wooden cabinet that holds our dishes is on its side; the glass is broken and all the dishes have spilled out and shattered.

Henry is lying in the midst of the mess, bleeding and covered with glass. Both Henrys look at me, one piteously, the other urgently. I kneel opposite Henry, over Henry. "Where's all this blood coming from?" I whisper. "I think it's all from the scalp," Henry whispers back. "Let's call an ambulance," I say. I start to pick the glass out of Henry's chest. He closes his eyes and says, "Don't." I stop.

"Holy cats." Gomez stands in the doorway. I see Charisse standing behind him on tiptoe, trying to see over his shoulder. "Wow," she says, pushing past Gomez. Henry throws a dish cloth over his prone duplicate's genitalia.

"Oh, Henry, don't worry about it, I've drawn a gazillion models—"

"I try to retain a modicum of privacy," Henry snaps. Charisse recoils as though he's slapped her.

"Listen, Henry—" Gomez rumbles.

I can't think with all this going on. "Everyone please shut up," I demand, exasperated. To my surprise they do. "What happens?" I ask Henry, who has been lying on the floor grimacing and trying not to move. He opens his eyes and stares up at me for a moment before answering.

"I'll be gone in a few minutes," he finally says, softly. He looks at Henry. "I want a drink." Henry bounds up and comes back with a juice glass full of Jack Daniels. I support Henry's head and he manages to down about a third of it.

"Is that wise?" Gomez asks.

"Don't know. Don't care," Henry assures him from the floor. "This hurts like hell." He gasps. "Stand back! Close your eyes—"

"Why?—" Gomez begins.

Henry is convulsing on the floor as though he is being electrified. His head is nodding violently and he yells "Clare!" and I close my eyes. There is a noise like a bed sheet being snapped but much louder and then there is a cascade of glass and china everywhere and Henry has vanished.

"Oh my God," says Charisse. Henry and I stare at each other. *That was different, Henry. That was violent and ugly. What is happening to you?* His white face tells me that he doesn't know either. He inspects the whiskey for glass fragments and then drinks it down.

"What's with all the glass?" Gomez demands, gingerly brushing himself off.

Henry stands up, offers me his hand. He's covered with a fine mist of blood and bits of crockery and crystal. I stand up and look at Charisse. She has a big cut on her face; blood is running down her cheek like a tear.

"Anything that's not part of my body gets left behind," Henry explains. He shows them the gap where he had a tooth pulled because he kept losing the filling. "So whenever I went back to, at least all the glass is gone, they won't have to sit there and pick it out with tweezers."

"No, but we will," Gomez says, gently removing glass from Charisse's hair. He has a point.

LIBRARY SCIENCE FICTION

••••••••••••••••••••••••••••••••••

Wednesday, March 8, 1995 (Henry is 31)

HENRY: Matt and I are playing Hide and Seek in the stacks in Special Collections. He's looking for me because we are supposed to be giving a calligraphy Show and Tell to a Newberry Trustee and her Ladies' Lettering Club. I'm hiding from him because I'm trying to get all of my clothes on my body before he finds me.

"Come *on*, Henry, they're waiting," Matt calls from somewhere in Early American Broadsides. I'm pulling on my pants in Twentieth-Century French *Livres d'artistes*. "Just a second, I just want to find this one thing," I call. I make a mental note to learn ventriloquism for moments like this. Matt's voice is coming closer as he says, "You know Mrs. Connelly is going to have kittens, just forget it, let's get *out* there—" He sticks his head into my row as I'm buttoning my shirt. "What are you doing?"

"Sorry?"

"You've been running around naked in the stacks again, haven't you?"

"Um, maybe." I try to sound nonchalant.

"Jesus, Henry. Give me the cart." Matt grabs the book-laden

cart and starts to wheel it off toward the Reading Room. The heavy metal door opens and closes. I put on my socks and shoes, knot my tie, dust off my jacket and put it on. Then I walk out into the Reading Room, face Matt over the long classroom table surrounded by middle-aged rich ladies, and begin to discourse on the various book hands of lettering genius Rudolf Koch. Matt lays out felts and opens portfolios and interjects intelligent things about Koch and by the end of the hour he seems like maybe he's not going to kill me this time. The happy ladies toddle off to lunch. Matt and I move around the table, putting books back into their boxes and onto the cart.

"I'm sorry about being late," I say.

"If you weren't brilliant," Matt replies, "we would have tanned you and used you to rebind *Das Manifest der Nacktkultur* by now."

"There's no such book."

"Wanna bet?"

"No." We wheel the cart back to the stacks and begin reshelving the portfolios and books. I buy Matt lunch at the Beau Thai, and all is forgiven, if not forgotten.

Tuesday, April 11, 1995 (Henry is 31)

HENRY: There is a stairwell in the Newberry Library that I am afraid of. It is located toward the east end of the long hallway that runs through each of the four floors, bisecting the Reading Rooms from the stacks. It is not grand, like the main staircase with its marble treads and carved balustrades. It has no windows. It has fluorescent lights, cinderblock walls, concrete stairs with yellow safety strips. There are metal doors with no windows on each floor. But these are not the things that frighten me. The thing about this stairwell that I don't like one bit is the Cage.

The Cage is four stories tall and runs up the center of the stairwell. At first glance it looks like an elevator cage, but there is no elevator and never was. No one at the Newberry seems to know what the Cage is for, or why it was installed. I assume it's there to stop people from throwing themselves from the stairs and landing in a broken heap. The Cage is painted beige. It is made of steel.

When I first came to work at the Newberry, Catherine gave me a tour of all the nooks and crannies. She proudly showed me the stacks, the artifact room, the unused room in the east link where Matt practices his singing, McAllister's amazingly untidy cubicle, the Fellows' carrels, the Staff Lunch Room. As Catherine opened the door to the stairwell, on our way up to Conservation, I had a moment of panic. I glimpsed the criss-crossed wire of the Cage and balked, like a skittish horse.

"What's that?" I asked Catherine.

"Oh, that's the Cage," she replied, casually.

"Is it an elevator?"

"No, it's just a cage. I don't think it does anything."

"Oh." I walked up to it, looked in. "Is there a door down there?"

"No. You can't get into it."

"Oh." We walked up the stairs and continued on with our tour.

Since then, I have avoided using that stairway. I try not to think about the Cage; I don't want to make a big deal out of it. But if I ever end up inside it, I won't be able to get out.

Friday, June 9, 1995 (Henry is 31)

HENRY: I materialize on the floor of the Staff Men's Room on the fourth floor of the Newberry. I've been gone for days, lost in 1973, rural Indiana, and I'm tired, hungry, and unshaven; worst of all, I've got a black eye and I can't find my clothes. I get up and lock myself in a stall, sit down and think. While I'm thinking someone comes in, unzips, and stands in front of the urinal pissing. When he's done he zips and then stands for a moment and right then I happen to sneeze.

"Who's there?" says Roberto. I sit silently. Through the space between the door and the stall I see Roberto slowly bend down and look under the door at my feet.

"Henry?" he says. "I will have Matt bring your clothes. Please get dressed and come to my office."

I slink into Roberto's office and sit down across from him. He's on the phone, so I sneak a look at his calendar. It's Friday. The clock above the desk says 2:17. I've been gone for a little more than twenty-two hours. Roberto places the phone gently in its cradle and turns to look at me. "Shut the door," he says. This is a mere formality because the walls of our offices don't actually go all the way up to the ceiling, but I do as he says.

Roberto Calle is an eminent scholar of the Italian Renaissance and the Head of Special Collections. He is ordinarily the most sanguine of men, golden, bearded, and encouraging; now he gazes at me sadly over his bifocals and says, "We really can't have this, you know."

"Yes," I say. "I know."

"May I ask how you acquired that rather impressive black eye?" Roberto's voice is grim.

"I think I walked into a tree."

"Of course. How silly of me not to think of that." We sit and look at each other. Roberto says, "Yesterday I happened to notice Matt walking into your office carrying a pile of clothing. Since it was not the first time I had seen Matt walking around with clothing I asked him where he had gotten this particular pile, and he said that he had found it in the Men's Room. And so I asked him why he felt compelled to transport this pile of clothing to your office and he said that it looked like what you were wearing, which it did. And since no one could find you, we simply left the clothing on your desk."

He pauses as though I'm supposed to say something, but I can't think of anything appropriate. He goes on, "This morning Clare called and told Isabelle you had the flu and wouldn't be in." I lean my head against my hand. My eye is throbbing. "Explain yourself," Roberto demands.

It's tempting to say, *Roberto, I got stuck in 1973 and I couldn't get out and I was in Muncie, Indiana, for days living in a barn and I got decked by the guy who owned the barn because he thought I was trying to mess with his sheep.* But of course I can't say that. I say, "I don't really remember, Roberto. I'm sorry."

"Ah. Well, I guess Matt wins the pool."

"What pool?"

Roberto smiles, and I think that maybe he's not going to fire me. "Matt bet that you wouldn't even attempt to explain. Amelia put her money on abduction by aliens. Isabelle bet that you were involved in an international drug-running cartel and had been kidnapped and killed by the Mafia."

"What about Catherine?"

"Oh, Catherine and I are convinced that this is all due to an unspeakably bizarre sexual kink involving nudity and books."

I take a deep breath. "It's more like epilepsy," I say.

Roberto looks skeptical. "Epilepsy? You disappeared yesterday afternoon. You have a black eye and scratches all over your face and hands. I had Security searching the building top to bottom for you yesterday; they tell me you are in the habit of taking off your clothing in the stacks."

I stare at my fingernails. When I look up, Roberto is staring out the window. "I don't know what to do with you, Henry. I would hate to lose you; when you are here and fully clothed you can be quite . . . competent. But this just *will not do*."

We sit and look at each other for minutes. Finally Roberto says, "Tell me it won't happen again."

"I can't. I wish I could."

Roberto sighs, and waves his hand at the door. "Go. Go catalogue the Quigley Collection, that'll keep you out of trouble for a while." (The Quigley Collection, recently donated, is over two thousand pieces of Victorian ephemera, mostly having to do with soap.) I nod my obedience and stand up.

As I open the door Roberto says, "Henry. Is it so bad that you can't tell me?"

I hesitate. "Yes," I say. Roberto is silent. I close the door behind me and walk to my office. Matt is sitting behind my desk, transferring stuff from his calendar into mine. He looks up as I come in. "Did he fire you?" Matt asks.

"No," I reply.

"Why not?"

"Dunno."

"Odd. By the way, I did your lecture for the Chicago Hand Bookbinders."

"Thanks. Buy you lunch tomorrow?"

"Sure." Matt checks the calendar in front of him. "We've got a Show and Tell for a History of Typography class from Columbia in forty-five minutes." I nod and start rummaging in my desk for the list of items we're about to show. "Henry?"

"Yeah?"

"Where were you?"

"Muncie, Indiana. 1973."

"Yeah, right." Matt rolls his eyes and grins sarcastically. "Never mind."

Sunday, December 17, 1995 (Clare is 24, Henry is 8)

CLARE: I'm visiting Kimy. It's a snowy Sunday afternoon in December. I've been Christmas shopping, and I'm sitting in Kimy's kitchen drinking hot chocolate, warming my feet by the baseboard radiator, regaling her with stories of bargains and decorations. Kimy plays solitaire while we talk; I admire her practiced shuffle, her efficient slap of red card on black card. A pot of stew simmers on the stove. There's a noise in the dining room; a chair falls over. Kimy looks up, turns.

"Kimy," I whisper. "There's a little boy under the dining room table."

Someone giggles. "Henry?" Kimy calls. No answer. She gets up and stands in the doorway. "Hey, buddy. Stop that. Put some clothes on, mister." Kimy disappears into the dining room. Whispering. More giggles. Silence. Suddenly a small naked boy is staring at me from the doorway, and just as suddenly he vanishes. Kimy comes back in, sits down at the table, and resumes her game.

"Wow," I say.

Kimy smiles. "That don't happen so much these days. Now he's a grown-up, when he comes. But he don't come as much as he used to."

"I've never seen him go forward like that, into the future."

"Well, you don't have so much future with him, yet."

It takes me a second to figure out what she means. When I do, I wonder what kind of future it will be, and then I think about the future expanding, gradually opening enough for Henry to come to me from the past. I drink my chocolate and stare out into Kimy's frozen yard.

"Do you miss him?" I ask her.

"Yeah, I miss him. But he's grown-up now. When he comes like a little boy, it's like a ghost, you know?" I nod. Kimy finishes her game, gathers up the cards. She looks at me, smiles. "When you guys gonna have a baby, huh?"

"I don't know, Kimy. I'm not sure we can."

She stands up, walks over to the stove and stirs the stew. "Well, you never know."

"True." You never know.

Later, Henry and I are lying in bed. Snow is still falling; the radiators make faint clucking noises. I turn to him and he looks at me and I say, "Let's make a baby."

Monday, March 11, 1996 (Henry is 32)

HENRY: I have tracked down Dr. Kendrick; he is affiliated with the University of Chicago Hospital. It is a vile wet cold day in March. March in Chicago seems like it ought to be an improvement over February, but sometimes it isn't. I get on the IC and sit facing backwards. Chicago streams out behind us and soon enough we are at 59th Street. I disembark and struggle through the sleety rain. It's 9:00 a.m., it's Monday. Everyone is drawn into themselves, resisting being back in the workweek. I like Hyde Park. It makes me feel as though I've fallen out of Chicago and into some other city, Cambridge, perhaps. The gray stone buildings are dark with rain and the trees drip fat icy drops on passersby. I feel the blank serenity of the fait accompli; I will be able to convince Kendrick, though I have failed to convince so many doctors, because I do convince him. He will be my doctor because in the future he is my doctor.

I enter a small faux-Mies building next to the hospital. I take the elevator to Three, open the glass door that bears the golden legend DRS. C. P. SLOANE AND D. L. KENDRICK, announce myself to the receptionist, and sit in one of the deep lavender upholstered chairs. The waiting room is pink and violet, I suppose to soothe the patients. Dr. Kendrick is a geneticist, and not incidentally, a philosopher; the latter, I think, must be of some use in coping with the harsh practical realities of the former. Today there is no one here but me. I'm ten minutes early. The wallpaper is broad stripes the exact color of Pepto-Bismol. It clashes with the painting of a watermill opposite me, mostly browns and greens. The furniture is pseudocolonial, but there's a pretty nice rug, some kind of soft Persian carpet, and I feel kind of sorry for it, stuck here in this ghastly waiting room. The receptionist is a kind-looking middle-aged woman with very deep wrinkles from years of tanning; she is deeply tanned now, in March in Chicago.

At 9:35 I hear voices in the corridor and a blond woman enters the waiting room with a little boy in a small wheelchair. The boy appears to have cerebral palsy or something like it. The woman smiles at me; I smile back. As she turns I see that she is pregnant. The receptionist says, "You may go in, Mr. DeTamble," and I smile at the boy as I pass him. His enormous eyes take me in, but he doesn't smile back.

As I enter Dr. Kendrick's office, he is making notes in a file. I sit down and he continues to write. He is younger than I thought he would be; late thirties. I always expect doctors to be old men. I can't help it, it's left over from my childhood of endless medical men. Kendrick is red-haired, thin-faced, bearded, with thick wire-rimmed glasses. He looks a little bit like D. H. Lawrence. He's wearing a nice charcoal-gray suit and a narrow dark green tie with a rainbow trout tie clip. An ashtray overflows at his elbow; the room is suffused with cigarette smoke, although he isn't smoking right now. Everything is very modern: tubular steel, beige twill, blond wood. He looks up at me and smiles.

"Good morning, Mr. DeTamble. What can I do for you?" He is looking at his calendar. "I don't seem to have any information about you, here? What seems to be the problem?"

"*Dasein.*"

Kendrick is taken aback. "*Dasein?* Being? How so?"

"I have a condition which I'm told will become known as Chrono-Impairment. I have difficulty staying in the present."

"I'm sorry?"

"I time travel. Involuntarily."

Kendrick is flustered, but subdues it. I like him. He is attempting to deal with me in a manner befitting a sane person, although I'm sure he is considering which of his psychiatrist friends to refer me to.

"But why do you need a geneticist? Or are you consulting me as a philosopher?"

"It's a genetic disease. Although it will be pleasant to have someone to chat with about the larger implications of the problem."

"Mr. DeTamble. You are obviously an intelligent man . . . I've never heard of this disease. I can't do anything for you."

"You don't believe me."

"Right. I don't."

Now I am smiling, ruefully. I feel horrible about this, but it has to be done. "Well. I've been to quite a few doctors in my life, but this is the first time I've ever had anything to offer in the way of proof. Of course no one ever believes me. You and your wife are expecting a child next month?"

He is wary. "Yes. How do you know?"

"In a few years I look up your child's birth certificate. I travel to my wife's past, I write down the information in this envelope. She gives it to me when we meet in the present. I give it to you, now. Open it after your son is born."

"We're having a daughter."

"No, you're not, actually," I say gently. "But let's not quibble about it. Save that, open it after the child is born. Don't throw it out. After you read it, call me, if you want to." I get up to leave. "Good luck," I say, although I do not believe in luck, these days. I am deeply sorry for him, but there's no other way to do this.

"Goodbye, Mr. DeTamble," Dr. Kendrick says coldly. I leave. As I get into the elevator I think to myself that he must be opening the envelope right now. Inside is a sheet of typing paper. It says:

Colin Joseph Kendrick
April 6, 1996 1:18 a.m.
6 lbs. 8 oz Caucasian male
Down syndrome

Saturday, April 6, 1996, 5:32 a.m. (Henry is 32, Clare is 24)

HENRY: We are sleeping all tangled together; all night we have been waking, turning, getting up, coming back to bed. The Kendricks' baby was born in the early hours of today. Soon the phone will ring. It does ring. The phone is on Clare's side of the bed, and she picks it up and says "Hello?" very quietly, and hands it to me.

"How did you know? *How did you know?*" Kendrick is almost whispering.

"I'm sorry. I'm so sorry." Neither of us says anything for a minute. I think Kendrick is crying.

"Come to my office."

"When?"

"Tomorrow," he says, and hangs up the phone.

Sunday, April 7, 1996 (Henry is 32 and 8, Clare is 24)

HENRY: Clare and I are driving to Hyde Park. We've been silent for most of the ride. It's raining, and the wipers provide the rhythm section for the water streaming off the car and the wind.

As though continuing a conversation we haven't exactly been having, Clare says, "It doesn't seem fair."

"What? Kendrick?"

"Yeah."

"Nature isn't fair."

"Oh—no. I mean, yeah, it's sad about the baby, but actually I meant us. It seems not fair that we're exploiting this."

"Unsporting, you mean?"

"Uh-huh."

I sigh. The 57th Street exit sign appears and Clare changes lanes and pulls off the drive. "I agree with you, but it's too late. And I tried. . . ."

"Well, it's too late, anyway."

"Right." We lapse into silence again. I direct Clare through the maze of one-way streets, and soon we are sitting in front of Kendrick's office building.

"Good luck."

"Thanks." I am nervous.

"Be nice." Clare kisses me. We look at each other, all our hopes submerged in feeling guilty about Kendrick. Clare smiles, and looks away. I get out of the car and watch as Clare drives off slowly down

59th Street and crosses the Midway. She has an errand to do at the Smart Gallery.

The main door is unlocked and I take the elevator up to Three. There's no one in Kendrick's waiting room, and I walk through it and down the hall. Kendrick's door is open. The lights are off. Kendrick stands behind his desk with his back to me, looking out the window at the rainy street below. I stand silently in the doorway for a long moment. Finally I walk into the office.

Kendrick turns and I am shocked at the difference in his face. Ravaged is not the word. He is emptied; something has gone that was there before. Security; trust; confidence. I am so accustomed to living on a metaphysical trapeze that I forget that other people tend to enjoy more solid ground.

"Henry DeTamble," says Kendrick.

"Hello."

"Why did you come to me?"

"Because I had come to you. It wasn't a matter of choice."

"Fate?"

"Call it whatever you want. Things get kind of circular, when you're me. Cause and effect get muddled."

Kendrick sits down at his desk. The chair squeaks. The only other sound is the rain. He reaches in his pocket for his cigarettes, finds them, looks at me. I shrug. He lights one, and smokes for a little while. I regard him.

"How did you know?" he says.

"I told you before. I saw the birth certificate."

"When?"

"1999."

"Impossible."

"Explain it, then."

Kendrick shakes his head. "I can't. I've been trying to work it out, and I can't. Everything—was correct. The hour, the day, the weight, the . . . abnormality." He looks at me desperately. "What if we had decided to name him something else—Alex, or Fred, or Sam . . . ?"

I shake my head, and stop when I realize I'm mimicking him. "But you didn't. I won't go so far as to say you *couldn't*, but you did not. All I was doing was reporting. I'm not a psychic."

"Do you have any children?"

"No." I don't want to discuss it, although eventually I will have to. "I'm sorry about Colin. But you know, he's really a wonderful boy."

Kendrick stares at me. "I tracked down the mistake. Our test results were accidentally switched with those of a couple named Kenwick."

"What would you have done if you had known?"

He looks away. "I don't know. My wife and I are Catholic, so I imagine the end result would be the same. It's ironic. . . ."

"Yes."

Kendrick stubs out his cigarette and lights another. I resign myself to a smoke-induced headache.

"How does it work?"

"What?"

"This supposed time travel thing that you supposedly do." He sounds angry. "You say some magic words? Climb in a machine?"

I try to explain plausibly. "No. I don't do anything. It just happens. I can't control it, I just—one minute everything is fine, the next I'm somewhere else, some other time. Like changing channels. I just suddenly find myself in another time and place."

"Well, what do you want me to do about it?"

I lean forward, for emphasis. "I want you to find out why, and stop it."

Kendrick smiles. It's not a friendly smile. "Why would you want to do that? It seems like it would be quite handy for you. Knowing all these things that other people don't know."

"It's dangerous. Sooner or later it's going to kill me."

"I can't say that I would mind that."

There's no point in continuing. I stand up, and walk to the door. "Goodbye, Dr. Kendrick." I walk slowly down the hall, giving him a chance to call me back, but he doesn't. As I stand in the elevator I reflect miserably that whatever went wrong, it just had to go that way, and sooner or later it will right itself. As I open the door I see Clare waiting for me across the street in the car. She turns her head and there is such an expression of hope, such anticipation in her face that I am overwhelmed by sadness, I am dreading telling her, and as I walk across the street to her my ears are buzzing and I lose my balance and I am falling but instead of pavement I hit carpeting and I lie where I fall until I hear a familiar child's voice saying "Henry, are you okay?" and I look up to see myself, age eight, sitting up in bed, looking at me.

"I'm fine, Henry." He looks dubious. "Really, I'm okay."

"You want some Ovaltine?"

"Sure." He gets out of bed, toddles across the bedroom and down the hall. It's the middle of the night. He fusses around in the kitchen for a while, and eventually returns with two mugs of hot chocolate. We drink them slowly, in silence. When we're done Henry takes the mugs back to the kitchen and washes them. No sense in leaving the evidence around. When he comes back I ask, "What's up?"

"Not much. We went to see another doctor today."

"Hey, me too. Which one?"

"I forget the name. An old guy with a lot of hair in his ears."

"How was it?"

Henry shrugs. "He didn't believe me."

"Uh-huh. You should just give up. None of them ever will believe you. Well, the one I saw today believed me, I think, but he didn't want to help."

"How come?"

"He just didn't like me, I guess."

"Oh. Hey, do you want some blankets?"

"Um, maybe just one." I strip the bedspread off Henry's bed and curl up on the floor. "Good night. Sleep tight." I see the flash of my small self's white teeth in the blueness of the bedroom, and then he turns away into a tight ball of sleeping boy and I am left staring at my old ceiling, willing myself back to Clare.

CLARE: Henry walks out of the building looking unhappy, and suddenly he cries out and he's gone. I jump out of the car and run over to the spot where Henry was, just an instant ago, but of course there's just a pile of clothing there, now. I gather everything up and stand for a few heartbeats in the middle of the street, and as I stand there I see a man's face looking down at me from a window on the third floor. Then he disappears. I walk back to the car and get in, and sit staring at Henry's light blue shirt and black pants, wondering if there's any point in staying here. I've got *Brideshead Revisited* in my purse, so I decide to hang around for a while in case Henry reappears soon. As I turn to find the book I see a red-haired man running toward the car. He stops at the passenger door and peers in at me. This must be Kendrick. I flip the lock and he climbs into the car, and then he doesn't know what to say.

"Hello," I say. "You must be David Kendrick. I'm Clare DeTamble."

"Yes—" he's completely flustered, "yes, yes. Your husband—"

"Just vanished in broad daylight."

"Yes!"

"You seem surprised."

"Well—"

"Didn't he tell you? He does that." So far I'm not very impressed with this guy, but I persevere. "I'm so sorry about your baby. But Henry says he's a darling kid, and that he draws really well and has a lot of imagination. And your daughter's very gifted, and it will all be fine. You'll see."

He's gaping at me. "We don't have a daughter. Just—Colin."

"But you will. Her name is Nadia."

"It's been a shock. My wife is very upset. . . ."

"But it will be okay. Really." To my surprise this stranger begins to cry, his shoulders shaking, his face buried in his hands. After a few minutes he stops, and raises his head. I hand him a Kleenex, and he blows his nose.

"I'm so sorry," he begins.

"Never mind. What happened in there, with you and Henry? It went badly."

"How do you know?"

"He was all stressed out, so he lost his grip on now."

"Where is he?" Kendrick looks around as though I might be hiding Henry in the back seat.

"I don't know. Not here. We were hoping you could help, but I guess not."

"Well, I don't see how—" At this instant Henry appears in exactly the same spot he disappeared from. There's a car about twenty feet away, and the driver slams his brakes as Henry throws himself across the hood of our car. The man rolls down his window and Henry sits up and makes a little bow, and the man yells something and drives off. My blood is singing in my ears. I look over at Kendrick, who is speechless. I jump out of the car, and Henry eases himself off the hood.

"Hi, Clare. That was close, huh?" I wrap my arms around him; he's shaking. "Have you got my clothes?"

"Yeah, right here—oh hey, Kendrick is here."

"What? Where?"

"In the car."

"Why?"

"He saw you disappear and it seems to have affected his brain."

Henry sticks his head in the driver's side door. "Hello." He grabs his clothing and starts to get dressed. Kendrick gets out of the car and trots around to us.

"Where were you?"

"1971. I was drinking Ovaltine with myself, as an eight-year-old, in my old bedroom, at one in the morning. I was there for about an hour. Why do you ask?" Henry regards Kendrick coldly as he knots his tie.

"Unbelievable."

"You can go on saying that as long as you want, but unfortunately it's true."

"You mean you became eight years old?"

"No. I mean I was sitting in my old bedroom in my dad's apartment, in 1971, just as I am, thirty-two years old, in the company of myself, at eight. Drinking Ovaltine. We were chatting about the incredulity of the medical profession." Henry walks around to the side of the car and opens the door. "Clare, let's vamoose. This is pointless."

I walk to the driver's side. "Goodbye, Dr. Kendrick. Good luck with Colin."

"Wait—" Kendrick pauses, collects himself. "This is a genetic disease?"

"Yes," says Henry. "It's a genetic disease, and we're trying to have a child."

Kendrick smiles, sadly. "A chancy thing to do."

I smile back at him. "We're used to taking chances. Goodbye." Henry and I get into the car, and drive away. As I pull onto Lake Shore Drive I glance at Henry, who to my surprise is grinning broadly.

"What are you so pleased about?"

"Kendrick. He is totally hooked."

"You think?"

"Oh, yeah."

"Well, great. But he seemed kind of dense."

"He's not."

"Okay." We drive home in silence, an entirely different quality of silence than we arrived with. Kendrick calls Henry that evening, and they make an appointment to begin the work of figuring out how to keep Henry in the here and now.

Friday, April 12, 1996 (Henry is 32)

HENRY: Kendrick sits with his head bowed. His thumbs move around the perimeter of his palms as though they want to escape from his hands. As the afternoon has passed the office has been illuminated with golden light; Kendrick has sat immobile except for those twitching thumbs, listening to me talk. The red Indian carpet, the beige twill armchairs' steel legs have flared bright; Kendrick's cigarettes, a pack of Camels, have sat untouched while he listened. The gold rims of his round glasses have been picked out by the sunlight; the edge of Kendrick's right ear has glowed red, his foxish hair and pink skin have been as burnished by the light as the yellow chrysanthemums in the brass bowl on the table between us. All afternoon, Kendrick has sat there in his chair, listening.

And I have told him everything. The beginning, the learning, the rush of surviving and the pleasure of knowing ahead, the terror of knowing things that can't be averted, the anguish of loss. Now we sit in silence and finally he raises his head and looks at me. In Kendrick's light eyes is a sadness that I want to undo; after laying everything before him I want to take it all back and leave, excuse him from the burden of having to think about any of this. He reaches for his cigarettes, selects one, lights it, inhales and then exhales a blue cloud that turns white as it crosses the path of the light along with its shadow.

"Do you have difficulty sleeping?" he asks me, his voice rasping from disuse.

"Yes."

"Is there any particular time of day that you tend to . . . vanish?"

"No . . . well, early morning maybe more than other times."

"Do you get headaches?"

"Yes."

"Migraines?"

"No. Pressure headaches. With vision distortion, auras."

"Hmm." Kendrick stands up. His knees crack. He paces around the office, smoking, following the edge of the rug. It's beginning to bug me when he stops and sits down again. "Listen," he says, frowning, "there are these things called clock genes. They govern circadian rhythms, keep you in sync with the sun, that sort of thing. We've found them in many different types of cells, all over the body, but they are especially tied to vision, and you seem to experience many of your symptoms visually. The suprachiasmatic nucleus of the hypothalamus, which is located right above your optic chiasm, serves as the reset button, as it were, of your sense of time—so that's what I want to begin with."

"Um, sure," I say, since he's looking at me as though he expects a reply. Kendrick gets up again and strides over to a door I haven't noticed before, opens it and disappears for a minute. When he returns he's holding latex gloves and a syringe.

"Roll up your sleeve," Kendrick demands.

"What are you doing?" I ask, rolling my sleeve above my elbow. He doesn't answer, unwraps the syringe, swabs my arm and ties it off, sticks me expertly. I look away. The sun has passed, leaving the office in gloom.

"Do you have health insurance?" he asks me, removing the needle and untying my arm. He puts cotton and a Band-Aid over the puncture.

"No. I'll pay for everything myself." I press my fingers against the sore spot, bend my elbow.

Kendrick smiles. "No, no. You can be my little science experiment, hitchhike on my NIH grant for this."

"For what?"

"We're not going to mess around, here." Kendrick pauses, stands holding the used gloves and the little vial of my blood that he's just drawn. "We're going to have your DNA sequenced."

"I thought that took years."

"It does, if you're doing the whole genome. We are going to begin by looking at the most likely sites; Chromosome 17, for example." Kendrick throws the latex and needle in a can labeled BIO-HAZARD and writes something on the little red vial of blood. He sits back down across from me and places the vial on the table next to the Camels.

"But the human genome won't be sequenced until 2000. What will you compare it to?"

"2000? So soon? You're sure? I guess you are. But to answer your question, a disease that is as—disruptive—as yours often appears as a kind of stutter, a repeated bit of code that says, in essence, Bad News. Huntington's disease, for instance, is just a bunch of extra CAG triplets on Chromosome 4."

I sit up and stretch. I could use some coffee. "So that's it? Can I run away and play now?"

"Well, I want to have your head scanned, but not today. I'll make an appointment for you at the hospital. MRI, CAT scan, and X-rays. I'm also going to send you to a friend of mine, Alan Larson; he has a sleep lab here on campus."

"Fun," I say, standing up slowly so the blood doesn't all rush to my head.

Kendrick tilts his face up at me. I can't see his eyes, his glasses are shiny opaque disks at this angle. "It *is* fun," he says. "It's such a great puzzle, and we finally have the tools to find out—"

"To find out what?"

"Whatever it is. Whatever you are." Kendrick smiles and I notice that his teeth are uneven and yellowed. He stands, extends his hand, and I shake it, thank him; there's an awkward pause: we are strangers again after the intimacies of the afternoon, and then I walk out of his office, down stairs, into the street, where the sun has been waiting for me. Whatever I am. What am I? *What am I?*

A VERY SMALL SHOE

•••••••••••••••••••••••••••••••••

Spring, 1996 (Clare is 24, Henry is 32)

CLARE: When Henry and I had been married for about two years we decided, without talking about it very much, to see if we could have a baby. I knew that Henry was not at all optimistic about our chances of having a baby and I was not asking him or myself why this might be because I was afraid that he had seen us in the future without any baby and I just didn't want to know about that. And I didn't want to think about the possibility that Henry's difficulties with time travel might be hereditary or somehow mess up the whole baby thing, as it were. So I was simply not thinking about a lot of important stuff because I was completely drunk with the notion of a baby: a baby that looked sort of like Henry, black hair and those intense eyes and maybe very pale like me and smelled like milk and talcum powder and skin, a sort of dumpling baby, gurgling and laughing at everyday stuff, a monkey baby, a small cooing sort of baby. I would dream about babies. In my dreams I would climb a tree and find a very small shoe in a nest; I would suddenly discover that the cat/book/sandwich I thought I was holding was really a baby; I would be swimming in the lake and find a colony of babies growing at the bottom.

I suddenly began to see babies everywhere; a sneezing red-haired girl in a sunbonnet at the A&P; a tiny staring Chinese boy, son of the owners, in the Golden Wok (home of wonderful vegetarian eggrolls); a sleeping almost bald baby at a Batman movie. In a fitting room in a JCPenney a very trusting woman actually let me hold her three-month-old daughter; it was all I could do to continue sitting in that pink-beige vinyl chair and not spring up and run madly away hugging that tiny soft being to my breasts.

My body wanted a baby. I felt empty and I wanted to be full. I wanted someone to love who would stay: stay and be there, always. And I wanted Henry to be in this child, so that when he was gone he wouldn't be entirely gone, there would be a bit of him with me . . . insurance, in case of fire, flood, act of God.

Sunday, October 2, 1966 (Henry is 33)

HENRY: I am sitting, very comfortable and content, in a tree in Appleton, Wisconsin, in 1966, eating a tuna fish sandwich and wearing a white T-shirt and chinos stolen from someone's beautiful sun-dried laundry. Somewhere in Chicago, I am three; my mother is still alive and none of this chrono-fuckupedness has started. I salute my small former self, and thinking about me as a child naturally gets me thinking about Clare, and our efforts to conceive. On one hand, I am all eagerness; I want to give Clare a baby, see Clare ripen like a flesh melon, Demeter in glory. I want a normal baby who will do the things normal babies do: suck, grasp, shit, sleep, laugh; roll over, sit up, walk, talk in nonsense mumblings. I want to see my father awkwardly cradling a tiny grandchild; I have given my father so little happiness—this would be a large redress, a balm.

And a balm to Clare, too; when I am snatched away from her, a part of me would remain.

But: but. I know, without knowing, that this is very unlikely. I know that a child of mine is almost certainly going to be The One Most Likely to Spontaneously Vanish, a magical disappearing baby who will evaporate as though carried off by fairies. And even as I pray, panting and gasping over Clare in extremities of desire, for the miracle of sex to somehow yield us a baby, a part of me is praying just as vehemently for us to be spared. I am reminded of the story of the monkey's paw, and the three wishes that followed so naturally and horribly from each other. I wonder if our wish is of a similar order.

I am a coward. A better man would take Clare by the shoulders and say, Love, this is all a mistake, let us accept it and go on, and be happy. But I know that Clare would never accept, would always be sad. And so I hope, against hope, against reason and I make love to Clare as though anything good might come of it.

ONE

• •

Monday, June 3, 1996 (Clare is 25)

CLARE: The first time it happens Henry is away. It's the eighth week of the pregnancy. The baby is the size of a plum, has a face and hands and a beating heart. It is early evening, early summer, and I can see magenta and orange clouds in the west as I wash the dishes. Henry disappeared almost two hours ago. He went out to water the lawn and after half an hour, when I realized that the sprinkler still wasn't on, I stood at the back door and saw the telltale pile of clothing sitting by the grape arbor. I went out and gathered up Henry's jeans and underwear and his ratty KILL YOUR TELEVISION T-shirt, folded them and put them on the bed. I thought about turning on the sprinkler but decided not to, reasoning that Henry won't like it if he appears in the backyard and gets drenched.

I have prepared and eaten macaroni and cheese and a small salad, have taken my vitamins, have consumed a large glass of skim milk. I hum as I do the dishes, imagine the little being inside me hearing the humming, filing the humming away for future reference at some subtle, cellular level, and as I stand there, conscientiously washing my salad bowl I feel a slight twinge somewhere deep inside, somewhere in my pelvis. Ten minutes later I am sitting in the living room minding my own business and reading Louis De-Bernieres and there it is again, a brief twang on my internal strings. I ignore it. Everything is fine. Henry's been gone for more than two hours. I worry about him for a second, then resolutely ignore that, too. I do not start to really worry for another half hour or so, because now the weird little sensations are resembling menstrual cramps, and I am even feeling that sticky blood feeling between my legs and I get up and walk into the bathroom and pull down my underpants there's a lot of blood oh my god.

I call Charisse. Gomez answers the phone. I try to sound okay, ask for Charisse, who gets on the phone and immediately says, "What's wrong?"

"I'm bleeding."

"Where's Henry?"

"I don't know."

"What kind of bleeding?"

"Like a period." The pain is becoming intense and I sit down on the floor. "Can you take me to Illinois Masonic?"

"I'll be right there, Clare." She hangs up, and I replace the receiver gently, as though I might hurt its feelings by handling it too roughly. I get to my feet with care, find my purse. I want to write Henry a note, but I don't know what to say. I write: "Went to IL Masonic. (Cramps.) Charisse drove me there. 7:20 p.m. C." I unlock the back door for Henry. I leave the note by the phone. A few minutes later Charisse is at the front door. When we get to the car, Gomez is driving. We don't talk much. I sit in the front seat, look out the window. Western to Belmont to Sheffield to Wellington. Everything is unusually sharp and emphatic, as though I need to remember, as though there will be a test. Gomez turns into the Unloading Zone for the Emergency Room. Charisse and I get out. I look back at Gomez, who smiles briefly and roars off to park the car. We walk through doors that open automatically as our feet press the ground, as in a fairy tale, as though we are expected. The pain has receded like an ebbing tide, and now it moves toward the shore again, fresh and fierce. There are a few people sitting abject and small in the brightly lit room, waiting their turn, encircling their pain with bowed heads and crossed arms, and I sink down among them. Charisse walks over to the man sitting behind the triage desk. I can't hear what she says, but when he says "Miscarriage?" it dawns on me that this is what is going on, this is what it is called, and the word expands in my head until it fills all crevices of my mind, until it has crowded out every other thought. I start to cry.

After they've done everything they could, it happens anyway. I find out later that Henry arrived just before the end, but they wouldn't let him come in. I have been sleeping, and when I wake up it's late at night and Henry is there. He is pale and hollow-eyed and he doesn't say a word. "Oh," I mumble, "where were you?" and Henry leans over and carefully embraces me. I feel his stubble against my cheek and I am rubbed raw, not on my skin but deep in me, a wound opens and Henry's face is wet but with whose tears?

Thursday, June 13 and Friday, June 14, 1996 (Henry is 32)

HENRY: I arrive at the sleep lab exhausted, as Dr. Kendrick has asked me to. This is the fifth night I've spent here, and by now I know the routine. I sit on the bed in the odd, fake, home-like bedroom wearing pajama bottoms while Dr. Larson's lab technician, Karen, puts cream on my head and chest and tapes wires in place. Karen is young and blond and Vietnamese. She's wearing long fake fingernails and says, "Oops, sorry," when she rakes my cheek with one of them. The lights are dim, the room is cool. There are no windows except a piece of one-way glass that looks like a mirror, behind which sits Dr. Larson, or whoever's watching the machines this evening. Karen finishes the wiring, bids me good night, leaves the room. I settle into the bed carefully, close my eyes, imagine the spider-legged tracings on long streams of graph paper gracefully recording my eye movements, respiration, brain waves on the other side of the glass. I'm asleep within minutes.

I dream of running. I'm running through woods, dense brush, trees, but somehow I am running through all of it, passing through like a ghost. I burst into a clearing, there's been a fire. . . .

I dream I am having sex with Ingrid. I know it's Ingrid, even though I can't see her face, it is Ingrid's body, Ingrid's long smooth legs. We are fucking in her parents' house, in their living room on the couch, the TV is on, tuned to a nature documentary in which a herd of antelope is running, and then there's a parade. Clare is sitting on a tiny float in the parade, looking sad while people are cheering all around her and suddenly Ing jumps up and pulls a bow and arrow from behind the couch and she shoots Clare. The arrow goes right into the TV and Clare claps her hands to her breast like Wendy in a silent version of *Peter Pan* and I leap up and I'm choking Ingrid, my hands around her throat, screaming at her—

I wake up. I'm cold with sweat and my heart is pounding. I'm in the sleep lab. I wonder for a moment if there's something they're not telling me, if they can somehow watch my dreams, see my thoughts. I turn onto my side and close my eyes.

I dream that Clare and I are walking through a museum. The museum is an old palace, all the paintings are in rococo gold frames, all the other visitors are wearing tall powdered wigs and immense dresses, frock coats, and breeches. They don't seem to notice us as we pass. We look at the paintings, but they aren't really paintings, they're poems, poems somehow given physical manifestation.

"Look," I say to Clare, "there's an Emily Dickinson." *The heart asks pleasure first; And then excuse from pain . . .* She stands in front of the bright yellow poem and seems to warm herself by it. We see Dante, Donne, Blake, Neruda, Bishop; linger in a room full of Rilke, pass quickly through the Beats and pause before Verlaine and Baudelaire. I suddenly realize that I've lost Clare, I am walking, then running, back through the galleries and then I abruptly find her: she is standing before a poem, a tiny white poem tucked into a corner. She is weeping. As I come up behind her I see the poem: *Now I lay me down to sleep, I pray the Lord my soul to keep, If I should die before I wake, I pray the Lord my soul to take.*

I'm thrashing in grass, it's cold, wind rushes over me, I'm naked and cold in darkness, there's snow on the ground, I am on my knees in the snow, blood drips onto the snow and I reach out—

"My god, he's bleeding—"

"How the hell did that happen?"

"Shit, he's ripped off all the electrodes, help me get him back on the bed—"

I open my eyes. Kendrick and Dr. Larson are crouched over me. Dr. Larson looks upset and worried, but Kendrick has a jubilant smile on his face.

"Did you get it?" I ask, and he replies, "It was perfect." I say, "Great," and then I pass out.

Two

....

Sunday, October 12, 1997 (Henry is 34, Clare is 26)

H E N R Y : I wake up and smell iron and it's blood. Blood is everywhere and Clare is curled up in the middle of it like a kitten.

I shake her and she says, "No."

"ComeonClarewakeupyou'rebleeding."

"I was dreaming. . . ."

"Clare, *please*. . . ."

She sits up. Her hands, her face, her hair are drenched in blood. Clare holds out her hand and on it reclines a tiny monster. She says, simply, "He died," and bursts into tears. We sit together on the edge of the blood-soaked bed, holding each other, and crying.

Monday, February 16, 1998 (Clare is 26, Henry is 34)

C L A R E : Henry and I are just about to go out. It's a snowy afternoon, and I'm pulling on my boots when the phone rings. Henry walks down the hall and into the living room to answer it. I hear him say, "Hello?" and then "Really?" and then "Well, hot damn!" Then he says, "Wait, let me get some paper—" and there's a long silence, punctuated once in a while with "Wait, explain that," and I take off my boots and my coat and pad into the living room in my socks. Henry is sitting on the couch with the phone cradled in his lap like a pet, furiously taking notes. I sit down next to him and he grins at me. I look at the pad; the top of the page starts off: *4 genes: per4, timeless1, Clock, new gene=timetraveler?? Chrom=17 x 2, 4, 25, 200+ repeats TAG, sex linked? no, +too many dopamine recpts, what proteins???* . . . and I realize: Kendrick has done it! He's figured it out! I can't believe it. He's done it. Now what?

Henry puts down the phone, turns to me. He looks as stunned as I feel.

"What happens next?" I ask him.

"He's going to clone the genes and put them into mice."

"*What?*"

"He's going to make time-traveling mice. Then he's going to cure them."

We both start to laugh at the same time, and then we are dancing, flinging each other around the room, laughing and dancing until we fall back onto the couch, panting. I look over at Henry, and I wonder that on a cellular level he is so different, so *other,* when he's just a man in a white button-down shirt and a pea jacket whose hand feels like skin and bone in mine, a man who smiles just like a human. *I always knew he was different,* what does it matter? a few letters of code? but somehow it must matter, and somehow we must change it, and somewhere on the other side of the city Dr. Kendrick is sitting in his office figuring out how to make mice that defy the rules of time. I laugh, but it's life and death, and I stop laughing and put my hand over my mouth.

INTERMEZZO

• •

Wednesday, August 12, 1998 (Clare is 27)

CLARE: Mama is asleep, finally. She sleeps in her own bed, in her own room; she has escaped from the hospital, at last, only to find her room, her refuge, transformed into a hospital room. But now she is past knowing. All night she talked, wept, laughed, yelled, called out "Philip!" and "Mama!" and "No, no, no . . ." All night the cicadas and the tree frogs of my childhood pulsed their electric curtain of sound and the night light made her skin look like beeswax, her bone hands flailing in supplication, clutching at the glass of water I held to her crusted lips. Now it is dawn. Mama's window looks out over the east. I sit in the white chair, by the window, facing the bed, but not looking, not looking at Mama so effaced in her big bed, not looking at the pill bottles and the spoons and the glasses and the IV pole with the bag hanging obese with fluid and the blinking red LED display and the bed pan and the little kidney-shaped receptacle for vomit and the box of latex gloves and the trash can with the BIOHAZARD warning label full of bloody syringes. I am looking out the window, toward the east. A few birds are singing. I can hear the doves that live in the wisteria waking up. The world is gray. Slowly color leaks into it, not rosy-fingered but like a slowly spreading stain of blood orange, one moment lingering at the horizon and then flooding the garden and then golden light, and then a blue sky, and then all the colors vibrant in their assigned places, the trumpet vines, the roses, the white salvia, the marigolds, all shimmering in the new morning dew like glass. The silver birches at the edges of the woods dangle like white strings suspended from the sky. A crow flies across the grass. Its shadow flies under it, and meets it as it lands under the window and caws, once. Light finds the window, and creates my hands, my body heavy in Mama's white chair. The sun is up.

I close my eyes. The air conditioner purrs. I'm cold, and I get up and walk to the other window, and turn it off. Now the room is silent. I walk to the bed. Mama is still. The laborious breathing that has haunted my dreams has stopped. Her mouth is open slightly and her eyebrows are raised as though in surprise, although her eyes are closed; she could be singing. I kneel by the bed, I pull back the covers and lay my ear against her heart. Her skin is warm. Nothing. No heart beats, no blood moves, no breath inflates the sails of her lungs. Silence.

I gather up her reeking, wasted body into my arms, and she is perfect, she is my own perfect beautiful Mama again, for just a moment, even as her bones jut against my breasts and her head lolls, even as her cancer-laden belly mimics fecundity she rises up in memory shining, laughing, released: free.

Footsteps in the hall. The door opens and Etta's voice.

"Clare? Oh—"

I lower Mama back to the pillows, smooth her nightgown, her hair.

"She's gone."

Saturday, September 12, 1998 (Henry is 35, Clare is 27)

HENRY: Lucille was the one who loved the garden. When we came to visit, Clare would walk through the front door of the Meadowlark House and straight out the back door to find Lucille, who was almost always in the garden, rain or shine. When she was well we would find her kneeling in the beds, weeding or moving plants or feeding the roses. When she was ill Etta and Philip would bring her downstairs wrapped in quilts and seat her in her wicker chair, sometimes by the fountain, sometimes under the pear tree where she could see Peter working, digging and pruning and grafting. When Lucille was well she would regale us with the doings of the garden: the red-headed finches who had finally discovered the new feeder, the dahlias that had done better than expected over by the sundial, the new rose that turned out to be a horrible shade of lavender but was so vigorous that she was loathe to get rid of it. One summer Lucille and Alicia conducted an experiment: Alicia spent several hours each day practicing the cello in the garden, to see if the plants would respond to the music. Lucille swore that her tomatoes had never been so plentiful, and she showed us a zucchini that was the size of my thigh. So the experiment was deemed a success, but was never repeated because it was the last summer Lucille was well enough to garden.

Lucille waxed and waned with the seasons, like a plant. In the summer, when we all showed up, Lucille would rally and the house rang with the happy shouts and pounding of Mark and Sharon's children, who tumbled like puppies in the fountain and cavorted sticky and ebullient on the lawn. Lucille was often grimy but always elegant. She would rise to greet us, her white and copper hair in a thick coil with fat strands straggling into her face, white kidskin gardening gloves and Smith & Hawken tools thrown down as she received our hugs. Lucille and I always kissed very formally, on both cheeks, as though we were very old French countesses who hadn't seen each other in a while. She was never less than kind to me, although she could devastate her daughter with a glance. I miss her. Clare . . . well, 'miss' is inadequate. Clare is bereft. Clare walks into rooms and forgets why she is there. Clare sits staring at a book without turning a page for an hour. But she doesn't cry. Clare smiles if I make a joke. Clare eats what I put in front of her. If I try to make love to her Clare will try to go along with it . . . and soon I leave her alone, afraid of the docile, tearless face that seems to be miles away. I miss Lucille, but it is Clare I am bereft of, Clare who has gone away and left me with this stranger who only looks like Clare.

Wednesday, November 26, 1998 (Clare is 27, Henry is 35)

CLARE: Mama's room is white and bare. All the medical paraphernalia is gone. The bed is stripped down to the mattress, which is stained and ugly in the clean room. I'm standing in front of Mama's desk. It's a heavy white Formica desk, modern and strange in an otherwise feminine and delicate room full of antique French furniture. Mama's desk stands in a little bay, windows embrace it, morning light washes across its empty surface. The desk is locked. I have spent an hour looking for the key, with no luck. I lean my elbows on the back of Mama's swivel chair, and stare at the desk. Finally, I go downstairs. The living room and dining room are empty. I hear laughter in the kitchen, so I push the door open. Henry and Nell are huddled over a cluster of bowls and a pastry cloth and a rolling pin.

"Easy, boy, easy! You gonna toughen 'em up, you go at 'em like that. You need a light touch, Henry, or they gonna have a texture like bubble gum."

"Sorry sorry sorry. I will be light, just don't whack me like that. Hey, Clare." Henry turns around smiling and I see that he is covered with flour.

"What are you making?"

"Croissants. I have sworn to master the art of folding pastry dough or perish in the attempt."

"Rest in peace, son," says Nell, grinning.

"What's up?" Henry asks as Nell efficiently rolls out a ball of dough and folds it and cuts it and wraps it in waxed paper.

"I need to borrow Henry for a couple of minutes, Nell." Nell nods and points her rolling pin at Henry. "Come back in fifteen minutes and we'll start the marinade."

"Yes'm."

Henry follows me upstairs. We stand in front of Mama's desk.

"I want to open it and I can't find the keys."

"Ah." He darts a look at me, so quick I can't read it. "Well, that's easy." Henry leaves the room and is back in minutes. He sits on the floor in front of Mama's desk, straightening out two large paper clips. He starts with the bottom left drawer, carefully probing and turning one paper clip, and then sticks the other one in after it. "*Voilà*," he says, pulling on the drawer. It's bursting with paper. Henry opens the other four drawers without any fuss. Soon they are all gaping, their contents exposed: notebooks, loose-leaf papers, gardening catalogs, seed packets, pens and short pencils, a checkbook, a Hershey's candy bar, a tape measure, and a number of other small items that now seem forlorn and shy in the daylight. Henry hasn't touched anything in the drawers. He looks at me; I glance at the door almost involuntarily and Henry takes the hint. I turn to Mama's desk.

The papers are in no order at all. I sit on the floor and pile the contents of a drawer in front of me. Everything with her handwriting on it I smooth and pile on my left. Some of it is lists, and notes to herself: *Do not ask P about S.* Or: *Remind Etta dinner B's Friday.* There are pages and pages of doodles, spirals and squiggles, black circles, marks like the feet of birds. Some of these have a sentence or a phrase embedded in them. *To part her hair with a knife.* And: *couldn't couldn't do it.* And: *If I am quiet it will pass me by.* Some sheets are poems so heavily marked and crossed out that very little remains, like fragments of Sappho:

> *Like old meat, ~~relaxed and tender~~*
> *no air ~~XXXXXXX~~ she said yes*
> *~~she said~~ ~~XXXXXXXXXXXXXXXX~~*

Or:

> *his hand ~~XXXXXXXXXXX~~*
> *~~XXXXX~~ to possess,*
> *~~XXXXXXXXXXXXXXXXXX~~*
> *in extreme ~~XXXXXXXXX~~*

Some poems have been typed:

> *At the moment*
> *all hope is weak*
> *and small.*
> *Music and beauty*
> *are salt in my sadness;*
> *a white void rips through my ice.*
> *Who could have said*
> *that the angel of sex*
> *was so sad?*
> *or known desire*
> *would melt this vast*
> *winter night into*
> *a flood of darkness.*

> *1/23/79*

The spring garden:
a ship of summer
swimming through
my winter vision.

4/6/79

1979 was the year Mama lost the baby and tried to kill herself. My stomach aches and my eyes blur. I know now how it was with her then. I take all of those papers and put them aside without reading any more. In another drawer I find more recent poems. And then I find a poem addressed to me:

The Garden Under Snow
for clare

    now the garden is under snow
    a blank page our footprints write on
    clare who was never mine
    but always belonged to herself
    Sleeping Beauty
    a crystalline blanket
    ~~*she waits*~~
    this is her spring
    this is her sleeping/awakening
    she is waiting
    everything is waiting
    ~~*for a kiss*~~
    the improbable shapes of ~~*tubers*~~ *roots*
    ~~*I never thought*~~
    my baby
    her ~~*almost*~~ *face*
    a garden, waiting

HENRY: It's almost dinner time and I'm in Nell's way, so when she says, "Shouldn't you go see what your woman is up to?" it seems like a good idea to go and find out.

Clare is sitting on the floor in front of her mother's desk surrounded by white and yellow papers. The desk lamp throws a pool of light around her, but her face is in shadow; her hair a flaming copper aura. She looks up at me, holds out a piece of paper, and says, "Look, Henry, she wrote me a poem." As I sit beside Clare and read the poem I forgive Lucille, a little, for her colossal selfishness and her monstrous dying, and I look up at Clare. "It's beautiful," I say, and she nods, satisfied, for a moment, that her mother really did love her. I think about my mother singing *lieder* after lunch on a summer afternoon, smiling at our reflection in a shop window, twirling in a blue dress across the floor of her dressing room. She loved me. I never questioned her love. Lucille was changeable as wind. The poem Clare holds is evidence, immutable, undeniable, a snapshot of an emotion. I look around at the pools of paper on the floor and I am relieved that something in this mess has risen to the surface to be Clare's lifeboat.

"She wrote me a poem," Clare says, again, in wonder. Tears are streaking down her cheeks. I put my arms around her, and she's back, my wife, Clare, safe and sound, on the shore at last after the shipwreck, weeping like a little girl whose mother is waving to her from the deck of the foundering boat.

New Year's Eve, One

•••••••••••••••••••••••••••••••

Friday, December 31, 1999, 11:55 p.m. (Henry is 36, Clare is 28)

HENRY: Clare and I are standing on a rooftop in Wicker Park with a multitude of other hardy souls, awaiting the turn of the so-called millennium. It's a clear night, and not that cold; I can see my breath, and my ears and nose are a bit numb. Clare is all muffled up in her big black scarf and her face is startlingly white in the moon/ street light. The rooftop belongs to a couple of Clare's artist friends. Gomez and Charisse are nearby, slow-dancing in parkas and mittens to music only they can hear. Everyone around us is drunkenly bantering about the canned goods they have stockpiled, the heroic measures they have taken to protect their computers from melt-down. I smile to myself, knowing that all this millennial nonsense will be completely forgotten by the time the Christmas trees are picked up off the curbs by Streets and San.

We are waiting for the fireworks to begin. Clare and I lean against the waist-high false front of the building and survey the City of Chicago. We are facing east, looking toward Lake Michigan. "Hello, everybody," Clare says, waving her mitten at the lake, at South Haven, Michigan. "It's funny," she says to me. "It's already the new year there. I'm sure they're all in bed."

We are six stories up, and I am surprised by how much I can see from here. Our house, in Lincoln Square, is somewhere to the north and west of here; our neighborhood is quiet and dark. Downtown, to the southeast, is sparkling. Some of the huge buildings are decorated for Christmas, sporting green and red lights in their windows. The Sears and the Hancock stare at each other like giant robots over the heads of lesser skyscrapers. I can almost see the building I lived in when I met Clare, on North Dearborn, but it's obscured by the taller, uglier building they put up a few years ago next to it. Chicago has so much excellent architecture that they feel obliged to tear some of it down now and then and erect terrible buildings just to help us all appreciate the good stuff. There isn't much traffic; everyone wants to be somewhere at midnight, not on the road. I can hear bursts of firecrackers here and there, punctuated occasionally with gunfire from the morons who seem to forget that guns do more than make loud noises. Clare says, "I'm freezing," and looks at her watch. "Two more minutes." Bursts of celebration around the neighborhood indicate that some people's watches are fast.

I think about Chicago in the next century. More people, many more. Ridiculous traffic, but fewer potholes. There will be a hideous building that looks like an exploding Coke can in Grant Park; the West Side will slowly rise out of poverty and the South Side will continue to decay. They will finally tear down Wrigley Field and build an ugly megastadium, but for now it stands blazing with light in the Northeast.

Gomez begins the countdown: "Ten, nine, eight . . ." and we all take it up: "seven, six, five, four, THREE! TWO! ONE! *Happy New Year!*" Champagne corks pop, fireworks ignite and streak across the sky, and Clare and I dive into each other's arms. Time stands still, and I hope for better things to come.

THREE

....

Saturday, March 13, 1999 (Henry is 35, Clare is 27)

HENRY: Charisse and Gomez have just had their third child, Rosa Evangeline Gomolinski. We allow a week to pass, then descend on them with presents and food.

Gomez answers the door. Maximilian, three years old, is clinging to his leg, and hides his face behind Gomez's knee when we say "Hi Max!" Joseph, more extroverted at one, races up to Clare babbling "Ba ba ba" and burps loudly as she picks him up. Gomez rolls his eyes, and Clare laughs, and Joe laughs, and even I have to laugh at the complete chaos. Their house looks as though a glacier with a Toys "R" Us store inside it has moved through, leaving pools of Legos and abandoned stuffed bears.

"Don't look," says Gomez. "None of this is real. We're just testing one of Charisse's virtual reality games. We call it 'Parenthood.'"

"Gomez?" Charisse's voice floats out of the bedroom. "Is that Clare and Henry?"

We all tromp down the hall and into the bedroom. I catch a glimpse of the kitchen as we pass. A middle-aged woman is standing at the sink, washing dishes.

Charisse is lying in bed with the baby in her arms. The baby is asleep. She is tiny and has black hair and a sort of Aztec look about her. Max and Joe are light-haired. Charisse looks awful (to me. Clare insists later that she looked "wonderful"). She has gained a lot of weight and looks exhausted and ill. She has had a caesarean. I sit down on the chair. Clare and Gomez sit on the bed. Max clambers over to his mother and snuggles under her free arm. He stares at me and puts his thumb in his mouth. Joe is sitting on Gomez's lap.

"She's beautiful," says Clare. Charisse smiles. "And you look great."

"I feel like shit," says Charisse. "But I'm done. We got our girl." She strokes the baby's face, and Rosa yawns and raises one tiny hand. Her eyes are dark slits.

"Rosa Evangeline," Clare coos to the baby. "That's so pretty."

"Gomez wanted to name her Wednesday, but I put my foot down," says Charisse.

"Well, she was born on a Thursday, anyway," explains Gomez.

"Wanna hold her?" Clare nods, and Charisse carefully hands her daughter into Clare's arms.

Seeing Clare with a baby in her arms, the reality of our miscarriages grabs me and for a moment I feel nauseous. I hope I'm not about to time travel. The feeling retreats and I am left with the actuality of what we've been doing: we have been losing children. Where are they, these lost children, wandering, hovering around confused?

"Henry, would you like to hold Rosa?" Clare asks me.

I panic. "No," I say, too emphatically. "I'm not feeling so hot," I explain. I get up and walk out of the bedroom, through the kitchen and out the back door. I stand in the backyard. It is raining lightly. I stand and breathe.

The back door slams. Gomez comes out and stands beside me.

"You okay?" he asks.

"I think so. I was getting claustrophobic in there."

"Yeah, I know what you mean."

We stand silently for minutes. I am trying to remember my father holding me when I was little. All I can remember is playing games with him, running, laughing, riding around on his shoulders. I realize that Gomez is looking at me, and that tears are coursing down my cheeks. I wipe my sleeve across my face. Somebody has to say something.

"Don't mind me," I say.

Gomez makes an awkward gesture. "I'll be right back," he says, and disappears into the house. I think he's gone for good, but he reappears with a lit cigarette in hand. I sit down on the decrepit picnic table, which is damp with rain and covered with pine needles. It's cold out here.

"You guys still trying to have a kid?"

I am startled by this until I realize that Clare probably tells Charisse everything, and Charisse probably tells Gomez nothing.

"Yeah."

"Is Clare still upset about that miscarriage?"

"Miscarriages. Plural. We've had three."

"'To lose one child, Mr. DeTamble, may be regarded as a misfortune; to lose three looks like carelessness.'"

"That's not really all that funny, Gomez."

"Sorry." Gomez does look abashed, for once. I don't want to talk about this. I have no words to talk about it, and I can barely talk about it with Clare, with Kendrick and the other doctors at whose feet we've laid our sad case. "Sorry," Gomez repeats.

I stand up. "We'd better go in."

"Ah, they don't want us, they want to talk about girl stuff."

"Mmm. Well, then. How about those Cubs?" I sit down again.

"Shut up." Neither of us follows baseball. Gomez is pacing back and forth. I wish he would stop, or, better yet, go inside. "So what's the problem?" he asks, casually.

"With what? The Cubs? No pitching, I'd say."

"No, dear Library Boy, not the Cubs. What is the problem that is causing you and Clare to be *sans* infants?"

"That is really not any of your business, Gomez."

He plunges on, unfazed. "Do they even know what the problem is?"

"Fuck off, Gomez."

"Tut, tut. Language. Because I know this great doctor . . ."

"Gomez—"

"Who specializes in fetal chromosomal disorders."

"Why on earth would you know—"

"Expert witness."

"Oh."

"Her name is Amit Montague," he continues, "she's a genius. She's been on TV and won all these awards. Juries adore her."

"Oh, well, if *juries* love her—" I begin, sarcastically.

"Just go and see her. Jesus, I'm trying to be helpful."

I sigh. "Okay. Um, thanks."

"Is that 'Thanks, we will run right out and do as you suggest, dear Comrade,' or 'Thanks, now go screw yourself'?"

I stand up, brush damp pine needles off the seat of my pants. "Let's go in," I say, and we do.

• •

Wednesday, July 21, 1999/September 8, 1998 (Henry is 36, Clare is 28)

H E N R Y : We are lying in bed. Clare is curled on her side, her back to me, and I am curled around her, facing her back. It's about two in the morning, and we have just turned out the light after a long and pointless discussion of our reproductive misadventures. Now I lie pressed against Clare, my hand cupping her right breast, and I try to discern if we are in this together or if I have been somehow left behind.

"Clare," I say softly, into her neck.

"Mmm?"

"Let's adopt." I've been thinking about this for weeks, months. It seems like a brilliant escape route: we will have a baby. It will be healthy. Clare will be healthy. We will be happy. It is the obvious answer.

Clare says, "But that would be fake. It would be pretending." She sits up, faces me, and I do the same.

"It would be a real baby, and it would be ours. What's pretend about that?"

"I'm sick of pretending. We pretend all the time. I want to really do this."

"We don't pretend all the time. What are you talking about?"

"We pretend to be normal people, having normal lives! I pretend it's perfectly okay with me that you're always disappearing God knows where. You pretend everything is okay even when you almost get killed and Kendrick doesn't know what the hell to do about it! I pretend I don't care when our babies die. . . ." She is sobbing, bent double, her face covered by her hair, a curtain of silk sheltering her face.

I'm tired of crying. I'm tired of watching Clare cry. I am helpless before her tears, there is nothing I can do that will change anything.

"Clare . . ." I reach out to touch her, to comfort her, to comfort myself, and she pushes me away. I get out of bed, and grab my clothes. I dress in the bathroom. I take Clare's keys from her purse, and I put on my shoes. Clare appears in the hall.

"Where are you going?"

"I don't know."

"Henry—"

I walk out the door, and slam it. It feels good to be outside. I can't remember where the car is. Then I see it across the street. I walk over to it and get in.

My first idea was to sleep in the car, but once I am sitting in it I decide to drive somewhere. The beach: I will drive to the beach. I know that this is a terrible idea. I'm tired, I'm upset, it would be madness to drive . . . but I just feel like driving. The streets are empty. I start the car. It roars to life. It takes me a minute to get out of the parking space. I see Clare's face in the front window. Let her worry. For once I don't care.

I drive down Ainslie to Lincoln, cut over to Western, and drive north. It's been a while since I've been out alone in the middle of the night in the present, and I can't even remember the last time I drove a car when I didn't absolutely have to. This is nice. I speed past Rosehill Cemetery and down the long corridor of car dealerships. I turn on the radio, punch through the presets to WLUW; they're playing Coltrane so I crank up the volume and wind the window down. The noise, the wind, the soothing repetition of stoplights and streetlights make me calm, anesthetize me, and after a while I kind of forget why I'm out here in the first place. At the Evanston border I cut over to Ridge, and then take Dempster to the lake. I park near the lagoon, leave the keys in the ignition, get out, and walk. It's cool and very quiet. I walk out onto the pier and stand at the end of it, looking down the shoreline at Chicago, flickering under its orange and purple sky.

I'm so tired. I'm tired of thinking about death. I'm tired of sex as a means to an end. And I'm frightened of where it all might end. I don't know how much pressure I can take from Clare.

What are these fetuses, these embryos, these clusters of cells we keep making and losing? What is it about them that is important enough to risk Clare's life, to tinge every day with despair? Nature is telling us to give up, Nature is saying: Henry, you're a very fucked-up organism and we don't want to make any more of you. And I am ready to acquiesce.

I have never seen myself in the future with a child. Even though I have spent quite a bit of time with my young self, even though I spend a lot of time with Clare as a child, I don't feel like my life is incomplete without one of my very own. No future self has ever encouraged me to keep plugging away at this. I actually broke down and asked, a few weeks ago; I ran into my self in the stacks at the Newberry, a self from 2004. *Are we ever going to have a baby?* I asked. My self only smiled and shrugged. *You just have to live it, sorry,* he replied, smug and sympathetic. *Oh, Jesus, just* tell *me,* I cried, raising my voice as he raised his hand and disappeared. *Asshole,* I said loudly, and Isabelle stuck her head in the security door and asked me why I was yelling in the stacks and did I realize that they could hear me in the Reading Room?

I just don't see any way out of this. Clare is obsessed. Amit Montague encourages her, tells her stories about miracle babies, gives her vitamin drinks that remind me of *Rosemary's Baby.* Maybe I could go on strike. Sure, that's it; a sex strike. I laugh to myself. The sound is swallowed by the waves gently lapping the pier. Fat chance. I'd be groveling on my knees within days.

My head hurts. I try to ignore it; I know it's because I'm tired. I wonder if I could sleep on the beach without anyone bothering me. It's a beautiful night. Just at this moment I am startled by an intense beam of light that pans across the pier and into my face

and suddenly

I'm in Kimy's kitchen, lying on my back under her kitchen table, surrounded by the legs of chairs. Kimy is seated in one of the chairs and is peering at me under the table. My left hip is pressing against her shoes.

"Hi, buddy," I say weakly. I feel like I'm about to pass out.

"You gonna give me a heart attack one of these days, buddy," Kimy says. She prods me with her foot. "Get out from under there and put on some clothes."

I flop over and back out from under the table on my knees. Then I curl up on the linoleum and rest for a moment, gathering my wits and trying not to gag.

"Henry . . . you okay?" She leans over me. "You want something to eat? You want some soup? I got minestrone soup . . . Coffee?" I shake my head. "You want to lie on the couch? You sick?"

"No, Kimy, it's okay, I'll be okay." I manage to get to my knees and then to my feet. I stagger into the bedroom and open Mr. Kim's closet, which is almost empty except for a few pairs of neatly pressed jeans in various sizes ranging from small boy to grown-up, and several crisp white shirts, my little clothing stash, ready and waiting. Dressed, I walk back to the kitchen, lean over Kimy, and give her a peck on the cheek. "What's the date?"

"September 8, 1998. Where you from?"

"Next July." We sit down at the table. Kimy is doing the *New York Times* crossword puzzle.

"What's going on, next July?"

"It's been a very cool summer, your garden's looking good. All the tech stocks are up. You should buy some Apple stock in January."

She makes a note on a piece of brown paper bag. "Okay. And you? How are you doing? How's Clare? You guys got a baby yet?"

"Actually, I am hungry. How about some of that soup you were mentioning?"

Kimy lumbers out of her chair and opens the fridge. She gets out a saucepan and starts to heat up some soup. "You didn't answer my question."

"No news, Kimy. No baby. Clare and I fight about it just about every waking moment. Please don't start on me."

Kimy has her back to me. She stirs the soup vigorously. Her back radiates chagrin. "I'm not 'starting on you.' I just ask, okay? I just wondering. Sheesh."

We are silent for a few minutes. The noise of the spoon scraping the bottom of the saucepan is getting to me. I think about Clare, looking out the window at me as I drove away.

"Hey, Kimy."

"Hey, Henry."

"How come you and Mr. Kim never had kids?"

Long silence. Then: "We did have child."

"You did?"

She pours the steaming soup into one of the Mickey Mouse bowls I loved when I was a kid. She sits down and runs her hands over her hair, smoothes the white straggling hairs into the little bun at the back. Kimy looks at me. "Eat your soup. I be right back." She gets up and walks out of the kitchen, and I hear her shuffling down the plastic runner that covers the carpeting in the hall. I eat the soup. It's almost gone when she comes back.

"Here. This is Min. She is my baby." The photograph is black and white, blurry. In it a young girl, perhaps five or six years old, stands in front of Mrs. Kim's building, this building, the building I grew up in. She is wearing a Catholic school uniform, smiling, and holding an umbrella. "It's her first day school. She is so happy, so scared."

I study the photo. I am afraid to ask. I look up. Kimy is staring out the window, over the river. "What happened?"

"Oh. She died. Before you were born. She had leukemia, she die."

I suddenly remember. "Did she used to sit out in a rocker in the backyard? In a red dress?"

Mrs. Kim stares at me, startled. "You see her?"

"Yes, I think so. A long time ago. When I was about seven. I was standing on the steps to the river, buck naked, and she told me I better not come into her yard, and I told her it was my yard and she didn't believe me. I couldn't figure it out." I laugh. "She told me her mom was gonna spank me if I didn't go away."

Kimy laughs shakily. "Well, she right, huh?"

"Yeah, she was just off by a few years."

Kimy smiles. "Yeah, Min, she a little firecracker. Her dad call her Miss Big Mouth. He loved her very much." Kimy turns her head, surreptitiously touches her hand to her eyes. I remember Mr. Kim as a taciturn man who spent most of his time sitting in his armchair watching sports on TV.

"What year was Min born?"

"1949. She died 1956. Funny, she would be middle-aged lady with kids now, herself. She would be forty-nine years old. Kids would be maybe in college, maybe a little older." Kimy looks at me, and I look back at her.

"We're trying, Kimy. We're trying everything we can think of."

"I didn't say nothing."

"Uh-huh."

Kimy bats her eyelashes at me like she's Louise Brooks or somebody. "Hey, buddy, I am stuck on this crossword. Nine down, starts with 'K' . . ."

CLARE: I watch the police divers swim out into Lake Michigan. It's an overcast morning, already very hot. I am standing on the Dempster Street pier. There are five fire engines, three ambulances, and seven squad cars standing on Sheridan Road with their lights blinking and flashing. There are seventeen firemen and six paramedics. There are fourteen policemen and one policewoman, a short fat white woman whose head seems squashed by her cap, who keeps saying stupid platitudes intended to comfort me until I want to push her off the pier. I'm holding Henry's clothes. It's five o'clock in the morning. There are twenty-one reporters, some of whom are TV reporters with trucks and microphones and video people, and some of whom are print reporters with photographers. There is an elderly couple hanging around the edges of the action, discreet but curious. I try not to think about the policeman's description of Henry jumping off the end of the pier, caught in the beam of the police car searchlight. I try not to think.

Two new policemen come walking down the pier. They confer with some of the police who are already here, and then one of them, the older one, detaches and walks to me. He has a handlebar mustache, the old-fashioned kind that ends in little points. He introduces himself as Captain Michels, and asks me if I can think of any reason my husband might have wanted to take his own life.

"Well, I really don't think he did, Captain. I mean, he's a very good swimmer, he's probably just swimming to, um, Wilmette or someplace"—I wave my hand vaguely to the north—"and he'll be back any time now. . . ."

The Captain looks dubious. "Does he make a habit of swimming in the middle of the night?"

"He's an insomniac."

"Had you been arguing? Was he upset?"

"No," I lie. "Of course not." I look out over the water. I am sure I don't sound very convincing. "I was sleeping and he must have decided to go swimming and he didn't want to wake me up."

"Did he leave a note?"

"No." As I rack my brains for a more realistic explanation I hear a splash near the shore. Hallelujah. Not a moment too soon. "There he is!" Henry starts to stand up in the water, hears me yell, and ducks down again and swims to the pier.

"Clare. What's going on?"

I kneel on the pier. Henry looks tired, and cold. I speak quietly. "They thought you drowned. One of them saw you throw yourself off the pier. They've been searching for your body for two hours."

Henry looks worried, but also amused. Anything to annoy the police. All the police have clustered around me and they are peering down at Henry silently.

"Are you Henry DeTamble?" asks the captain.

"Yes. Would you mind if I got out of the water?" We all follow Henry to the shore, Henry swimming and the rest of us walking along beside him on the pier. He climbs out of the water and stands dripping on the beach like a wet rat. I hand him his shirt, which he uses to dry himself off. He puts on the rest of his clothes, and stands calmly, waiting for the police to figure out what they want to do with him. I want to kiss him and then kill him. Or vice versa. Henry puts his arm around me. He is clammy and damp. I lean close to him, for his coolness, and he leans into me, for warmth. The police ask him questions. He answers them very politely. These are the Evanston police, with a few Morton Grove and Skokie police who have come by just for the heck of it. If they were Chicago police they would know Henry, and they would arrest him.

"Why didn't you respond when the officer told you to get out of the water?"

"I was wearing earplugs, Captain."

"Earplugs?"

"To keep the water out of my ears." Henry makes a show of digging in his pockets. "I don't know where they got to. I always wear earplugs when I swim."

"Why were you swimming at three o'clock in the morning?"

"I couldn't sleep."

And so on. Henry lies seamlessly, marshaling the facts to support his thesis. In the end, grudgingly, the police issue him a citation, for swimming when the beach is officially closed. It's a $500 fine. When the police let us go, the reporters and photographers and TV cameras converge on us as we walk to the car. No comment. Just out for a swim. Please, we would really rather not have our picture taken. Click. We finally make it to the car, which is sitting all by itself with the keys in it on Sheridan Road. I start the ignition and roll down my window. The police and the reporters and the elderly couple are all standing on the grass, watching us. We are not looking at each other.

"Clare."

"Henry."

"I'm sorry."

"Me too." He looks over at me, touches my hand on the steering wheel. We drive home in silence.

Friday, January 14, 2000 (Clare is 28, Henry is 36)

CLARE: Kendrick leads us through a maze of carpeted, drywalled, acoustical-tiled hallways and into a conference room. There are no windows, only blue carpet and a long, polished black table surrounded by padded swivel chairs. There's a whiteboard and a few Magic Markers, a clock over the door, and a coffee urn with cups, cream, and sugar ready beside it. Kendrick and I sit at the table, but Henry paces around the room. Kendrick takes off his glasses and massages the sides of his small nose with his fingers. The door opens and a young Hispanic man in surgical scrubs wheels a cart into the room. On the cart is a cage covered with a cloth. "Where d'ya want it?" the young man asks, and Kendrick says, "Just leave the whole cart, if you don't mind," and the man shrugs and leaves. Kendrick walks to the door and turns a knob and the lights dim to twilight. I can barely see Henry standing next to the cage. Kendrick walks to him and silently removes the cloth.

The smell of cedar wafts from the cage. I stand and stare into it. I don't see anything but the core of a roll of toilet paper, some food bowls, a water bottle, an exercise wheel, fluffy cedar chips. Kendrick opens the top of the cage and reaches in, scoops out something small and white. Henry and I crowd around, staring at the tiny mouse that sits blinking on Kendrick's palm. Kendrick takes a tiny penlight out of his pocket, turns it on and rapidly flashes it over the mouse. The mouse tenses, and then it is gone.

"Wow," I say. Kendrick places the cloth back over the cage and turns the lights up.

"It's being published in next week's issue of *Nature*," he says, smiling. "It's the lead article."

"Congratulations," Henry says. He glances at the clock. "How long are they usually gone? And where do they go?"

Kendrick gestures at the urn and we both nod. "They tend to be gone about ten minutes or so," he says, pouring three cups of coffee as he speaks and handing us each one. "They go to the Animal Lab in the basement, where they were born. They don't seem to be able to go more than a few minutes either way."

Henry nods. "They'll go longer as they get older."

"Yes, that's been true so far."

"How did you do it?" I ask Kendrick. I still can't quite believe that he *has* done it.

Kendrick blows on his coffee and takes a sip, makes a face. The coffee is bitter, and I add sugar to mine. "Well," he says, "it helped a lot that Celera has been sequencing the whole mouse genome. It told us where to look for the four genes we were targeting. But we could have done it without that.

"We started by cloning your genes and then used enzymes to snip out the damaged portions of DNA. Then we took those pieces and snuck them into mouse embryos at the four-cell-division stage. That was the easy part."

Henry raises his eyebrows. "Sure, of course. Clare and I do that all the time in our kitchen. So what was the hard part?" He sits on the table and sets his coffee beside him. In the cage I can hear the squeaking of the exercise wheel.

Kendrick glances at me. "The hard part was getting the dams, the mother mice, to carry the altered mice to term. They kept dying, hemorrhaging to death."

Henry looks very alarmed. "The mothers died?"

Kendrick nods. "The mothers died, and the babies died. We couldn't figure it out, so we started watching them around the clock, and then we saw what was going on. The embryos were traveling out of their dam's womb, and then in again, and the mothers bled to death internally. Or they would just abort the fetus at the ten-day mark. It was very frustrating."

Henry and I exchange looks and then look away. "We can relate to that," I tell Kendrick.

"Ye-ess," he says. "But we solved the problem."

"How?" Henry asks.

"We decided that it might be an immune reaction. Something about the fetal mice was so foreign that the dams' immune systems were trying to fight them as though they were a virus or something. So we suppressed the dams' immune systems, and then it all worked like magic."

My heart is beating in my ears. *Like magic.*

Kendrick suddenly stoops and grabs for something on the floor. "Gotcha," he says, displaying the mouse in his cupped hands.

"Bravo!" Henry says. "What's next?"

"Gene therapy," Kendrick tells him. "Drugs." He shrugs. "Even though we can *make* it happen, we still don't know why it happens. Or how it happens. So we try to understand that." He offers Henry the mouse. Henry cups his hands and Kendrick tips the mouse into them. Henry inspects it curiously.

"It has a tattoo," he says.

"It's the only way we can keep track of them," Kendrick tells him. "They drive the Animal Lab technicians nuts, they're always escaping."

Henry laughs. "That's our Darwinian advantage," he says. "We escape." He strokes the mouse, and it shits on his palm.

"Zero tolerance for stress," says Kendrick, and puts the mouse back in its cage, where it flees into the toilet-paper core.

As soon as we get home I am on the phone to Dr. Montague, babbling about immuno-suppressants and internal bleeding. She listens carefully and then tells me to come in next week, and in the meantime she will do some research. I put down the phone and Henry regards me nervously over the *Times* business section. "It's worth a try," I tell him.

"Lots of dead mouse moms before they figured it out," Henry says.

"But it worked! Kendrick made it work!"

Henry just says, "Yeah," and goes back to reading. I open my mouth and then change my mind and walk out to the studio, too excited to argue. *It worked like magic. Like magic.*

FIVE

••••••••••••••••••••••••••••••••

Thursday, May 11, 2000 (Henry is 39, Clare is 28)

HENRY: I'm walking down Clark Street in late spring, 2000. There's nothing too remarkable about this. It's a lovely warm evening in Andersonville, and all the fashionable youth are sitting at little tables drinking fancy cold coffee at Kopi's, or sitting at medium-sized tables eating couscous at Reza's, or just strolling, ignoring the Swedish knickknacks stores and exclaiming over each other's dogs. I should be at work, in 2002, but oh, well. Matt will have to cover for my afternoon Show and Tell, I guess. I make a mental note to take him out to dinner.

As I idle along, I unexpectedly see Clare across the street. She is standing in front of George's, the vintage clothing store, looking at a display of baby clothes. Even her back is wistful, even her shoulders sigh with longing. As I watch her, she leans her forehead against the shop window and stands there, dejected. I cross the street, dodging a UPS van and a Volvo, and stand behind her. Clare looks up, startled, and sees my reflection in the glass.

"Oh, it's you," she says, and turns. "I thought you were at the movies with Gomez." Clare seems a little defensive, a little guilty, as though I have caught her doing something illicit.

"I probably am. I'm supposed to be at work, actually. In 2002."

Clare smiles. She looks tired, and I do the dates in my head and realize that our fifth miscarriage was three weeks ago. I hesitate, and then I put my arms around her, and to my relief she relaxes against me, leans her head on my shoulder.

"How are you?" I ask.

"Terrible," she says softly. "Tired." I remember. She stayed in bed for weeks. "Henry, I quit." She watches me, trying to gauge my reaction to this, weighing her intention against my knowledge. "I give up. It isn't going to happen."

Is there anything to stop me from giving her what she needs? I can't think of a single reason not to tell her. I stand and rack my brain for anything that would preclude Clare knowing. All I remember is her certainty, which I am about to create.

"Persevere, Clare."

"What?"

"Hang in there. In my present we have a baby."

Clare closes her eyes, whispers, "Thank you." I don't know if she's talking to me or to God. It doesn't matter. "Thank you," she says, again, looking at me, talking to me, and I feel as though I am an angel in some demented version of the Annunciation. I lean over and kiss her; I can feel resolve, joy, purpose coursing through Clare. I remember the tiny head full of black hair crowning between Clare's legs and I marvel at how this moment creates that miracle, and vice versa. Thank you. Thank you.

"Did you know?" Clare asks me.

"No." She looks disappointed. "Not only did I not know, I did everything I could think of to prevent you from getting pregnant again."

"Great." Clare laughs. "So whatever happens, I just have to be quiet and let it rip?"

"Yep."

Clare grins at me, and I grin back. Let it rip.

· ·

Saturday, June 3, 2000 (Clare is 29, Henry is 36)

CLARE: I'm sitting at the kitchen table idly flipping through the *Chicago Tribune* and watching Henry unpack the groceries. The brown paper bags stand evenly lined up on the counter and Henry produces ketchup, chicken, gouda cheese from them like a magician. I keep waiting for the rabbit and the silk scarves. Instead it's mushrooms, black beans, fettucine, lettuce, a pineapple, skim milk, coffee, radishes, turnips, a rutabaga, oatmeal, butter, cottage cheese, rye bread, mayonnaise, eggs, razors, deodorant, Granny Smith apples, half-and-half, bagels, shrimp, cream cheese, Frosted Mini-Wheats, marinara sauce, frozen orange juice, carrots, condoms, sweet potatoes . . . condoms? I get up and walk to the counter, pick up the blue box and shake it at Henry.

"What, are you having an affair?"

He looks up at me defiantly as he rummages in the freezer. "No, actually, I had an epiphany. I was standing in the toothpaste aisle when it happened. Want to hear it?"

"No."

Henry stands up and turns to me. His expression is like a sigh. "Well, here it is anyway: we can't keep trying to have a baby."

Traitor. "We agreed . . ."

". . . to keep trying. I think five miscarriages is enough. I think we have tried."

"*No.* I mean—why not, try again?" I try to keep the pleading out of my voice, to keep the anger that rises up in my throat from spilling into my words.

Henry walks around the counter, stands in front of me, but doesn't touch me, knows that he can't touch me. "Clare. The next time you miscarry it's going to kill you, and I am not going to keep doing something that's going to end up with you dead. Five pregnancies . . . I know you want to try again, but I can't. I can't take it anymore, Clare. I'm sorry."

I walk out the back door and stand in the sun, by the raspberry bushes. Our children, dead and wrapped in silky gampi tissue paper, cradled in tiny wooden boxes, are in shade now, in the late afternoon, by the roses. I feel the heat of the sun on my skin and shiver for them, deep in the garden, cool on this mild June day. *Help,* I say in my head, to our future child. *He doesn't know, so I can't tell him. Come soon.*

Friday, June 9, 2000/November 19, 1986 (Henry is 36, Clare is 15)

HENRY: It's 8:45 a.m. on a Friday morning and I'm sitting in the waiting room of a certain Dr. Robert Gonsalez. Clare doesn't know I'm here. I've decided to get a vasectomy.

Dr. Gonsalez's office is on Sheridan Road, near Diversey, in a posh medical center just up the way from the Lincoln Park Conservatory. This waiting room is decorated in browns and hunter green, lots of paneling and framed prints of Derby winners from the

1880s. Very manly. I feel as though I should be wearing a smoking jacket and clenching a large cigar between my jaws. I need a drink.

The nice woman at Planned Parenthood assured me in her soothing, practiced voice that this would hardly hurt a bit. There are five other guys sitting here with me. I wonder if they've got the clap, or maybe their prostates are acting up. Maybe some of them are like me, sitting here waiting to end their careers as potential dads. I feel a certain solidarity with these unknown men, all of us sitting here together in this brown wooden leather room on this gray morning waiting to walk into the examining room and take off our pants. There's a very old man who sits leaning forward with his hands clasped around his cane, his eyes closed behind thick glasses that magnify his eyelids. He's probably not here to get snipped. The teenage boy who sits leafing through an ancient copy of *Esquire* is feigning indifference. I close my eyes and imagine that I am in a bar and the bartender has her back to me now as she mixes a good single-malt Scotch with just a small amount of tepid water. Perhaps it's an English pub. Yes, that would account for the decor. The man on my left coughs, a deep lung-shaking sort of cough, and when I open my eyes I'm still sitting in a doctor's waiting room. I sneak a look at the watch of the guy on my right. He's got one of those immense sports watches that you can use to time sprints or call the mothership. It's 9:58. My appointment is in two minutes. The doctor seems to be running late, though. The receptionist calls, "Mr. Liston," and the teenager stands up abruptly and walks through the heavy paneled door into the office. The rest of us look at each other, furtively, as though we are on the subway and someone is trying to sell us *Streetwise*.

I am rigid with tension and I remind myself that this is a necessary and good thing that I am about to do. I am not a traitor. I am not a traitor. I am saving Clare from horror and pain. She will never know. It will not hurt. Maybe it will hurt a little. Someday I will tell her and she will realize I had to do it. We tried. I have no choice. I am not a traitor. Even if it hurts it will be worth it. I am doing it because I love her. I think of Clare sitting on our bed, covered in blood, weeping, and I feel sick.

"Mr. DeTamble." I rise, and now I really feel sick. My knees buckle. My head swims, and I'm bent over, retching, I'm on my hands and knees, the ground is cold and covered with the stubble of dead grass. There's nothing in my stomach, I'm spitting up mucus. It's cold. I look up. I'm in the clearing, in the Meadow. The trees are bare, the sky is flat clouds with early darkness approaching. I'm alone.

I get up and find the clothes box. Soon I am wearing a Gang of Four T-shirt and a sweater and jeans, heavy socks and black military boots, a black wool overcoat and large baby blue mittens. Something has chewed its way into the box and made a nest. The clothes indicate the mid-eighties. Clare is about fifteen or sixteen. I wonder whether to hang around and wait for her or just go. I don't know if I can face Clare's youthful exuberance right now. I turn and walk toward the orchard.

It looks like late November. The Meadow is brown, and makes a rattling noise in the wind. Crows are fighting over windfall apples at the edge of the orchard. Just as I reach them I hear someone panting, running behind me. I turn, and it's Clare.

"Henry—" she's out of breath, she sounds like she has a cold. I let her stand, rasping, for a minute. I can't talk to her. She stands, breathing, her breath steaming in front of her in white clouds, her hair vivid red in the gray and brown, her skin pink and pale.

I turn and walk into the orchard.

"Henry—" Clare follows me, catches my arm. "What? What did I do? Why won't you talk to me?"

THE TIME TRAVELER'S WIFE

Oh God. "I tried to do something for you, something important, and it didn't work. I got nervous, and ended up here."

"What was it?"

"I can't tell you. I wasn't even going to tell you about it in the present. You wouldn't like it."

"Then why did you want to do it?" Clare shivers in the wind.

"It was the only way. I couldn't get you to listen to me. I thought we could stop fighting if I did it." I sigh. I will try again, and, if necessary, again.

"Why are we fighting?" Clare is looking up at me, tense and anxious. Her nose is running.

"Have you got a cold?"

"Yes. What are we fighting about?"

"It all began when the wife of your ambassador slapped the mistress of my prime minister at a *soirée* being held at the embassy. This affected the tariff on oatmeal, which led to high unemployment and rioting—"

"*Henry.*"

"Yes?"

"Just once, *just once,* would you stop making fun of me and tell me something I am asking you?"

"I can't."

Without apparent premeditation, Clare slaps me, hard. I step back, surprised, glad.

"Hit me again."

She is confused, shakes her head. "Please, Clare."

"No. Why do you want me to hit you? I wanted to *hurt* you."

"I want you to hurt me. Please." I hang my head.

"*What is the matter with you?*"

"Everything is terrible and I can't seem to feel it."

"*What* is terrible? What is going on?"

"Don't ask me." Clare comes up, very close to me, and takes my hand. She pulls off the ridiculous blue mitten, brings my palm to her mouth, and bites. The pain is excruciating. She stops, and I look at my hand. Blood comes slowly, in tiny drops, around the bite mark. I will probably get blood poisoning, but at the moment I don't care.

"Tell me." Her face is inches from mine. I kiss her, very roughly. She is resistant. I release her, and she turns her back on me.

"That wasn't very nice," she says in a small voice.

What is wrong with me? Clare, at fifteen, is not the same person who's been torturing me for months, refusing to give up on having a baby, risking death and despair, turning lovemaking into a battle-field strewn with the corpses of children. I put my hands on her shoulders. "I'm sorry. I'm very sorry, Clare, it's not you. Please."

She turns. She's crying, and she's a mess. Miraculously, there's a Kleenex in my coat pocket. I dab at her face, and she takes the tissue from me and blows her nose.

"You never kissed me before." Oh, no. My face must be funny, because Clare laughs. I can't believe it. What an idiot I am.

"Oh, Clare. Just—forget that, okay? Just erase it. It never happened. Come here. Take two, yes? Clare?"

She tentatively steps toward me. I put my arms around her, look at her. Her eyes are rimmed red, her nose is swollen, and she definitely has a bad cold. I place my hands over her ears and tip her head back, and kiss her, and try to put my heart into hers, for safe-keeping, in case I lose it again.

Friday, June 9, 2000 (Clare is 29, Henry is 36)

CLARE: Henry has been terribly quiet, distracted, and pensive all evening. All through dinner he seemed to be mentally searching imaginary stacks for a book he'd read in 1942 or something. Plus his right hand is all bandaged up. After dinner he went into the bedroom and lay face down on the bed with his head hanging over the foot of the bed and his feet on my pillow. I went to the studio and scrubbed molds and deckles and drank my coffee, but I wasn't enjoying myself because I couldn't figure out what Henry's problem was. Finally I go back into the house. He is still lying in the same position. In the dark.

I lie down on the floor. My back makes loud cracking sounds as I stretch out.

"Clare?"

"Mmmm?"

"Do you remember the first time I kissed you?"

"Vividly."

"I'm sorry." Henry rolls over.

I'm burning up with curiosity. "What were you so upset about? You were trying to do something, and it didn't work, and you said I wouldn't like it. What was it?"

"How do you manage to remember all that?"

"I am the original elephant child. Are you going to tell me now?"

"No."

"If I guess will you tell me if I'm right?"

"Probably not."

"Why not?"

"Because I am exhausted, and I don't want to fight tonight."

I don't want to fight either. I like lying here on the floor. It's kind of cold but very solid. "You went to get a vasectomy."

Henry is silent. He is so silent for so long that I want to put a mirror in front of his mouth to see if he's breathing. Finally: "How did you know?"

"I didn't exactly know. I was afraid that might be it. And I saw the note you made for the appointment with the doctor this morning."

"I *burned* that note."

"I saw the impression on the sheet below the one you wrote on."

Henry groans. "Okay, Sherlock. You got me."

We continue to lie peaceably in the dark. "Go ahead."

"What?"

"Get a vasectomy. If you have to."

Henry rolls over again and looks at me. All I see is his dark head against the dark ceiling. "You're not yelling at me."

"No. I can't do this anymore, either. I give up. You win, we'll stop trying to have a baby."

"I wouldn't exactly describe that as winning. It just seems— necessary."

"Whatever."

Henry climbs off the bed and sits on the floor with me. "Thank you."

"You're welcome." He kisses me. I imagine the bleak November day in 1986 that Henry has just come from, the wind, the warmth of his body in the cold orchard. Soon, for the first time in many months, we are making love without worrying about the consequences. Henry has caught the cold I had sixteen years ago. Four weeks later, Henry has had his vasectomy and I discover that I am pregnant for the sixth time.

BABY DREAMS

. . . .

September 2000 (Clare is 29)

CLARE: I dream I'm walking down stairs into my grandmother Abshire's basement. The long soot mark from the time the crow flew down the chimney is still there on the left-hand wall; the steps are dusty and the handrail leaves gray marks on my hand as I steady myself; I descend and walk into the room that always scared me when I was little. In this room are deep shelves with rows and rows of canned goods, tomatoes and pickles, corn relish and beets. They look embalmed. In one of the jars is the small fetus of a duck. I carefully open the jar and pour the duckling and the fluid into my hand. It gasps and retches. "Why did you leave me?" it asks, when it can speak. "I've been waiting for you."

I dream that my mother and I are walking together down a quiet residential street in South Haven. I am carrying a baby. As we walk, the baby becomes heavier and heavier, until I can barely lift it. I turn to Mama and tell her that I can't carry this baby any farther; she takes it from me easily and we continue on. We come to a house and walk down the small walkway to its backyard. In the yard there are two screens and a slide projector. People are seated in lawn chairs, watching slides of trees. Half of a tree is on each screen. One half is summer and the other winter; they are the same tree, different seasons. The baby laughs and cries out in delight.

I dream I am standing on the Sedgwick El platform, waiting for the Brown Line train. I am carrying two shopping bags, which upon inspection turn out to contain boxes of saltine crackers and a very small, stillborn baby with red hair, wrapped in Saran Wrap.

I dream I am at home, in my old room. It's late at night, the room is dimly illuminated by the aquarium light. I suddenly realize, with horror, that there is a small animal swimming round and round the tank; I hastily remove the lid and net the animal, which turns out to be a gerbil with gills. "I'm so sorry," I say. "I forgot about you." The gerbil just stares at me reproachfully.

I dream I am walking up stairs in Meadowlark House. All the furniture is gone, the rooms are empty, dust floats in the sunlight which makes golden pools on the polished oak floors. I walk down the long hall, glancing in the bedrooms, and come to my room, in which a small wooden cradle sits alone. There is no sound. I am afraid to look into the cradle. In Mama's room white sheets are spread over the floor. At my feet is a tiny drop of blood, which touches the tip of a sheet and spreads as I watch until the entire floor is covered in blood.

Saturday, September 23, 2000 (Clare is 29, Henry is 37)

CLARE: I'm living under water. Everything seems slow and far away. I know there's a world up there, a sunlit quick world where time runs like dry sand through an hourglass, but down here, where I am, air and sound and time and feeling are thick and dense. I'm in a diving bell with this baby, just the two of us trying to survive in this alien atmosphere, but I feel very alone. *Hello? Are you there?* No answer comes back. *He's dead,* I tell Amit. *No,* she says, smiling anxiously, *no, Clare, see, there's his heartbeat.* I can't explain. Henry hovers around trying to feed me, massage me, cheer me up, until I snap at him. I walk across the yard, into my studio. It's like a museum, a mausoleum, so still, nothing living or breathing, no ideas here, just things, things that stare at me accusingly. *I'm sorry,* I tell my blank, empty drawing table, my dry vats and molds, the half-made sculptures. *Stillborn,* I think, looking at the blue iris paper-wrapped armature that seemed so hopeful in June. My hands are clean and soft and pink. I hate them. I hate this emptiness. I hate this baby. *No.* No, I don't hate him. I just can't find him.

I sit at my drawing board with a pencil in my hand and a sheet of white paper before me. Nothing comes. I close my eyes and all I can think of is red. So I get a tube of watercolor, cadmium red dark, and I get a big mop of a brush, and I fill a jar with water, and I begin to cover the paper with red. It glistens. The paper is limp with moisture, and darkens as it dries. I watch it drying. It smells of gum arabic. In the center of the paper, very small, in black ink, I draw a heart, not a silly Valentine but an anatomically correct heart, tiny, doll-like, and then veins, delicate road maps of veins, that reach all the way to the edges of the paper, that hold the small heart enmeshed like a fly in a spiderweb. *See, there's his heartbeat.*

It has become evening. I empty the water jar and wash the brush. I lock the studio door, cross the yard, and let myself in the back door. Henry is making spaghetti sauce. He looks up as I come in.

"Better?" he asks.

"Better," I reassure him, and myself.

Wednesday, September 27, 2000 (Clare is 29)

CLARE: It's lying on the bed. There's some blood, but not so much. It's lying on its back, trying to breathe, its tiny ribcage quivering, but it's too soon, it's convulsing, and blood is gushing from the cord in time with the beating of its heart. I kneel beside the bed and pick it up, pick him up, my tiny boy, jerking like a small freshly caught fish, drowning in air. I hold him, so gently, but he doesn't know I'm here, holding him, he is slippery and his skin is almost imaginary, his eyes are closed and I think wildly of mouth-to-mouth resuscitation, of 911 and Henry, *oh, don't go before Henry can see you!* but his breath is bubbling with fluid, small sea creature breathing water and then he opens his mouth wide and I can see right through him and my hands are empty and he's gone, gone.

I don't know how long, time passes. I am kneeling. Kneeling, I pray. *Dear God. Dear God. Dear God.* The baby stirs in my womb. *Hush. Hide.*

I wake up in the hospital. Henry is there. The baby is dead.

SEVEN

....

Thursday, December 28, 2000 (Henry is 33, and 37, Clare is 29)

HENRY: I am standing in our bedroom, in the future. It's night, but moonlight gives the room a surreal, monochromatic distinctness. My ears are ringing, as they often do, in the future. I look down on Clare and myself, sleeping. It feels like death. I am sleeping tightly balled up, knees to chest, wound up in blankets, mouth slightly open. I want to touch me. I want to hold me in my arms, look into my eyes. But it won't happen that way; I stand for long minutes staring intently at my sleeping future self. Eventually I walk softly to Clare's side of the bed, kneel. It feels immensely like the present. I will myself to forget the other body in the bed, to concentrate on Clare.

She stirs, her eyes open. She isn't sure where we are. Neither am I.

I am overwhelmed by desire, by a longing to be connected to Clare as strongly as possible, to be here, now. I kiss her very lightly, lingering, thinking about nothing. She is drunk with sleep, moves her hand to my face and wakes more as she feels the solidity of me. Now she is present; she runs her hand down my arm, a caress. I carefully peel the sheet from her, so as not to disturb the other me, of whom Clare is still not aware. I wonder if this other self is somehow impervious to waking, but decide not to find out. I am lying on top of Clare, covering her completely with my body. I wish I could stop her from turning her head, but she will turn her head any minute now. As I penetrate Clare she looks at me and I think I don't exist and a second later she turns her head and sees me. She cries out, not loudly, and looks back at me, above her, in her. Then she remembers, accepts it, *this is pretty strange but it's okay,* and in this moment I love her more than life.

Monday, February 12, 2001 (Henry is 37, Clare is 29)

HENRY: Clare has been in a strange mood all week. She's distracted. It is as though something only Clare can hear has riveted her attention, as though she's receiving revelations from God through her fillings, or trying to decode satellite transmissions of Russian cryptology in her head. When I ask her about it, she just smiles and shrugs. This is so unlike Clare that I am alarmed, and immediately desist.

I come home from work one evening and I can see just by looking at Clare that something awful has happened. Her expression is scared and pleading. She comes close to me and stops, and doesn't say anything. Someone has died, I think. Who has died? Dad? Kimy? Philip?

"Say something," I ask. "What's happened?"

"I'm pregnant."

"How can you—" Even as I say it I know exactly how. "Never mind, I remember." For me, that night was years ago, but for Clare it is only weeks in the past. I was coming from 1996, when we were trying desperately to conceive, and Clare was barely awake. I curse myself for a careless fool. Clare is waiting for me to say something. I force myself to smile.

"Big surprise."

"Yeah." She looks a little teary. I take her into my arms, and she holds me tightly.

"Scared?" I murmur into Clare's hair.

"Uh-huh."

"You were never scared, before."

"I was crazy, before. Now I know . . ."

"What it is."

"What can happen." We stand and think about what can happen.

I hesitate. "We could . . ." I let it hang.

"No. I can't." It's true. Clare can't. Once a Catholic, always a Catholic.

I say, "Maybe it will be good. A happy accident."

Clare smiles, and I realize that she wants this, that she actually hopes that seven will be our lucky number. My throat contracts, and I have to turn away.

Tuesday, February 20, 2001 (Clare is 29, Henry is 37)

CLARE: The clock radio clicks on at 7:46 a.m. and National Public Radio sadly tells me that there has been a plane crash somewhere and eighty-six people are dead. I'm pretty sure I am one of them. Henry's side of the bed is empty. I close my eyes and I am in a little berth in a cabin on an oceanliner, pitching over rough seas. I sigh and gingerly creep out of bed and into the bathroom. I'm still throwing up ten minutes later when Henry sticks his head in the door and asks me if I'm okay.

"Great. Never better."

He perches on the edge of the tub. I would just as soon not have an audience for this. "Should I be worried? You never threw up at all before."

"Amit says this is good; I'm supposed to throw up." It's something about my body recognizing the baby as part of me, instead of a foreign body. Amit has been giving me this drug they give people who have organ transplants.

"Maybe I should bank some more blood for you today." Henry and I are both type O. I nod, and throw up. We are avid blood bankers; he has needed transfusions twice, and I have had three, one of them requiring a huge amount. I sit for a minute and then stagger to my feet. Henry steadies me. I wipe my mouth and brush my teeth. Henry goes downstairs to make breakfast. I suddenly have an overpowering desire for oatmeal.

"Oatmeal!" I yell down the stairs.

"Okay!"

I begin to brush out my hair. My reflection in the mirror shows me pink and puffy. I thought pregnant women were supposed to glow. I am not glowing. Oh, well. I'm still pregnant, and that's all that counts.

Thursday, April 19, 2001 (Henry is 37, Clare is 29)

HENRY: We are at Amit Montague's office for the ultrasound. Clare and I have been both eager and reluctant to have an ultrasound. We have refused amniocentesis because we are sure we will lose the baby if we poke a huge long needle at it. Clare is eighteen weeks pregnant. Halfway there; if we could fold time in half right now like a Rorschach test, this would be the crease down the middle. We live in a state of holding breath, afraid to exhale for fear of breathing out the baby too soon.

We sit in the waiting room with other expectant couples and mothers with strollers and toddlers who run around bumping into things. Dr. Montague's office always depresses me, because we have spent so much time here being anxious and hearing bad news. But today is different. Today everything will be okay.

A nurse calls our names. We repair to an examining room. Clare gets undressed, and gets on the table, and is greased and scanned. The technician watches the monitor. Amit Montague, who is tall and regal and French Moroccan, watches the monitor. Clare and I hold hands. We watch the monitor, too. Slowly the image builds itself, bit by bit.

On the screen is a weather map of the world. Or a galaxy, a swirl of stars. Or a baby.

"Bien joué, une fille," Dr. Montague says. "She is sucking her thumb. She is very pretty. And very big."

Clare and I exhale. On the screen a pretty galaxy is sucking her thumb. As we watch she takes her hand away from her mouth. Dr. Montague says, "She smiles." And so do we.

Monday, August 20, 2001 (Clare is 30, Henry is 38)

CLARE: The baby is due in two weeks and we still haven't settled on a name for her. In fact, we've barely discussed it; we've been avoiding the whole subject superstitiously, as though naming the baby will cause the Furies to notice her and torment her. Finally Henry brings home a book called *Dictionary of Given Names.*

We are in bed. It's only 8:30 p.m. and I'm wiped out. I lie on my side, my belly a peninsula, facing Henry, who lies on his side facing me with his head propped on his arm, the book on the bed between us. We look at each other, smile nervously.

"Any thoughts?" he says, leafing through the book.

"Jane," I reply.

He makes a face. "Jane?"

"I used to name all my dolls and stuffed animals Jane. Every one of them."

Henry looks it up. "It means *'Gift of God.'*"

"That works for me."

"Let's have something a little unusual. How about Irette? Or Jodotha?" He riffs through the pages. "Here's a good one: Loololu-luah. It's Arabic for pearl."

"How about Pearl?" I picture the baby as a smooth iridescent white ball.

Henry runs his finger downs the columns. "Okay: *'(Latin) A probable variant of* perula, *in reference to the most valued form of this product of disease.'*"

"Ugh. What's wrong with this book?" I take it from Henry and, for kicks, look up *"'Henry (Teutonic) Ruler of the home: chief of the dwelling.'"*

He laughs. "Look up Clare."

"It's just another form of *'Clara (Latin) Illustrious, bright.'*"

"That's good," he says.

I flip through the book randomly. "Philomele?"

"I like that," says Henry. "But what of the horrible nickname issue? Philly? Mel?"

"Pyrene (Greek) Red-haired."

"But what if she isn't?" Henry reaches over the book and picks up a handful of my hair, and puts the ends in his mouth. I pull it away from him and push all my hair behind me.

"I thought we knew everything there was to know about this kid. Surely Kendrick tested for red hair?" I say.

Henry retrieves the book from me. "Yseult? Zoe? I like Zoe. Zoe has possibilities."

"What's it mean?"

"*Life.*"

"Yeah, that's very good. Bookmark that."

"Eliza," Henry offers.

"Elizabeth."

Henry looks at me, hesitates. "Annette."

"Lucy."

"No," Henry says firmly.

"No," I agree.

"What we need," Henry says, "is a fresh start. A blank slate. Let's call her Tabula Rasa."

"Let's call her Titanium White."

"Blanche, Blanca, Bianca . . ."

"Alba," I say.

"As in Duchess of?"

"Alba DeTamble." It rolls around in my mouth as I say it.

"That's nice, all the little iambs, tripping along . . ." He's flipping through the book. "'*Alba (Latin) White. (Provençal) Dawn of day.*' Hmm." He laboriously clambers off the bed. I can hear him rummaging around in the living room; he returns after a few minutes with Volume I of the OED, the big Random House dictionary, and my decrepit old *Encyclopedia Americana* Book I, A to Annuals. "'A dawn song of the Provençal poets . . . in honor of their mistresses. *Réveillés, à l'aurore, par le cri du guetteur, deux amants qui viennent de passer la nuit ensemble se séparent en maudissant le jour qui vient trop tôt; tel est le thème, non moins invariable que celui de la pastourelle, d'un genre dont le nom est emprunté au mot alba, qui figure parfois au début de la pièce. Et régulièrement à la fin de chaque couplet, où il forme refrain.*' How sad. Let's try Random House. This is better. 'A white city on a hill. A fortress.'" He jettisons Random House off the bed and opens the encyclopedia. "Æsop, Age of Reason, Alaska . . .

okay, here, Alba." He scans the entry. "A bunch of now wiped-out towns in ancient Italy. And the Duke of Alba."

I sigh and turn onto my back. The baby stirs. She must have been sleeping. Henry is back to perusing the OED. "Amour. Amourous. Armadillo. Bazooms. Goodness, the things they print these days in works of reference." He slides his hand under my nightgown, runs it slowly over my taut stomach. The baby kicks, hard, just where his hand is, and he starts, and looks at me, amazed. His hands are roaming, finding their way across familiar and unfamiliar terrain. "How many DeTambles can you fit in there?"

"Oh, there's always room for one more."

"Alba," he says, softly.

"A white city. An impregnable fortress on a white hill."

"She'll like it." Henry is pulling my underwear down my legs and over my ankles. He tosses it off the bed and looks at me.

"Careful . . . ," I tell him.

"Very careful," he agrees, as he strips off his clothes.

I feel immense, like a continent in a sea of pillows and blankets. Henry bends over me from behind, moves over me, an explorer mapping my skin with his tongue. "Slowly, slowly . . ." I am afraid.

"A song sung by the troubadours at dawn . . . ," he is whispering to me as he enters me.

". . . To their mistresses," I reply. My eyes are closed and I hear Henry as though from the next room:

"Just . . . so." And then: "Yes. *Yes.*"

Alba, an Introduction

....

Wednesday, November 16, 2011 (Henry is 38, Clare is 40)

HENRY: I'm in the Surrealist Galleries at the Art Institute of Chicago, in the future. I am not perfectly dressed; the best I could do was a long black winter coat from the coat check room and pants from a guard's locker. I did manage to find shoes, which are always the most difficult thing to get. So I figure I'll lift a wallet, buy a T-shirt in the museum store, have lunch, see some art, and then launch myself out of the building and into the world of shops and hotel rooms. I have no idea where I am in time. Not too far out there; the clothing and haircuts are not too different from 2001. I'm simultaneously excited about this little sojourn and disturbed, because in my present Clare is about to have Alba at any moment, and I absolutely want to be there, but on the other hand this is an un-usually high-quality slice of forward time travel. I feel strong and really present, really good. So I stand quietly in a dark room full of spot-lit Joseph Cornell boxes, watching a school group following a docent, carrying little stools which they obediently sit on when she tells them to park themselves.

I observe the group. The docent is the usual: a well-groomed woman in her fifties with impossibly blond hair and taut face. The teacher, a good-humored young woman wearing light blue lipstick, stands at the back of the flock of students, ready to contain any who get boisterous. It's the students who interest me. They are all about ten or so, fifth grade, I guess that would be. It's a Catholic school, so they all wear identical clothes, green plaid for the girls and navy blue for the boys. They are attentive and polite, but not excited. Too bad; I would think Cornell would be perfect for kids. The docent seems to think they are younger than they are; she talks to them as though they are little children. There's a girl in the back row who seems more engaged than the rest. I can't see her face. She has long curly black hair and a peacock-blue dress, which sets her apart from her peers. Every time the docent asks a question, this girl's hand goes up, but the docent never calls on her. I can see that the girl is getting fed up.

The docent is talking about Cornell's *Aviary* boxes. Each box is bleak, and many have white, painted interiors with perches and the kind of holes that a birdhouse would have, and some have pictures of birds. They are the starkest and most austere of his pieces, without the whimsy of the *Soap Bubble Sets* or the romance of the *Hotel* boxes.

"Why do you think Mr. Cornell made these boxes?" The docent brightly scans the children for a reply, ignoring the peacock-blue girl, who is waving her hand like she has Saint Vitus' Dance. A boy in the front says shyly that the artist must have liked birds. This is too much for the girl. She stands up with her hand in the air. The docent reluctantly says, "Yes?"

"He made the boxes because he was lonely. He didn't have anyone to love, and he made the boxes so he could love them, and so people would know that he existed, and because birds are free and the boxes are hiding places for the birds so they will feel safe, and he wanted to be free and be safe. The boxes are for him so he can be a bird." The girl sits down.

I am blown away by her answer. This is a ten-year-old who can empathize with Joseph Cornell. Neither the docent nor the class exactly knows what to make of this, but the teacher, who is obviously used to her, says, "Thank you, Alba, that's very perceptive." She turns and smiles gratefully at the teacher, and I see her face, and I am looking at my daughter. I have been standing in the next gallery, and I take a few steps forward, to look at her, to see her, and she sees me, and her face lights up, and she jumps up, knocks over her little folding chair, and almost before I know it I am holding Alba in my arms, holding her tight, kneeling before her with my arms around her as she says "Daddy," over and over.

Everyone is gaping at us. The teacher hurries over.

She says, "Alba, who is this? Sir, who are you?"

"I'm Henry DeTamble, Alba's father."

"He's my daddy!"

The teacher is almost wringing her hands. "Sir, Alba's father is dead."

I am speechless. But Alba, daughter mine, has a grip on the situation.

"He's dead," she tells her teacher. "But he's not *continuously* dead."

I find my wits. "It's kind of hard to explain—"

"He's a CDP," says Alba. "Like me." This seems to make perfect sense to the teacher although it means nothing to me. The teacher is a bit pale under her makeup but she looks sympathetic. Alba squeezes my hand. Say something, is what she means.

"Ah, Ms.—"

"Cooper."

"Ms. Cooper, is there any possibility that Alba and I could have a few minutes, here, to talk? We don't see each other much."

"Well . . . I just . . . we're on a field trip . . . the group . . . I can't let you just take the child away from the group, and I don't really know that you *are* Mr. DeTamble, you see . . ."

"Let's call Mama," says Alba. She runs over to her school bag and whips out a cell phone. She presses a key and I hear the phone ringing and I'm rapidly realizing that there are possibilities here: someone picks up on the other end, and Alba says "Mama? . . . I'm at the Art Institute . . . No, I'm okay . . . Mama, Daddy's here! Tell Mrs. Cooper it's really Daddy, okay? . . . Yeah, 'k, bye!" She hands me the phone. I hesitate, pull my head together.

"Clare?" There's a sharp intake of breath. "Clare?"

"*Henry!* Oh, God, I can't believe it! Come home!"

"I'll try . . ."

"When are you from?"

"2001. Just before Alba was born." I smile at Alba. She is leaning against me, holding my hand.

"Maybe I should come down there?"

"That would be faster. Listen, could you tell this teacher that I'm really me?"

"Sure—where will you be?"

"At the lions. Come as fast as you can, Clare. It won't be much longer."

"I love you."

"I love you, Clare." I hesitate, and then hand the phone to Mrs. Cooper. She and Clare have a short conversation, in which Clare somehow convinces her to let me take Alba to the museum entrance, where Clare will meet us. I thank Mrs. Cooper, who has been pretty graceful in a weird situation, and Alba and I walk hand in hand out of the Morton Wing, down the spiral staircase and into Chinese ceramics. My mind is racing. What to ask first?

Alba says, "Thank you for the videos. Mama gave them to me for my birthday." What videos? "I can do the Yale and the Master, and I'm working on the Walters."

Locks. She's learning to pick locks. "Great. Keep at it. Listen, Alba?"

"Daddy?"

"What's a CDP?"

"Chrono-Displaced Person." We sit down on a bench in front of a Tang Dynasty porcelain dragon. Alba sits facing me, with her hands in her lap. She looks exactly like me at ten. I can hardly believe any of this. Alba isn't even born yet and here she is, Athena sprung full blown. I level with her.

"You know, this is the first time I've met you."

Alba smiles. "How do you do?" She is the most self-possessed child I've ever met. I scrutinize her: where is Clare in this child?

"Do we see each other much?"

She considers. "Not much. It's been about a year. I saw you a few times when I was eight."

"How old were you when I died?" I hold my breath.

"Five." Jesus. I can't deal with this.

"I'm sorry! Should I not have said that?" Alba is contrite. I hug her to me.

"It's okay. I asked, didn't I?" I take a deep breath. "How is Clare?"

"Okay. Sad." This pierces me. I realize I don't want to know anything more.

"What about you? How's school? What are you learning?"

Alba grins. "I'm not learning much in *school*, but I'm reading all about early instruments, and Egypt, and Mama and I are reading *Lord of the Rings,* and I'm learning a tango by Astor Piazzolla."

At ten? Heavens. "Violin? Who's your teacher?"

"Gramps." For a moment I think she means my grandfather, and then I realize she means Dad. This is great. If Dad is spending time with Alba, she must actually be good.

"Are you good?" What a rude question.

"Yes. I'm *very* good." Thank God.

"I was never any good at music."

"That's what Gramps says." She giggles. "But you like music."

"I love music. I just can't play it, myself."

"I heard Grandma Annette sing! She was *so* beautiful!"

"Which recording?"

"I saw her for real. At the Lyric. She was singing Aïda."

He's a CDP, like me. Oh, shit. "You time travel."

"Sure." Alba smiles happily. "Mama always says you and I are exactly alike. Dr. Kendrick says I am a prodigy."

"How so?"

"Sometimes I can go when and where I want." Alba looks pleased with herself; I'm so envious.

"Can you not go at all if you don't want to?"

"Well, no." She looks embarrassed. "But I like it. I mean, sometimes it's not *convenient,* but . . . it's *interesting,* you know?" Yes. I know.

"Come and visit me, if you can be anytime you want."

"I tried. I saw you once on the street; you were with a blond woman. You seemed like you maybe were busy, though." Alba blushes and all of a sudden Clare peeks out at me, for just a tiny fraction of a second.

"That was Ingrid. I dated her before I met your mom." I wonder what we were doing, Ing and I, back then, that Alba is so discomfited by; I feel a pang of regret, that I made a poor impression on this sober and lovely girl. "Speaking of your mom, we should go out front and wait for her." The high-pitched whining noise has set in, and I just hope Clare will get here before I'm gone. Alba and I get up and quickly make our way to the front steps. It's late fall, and Alba doesn't have a coat, so I wrap mine around both of us. I am leaning against the granite slab that supports one of the lions, facing south, and Alba leans against me, encased in my coat, pressed against my bare torso with just her face sticking out at the level of my chest. It's a rainy day. Traffic swims along on Michigan Avenue. I am drunk with the overwhelming love I feel for this amazing child, who presses against me as though she belongs to me, as though we will never be separated, as though we have all the time in the world. I am clinging to this moment, fighting fatigue and the pulling of my own time. Let me stay, I implore my body, God, Father Time, Santa, anybody who might be listening. Just let me see Clare, and I'll come along peacefully.

"There's Mama," says Alba. A white car, unfamiliar to me, is speeding toward us. It pulls up to the intersection and Clare jumps out, leaving it where it is, blocking traffic.

"Henry!" I try to run to her, she is running, and I collapse onto the steps, and I stretch out my arms toward Clare: Alba is holding me and yelling something and Clare is only a few feet from me and I use my last reserves of will to look at Clare who seems so far away and I say as clearly as I can "I love you," and I'm gone. Damn. *Damn.*

7:20 p.m. Friday, August 24, 2001 (Clare is 30, Henry is 38)

CLARE: I am lying on the battered chaise lounge in the backyard with books and magazines cast adrift all around me and a half-drunk glass of lemonade now diluted with melted ice cubes at my

elbow. It's beginning to cool off a bit. It was eighty-five degrees earlier; now there's a breeze and the cicadas are singing their late summer song. Fifteen jets have passed over me on their way to O'Hare
from distances unknown. My belly looms before me, anchoring me
to this spot. Henry has been gone since eight o'clock yesterday
morning and I am beginning to be afraid. What if I go into labor
and he's not here? What if I have the baby and he still isn't back?
What if he's hurt? What if he's dead? What if I die? These thoughts
chase each other like those weird fur pieces old ladies used to wear
around their necks with the tail in the mouth, circling around until
I can't stand one more minute of it. Usually I like to fret in a whirl
of activity; I worry about Henry while I scrub down the studio or
do nine loads of wash or pull three posts of paper. But now I lie
here, beached by my belly in the early evening sun of our backyard
while Henry is out there . . . doing whatever it is that he is doing.
Oh, God. Bring him back. Now.

But nothing happens. Mr. Panetta drives down the alley and his
garage door screeches open and then closed. A Good Humor truck
comes and goes. The fireflies begin their evening revels. But no
Henry.

I am getting hungry. I am going to starve to death in the backyard because Henry is not here to make dinner. Alba is squirming
around and I consider getting up and going into the kitchen and
fixing some food and eating it. But then I decide to do the same
thing I always do when Henry isn't around to feed me. I get up,
slowly, in increments, and walk sedately into the house. I find my
purse, and I turn on a few lights, and I let myself out the front door
and lock it. It feels good to be moving. Once again I am surprised,
and am surprised to be surprised, that I am so huge in one part of
my body only, like someone whose plastic surgery has gone wrong,
like one of those women in an African tribe whose idea of beauty

requires extremely elongated necks or lips or earlobes. I balance my weight against Alba's, and in this Siamese twin dancing manner we walk to the Opart Thai Restaurant.

The restaurant is cool and full of people. I am ushered to a table in the front window. I order spring rolls and Pad Thai with tofu, bland and safe. I drink a whole glass of water. Alba presses against my bladder; I go to the restroom and when I come back food is on the table. I eat. I imagine the conversation Henry and I would be having if he were here. I wonder where he might be. I mentally comb through my memory, trying to fit the Henry who vanished while putting on his pants yesterday with any Henry I have seen in my childhood. This is a waste of time; I'll just have to wait for the story from Himself. Maybe he's back. I have to stop myself from bolting out of the restaurant to go check. The entrée arrives. I squeeze lime over the noodles and scoop them into my mouth. I picture Alba, tiny and pink, curled inside me, eating Pad Thai with tiny delicate chopsticks. I picture her with long black hair and green eyes. She smiles and says, "Thanks, Mama." I smile and tell her, "You're welcome, so very welcome." She has a tiny stuffed animal in there with her named Alfonzo. Alba gives Alfonzo some tofu. I finish eating. I sit for a few minutes, resting. Someone at the next table lights up a cigarette. I pay, and leave.

I toddle down Western Avenue. A car full of Puerto Rican teenagers yells something at me, but I don't catch it. Back at the ranch I fumble for my keys and Henry swings the door open and says, "Thank God," and flings his arms around me.

We kiss. I am so relieved to see him that it takes me a few minutes to realize that he is also extremely relieved to see me.

"Where have you been?" Henry demands.

"Opart. Where have you been?"

"You didn't leave a note, and I came home, and you weren't

here, and I thought you were at the hospital. So I called, but they said you weren't . . ."

I start laughing, and it's hard to stop. Henry looks perplexed. When I can say something I tell him, "Now you know how it feels."

He smiles. "Sorry. But I just—I didn't know where you were, and I sort of panicked. I thought I'd missed Alba."

"But where were you?"

Henry grins. "Wait till you hear this. Just a minute. Let's sit down."

"Let's lie down. I'm beat."

"Whadja do all day?"

"Laid around."

"Poor Clare, no wonder you're tired." I go into the bedroom and turn on the air conditioner and pull the shades. Henry veers into the kitchen and appears after a few minutes with drinks. I arrange myself on the bed and receive ginger ale; Henry kicks off his shoes and joins me with a beer in hand.

"Tell all."

"Well." He raises one eyebrow and opens his mouth and closes it. "I don't know how to begin."

"Spit it out."

"I have to start by saying that this is by far the weirdest thing that has ever happened to me."

"Weirder than you and me?"

"Yeah. I mean, that felt reasonably natural, boy meets girl . . ."

"Weirder than watching your mom die over and over?"

"Well, that's just a horrible routine, by now. It's a bad dream I have every so often. No, this was just surreal." He runs his hand over my belly. "I went forward, and I was really there, you know, coming in strong, and I ran into our little girl, here."

"Oh, my god. I'm so jealous. But wow."

"Yeah. She was about ten. Clare, she is so amazing—she's smart and musical and just . . . really confident and nothing fazed her . . ."

"What does she look like?"

"Me. A girl version of me. I mean, she's beautiful, she's got your eyes, but basically she looks a lot like me: black hair, pale, with a few freckles, and her mouth is smaller than mine was, and her ears don't stick out. She had long curly hair, and my hands with the long fingers, and she's tall. . . . She was like a young cat."

Perfect. Perfect.

"I'm afraid my genes have had their way with her. . . . She was like you in personality, though. She had the most amazing presence. . . . I saw her in a group of schoolchildren at the Art Institute and she was talking about Joseph Cornell's *Aviary* boxes, and she said something heartrending about him . . . and somehow *I knew who she was.* And she recognized me."

"Well, I would hope so." I have to ask. "Does she—is she—?"

Henry hesitates. "Yes," he finally says. "She does." We are both silent. He strokes my face. "I know."

I want to cry.

"Clare, she seemed happy. I asked her—she said she likes it." He smiles. "She said it was *interesting.*"

We both laugh, a little ruefully at first, and then, it hits me, and we laugh in earnest, until our faces hurt, until tears are streaming down our cheeks. Because, of course, it *is* interesting. *Very* interesting.

BIRTHDAY

· ·

Wednesday, September 5–Thursday, September 6, 2001
(Henry is 38, Clare is 30)

HENRY: Clare has been pacing around the house all day like a tiger. The contractions come every twenty minutes or so. "Try to get some sleep," I tell her, and she lies on the bed for a few minutes and then gets up again. At two in the morning she finally goes to sleep. I lie next to her, wakeful, watching her breathe, listening to the little fretful sounds she makes, playing with her hair. I am worried, even though I know, even though I have seen with my own eyes that she will be okay, and Alba will be okay. Clare wakes up at 3:30.

"I want to go to the hospital," she tells me.

"Maybe we should call a cab," I say. "It's awfully late."

"Gomez said to call no matter what time it was."

"Okay." I dial Gomez and Charisse. The phone rings sixteen times, and then Gomez picks up, sounding like a man on the bottom of the sea.

"Muh?" says Gomez.

"Hey, Comrade. It's time."

He mutters something that sounds like "mustard eggs." Then Charisse gets on the phone and tells me that they are on their way. I hang up and call Dr. Montague, and leave a message with her answering service. Clare is crouched on all fours, rocking back and forth. I get down on the floor with her.

"Clare?"

She looks up at me, still rocking. "Henry . . . why did we decide to do this again?"

"Supposedly when it's over they hand you a baby and let you keep it."

"Oh, yeah."

Fifteen minutes later we are climbing into Gomez's Volvo. Gomez yawns as he helps me maneuver Clare into the back seat. "Do not even think of drenching my car in amniotic fluid," he says to Clare amiably. Charisse runs into the house for garbage bags and covers the seats. We hop in and away we go. Clare leans against me and clenches my hands in hers.

"Don't leave me," she says.

"I won't," I tell her. I meet Gomez's eyes in the rearview mirror.

"It hurts," Clare says. "Oh, God, it hurts."

"Think of something else. Something nice," I say. We are racing down Western Avenue, headed south. There's hardly any traffic.

"Tell me . . ."

I cast about and come up with my most recent sojourn into Clare's childhood. "Remember the day we went to the lake, when you were twelve? And we went swimming, and you were telling me about getting your period?" Clare is gripping my hands with bone-shattering strength.

"Did I?"

"Yeah, you were sort of embarrassed but also real proud of

yourself. . . . You were wearing a pink and green bikini, and these yellow sunglasses with hearts molded into the frames."

"I remember—ah!—oh, Henry, it hurts, it hurts!"

Charisse turns around and says, "Come on, Clare, it's just the baby leaning on your spine, you've got to turn, okay?" Clare tries to change her position.

"Here we are," Gomez says, turning into Mercy Hospital's Emergency Unloading Zone.

"I'm leaking," Clare says. Gomez stops the car, jumps out, and we gently remove Clare from the car. She takes two steps and her water breaks.

"Good timing, kitten," Gomez says. Charisse runs ahead with our paperwork, and Gomez and I walk Clare slowly through ER and down long corridors to the OB wing. She stands leaning against the nurses' station while they nonchalantly prepare a room for her.

"Don't leave me," Clare whispers.

"I won't," I tell her again. I wish I could be sure about this. I am feeling cold and a little nauseous. Clare turns and leans into me. I wrap my arms around her. The baby is a hard roundness between us. *Come out, come out wherever you are.* Clare is panting. A fat blond nurse comes and tells us the room is ready. We all troop in. Clare immediately gets down on the floor on her hands and knees. Charisse starts putting things away, clothes in the closet, toiletries in the bathroom. Gomez and I stand watching Clare helplessly. She is moaning. We look at each other. Gomez shrugs.

Charisse says, "Hey Clare, how about a bath? You'll feel better in warm water."

Clare nods. Charisse makes a motion with her hands at Gomez that means *shoo*. Gomez says, "I think I'll go have a smoke," and leaves.

"Should I stay?" I ask Clare.

"Yes! Don't go—stay where I can see you."

"Okay." I walk into the bathroom to run the bathwater. Hospital bathrooms creep me out. They always smell like cheap soap and diseased flesh. I turn on the tap, wait for the water to get warm.

"Henry! Are you there?" Clare calls out.

I stick my head back into the room. "I'm here."

"Stay in here," Clare commands, and Charisse takes my place in the bathroom. Clare makes a sound that I have never heard a human being make before, a deep despairing groan of agony. What have I done to her? I think of twelve-year-old Clare laughing and covered with wet sand on a blanket, in her first bikini, at the beach. Oh, Clare, I'm sorry, I'm sorry. An older black nurse comes in and checks Clare's cervix.

"Good girl," she coos to Clare. "Six centimeters."

Clare nods, smiles, and then grimaces. She clutches her belly and doubles over, moaning louder. The nurse and I hold her. Clare gasps for breath, and then starts to scream. Amit Montague walks in and rushes to her.

"Baby baby baby, hush—" The nurse is giving Dr. Montague a bunch of information that means nothing to me. Clare is sobbing. I clear my throat. My voice comes out in a croak. "How about an epidural?"

"Clare?"

Clare nods. People crowd into the room with tubes and needles and machines. I sit holding Clare's hand, watching her face. She is lying on her side, whimpering, her face wet with sweat and tears as the anesthesiologist hooks up an IV and inserts a needle into her spine. Dr. Montague is examining her, and frowning at the fetal monitor.

"What's wrong?" Clare asks her. "Something's wrong."

"The heartbeat is very fast. She is scared, your little girl. You have to be calm, Clare, so the baby can be calm, yes?"

"It hurts so much."

"That is because she is big." Amit Montague's voice is quiet, soothing. The burly walrus-mustachioed anesthesiologist looks at me, bored, over Clare's body. "But now we are giving you a little cocktail, eh, some narcotic, some analgesic, soon you will relax, and the baby will relax, yes?" Clare nods, yes. Dr. Montague smiles. "And Henry, how are you?"

"Not very relaxed." I try to smile. I could use some of whatever it is they are giving Clare. I am experiencing slight double vision; I breathe deeply and it goes away.

"Things are improving: see?" says Dr. Montague. "It is like a cloud that passes over, the pain goes away, we take it somewhere and leave it by the side of the road, all by itself, and you and the little one are still here, yes? It is pleasant here, we will take our time, there is no hurry. . . ." The tension has left Clare's face. Her eyes are fixed on Dr. Montague. The machines beep. The room is dim. Outside the sun is rising. Dr. Montague is watching the fetal monitor. "Tell her you are fine, and she is fine. Sing her a song, yes?"

"Alba, it's okay," Clare says softly. She looks at me. "Say the poem about the lovers on the carpet."

I blank, and then I remember. I feel self-conscious reciting Rilke in front of all these people, and so I begin: *"Engel!: Es wäre ein Platz, den wir nicht wissen—"*

"Say it in English," Clare interrupts.

"Sorry." I change my position, so that I am sitting by Clare's belly with my back to Charisse and the nurse and the doctor, I slide my hand under Clare's button-strained shirt. I can feel the outline of Alba through Clare's hot skin.

"Angel!" I say to Clare, as though we are in our own bed, as though we have been up all night on less momentous errands,

> *Angel!: If there were a place that we didn't know of, and there,*
> *on some unsayable carpet, lovers displayed*
> *what they could never bring to mastery here—the bold*
> *exploits of their high-flying hearts,*
> *their towers of pleasure, their ladders*
> *that have long since been standing where there was no ground,*
>   *leaning*
> *just on each other, trembling,— and could master all this,*
> *before the surrounding spectators, the innumerable soundless dead:*
>   *Would these, then, throw down their final, forever saved-up,*
> *forever hidden, unknown to us, eternally valid*
> *coins of happiness before the at last*
> *genuinely smiling pair on the gratified*
> *carpet?*

"There," says Dr. Montague, clicking off the monitor. "Everyone is serene." She beams at us all, and glides out the door, followed by the nurse. I accidentally catch the eye of the anesthesiologist, whose expression plainly says *What kind of a pussy are you, anyway?*

CLARE: The sun is coming up and I am lying numb on this strange bed in this pink room and somewhere in the foreign country that is my uterus Alba is crawling toward home, or away from home. The pain has left but I know that it has not gone far, that it is sulking somewhere in a corner or under the bed and it will jump out when I least expect it. The contractions come and go, remote, muffled like the peal of bells through fog. Henry lies down next to me. People come and go. I feel like throwing up, but I don't.

Charisse gives me shaved ice out of a paper cup; it tastes like stale snow. I watch the tubes and the red blinking lights and I think about Mama. I breathe. Henry watches me. He looks so tense and unhappy. I start to worry again that he will vanish. "It's okay," I say. He nods. He strokes my belly. I'm sweating. It's so hot in here. The nurse comes in and checks on me. Amit checks on me. I am somehow alone with Alba in the midst of everyone. *It's okay,* I tell her. *You're doing fine, you're not hurting me.* Henry gets up and paces back and forth until I ask him to stop. I feel as though all my organs are becoming creatures, each with its own agenda, its own train to catch. Alba is tunneling headfirst into me, a bone and flesh excavator of my flesh and bone, a deepener of my depths. I imagine her swimming through me, I imagine her falling into the stillness of a morning pond, water parting at her velocity. I imagine her face, I want to see her face. I tell the anesthesiologist I want to feel something. Gradually the numbness recedes and the pain comes back, but it's different pain now. It's okay pain. Time passes.

Time passes and the pain begins to roll in and out as though it's a woman standing at an ironing board, passing the iron back and forth, back and forth across a white tablecloth. Amit comes in and says it's time, time to go to the delivery room. I am shaved and scrubbed and moved onto a gurney and rolled through hallways. I watch the ceilings of the hallways roll by, and Alba and I are rolling toward meeting each other, and Henry is walking beside us. In the delivery room everything is green and white. I smell detergent, it reminds me of Etta, and I want Etta but she is at Meadowlark, and I look up at Henry who is wearing surgical scrubs and I think why are we here we should be at home and then I feel as though Alba is surging, rushing and I push without thinking and we do this again and again like a game, like a song. Someone says *Hey, where'd the Dad go?* I look around but Henry is gone, he is nowhere not here and I think God damn him, but no, I don't mean it God, but Alba is coming, she is coming and then I see Henry, he stumbles into my vision, disoriented and naked but here, he's here! and Amit says *Sacre Dieu!* and then *Ah, she has crowned,* and I push and Alba's head comes out and I put my hand down to touch her head, her delicate slippery wet velvet head and I push and push and Alba tumbles into Henry's waiting hands and someone says *Oh!* and I am empty and released and I hear a sound like an old vinyl record when you put the needle in the wrong groove and then Alba yells out and suddenly she is here, someone places her on my belly and I look down and her face, Alba's face, is so pink and creased and her hair is so black and her eyes blindly search and her hands reach out and Alba pulls herself up to my breasts and she pauses, exhausted by the effort, by the sheer fact of everything.

Henry leans over me and touches her forehead, and says, "Alba."

Later:

CLARE: It's the evening of Alba's first day on earth. I'm lying in bed in the hospital room surrounded by balloons and teddy bears and flowers with Alba in my arms. Henry is sitting cross-legged on the foot of the bed taking pictures of us. Alba has just finished nursing and she blows colostrum bubbles from her tiny lips and then falls asleep, a soft warm bag of skin and fluid against my nightgown. Henry finishes the roll of film and unloads the camera.

"Hey," I say, suddenly remembering. "Where did you go? In the delivery room?"

Henry laughs. "You know, I was hoping you hadn't noticed that. I thought maybe you were so preoccupied—"

"Where were you?"

"I was wandering around my old elementary school in the middle of the night."

"For how long?" I ask.

"Oh, god. Hours. It was beginning to get light when I left. It was winter and they had the heat turned way down. How long was I gone?"

"I'm not sure. Maybe five minutes?"

Henry shakes his head. "I was frantic. I mean, I had just abandoned you, and there I was just drifting around uselessly through the hallways of Francis Parker. . . . It was so . . . I felt so . . ." Henry smiles. "But it turned out okay, hmm?"

I laugh. "'All's well that ends well.'"

"'Thou speakest wiser than thou art ware of.'" There is a quiet knock on the door; Henry says, "Come in!" and Richard steps into the room and then stops, hesitant. Henry turns and says, "Dad—" and then stops, and then jumps off the bed and says, "Come in, have a seat." Richard is carrying flowers and a small teddy bear which Henry adds to the pile on the windowsill.

"Clare," says Richard. "I—congratulations." He sinks slowly into the chair beside the bed.

"Um, would you like to hold her?" Henry asks softly. Richard nods, looking at me to see if I agree. Richard looks as though he hasn't slept for days. His shirt needs ironing and he stinks of sweat and the iodine reek of old beer. I smile at him although I am wondering if this is such a hot idea. I hand Alba over to Henry who carefully transfers her into Richard's awkward arms. Alba turns her pink round face up to Richard's long unshaven one, turns toward his chest and searches for a nipple. After a moment she gives up and yawns, then goes back to sleep. He smiles. I had forgotten how Richard's smile can transform his face.

"She's beautiful," he tells me. And, to Henry, "She looks like your mother."

Henry nods. "There's your violinist, Dad." He smiles. "It skipped a generation."

"A violinist?" Richard looks down at the sleeping baby, black hair and tiny hands, fast asleep. No one ever looked less like a concert violinist than Alba does right now. "A violinist." He shakes his head. "But how do you—No, never mind. So you are a violinist, are you now, little girl?" Alba sticks out her tongue a tiny bit and we all laugh.

"She'll need a teacher, once she's old enough," I suggest.

"A teacher? Yes. . . . You're not going to hand her over to those Suzuki idiots, are you?" Richard demands.

Henry coughs. "Er, actually we were hoping that if you had nothing better to do . . ."

Richard gets it. It's a pleasure to see him comprehend, to see him realize that someone needs him, that only he can give his only granddaughter the training she will need.

"I'd be delighted," he says, and Alba's future unrolls in front of her like a red carpet as far as the eye can see.

Tuesday, September 11, 2001 (Clare is 30, Henry is 38)

CLARE: I wake up at 6:43 and Henry is not in bed. Alba isn't in her crib, either. My breasts hurt. My cunt hurts. Everything hurts. I get out of bed very carefully, go to the bathroom. I walk through the hall, the dining room, slowly. In the living room Henry is sitting on the couch with Alba cradled in his arms, not watching the little black and white television with the sound turned low. Alba is asleep. I sit down next to Henry. He puts his arm around me.

"How come you're up?" I ask him. "I thought you said it wasn't for a couple of hours yet?" On the TV a weatherman is smiling and pointing at a satellite picture of the Midwest.

"I couldn't sleep," Henry says. "I wanted to listen to the world being normal for a little while longer."

"Oh." I lean my head on Henry's shoulder and close my eyes. When I open them again a commercial for a cell phone company is ending and a commercial for bottled water comes on. Henry hands Alba to me and gets up. In a minute I hear him making breakfast. Alba wakes up and I undo my nightgown and feed her. My nipples hurt. I watch the television. A blond anchorperson tells me something, smiling. He and the other anchorperson, an Asian woman, laugh and smile at me. At City Hall, Mayor Daley is answering questions. I doze. Alba sucks at me. Henry brings in a tray of eggs, toast, and orange juice. I want coffee. Henry has tactfully drunk his in the kitchen, but I can smell it on his breath. He sets the tray on the coffee table and puts my plate on my lap. I eat my eggs as Alba nurses. Henry mops up yolk with his toast. On TV a bunch of kids are skidding across grass, to demonstrate the effectiveness of some laundry detergent. We finish eating; Alba finishes, too. I burp her and Henry takes all the dishes to the kitchen. When he comes back I pass her to him and head to the bathroom. I take a shower. The water is so hot I almost can't stand it, but it feels heavenly on my sore body. I breathe the steamy air, dry my skin gingerly, rub balm on my lips, breasts, stomach. The mirror is all steamed up, so I don't have to see myself. I comb my hair. I pull on sweatpants and a sweater. I feel deformed, deflated. In the living room Henry is sitting with his eyes closed, and Alba is sucking her thumb. As I sit down again Alba opens her eyes and makes a mewing sound. Her thumb slips out of her mouth and she looks confused. A Jeep is driving through a desert landscape. Henry has turned off the sound. He massages his eyes with his fingers. I fall asleep again.

Henry says, "Wake up, Clare." I open my eyes. The television picture swerves around. A city street. A sky. A white skyscraper on fire. An airplane, toylike, slowly flies into the second white tower. Silent flames shoot up. Henry turns up the sound. "Oh my god," says the voice of the television. "Oh my god."

Tuesday, June 11, 2002 (Clare is 31)

CLARE: I'm making a drawing of Alba. At this moment Alba is nine months and five days old. She is sleeping on her back, on a small light blue flannel blanket, on the yellow ochre and magenta Chinese rug on the living room floor. She has just finished nursing. My breasts are light, almost empty. Alba is so very asleep that I feel perfectly okay about walking out the back door and across the yard into my studio.

For a minute I stand in the doorway inhaling the slightly musty unused studio odor. Then I rummage around in my flat file, find some persimmon-tanned paper that looks like cowhide, grab a few pastels and other implements and a drawing board and walk (with only a small pang of regret) out the door and back into the house.

The house is very quiet. Henry is at work (I hope) and I can hear the washing machine churning away in the basement. The air conditioner whines. There's a faint rumble of traffic on Lincoln Avenue. I sit down on the rug next to Alba. A trapezoid of sunlight is inches away from her small pudgy feet. In half an hour it will cover her.

I clip my paper to the drawing board and arrange my pastels next to me on the rug. Pencil in hand, I consider my daughter.

Alba is sleeping deeply. Her ribcage rises and falls slowly and I can hear the soft grunt she makes with each exhalation. I wonder if she's getting a cold. It's warm in here, on this June late afternoon, and Alba's wearing a diaper and nothing else. She's a little flushed. Her left hand is clenching and unclenching rhythmically. Maybe she's dreaming music.

I begin to rough in Alba's head, which is turned toward me. I am not thinking about this, really. My hand is moving across the paper like the needle of a seismograph, recording Alba's form as I absorb it with my eyes. I note the way her neck disappears in the folds of baby fat under her chin, how the soft indentations above her knees alter slightly as she kicks, once, and is still again. My pencil describes the convexity of Alba's full belly which submerges into the top of her diaper, an abrupt and angular line cutting across her roundness. I study the paper, adjust the angle of Alba's legs, redraw the crease where her right arm joins her torso.

I begin to lay in pastel. I start by sketching in highlights in white—down her tiny nose, along her left side, across her knuckles, her diaper, the edge of her left foot. Then I rough in shadows, in dark green and ultramarine. A deep shadow clings to Alba's right side where her body meets the blanket. It's like a pool of water, and I put it in solidly. Now the Alba in the drawing suddenly becomes three-dimensional, leaps off the page.

I use two pink pastels, a light pink the hue of the inside of a shell and a dark pink that reminds me of raw tuna. With rapid strokes I make Alba's skin. It is as though Alba's skin was hidden in the paper, and I am removing some invisible substance that concealed it. Over this pastel skin I use a cool violet to make Alba's ears and nose and mouth (her mouth is slightly open in a tiny O). Her black and abundant hair becomes a mixture of dark blue and black and red on the paper. I take care with her eyebrows, which seem so much like furry caterpillars that have found a home on Alba's face.

The sunlight covers Alba now. She stirs, brings her small hand over her eyes, and sighs. I write her name, and my name, and the date at the bottom of the paper.

The drawing is finished. It will serve as a record—I loved you, I made you, and I made this for you—long after I am gone, and Henry is gone, and even Alba is gone. It will say, we made you, and here you are, here and now.

Alba opens her eyes and smiles.

SECRET

••••••••••••••••••••••••••••••••

Sunday, October 12, 2003 (Clare is 32, Henry is 40)

CLARE: This is a secret: sometimes I am glad when Henry is gone. Sometimes I enjoy being alone. Sometimes I walk through the house late at night and I shiver with the pleasure of not talking, not touching, just walking, or sitting, or taking a bath. Sometimes I lie on the living room floor and listen to Fleetwood Mac, the Bangles, the B-52's, the Eagles, bands Henry can't stand. Sometimes I go for long walks with Alba and I don't leave a note saying where I am. Sometimes I meet Celia for coffee, and we talk about Henry, and Ingrid, and whoever Celia's seeing that week. Sometimes I hang out with Charisse and Gomez, and we don't talk about Henry, and we manage to enjoy ourselves. Once I went to Michigan and when I came back Henry was still gone and I never told him I had been anywhere. Sometimes I get a babysitter and I go to the movies or I ride my bicycle after dark along the bike path by Montrose beach with no lights; it's like flying.

Sometimes I am glad when Henry's gone, but I'm always glad when he comes back.

EXPERIENCING TECHNICAL
DIFFICULTIES

•••••••••••••••••••••••••••••••••

Friday, May 7, 2004 (Henry is 40, Clare is 32)

HENRY: We are at the opening of Clare's exhibit at the Chicago
Cultural Center. She has been working nonstop for a year, building
huge, ethereal bird skeletons out of wire, wrapping them in translucent strips of paper, coating them with shellac until they transmit
light. Now the sculptures hang from the high ceiling, and squat on
the floor. Some of them are kinetic, motorized: a few beat their
wings, and there are two cock skeletons slowly demolishing each
other in a corner. An eight-foot-tall pigeon dominates the entrance.
Clare is exhausted, and ecstatic. She's wearing a simple black silk
dress, her hair is piled high on her head. People have brought her
flowers; she has a bouquet of white roses in her arms, there's a heap
of plastic-wrapped bouquets next to the guest book. It's very
crowded. People circle around, exclaim over each piece, crane their
heads back to look at the flying birds. Everyone congratulates Clare.
There was a glowing review in this morning's *Tribune.* All our
friends are here, and Clare's family has driven in from Michigan.
They surround Clare now, Philip, Alicia, Mark and Sharon and

their kids, Nell, Etta. Charisse takes pictures of them, and they all smile for her. When she gives us copies of the pictures, a few weeks from now, I will be struck by the dark circles under Clare's eyes, and by how thin she looks.

I am holding Alba's hand. We stand by the back wall, out of the crowd. Alba can't see anything, because everyone is tall, and so I lift her on to my shoulders. She bounces.

Clare's family has dispersed and she is being introduced to a very well-dressed elderly couple by Leah Jacobs, her dealer. Alba says, "I want Mama."

"Mama's busy, Alba," I say. I am feeling queasy. I bend over and set Alba on the floor. She puts her arms up. "*No. I want Mama.*" I sit on the floor and put my head between my knees. I need to find a place where no one can see me. Alba is pulling my ear. "Don't, Alba," I say. I look up. My father is making his way to us through the crowd. "Go," I tell Alba. I give her a little push. "Go see Grandpa." She starts to whimper. "I don't *see* Grandpa. I want *Mama*." I am crawling toward Dad. I bump into someone's legs. I hear Alba screaming, "Mama!" as I vanish.

CLARE: There are masses of people. Everyone presses at me, smiling. I smile at them. The show looks great, and it's done, it's up! I'm so happy, and so tired. My face hurts from smiling. Everyone I know is here. I'm talking to Celia when I hear a commotion at the back of the gallery, and then I hear Alba screaming, "Mama!" Where is Henry? I try to get through the crowd to Alba. Then I see her: Richard has lifted her up. People part to let me through. Richard hands Alba to me. She locks her legs around my waist, buries her face in my shoulder, wraps her arms around my neck. "Where's Daddy?" I ask her softly. "Gone," says Alba.

NATURE MORTE

•••••••••••••••••••••••••••••••••

Sunday, July 11, 2004 (Clare is 33, Henry is 41)

CLARE: Henry is sleeping, bruised and caked with blood, on the kitchen floor. I don't want to move him or wake him. I sit with him on the cool linoleum for a while. Eventually I get up and make coffee. As the coffee streams into the pot and the grounds make little exploding pufts, Henry whimpers and puts his hands over his eyes. It's obvious that he has been beaten. One eye is swollen shut. The blood seems to have come from his nose. I don't see any wounds, just radiant purple fist-sized bruises all over his body. He is very thin; I can see all his vertebrae and ribs. His pelvis juts, his cheeks are hollow. His hair has grown down almost to his shoulders, there is gray shot through it. There are cuts on his hands and feet, and insect bites everywhere on his body. He is very tanned, and filthy, grime under nails, dirt sweated into creases of his skin. He smells of grass, blood, and salt. After watching him and sitting with him for a while, I decide to wake him. "Henry," I say very softly, "wake up, now, you're home. . . ." I stroke his face, carefully, and he opens his eye. I can tell he's not quite awake. "Clare," he mumbles. "Clare."

Tears begin to stream from his good eye, he is shaking with sobbing, and I pull him into my lap. I am crying. Henry is curled in my lap, there on the floor, we shake tightly together, rocking, rocking, crying our relief and our anguish together.

Thursday, December 23, 2004 (Clare is 33, Henry is 41)

CLARE: It's the day before Christmas Eve. Henry is at Water Tower Place, taking Alba to see Santa at Marshall Field's while I finish the shopping. Now I'm sitting in the cafe at Borders, drinking cappuccino at a table by the front window and resting my feet with a pile of bulging shopping bags leaning against my chair. Outside the window the day is fading and tiny white lights describe every tree. Shoppers hurry up and down Michigan Avenue, and I can hear the muted clang of the Salvation Army Santa's bell below me. I turn back to the store, scanning for Henry and Alba, and someone calls my name. Kendrick is coming toward me with his wife, Nancy, and Colin and Nadia in tow.

I can see at a glance that they've just come from FAO Schwarz; they have the shell-shocked look of parents freshly escaped from toy-store hell. Nadia comes running up to me squealing "Aunt Clare, Aunt Clare! Where's Alba?" Colin smiles shyly and holds out his hand to show me that he has a tiny yellow tow truck. I congratulate him and tell Nadia that Alba's visiting Santa, and Nadia replies that she already saw Santa last week. "What did you ask for?" I query. "A boyfriend," says Nadia. She's three years old. I grin at Kendrick and Nancy. Kendrick says something, *sotto voce,* to Nancy, and she says, "Come on, troops, we have to find a book for Aunt Silvie," and the three of them go pelting off to the bargain tables. Kendrick gestures at the empty chair across from me. "May I?"

"Sure."

He sits down, sighing deeply. "I hate Christmas."

"You and Henry both."

"Does he? I didn't know that." Kendrick leans against the window and closes his eyes. Just as I think that he's actually asleep he opens them and says, "Is Henry following his drug regimen?"

"Um, I guess. I mean, as closely as he can, considering that he's been time traveling a lot lately."

Kendrick drums his fingers on the table. "How much is a lot?"

"Every couple days."

Kendrick looks furious. "Why doesn't he *tell* me these things?"

"I think he's afraid you'll get upset with him and quit."

"He's the only test subject I have who can *talk* and he never tells me anything!"

I laugh. "Join the club."

Kendrick says, "I'm trying to do science. I need him to tell me when something doesn't work. Otherwise we're all just spinning our wheels."

I nod. Outside it has started to snow.

"Clare?"

"Hmm?"

"Why won't you let me look at Alba's DNA?"

I've had this conversation a hundred times with Henry. "Because first you'd just want to locate all the markers in her genes, and that would be okay. But then you and Henry would start to badger me to let you try out drugs on her, and that is not okay. That's why."

"But she's still very young; she has a better chance of responding positively to the medication."

"I said *no*. When Alba is eighteen she can decide for herself. So far, everything you've given Henry has been a nightmare." I can't look at Kendrick. I say this to my hands, tightly folded on the table.

"But we might be able to develop gene therapy for her—"

"People have *died* from gene therapy."

Kendrick is silent. The noise level in the store is overwhelming. Then from the babble I hear Alba calling, "Mama!" I look up and see her riding on Henry's shoulders, clutching his head with her hands. Both of them are wearing coonskin caps. Henry sees Kendrick and for a brief moment he looks apprehensive and I wonder what secrets these two men are keeping from me. Then Henry smiles and comes striding toward us, Alba bobbing happily above the crowd. Kendrick rises to greet him, and I push the thought away.

BIRTHDAY

· ·

Wednesday, May 24, 1989 (Henry is 41, Clare is 18)

HENRY: I come to with a thud and skid across the painful
stubble of the Meadow on my side, ending up dirty and bloody at
Clare's feet. She is sitting on the rock, coolly immaculate in a white
silk dress, white stockings and shoes, and short white gloves. "Hello,
Henry," she says, as though I have just dropped in for tea.

"What's up?" I ask. "You look like you're on your way to your
first communion."

Clare sits up very straight and says, "Today is May 24, 1989."

I think fast. "Happy birthday. Do you happen to have a Bee
Gees outfit squirreled away somewhere around here for me?" Without deigning to reply, Clare glides off the rock and, reaching behind
it, produces a garment bag. With a flourish she unzips it to reveal a
tuxedo, pants, and one of those infernal formal shirts that require
studs. She produces a suitcase containing underwear, a cummer-
bund, a bow tie, studs, and a gardenia. I am seriously alarmed, and
not forewarned. I ponder the available data. "Clare. We're not getting married today or anything insane like that, are we? Because I

know for a fact that our anniversary is in the fall. October. Late October."

Clare turns away while I am dressing. "You mean you can't remember our anniversary? How male."

I sigh. "Darling, you know I know, I just can't get at it right now. But anyway. Happy Birthday."

"I'm eighteen."

"Heavens, so you are. It seems like only yesterday that you were six."

Clare is intrigued, as always, with the notion that I have recently visited some other Clare, older or younger. "Have you seen me when I was six lately?"

"Well, just now I was lying in bed with you reading *Emma*. You were thirty-three. I am forty-one at the moment, and feeling every minute." I comb through my hair with my fingers and run my hand over my stubble. "I'm sorry, Clare. I'm afraid I'm not at my best for your birthday." I fasten the gardenia through the buttonhole of the tuxedo and start to do up the studs. "I saw you at six about two weeks ago. You drew me a picture of a duck."

Clare blushes. The blush spreads like drops of blood in a bowl of milk.

"Are you hungry? I made us a feast!"

"Of course I'm hungry. I'm famished, gaunt, and considering cannibalism."

"That won't be necessary just yet."

There is something in her tone that pulls me up. Something is going on that I don't know about, and Clare expects me to know it. She is practically humming with excitement. I contemplate the relative merits of a simple confession of ignorance versus continuing to fake it. I decide to let it go for a while. Clare is spreading out a blanket which will later end up on our bed. I carefully sit down on it and am comforted by its pale green familiarity. Clare unpacks sandwiches, little paper cups, silverware, crackers, a tiny black jar of supermarket caviar, Thin Mint Girl Scout cookies, strawberries, a bottle of Cabernet with a fancy label, Brie cheese which looks a bit melted, and paper plates.

"Clare. Wine! Caviar!" I am impressed, and somehow not amused. She hands me the Cabernet and the corkscrew. "Um, I don't think I've ever mentioned this, but I'm not supposed to drink. Doctor's orders." Clare looks crestfallen. "But I can certainly eat . . . I can pretend to be drinking. I mean, if that would be helpful." I can't shake the feeling that we are playing house. "I didn't know you drank. Alcohol. I mean, I've hardly ever seen you drink any."

"Well, I don't really like it, but since this is a momentous occasion I thought it would be nice to have wine. Champagne probably would have been better, but this was in the pantry, so I brought it along."

I open the wine and pour us each a small cup. We toast each other silently. I pretend to sip mine. Clare takes a mouthful, swallows it in a businesslike fashion, and says, "Well, that's not so bad."

"That's a twenty-something-dollar bottle of wine."

"Oh. Well, that was marvelous."

"Clare." She is unwrapping dark rye sandwiches which seem to be overflowing with cucumbers. "I hate to be obtuse . . . I mean, obviously it's your birthday . . ."

"My eighteenth birthday," she agrees.

"Um, well, to begin with, I'm really upset that I don't have a present for you. . . ." Clare looks up, surprised, and I realize that I'm warm, I'm on to something here, "but you know I never know when I'm coming, and I can't bring anything with me. . . ."

"I know all that. But don't you remember, we worked it all out last time you were here; because on the List today is the last day left

419

and also my birthday. You don't remember?" Clare is looking at me very intently, as though concentration can move memory from her mind to mine.

"Oh. I haven't been there yet. I mean, that conversation is still in my future. I wonder why I didn't tell you then? I still have lots of dates on the list left to go. Is today really the last day? You know, we'll be meeting each other in the present in a couple years. We'll see each other then."

"But that's a long time. For me."

There is an awkward pause. It's strange to think that right now I am in Chicago, twenty-five years old, going about my business, completely unaware of Clare's existence, and for that matter, oblivious to my own presence here in this lovely Michigan meadow on a gorgeous spring day which is the eighteenth anniversary of her birth. We are using plastic knives to apply caviar to Ritz crackers. For a while there is much crunching and furious consumption of sandwiches. The conversation seems to have foundered. And then I wonder, for the first time, if perhaps Clare is being entirely truthful with me here, knowing as she does that I am on slippery terms with statements that begin "I never," since I never have a complete inventory of my past handy at any given moment, since my past is inconveniently compounded with my future. We move on to the strawberries.

"Clare." She smiles, innocently. "What exactly did we decide, the last time you saw me? What were we planning to do for your birthday?"

She's blushing again. "Well, this," she says, gesturing at our picnic.

"Anything else? I mean, this is wonderful."

"Well. Yes." I'm all ears, because I think I know what's coming. "Yes?"

Clare is quite pink but manages to look otherwise dignified as she says, "We decided to make love."

"Ah." I have, actually, always wondered about Clare's sexual experiences prior to October 26, 1991, when we met for the first time in the present. Despite some pretty amazing provocation on Clare's part I have refused to make love to her and have spent many amusing hours chatting with her about this and that while trying to ignore painful hard-ons. But today, Clare is legally, if perhaps not emotionally, an adult, and surely I can't warp her life too much . . . that is to say, I've already given her a pretty weird childhood just by being in her childhood at all. How many girls have their very own eventual husband appearing at regular intervals buck naked before their eyes? Clare is watching me think this through. I am thinking about the first time I made love to Clare and wondering if it was the first time she made love to me. I decide to ask her about this when I get back to my present. Meanwhile, Clare is tidying things back into the picnic basket.

"So?"

What the hell. "Yes."

Clare is excited and also scared. "Henry. You've made love to me lots of times . . ."

"Many, many times."

She's having trouble saying it.

"It's always beautiful," I tell her. "It's the most beautiful thing in my life. I will be very gentle." Having said this I am suddenly nervous. I'm feeling responsible and Humbert Humbertish and also as though I am being watched by many people, and all of those people are Clare. I have never felt less sexual in my life. Okay. Deep breath. "I love you."

We both stand up, lurching a bit on the uneven surface of the blanket. I open my arms and Clare moves into them. We stand, still, embracing there in the Meadow like the bride and groom on top of a wedding cake. And after all, this is Clare, come to my forty-one-year-old self almost as she was when we first met. No fear. She leans her head back. I lean forward and kiss her.

"Clare."

"Mmmm?"

"You're absolutely sure we're alone?"

"Everyone except Etta and Nell is in Kalamazoo."

"Because I feel like I'm on *Candid Camera*, here."

"Paranoid. Very sad."

"Never mind."

"We could go to my room."

"Too dangerous. God, it's like being in high school."

"What?"

"Never mind."

Clare steps back from me and unzips her dress. She pulls it over her head and drops it on the blanket with admirable unconcern. She steps out of her shoes and peels off her stockings. She unhooks her bra, discards it, and steps out of her panties. She is standing before me completely naked. It is a sort of miracle: all the little marks I have become fond of have vanished; her stomach is flat, no trace of the pregnancies that will bring us such grief, such happiness. This Clare is a little thinner, and a lot more buoyant than the Clare I love in the present. I realize again how much sadness has overtaken us. But today all of that is magically removed; today the possibility of joy is close to us. I kneel, and Clare comes over and stands in front of me. I press my face to her stomach for a moment, and then look up; Clare is towering over me, her hands in my hair, with the cloudless blue sky around her.

I shrug off my jacket and undo the tie. Clare kneels and we remove the studs deftly and with the concentration of a bomb squad.

I take off the pants and underwear. There's no way to do this grace-fully. I wonder how male strippers deal with this problem. Or do they just hop around on stage, one leg in, one out? Clare laughs. "I've never seen you get *undressed*. Not a pretty sight."

"You wound me. Come here and let me wipe that smirk off your face."

"Uh-oh." In the next fifteen minutes I'm proud to say that I have indeed removed all traces of superiority from Clare's face. Un-fortunately she's getting more and more tense, more . . . defended. In fourteen years and heaven only knows how many hours and days spent happily, anxiously, urgently, languorously making love with Clare, this is utterly new to me. I want, if at all possible, for her to feel the sense of wonder I felt when I met her and we made love for what I thought (silly me) was the first time. I sit up, panting. Clare sits up as well, and circles her arms around her knees, protectively.

"You okay?"

"I'm afraid."

"That's okay." I'm thinking. "I swear to you that the next time we meet you're going to practically rape me. I mean, you are really exceptionally talented at this."

"I am?"

"You are incandescent." I am rummaging through the picnic basket: cups, wine, condoms, towels. "Clever girl." I pour us each a cup of wine. "To virginity. *'Had we but world enough, and time.'* Drink up." She does, obediently, like a small child taking medicine. I refill her cup, and down my own.

"But you aren't supposed to drink."

"It's a momentous occasion. Bottoms up." Clare weighs about 120 pounds, but these are Dixie cups. "One more."

"More? I'll get sleepy."

"You'll relax." She gulps it down. We squash up the cups and throw them in the picnic basket. I lie down on my back with my arms stretched out like a sunbather, or a crucifixion. Clare stretches out beside me. I gather her in so that we are side by side, facing each other. Her hair falls across her shoulders and breasts in a very beautiful and touching way and I wish for the zillionth time that I was a painter.

"Clare?"

"Hmmm?"

"Imagine yourself as open; empty. Someone's come along and taken out all your innards, and left only nerve endings." I've got the tip of my index finger on her clit.

"Poor little Clare. No innards."

"Ah, but it's a good thing, you see, because there's all this extra room in there. Think of all the stuff you could put inside you if you didn't have all those silly kidneys and stomachs and pancreases and what not."

"Like what?" She's very wet. I remove my hand and carefully rip open the condom packet with my teeth, a maneuver I haven't performed in years.

"Kangaroos. Toaster ovens. Penises."

Clare takes the condom from me with fascinated distaste. She's lying on her back and she unfurls it and sniffs it. "Ugh. Must we?"

Although I often refuse to tell Clare things, I seldom actually lie to her. I feel a twinge of guilt as I say, "'Fraid so." I retrieve it from her, but instead of putting it on I decide that what we really need here is cunnilingus. Clare, in her future, is addicted to oral sex and will leap tall buildings in a single bound and wash the dishes when it's not her turn in order to get it. If cunnilingus were an Olympic event I would medal, no doubt about it. I spread her out and apply my tongue to her clit.

"Oh *God,*" Clare says in a low voice. "Sweet *Jesus.*"

"No yelling," I warn. Even Etta and Nell will come down to the Meadow to see what's wrong if Clare really gets going. In the next fifteen minutes I take Clare several steps down the evolutionary ladder until she's pretty much a limbic core with a few cerebral cortex peripherals. I roll on the condom and slowly, carefully slide into Clare, imagining things breaking and blood cascading around me. She has her eyes closed and at first I think she's not even aware that I'm actually inside her even though I'm directly over her but then she opens her eyes and smiles, triumphant, beatific.

I manage to come fairly quickly; Clare is watching me, concentrating, and as I come I see her face turn to surprise. How strange things are. What odd things we animals do. I collapse onto her. We are bathed in sweat. I can feel her heart beating. Or perhaps it's mine.

I pull out carefully and dispose of the condom. We lie, side by side, looking at the very blue sky. The wind is making a sea sound with the grass. I look over at Clare. She looks a bit stunned.

"Hey. Clare."

"Hey," she says weakly.

"Did it hurt?"

"Yes."

"Did you like it?"

"Oh, yes!" she says, and starts to cry. We sit up, and I hold her for a while. She is shaking.

"Clare. Clare. What's wrong?"

I can't make out her reply at first, then: "You're going away. Now I won't see you for years and years."

"Only two years. Two years and a few months." She is quiet. "Oh, Clare. I'm sorry. I can't help it. It's funny, too, because I was just lying here thinking what a blessing today was. To be here with you making love instead of being chased by thugs or freezing to death in some barn or some of the other stupid shit I get to deal with. And when I go back, I'm with you. And today was wonderful." She is smiling, a little. I kiss her.

"How come I always have to wait?"

"Because you have perfect DNA and you aren't being thrown around in time like a hot potato. Besides, patience is a virtue." Clare is pummeling my chest with her fists, lightly. "Also, you've known me your whole life, whereas I only meet you when I'm twenty-eight. So I spend all those years before we meet—"

"Fucking other women."

"Well, yeah. But, unbeknownst to me, it's all just practice for when I meet you. And it's very lonely and weird. If you don't believe me, try it yourself. I'll never know. It's different when you don't care."

"I don't want anybody else."

"Good."

"Henry, just give me a hint. Where do you live? Where do we meet? What day?"

"One hint. Chicago."

"More."

"Have faith. It's all there, in front of you."

"Are we happy?"

"We are often insane with happiness. We are also very unhappy for reasons neither of us can do anything about. Like being separated."

"So all the time you're here now you're not with me then?"

"Well, not exactly. I may end up missing only ten minutes. Or ten days. There's no rule about it. That's what makes it hard, for you. Also, I sometimes end up in dangerous situations, and I come back to you broken and messed up, and you worry about me when I'm gone. It's like marrying a policeman." I'm exhausted. I wonder how old I actually am, in real time. In calendar time I'm forty-one, but with all this coming and going perhaps I'm really forty-five or -six. Or maybe I'm thirty-nine. Who knows? There's something I have to tell her; what was it?

"Clare?"

"Henry."

"When you see me again, remember that I won't know you; don't be upset when you see me and I treat you like a total stranger, because to me you will be brand new. And please don't blow my mind with everything all at once. Have mercy, Clare."

"I will! Oh, Henry, stay!"

"Shh. I'll be with you." We lie down again. The exhaustion permeates me and I will be gone in a minute.

"I love you, Henry. Thank you for . . . my birthday present."

"I love you, Clare. Be good."

I'm gone.

SECRET

•••••••••••••••••••••••••••••••••

Thursday, February 10, 2005 (Clare is 33, Henry is 41)

CLARE: It's Thursday afternoon and I'm in the studio making pale yellow kozo paper. Henry's been gone for almost twenty-four hours now, and as usual I'm torn between thinking obsessively about when and where he might be and being pissed at him for not being here and worrying about when he'll be back. It's not helping my concentration and I'm ruining a lot of sheets; I plop them off the su and back into the vat. Finally I take a break and pour myself a cup of coffee. It's cold in the studio, and the water in the vat is supposed to be cold although I have warmed it a little to save my hands from cracking. I wrap my hands around the ceramic mug. Steam wafts up. I put my face over it, inhale the moisture and coffee smell. And then, oh thank you, God, I hear Henry whistling as he comes up the path through the garden, into the studio. He stomps the snow off his boots and shrugs off his coat. He's looking marvelous, really happy. My heart is racing and I take a wild guess: "May 24, 1989?"

"*Yes*, oh, yes!" Henry scoops me up, wet apron and Wellingtons and all, and swings me around. Now I'm laughing, we're both laughing. Henry exudes delight. "Why didn't you *tell* me? I've been needlessly wondering all these years. Vixen! Minx!" He's biting my neck and tickling me.

"But you didn't know, so I couldn't tell you."

"Oh. Right. My God, you're amazing." We sit on the grungy old studio couch. "Can we turn up the heat in here?"

"Sure." Henry jumps up and turns the thermostat higher. The furnace kicks in. "How long was I gone?"

"Almost a whole day."

Henry sighs. "Was it worth it? A day of anxiety in exchange for a few really beautiful hours?"

"Yes. That was one of the best days of my life." I am quiet, remembering. I often invoke the memory of Henry's face above me, surrounded by blue sky, and the feeling of being permeated by him. I think about it when he's gone and I'm having trouble sleeping.

"Tell me . . ."

"Mmmm?" We are wrapped around each other, for warmth, for reassurance.

"What happened after I left?"

"I picked everything up and made myself more or less presentable and went back up to the house. I got upstairs without running into anyone and I took a bath. After a while Etta started hammering on the door wanting to know why I was in the tub in the middle of the day and I had to pretend I was sick. And I was, in a way . . . I spent the summer lounging around, sleeping a lot. Reading. I just kind of rolled up into myself. I spent some time down in the Meadow, sort of hoping you might show up. I wrote you letters. I burned them. I stopped eating for a while and Mom dragged me to her therapist and I started eating again. At the end of August my parents informed me that if I didn't 'perk up' I wouldn't be going to school that fall, so I immediately perked up because my whole goal in life was to get out of the house and go to Chicago. And school was a good thing; it was new, I had an apartment, I loved the city. I had something to think about besides the fact that I had no idea where you were or how to find you. By the time I finally did run into you I was doing pretty well; I was into my work, I had friends, I got asked out quite a bit—"

"Oh?"

"Sure."

"Did you go? Out?"

"Well, yeah. I did. In the spirit of research . . . and because I occasionally got mad that somewhere out there you were obliviously dating other women. But it was all a sort of black comedy. I would go out with some perfectly nice pretty young art boy, and spend the whole evening thinking about how boring and futile it was and checking my watch. I stopped after five of them because I could see that I was really pissing these guys off. Someone put the word out at school that I was a dyke and then I got a wave of girls asking me out."

"I could see you as a lesbian."

"Yeah; behave yourself or I'll convert."

"I've always wanted to be a lesbian." Henry is looking dreamy and heavy-lidded; not fair when I am wound up and ready to jump on him. He yawns. "Oh, well, not in this lifetime. Too much surgery."

In my head I hear the voice of Father Compton behind the grille of the confessional, softly asking me if there's anything else I want to confess. No, I tell him firmly. No, there isn't. That was a mistake. I was drunk, and it doesn't count. The good Father sighs, and pushes the curtain across. End of confession. My penance is to lie to Henry, by omission, as long as we both shall live. I look at him, happily postprandial, sated with the charms of my younger self, and the image of Gomez sleeping, Gomez's bedroom in morning light flashes across my mental theater. It was a mistake, Henry, I tell him silently. I was waiting, and I got sideswiped, just once. Tell him, says Father Compton, or somebody, in my head. I can't, I retort. He'll hate me.

"Hey," Henry says gently. "Where are you?"

"Thinking."

"You look so sad."

"Do you worry sometimes that all the really great stuff has already happened?"

"No. Well, sort of, but in a different way than you mean. I'm still moving through the time you're reminiscing about, so it's not really gone, for me. I worry that we aren't paying close attention here and now. That is, time travel is sort of an altered state, so I'm more . . . aware when I'm out there, and it seems important, somehow, and sometimes I think that if I could just be that aware here and now, that things would be perfect. But there's been some great things, lately." He smiles, that beautiful crooked radiant smile, all innocence, and I allow my guilt to subside, back to the little box where I keep it crammed in like a parachute.

"Alba."

"Alba is perfect. And you are perfect. I mean, as much as I love you, back there, it's the shared life, the knowing each other . . ."

"Through thick and thin . . ."

"The fact that there are bad times makes it more real. It's the reality that I want."

Tell him, tell him.

"Even reality can be pretty unreal. . . ." If I'm ever going to say it, now's the time. He waits. I just. Can't.

"Clare?" I regard him miserably, like a child caught in a complicated fib, and then I say it, almost inaudibly.

"I slept with someone." Henry's face is frozen, disbelieving.

"Who?" he asks, without looking at me.

"Gomez."

"Why?" Henry is still, waiting for the blow.

"I was drunk. We were at a party, and Charisse was in Boston—"

"Wait a minute. When was this?"

"1990."

He starts to laugh. "Oh, God. Clare, don't do that to me, shit. 1990. Jesus, I thought you were telling me something that happened, like, last week." I smile, weakly. He says, "I mean, it's not like I'm overjoyed about it, but since I just got through telling you to go out and experiment I can't really . . . I dunno." He's getting restless. He gets up and starts pacing around the studio. I am incredulous. For fifteen years I've been paralyzed with fear, fear that Gomez would say something, do something in his big lumbering Gomez callousness, and Henry doesn't mind. Or does he?

"How was it?" he asks, quite casually, with his back to me as he messes with the coffeemaker.

I pick my words with care. "Different. I mean, without getting real critical of Gomez—"

"Oh, go ahead."

"It was sort of like being a china shop, and trying to get off with a bull."

"He's bigger than me." Henry states this as fact.

"I wouldn't know about now, but back then he had no finesse at all. He actually smoked a cigarette while he was fucking me." Henry winces. I get up, walk over to him. "I'm sorry. It was a mistake." He pulls me to him, and I say, softly, into his collar, "I was waiting very patiently . . ." but then I can't go on. Henry is stroking my hair. "It's okay, Clare," he says. "It's not so bad." I wonder if he is comparing the Clare he has just seen, in 1989, with the duplicitous me in his arms, and, as if reading my mind he says, "Any other surprises?"

"That was it."

"God, you can really keep a secret." I look at Henry, and he stares back at me, and I can tell that I have altered for him somehow.

"It made me understand, better . . . it made me appreciate . . ."

"You're trying to tell me that I did not suffer by comparison?"

"Yes." I kiss him, tentatively, and after a moment of hesitation Henry begins to kiss me back, and before too long we are on our way to being all right again. Better than all right. I told him, and it was okay, and he still loves me. My whole body feels lighter, and I sigh with the goodness of confessing, finally, and not even having a penance, not one Hail Mary or Our Father. I feel like I've walked away scot free from a totaled car. Out there, somewhere, Henry and I are making love on a green blanket in a meadow, and Gomez is looking at me sleepily and reaching for me with his enormous hands, and everything, everything is happening now, but it's too late, as usual, to change any of it, and Henry and I unwrap each other on the studio couch like brand new never before boxes of chocolate and it's not too late, not yet, anyway.

Saturday, April 14, 1990 (Clare is 18)
(6:43 a.m.)

CLARE: I open my eyes and I don't know where I am. Cigarette smell. Venetian blind shadow across cracked yellow wall. I turn my head and beside me, sleeping, in his bed, is Gomez. Suddenly I remember, and I panic.

Henry. Henry will kill me. Charisse will hate me. I sit up. Gomez's bedroom is a wreck of overfilled ashtrays, clothes, law textbooks, newspapers, dirty dishes. My clothes lie in a small, accusing pile on the floor beside me.

Gomez sleeps beautifully. He looks serene, not like a guy who's just cheated on his girlfriend with his girlfriend's best friend. His blond hair is wild, not in its usual perfect controlled state. He looks like an overgrown boy, exhausted from too many boyish games.

My head is pounding. My insides feel like they've been beaten. I get up, shakily, and walk down the hall to the bathroom, which is dank and mold-infested and filled with shaving paraphernalia and damp towels. Once I'm in the bathroom I'm not sure what I wanted; I pee and I wash my face with the hard soap sliver, and I look at myself in the mirror to see if I look any different, to see if Henry will be able to tell just by looking at me . . . I look kind of nauseous, but otherwise I just look the way I look at seven in the morning.

The house is quiet. There's a clock ticking somewhere nearby. Gomez shares this house with two other guys, friends who are also at Northwestern's Law School. I don't want to run into anyone. I go back to Gomez's room and sit on the bed.

"Good morning." Gomez smiles at me, reaches out to me. I recoil, and burst into tears. "Whoa. Kitten! Clare, baby, hey, hey . . ." He scrambles up and soon I am weeping in his arms. I think of all the times I have cried on Henry's shoulder. *Where are you?* I wonder desperately. *I need you, here and now.* Gomez is saying my name, over and over. What am I doing here, without any clothes on, crying in the embrace of an equally naked Gomez? He reaches over and hands me a box of tissue, and I blow my nose, and wipe my eyes, and then I look at him with a look of unconditional despair, and he looks back at me in confusion.

"Okay now?"

No. How can I be okay? "Yeah."

"What's wrong?"

I shrug. Gomez shifts into cross-examining fragile witness mode.

"Clare, have you ever had sex before?" I nod. "Is it Charisse? You feel bad about it 'cause of Charisse?" I nod. "Did I do something wrong?" I shake my head. "Clare, who is Henry?" I gape at him incredulously.

"How do you know? . . ." Now I've done it. Shit. Son of a bitch.

Gomez leans over and grabs his cigarettes from the bedside table, and lights one. He waves out the match and takes a deep drag. With a cigarette in his hand, Gomez seems more . . . dressed, somehow, even though he's not. He silently offers me one, and I take it, even though I don't smoke. It just seems like the thing to do, and it buys me time to think about what to say. He lights it for me, gets up, rummages around in his closet, finds a blue bathrobe that doesn't look all that clean, and hands it to me. I put it on; it's huge. I sit on the bed, smoking and watching Gomez put on a pair of jeans. Even in my wretchedness I observe that Gomez is beautiful, tall and broad and . . . large, an entirely different sort of beauty from Henry's lithe panther wildness. I immediately feel horrible for comparing. Gomez sets an ashtray next to me, and sits down on the bed, and looks at me.

"You were talking in your sleep to someone named Henry."

Damn. Damn. "What did I say?"

"Mostly just 'Henry' over and over, like you were calling someone to come to you. And 'I'm sorry.' And once you said 'Well, you weren't here,' like you were really angry. Who is Henry?"

"Henry is my lover."

"Clare, you don't have a lover. Charisse and I have seen you almost every day for six months, and you never date anyone, and no one ever calls you."

"Henry is my lover. He's been gone for a while, and he'll be back in the fall of 1991."

"Where is he?" Somewhere nearby.

"I don't know." Gomez thinks I am making this up. For no reason I am determined to make him believe me. I grab my purse, open my wallet, and show Gomez the photo of Henry. He studies it carefully.

"I've seen this guy. Well, no: someone a lot like him. This guy is too old to be the same person. But that guy's name was Henry."

My heart is beating like a mad thing. I try to be casual as I ask, "Where did you see him?"

"At clubs. Mostly Exit, and Smart Bar. But I can't imagine that he's your guy; he's a maniac. Chaos attends his every move. He's an alcoholic, and he's just . . . I don't know, he's really rough on women. Or so I hear."

"Violent?" I can't imagine Henry hitting a woman.

"No. I don't know."

"What's his last name?"

"I don't know. Listen, kitten, this guy would chew you up and spit you out . . . he's not at all what you need."

I smile. He's exactly what I need, but I know that it is futile to go chasing through clubland trying to find him. "What do I need?"

"Me. Except you don't seem to think so."

"You have Charisse. What do you want me for?"

"I just want you. I don't know why."

"You a Mormon or something?"

Gomez says very seriously, "Clare, I . . . look, Clare—"

"Don't say it."

"Really, I—"

"No. I don't want to know." I get up, stub out my cigarette, and start to put my clothes on. Gomez sits very still and watches me dress. I feel stale and dirty and creepy putting on last night's party dress in front of Gomez, but I try not to let it show. I can't do the long zipper in the back of the dress and Gomez gravely helps me with it.

"Clare, don't be mad."

"I'm not mad at you. I'm mad at myself."

"This guy must be really something if he can walk away from a girl like you and expect you to be around two years later."

I smile at Gomez. "He is *amazing.*" I can see that I have hurt Gomez's feelings. "Gomez, I'm sorry. If I was free, and you were free . . ." Gomez shakes his head, and before I know it, he's kissing me. I kiss back, and there's just a moment when I wonder. . . . "I've got to go now, Gomez."

He nods.

I leave.

Friday, April 27, 1990 (Henry is 26)

HENRY: Ingrid and I are at the Riviera Theater, dancing our tiny brains out to the dulcet tones of Iggy Pop. Ingrid and I are always happiest together when we are dancing or fucking or anything else that involves physical activity and no talking. Right now we are in heaven. We're way up front and Mr. Pop is whipping us all into a compact ball of manic energy. I told Ing once that she dances like a German and she didn't like it, but it's true: she dances seriously, like lives are hanging in the balance, like precision dancing can save the starving children in India. It's great. The Iggster is crooning *"I'm so pent up, like this I can't stay . . ."* and I know exactly how he feels. It's moments like this that I see the point of me and Ingrid. We slash and burn our way through "Lust for Life," "China Doll," "Funtime." Ingrid and I have taken enough speed to launch a mission to Pluto, and I have that weird high-pitched feeling and a deep conviction that I could do this, be here, for the rest of my life and be perfectly content. Ingrid is sweating. Her white T-shirt has glued itself to her body in an interesting and aesthetically pleasing way and I consider peeling it off of her but refrain, because she's not wearing a bra and I'll never hear the end of it. We dance, Iggy Pop sings, and sadly, inevitably, after three encores, the concert finally ends. I feel great. As we file out with our fellow elated and pumped-up concertgoers, I wonder what we should do next. Ingrid takes off to go and stand in the long line for the ladies' room, and I wait for her out on Broadway. I'm watching a yuppie in a BMW argue with a valet-parking kid over an illegal space when this huge blond guy walks up to me.

"Henry?" he asks. I wonder if I'm about to be served with a court summons or something.

"Yeah?"

"Clare says hello." Who the hell is Clare?

"Sorry, wrong number." Ingrid walks up, looking once again like her usual Bond Girl self. She sizes up this guy, who's a pretty fine specimen of guyhood. I put my arm around her.

The guy smiles. "Sorry. You must have a double out there." My heart contracts; something's going on that I don't get, a little of my future seeping into now, but now is not the moment to investigate. He seems pleased about something, and excuses himself, and walks away.

"What was that all about?" says Ingrid.

"I think he thought I was someone else." I shrug. Ingrid looks worried. Just about everything about me seems to worry Ingrid, so I ignore it. "Hey, Ing, what shall we do next?" I feel like leaping tall buildings in a single bound.

"My place?"

"Brilliant." We stop at Margie's Candies for ice cream, and soon we're in the car chanting "I scream, you scream, we all scream for ice cream," and laughing like deranged children. Later, in bed with Ingrid, I wonder who Clare is, but then I figure there's probably no answer to that, so I forget about it.

Friday, February 18, 2005 (Henry is 41, Clare is 33)

HENRY: I'm taking Charisse to the opera. It's *Tristan und Isolde*. The reason I am here with Charisse and not Clare has to do with Clare's extreme aversion to Wagner. I'm not a huge Wagnerite either, but we have season tickets and I'd just as soon go as not. We were discussing this one evening at Charisse and Gomez's place, and Charisse wistfully said that she'd never been to the opera. The upshot of it all is that Charisse and I are getting out of a taxi in front of the Lyric Opera House and Clare is at home minding Alba and playing Scrabble with Alicia, who's visiting us this week.

I'm not really in the mood for this. When I stopped at their house to collect Charisse, Gomez winked at me and said "Don't keep her out too late, son!" in his best clueless-parent voice. I can't remember the last time Charisse and I did anything by ourselves. I like Charisse, very much, but I don't have much of anything to say to her.

I shepherd Charisse through the crowd. She moves slowly, taking in the splendid lobby, marble and sweeping high galleries full of elegantly understated rich people and students with faux fur and pierced noses. Charisse smiles at the libretto vendors, two tuxedoed gents who stand at the entrance to the lobby singing "Libretto! Libretto! Buy yourself a libretto!" in two-part harmony. No one I know is here. Wagnerites are the Green Berets of opera fans; they're made of sterner stuff, and they all know each other. There's a lot of air kissing going on as Charisse and I walk upstairs to the mezzanine.

Clare and I have a private box; it's one of our indulgences. I pull back the curtain and Charisse steps in and says, "Oh!" I take her coat and drape it over a chair, and do the same with mine. We settle ourselves. Charisse crosses her ankles and folds her small hands in her lap. Her black hair gleams in the low soft light, and with her dark lipstick and dramatic eyes Charisse is like an exquisite, wicked child, all dressed up, allowed to stay up late with the grown-ups. She sits and drinks in the beauty of the Lyric, the ornate gold and green screen that shields the stage, the ripples of cascading plaster that rim every arch and dome, the excited murmur of the crowd. The lights go down and Charisse flashes me a grin. The screen rises, and we are on a boat, and Isolde is singing. I lean back in my chair and lose myself in the current of her voice.

Four hours, one love potion, and a standing ovation later, I turn to Charisse. "Well, how did you like it?"

She smiles. "It was silly, wasn't it? But the singing made it not silly."

I hold out her coat and she feels around for the arm hole; finds it and shrugs on the coat. "Silly? I guess. But I'm willing to pretend that Jane Egland is young and beautiful instead of a three-hundred-pound cow because she has the voice of Euterpe."

"Euterpe?"

"The muse of music." We join the stream of exiting, satiated listeners. Downstairs we flow out into the cold. I march us up Wacker Drive a bit and manage to snare a cab after only a few minutes. I'm about to give the cabbie Charisse's address when she says, "Henry, let's go have coffee. I don't want to go home yet." I tell the cabbie to take us to Don's Coffee Club, which is on Jarvis, at the northern edge of the city. Charisse chats about the singing, which was sublime; about the sets, which we both agree were not inspired; about the moral difficulties of enjoying Wagner when you know he was an anti-Semitic asshole whose biggest fan was Hitler. When we get to Don's, the joint is jumping; Don is holding court in an orange Hawaiian shirt and I wave to him. We find a small table in the back. Charisse orders cherry pie à la mode and coffee, and I order my usual peanut butter and jelly sandwich and coffee. Perry Como is crooning from the stereo and there's a haze of cigarette smoke drifting over the dinette sets and garage sale paintings. Charisse leans her head on her hand and sighs.

"This is so great. I feel like sometimes I forget what it was like to be a grown-up."

"You guys don't go out much?"

Charisse mushes her ice cream around with her fork, laughs. "Joe does this. He says it tastes better if it's mushy. God, I'm picking up their bad habits instead of them learning my good ones." She eats a bite of pie. "To answer your question, we do go out, but it's almost always to political stuff. Gomez is thinking about running for alderman."

I swallow my coffee the wrong way and start to cough. When I can talk again I say, "You're joking. Isn't that going over to the dark side? Gomez is always slamming the city administration."

Charisse gives me a wry look. "He's decided to change the system from within. He's burned out on horrible child abuse cases. I think he's convinced himself that he could actually improve things if he had some clout."

"Maybe he's right."

Charisse shakes her head. "I liked it better when we were young anarchist revolutionaries. I'd rather blow things up than kiss ass."

I smile. "I never realized that you were more radical than Gomez."

"Oh, yeah. Actually, it's just that I'm not as patient as Gomez. I want action."

"Gomez is patient?"

"Oh, sure. I mean, look at the whole thing with Clare—" Charisse abruptly stops, looks at me.

"What whole thing?" I realize as I ask the question that this is why we are here, that Charisse has been waiting to talk about this. I wonder what she knows that I don't know. I wonder if I want to know what Charisse knows. I don't think I want to know anything.

Charisse looks away, and then back at me. She looks down at her coffee, puts her hands around the cup. "Well, I thought you knew, but, like—Gomez is in love with Clare."

"Yes." I'm not helping her out with this.

Charisse is tracing the grain of the table's veneer with her finger. "So . . . Clare has been telling him to take a hike, and he thinks that if he just hangs in there long enough, something will happen, and he'll end up with her."

"Something will happen . . . ?"

"To you." Charisse meets my eyes.

I feel ill. "Excuse me," I say to her. I get up and make my way to the tiny Marilyn Monroe-plastered bathroom. I splash my face with cold water. I lean against the wall with my eyes closed. When it becomes obvious that I'm not going anywhere I walk back into the cafe and sit down. "Sorry. You were saying?"

Charisse looks scared and small. "Henry," she says quietly. "Tell me."

"Tell you what, Charisse?"

"Tell me you aren't going anywhere. Tell me Clare doesn't want Gomez. Tell me everything's going to work out. Or tell me it's all shit, I don't know—just tell me what happens!" Her voice shakes. She puts her hand on my arm, and I force myself not to pull away.

"You'll be fine, Charisse. It'll be okay." She stares at me, not believing and wanting to believe. I lean back in my chair. "He won't leave you."

She sighs. "And you?"

I am silent. Charisse stares at me, and then she bows her head. "Let's go home," she says, finally, and we do.

Sunday, June 12, 2005 (Clare is 34, Henry is 41)

CLARE: It's a sunny Sunday afternoon, and I walk into the kitchen to find Henry standing by the window staring out at the backyard. He beckons me over. I stand beside him and look out. Alba is playing in the yard with an older girl. The girl is about seven. She has long dark hair and she is barefoot. She wears a dirty T-shirt with the Cubs' logo on it. They are both sitting on the ground, facing each other. The girl has her back to us. Alba is smiling at her and gesturing with her hands as though she is flying. The girl shakes her head and laughs.

I look at Henry. "Who is that?"

"That's Alba."

"Yes, but who's with her?"

Henry smiles, but his eyebrows pull together so that the smile seems worried. "Clare, that's Alba when she's older. She's time traveling."

"My God." I stare at the girl. She swivels and points at the house, and I see a quick profile and then she turns away again. "Should we go out there?"

"No, she's fine. If they want to come in here they will."

"I'd love to meet her. . . ."

"Better not—" Henry begins, but as he speaks the two Albas jump up and come racing toward the back door, hand in hand.

They burst into the kitchen laughing. "Mama, Mama," says my Alba, three-year-old Alba, pointing, "look! A big girl Alba!"

The other Alba grins and says, "Hi, Mama," and I am smiling and I say, "Hello, Alba," when she turns and sees Henry and cries out, "Daddy!" and runs to him, throws her arms around him, and starts to cry. Henry glances at me, bends over Alba, rocking her, and whispers something in her ear.

HENRY: Clare is white-faced; she stands watching us, holding small Alba's hand, Alba who stands watching open-mouthed as her older self clings to me, weeping. I lean down to Alba, whisper in her ear: *"Don't tell Mama I died, okay?"* She looks up at me, tears clinging to her long lashes, lips quivering, and nods. Clare is holding a tissue, telling Alba to blow her nose, hugging her. Alba allows herself to be led off to wash her face. Small Alba, present Alba, wraps herself around my leg. "Why, Daddy? Why is she sad?" Fortunately I don't have to answer because Clare and Alba have returned; Alba is wearing one of Clare's T-shirts and a pair of my cutoffs. Clare says, "Hey, everybody. Why don't we go get an ice cream?" Both Albas smile; small Alba dances around us yelling "I scream, you scream, I scream, you scream . . ." We pile into the car, Clare driving, three-year-old Alba in the front seat and seven-year-old Alba in the backseat with me. She leans against me; I put my arm around her. Nobody says a word except little Alba, who says, "Look, Alba, a doggie! Look, Alba, look, Alba . . ." until her older self says, "Yeah, Alba, I see." Clare drives us to Zephyr; we settle into a blue glitter vinyl booth and order two banana splits, a chocolate malt, and a soft-serve vanilla cone with sprinkles. The girls suck down their banana splits like vacuum cleaners; Clare and I toy with our ice cream, not looking at each other. Clare says, "Alba, what's going on, in your present?"

Alba darts a look at me. "Not much," she says. "Gramps is teaching me Saint-Saëns' second violin concerto."

"You're in a play, at school," I prompt.

"I am?" she says. "Not yet, I guess."

"Oh, sorry," I say. "I guess that's not till next year." It goes on like this. We make halting conversation, working around what we know, what we must protect Clare and small Alba from knowing. After a while older Alba puts her head in her arms on the table. "Tired?" Clare asks her. She nods. "We'd better go," I tell Clare. We pay, and I pick Alba up; she's limp, almost asleep in my arms. Clare scoops up little Alba, who's hyper from all the sugar. Back in the car, as we're cruising up Lincoln Avenue, Alba vanishes. "She's gone back," I say to Clare. She holds my eyes in the rearview mirror for a few moments. "Back where, Daddy?" asks Alba. "Back where?"

Later:

CLARE: I've finally managed to get Alba to take a nap. Henry is sitting on our bed, drinking Scotch and staring out the window at some squirrels chasing each other around the grape arbor. I walk over and sit down next to him. "Hey," I say. Henry looks at me, puts his arm around me, pulls me to him. "Hey," he says.

"Are you going to tell me what that was all about?" I ask him.

Henry puts down his drink and starts to undo the buttons on my shirt. "Can I get away with not telling you?"

"No." I unbuckle his belt and open the button of his jeans.

"Are you sure?" He's kissing my neck.

"Yes." I slide his zipper down, run my hand under his shirt, over his stomach.

"Because you don't really want to know." Henry breathes into my ear and runs his tongue around the rim. I shiver. He takes off my shirt, undoes the clasp of my bra. My breasts fall loose and I lie back, watching Henry stripping off his jeans and underwear and shirt. He climbs onto the bed and I say, "Socks."

"Oh, yeah." He takes off his socks. We look at each other.

"You're just trying to distract me," I say.

Henry caresses my stomach. "I'm trying to distract myself. If I also manage to distract you, that's a bonus."

"You have to tell me."

"No, I don't." He cups my breasts in his hands, runs his thumbs over my nipples.

"I'll imagine the worst."

"Go ahead." I raise my hips and Henry pulls off my jeans and my underwear. He straddles me, leans over me, kisses me. *Oh, God,* I think, *what can it be? What is the worst?* I close my eyes. *A memory: the Meadow, a cold day in my childhood, running over dead grass, there was a noise, he called my name—*

"Clare?" Henry is biting my lips, gently. "Where are you?"

"1984."

Henry pauses and says, "Why?"

"I think that's where it happens."

"Where what happens?"

"Whatever it is you're afraid to tell me."

Henry rolls off of me and we are lying side by side. "Tell me about it," he says.

"It was early. A day in the fall. Daddy and Mark were out deer hunting. I woke up; I thought I heard you calling me, and I ran out into the meadow, and you were there, and you and Daddy and Mark were all looking at something, but Daddy made me go back to the house, so I never saw what you were looking at."

"Oh?"

"I went back there later in the day. There was a place in the grass all soaked in blood."

Henry says nothing. He presses his lips together. I wrap my arms around him, hold him tightly. I say, "The worst—"

"Hush, Clare."

"But—"

"Shh." Outside it is still a golden afternoon. Inside we are cold, and we cling together for warmth. Alba, in her bed, sleeps, and dreams of ice cream, dreams the small contented dreams of three, while another Alba, somewhere in the future, dreams of wrapping her arms around her father, and wakes up to find . . . what?

THE EPISODE OF THE MONROE
STREET PARKING GARAGE

....

Monday, January 7, 2006 (Clare is 34, Henry is 42)

CLARE: We are sleeping deep early morning winter sleep when the phone rings. I snap into wakefulness, my heart surging and realize Henry is there beside me. He reaches over me and picks up the phone. I glance at the clock; it's 4:32 a.m. "'Lo," says Henry. He listens for a long minute. I am wide awake now. Henry is expressionless. "Okay. Stay there. We'll leave right now." He leans over and replaces the receiver.

"Who was it?"

"Me. It was me. I'm down in the Monroe Street Parking Garage, no clothes, fifteen degrees below zero. God, I hope the car starts."

We jump out of bed and throw on yesterday's clothes. Henry is booted and has his coat on before I'm in my jeans and he runs out to start the car. I stuff Henry's shirt and long underwear and jeans and socks and boots and extra coat and mittens and a blanket into a shopping bag, wake Alba and stuff her into her coat and boots, fly into my coat and out the door. I pull out of the garage before the car is warmed up and it dies. I restart it, we sit for a minute and I try again. It snowed six inches yesterday and Ainslie is rutted with ice.

Alba is whining in her car seat and Henry shushes her. When we get to Lawrence I speed up and in ten minutes we are on the Drive; there's no one out at this hour. The Honda's heater purrs. Over the lake the sky is becoming lighter. Everything is blue and orange, brittle in the extreme cold. As we sail down Lake Shore Drive I have a strong *déja vu:* the cold, the lake in dreamy silence, the sodium glow of the streetlights: I've been here before, been here before. I'm deeply enmeshed in this moment and it stretches on, carrying me away from the strangeness of the thing into awareness of the duplicity of now; although we are speeding through this winter cityscape time stands immobile. We pass Irving, Belmont, Fullerton, LaSalle: I exit at Michigan. We fly down the deserted corridor of expensive shops, Oak Street, Chicago, Randolph, Monroe, and now we are diving down into the subterranean concrete world of the parking garage. I take the ticket the ghostly female machine voice offers me. "Drive to the northwest end," says Henry. "The pay phone by the security station." I follow his instructions. The *déja vu* is gone. I feel as though I've been abandoned by a protective angel. The garage is virtually empty. I speed across acres of yellow lines to the pay phone: the receiver dangles from its cord. No Henry.

"Maybe you got back to the present?"

"But maybe not . . ." Henry is confused, and so am I. We get out of the car. It's cold down here. My breath condenses and vanishes. I don't feel as though we should leave, but I don't have any idea what might have happened. I walk over to the security station and peer in the window. No guard. The video monitors show empty concrete. "Shit. Where would I go? Let's drive around." We get back into the car and cruise slowly through the vast pillared chambers of vacant space, past signs directing us to Go Slow, More Parking, Remember Your Car's Location. No Henry anywhere. We look at each other in defeat.

"When were you coming from?"

"I didn't say."

We drive home in silence. Alba is sleeping. Henry stares out the window. The sky is cloudless and pink in the east, and there are more cars out now, early commuters. As we wait for the stoplight at Ohio Street I hear seagulls squawking. The streets are dark with salt and water. The city is soft, white, obscured by snow. Everything is beautiful. I am detached, I am a movie. We are seemingly unscathed, but sooner or later there will be hell to pay.

∙∙∙∙∙∙∙∙∙∙∙∙∙∙∙∙∙∙∙∙∙∙∙∙∙∙∙∙∙∙∙∙∙

Thursday, June 15, 2006 (Clare is 35)

CLARE: Tomorrow is Henry's birthday. I'm in Vintage Vinyl, trying to find an album he will love that he doesn't already have. I was kind of counting on asking Vaughn, the owner of the shop, for help, because Henry's been coming here for years. But there's a high school kid behind the counter. He's wearing a Seven Dead Arson T-shirt and probably wasn't even born when most of the stuff in the shop was being recorded. I flip through the bins. Sex Pistols, Patti Smith, Supertramp, Matthew Sweet. Phish, Pixies, Pogues, Pretenders. B-52's, Kate Bush, Buzzcocks. Echo and the Bunnymen. The Art of Noise. The Nails. The Clash, the Cramps, the Cure. Television. I pause over an obscure Velvet Underground retread, trying to remember if I've seen it lying around the house, but on closer scrutiny I realize it's just a mishmash of stuff Henry has on other albums. Dazzling Killmen, Dead Kennedys. Vaughn comes in carrying a huge box, heaves it behind the counter, and goes back out. He does this a few more times, and then he and the kid start to unpack the boxes, piling LPs onto the counter, exclaiming over various things I've never heard of. I walk over to Vaughn and mutely fan three LPs before him. "Hi, Clare," he says, grinning hugely. "How's it going?"

"Hi, Vaughn. Tomorrow's Henry's birthday. Help."

He eyeballs my selections. "He's already got those two," he says nodding at Lilliput and the Breeders, "and that's really awful," indicating the Plasmatics. "Great cover, though, huh?"

"Yeah. Do you have anything in that box he might like?"

"Nah, this is all fifties. Some old lady died. You might like this, I just got this yesterday." He pulls a Golden Palominos compilation out of the New Arrivals bin. There's a couple new things on it, so I take it. Suddenly Vaughn grins at me. "I've got something really oddball for you—I've been saving it for Henry." He steps behind the counter and fishes around in the depths for a minute. "Here." Vaughn hands me an LP in a blank white jacket. I slide the record out and read the label: *"Annette Lyn Robinson, Paris Opera, May 13, 1968, Lulu."* I look at Vaughn, questioningly. "Yeah, not his usual thing, huh? It's a bootleg of a concert; it doesn't officially exist. He asked me to keep an eye out for her stuff a while back, but it's not my usual thing, either, so I found it and then I kept forgetting to tell him. I listened to it; it's really nice. Good sound quality."

"Thank you," I whisper.

"You're welcome. Hey, what's the big deal?"

"She's Henry's mother."

Vaughn raises his eyebrows and his forehead scrunches up comically. "No kidding? Yeah . . . he looks like her. Huh, that's interesting. You'd think he would have mentioned it."

"He doesn't talk about her much. She died when he was little. In a car accident."

"Oh. That's right, I sort of remember that. Well, can I find anything else for you?"

"No, that's it." I pay Vaughn and leave, hugging the voice of Henry's mother to me as I walk down Davis Street in an ecstasy of anticipation.

Friday, June 16, 2006 (Henry is 43, Clare is 35)

HENRY: It's my forty-third birthday. My eyes pop open at 6:46 a.m. even though I have the day off from work, and I can't get back to sleep. I look over at Clare and she's utterly abandoned to slumber, arms cast apart and hair fanned over her pillow willy-nilly. She looks beautiful, even with creases from the pillowcase across her cheeks. I get out of bed carefully, go to the kitchen, and start the coffee. In the bathroom I run the water for a while, waiting for it to get hot. We should get a plumber in here, but we never get around to it. Back in the kitchen I pour a cup of coffee, carry it to the bathroom, and balance it on the sink. I lather my face, and start to shave. Ordinarily, I am expert at shaving without actually looking at myself, but today, in honor of my birthday, I take inventory.

My hair has gone almost white; there's a bit of black left at the temples and my eyebrows are still completely black. I've grown it out some, not as long as I used to wear it before I met Clare, but not short, either. My skin is wind-roughened and there are creases at the edges of my eyes and across my forehead and lines that run from my nostrils to the corners of my mouth. My face is too thin. All of me is too thin. Not Auschwitz thin, but not normal thin, either. Early stages of cancer thin, perhaps. Heroin addict thin. I don't want to think about it, so I continue shaving. I rinse off my face, apply aftershave, step back, and survey the results.

At the library yesterday someone remembered that it's my birthday and so Roberto, Isabelle, Matt, Catherine, and Amelia gathered me up and took me to Beau Thai for lunch. I know there's been some talk at work about my health, about why I have suddenly lost so much weight and the fact that I have recently aged rapidly. Everyone was extra nice, the way people are to AIDS victims and chemotherapy patients. I almost long for someone to just ask me, so I can lie to them and get it over with. But instead we joked around and ate pad Thai and prik king, cashew chicken and pad seeuw. Amelia gave me a pound of killer Colombian coffee beans. Catherine, Matt, Roberto, and Isabelle splurged and got me the Getty facsimile of the *Mira Calligraphiae Monumenta,* which I have been lusting after in the Newberry bookstore for ages. I looked up at them, heartstruck, and I realized that my co-workers think I am dying. "You guys . . ." I said, and I couldn't think how to go on, so I didn't. It's not often that words fail me.

Clare gets up, Alba wakes up. We all get dressed, and pack the car. We're going to Brookfield Zoo with Gomez and Charisse and their kids. We spend the day ambling around, looking at monkeys and flamingoes, polar bears and otters. Alba likes the big cats best. Rosa holds Alba's hand and tells her about dinosaurs. Gomez does a great impression of a chimp, and Max and Joe rampage around, pretending to be elephants and playing hand-held video games. Charisse and Clare and I stroll aimlessly, talking about nothing, soaking in the sunlight. At four o'clock the kids are all tired and cranky and we pack them back in the cars, promise to do it again soon, and go home.

The baby-sitter arrives promptly at seven. Clare bribes and threatens Alba to be good, and we escape. We are dressed to the nines, at Clare's insistence, and as we sail south on Lake Shore Drive I realize that I don't know where we're going. "You'll see," says Clare. "It's not a surprise party, is it?" I ask apprehensively. "No," she assures me. Clare exits the Drive at Roosevelt and threads her way through Pilsen, a Hispanic neighborhood just south of downtown. Groups of kids are playing in the streets, and we weave around them and finally park near 20th and Racine. Clare leads me to a run-down two-flat and rings the bell at the gate. We are buzzed in, and we make our way through the trash-littered yard and up precarious stairs. Clare knocks on one of the doors and it is opened by Lourdes, a friend of Clare's from art school. Lourdes smiles and beckons us inside, and as we step in I see that the apartment has been transformed into a restaurant with only one table. Beautiful smells are wafting around, and the table is laid with white damask, china, candles. A record player stands on a heavy carved sideboard. In the living room are cages full of birds: parrots, canaries, tiny lovebirds. Lourdes kisses my cheek and says, "Happy birthday, Henry," and a familiar voice says, "Yeah, happy birthday!" I stick my head into the kitchen and there's Nell. She's stirring something in a saucepan and she doesn't stop even when I wrap my arms around her and lift her slightly off the ground. "Whooee!" she says. "You been eatin' your Wheaties!" Clare hugs Nell and they smile at each other. "He looks pretty surprised," Nell says, and Clare just smiles even more broadly. "Go on and sit down," Nell commands. "Dinner is ready."

We sit facing each other at the table. Lourdes brings small plates of exquisitely arranged antipasti: transparent prosciutto with pale yellow melon, mussels that are mild and smoky, slender strips of carrot and beet that taste of fennel and olive oil. In the candlelight Clare's skin is warm and her eyes are shadowed. The pearls she's wearing delineate her collar bones and the pale smooth area above her breasts; they rise and fall with her breath. Clare catches me staring at her and smiles and looks away. I look down and realize that I have finished eating my mussels and am sitting there holding a tiny fork in the air like an idiot. I put it down and Lourdes removes our plates and brings the next course.

We eat Nell's beautiful rare tuna, braised with a sauce of tomatoes, apples, and basil. We eat small salads full of radicchio and orange peppers and we eat little brown olives that remind me of a meal I ate with my mother in a hotel in Athens when I was very young. We drink Sauvignon Blanc, toasting each other repeatedly. ("To olives!" "To baby-sitters!" "To Nell!") Nell emerges from the kitchen carrying a small flat white cake that blazes with candles. Clare, Nell, and Lourdes sing "Happy Birthday" to me. I make a wish and blow out the candles in one breath. "That means you'll get your wish," says Nell, but mine is not a wish that can be granted. The birds talk to each other in strange voices as we all eat cake and then Lourdes and Nell vanish back into the kitchen. Clare says, "I got you a present. Close your eyes." I close my eyes. I hear Clare push her chair back from the table. She walks across the room. Then there is the noise of a needle hitting vinyl ... a hiss ... violins ... a pure soprano piercing like sharp rain through the clamor of the orchestra ... my mother's voice, singing Lulu. I open my eyes. Clare sits across the table from me, smiling. I stand up and pull her from her chair, embrace her. "Amazing," I say, and then I can't continue so I kiss her.

Much later, after we have said goodbye to Nell and Lourdes with many teary expressions of gratitude, after we have made our way home and paid the baby-sitter, after we have made love in a daze of exhausted pleasure, we lie in bed on the verge of sleep, and Clare says, "Was it a good birthday?"

"Perfect," I say. "The best."

"Do you ever wish you could stop time?" Clare asks. "I wouldn't mind staying here forever."

"Mmm," I say, rolling onto my stomach. As I slide into sleep Clare says, "I feel like we're at the top of a roller coaster," but then I am asleep and I forget to ask her, in the morning, what she means.

An Unpleasant Scene

....

Wednesday, June 28, 2006 (Henry is 43, and 43)

HENRY: I come to in the dark, on a cold concrete floor. I try to sit up, but I get dizzy and I lie down again. My head is aching. I explore with my hands; there's a big swollen area just behind my left ear. As my eyes adjust, I see the faint outlines of stairs, and Exit signs, and far above me a lone fluorescent bulb emitting cold light. All around me is the criss-crossed steel pattern of the Cage. I'm at the Newberry, after hours, inside the Cage.

"Don't panic," I say to myself out loud. "It's okay. It's okay. It's okay." I stop when I realize that I'm not listening to myself. I manage to get to my feet. I'm shivering. I wonder how long I have to wait. I wonder what my co-workers will say when they see me. Because this is it. I'm about to be revealed as the tenuous freak of nature that I really am. I have not been looking forward to this, to say the least.

I try pacing back and forth to keep warm, but this makes my head throb. I give it up, sit down in the middle of the floor of the Cage and make myself as compact as possible. Hours go by. I replay this whole incident in my head, rehearsing my lines, considering all the ways it could have gone better, or worse. Finally I get tired of that and play records for myself in my head. "That's Entertainment" by the Jam, "Pills and Soap" by Elvis Costello, "Perfect Day" by Lou Reed. I'm trying to remember all the words to the Gang of Four's "I Love a Man in a Uniform" when the lights blink on. Of course it's Kevin the Security Nazi, opening the library. Kevin is the last person on the entire planet I would want to encounter while naked and trapped in the Cage, so naturally he spots me as soon as he walks in. I am curled up on the floor, playing possum.

"Who's there?" Kevin says, louder than necessary. I imagine Kevin standing there, pasty and hung over in the dank light of the stairwell. His voice bounces around, echoing off the concrete. Kevin walks down the stairs and stands at the bottom, about ten feet away from me. "How'd you get in there?" He walks around the Cage. I continue to pretend to be unconscious. Since I can't explain, I might as well not be bothered. "My God, it's DeTamble." I can feel him standing there, gaping. Finally he remembers his radio. "Ah, ten-four, hey, Roy." Unintelligible static. "Ah, yeah, Roy it's Kevin, ah, could you come on down to A46? Yeah, at the bottom." Squawks. "Just come on down here." He turns the radio off. "Lord, DeTamble, I don't know what you think you're trying to prove, but you sure have done it now." I hear him moving around. His shoes squeak and he makes a soft grunting noise. I imagine he must be sitting on the stairs. After a few minutes a door opens upstairs and Roy comes down. Roy is my favorite security guy. He's a huge African-American gentleman who always has a beautiful smile on his face. He's the King of the Main Desk, and I'm always glad to arrive at work and bask in his magnificent good cheer.

"Whoa," Roy says. "What have we here?"

"It's DeTamble. I can't figure out how he got in there."

"DeTamble? My my. That boy sure has a thing for airing out his johnson. I ever tell you 'bout the time I found him running around the third-floor Link in his altogether?"

"Yeah, you did."

"Well, I guess we got to get him out of there."

"He's not moving."

"Well, he's breathing. You think he's hurt? Maybe we should call an ambulance."

"We're gonna need the fire department, cut him out with those Jaws of Life things they use on wrecks." Kevin sounds excited. I don't want the fire department or paramedics. I groan and sit up.

"Good *morning*, Mr. DeTamble," Roy croons. "You're here a bit early, aren't you?"

"Just a bit," I agree, pulling my knees to my chin. I'm so cold my teeth hurt from being clenched. I contemplate Kevin and Roy, and they return my gaze. "I don't suppose I could bribe you gentlemen?"

They exchange glances. "Depends," Kevin says, "on what you have in mind. We can't keep our mouths shut about this because we can't get you out by ourselves."

"No, no, I wouldn't expect that." They look relieved. "Listen. I will give each of you one hundred dollars if you will do two things for me. The first thing is, I would like one of you to go out and get me a cup of coffee."

Roy's face breaks into his patented King of the Main Desk smile. "Hell, Mr. DeTamble, I'll do that for free. 'Course, I don't know how you're gonna drink it."

"Bring a straw. And don't get it from the machines in the lounge. Go out and get real coffee. Cream, no sugar."

"Will do," says Roy.

"What's the second thing?" asks Kevin.

"I want you to go up to Special Collections and grab some

clothes out of my desk, lower right-hand drawer. Bonus points if you can do it without anyone noticing what you're up to."

"No sweat," Kevin says, and I wonder why I ever disliked the man.

"Better lock off this stairwell," Roy says to Kevin, who nods and walks off to do it. Roy stands at the side of the Cage and looks at me with pity. "So, how'd you get yourself in there?"

I shrug. "I don't have a really good answer for that."

Roy smiles, shakes his head. "Well, think about it and I'll go get you that cup of coffee."

About twenty minutes pass. Finally, I hear a door being unlocked and Kevin comes down the stairs, followed by Matt and Roberto. Kevin catches my eye and shrugs as though to say, *I tried.* He feeds my shirt through the mesh of the Cage, and I put it on while Roberto stands regarding me coldly with his arms crossed. The pants are a little bulky and it takes some effort to get them into the Cage. Matt is sitting on the stairs with a doubtful expression. I hear the door opening again. It's Roy, bringing coffee and a sweet roll. He places a straw in my coffee and sets it on the floor next to the roll. I have to drag my eyes away from it to look at Roberto, who turns to Roy and Kevin and asks, "May we have some privacy?"

"Certainly, Dr. Calle." The security guards walk upstairs and out the first-floor door. Now I am alone, trapped, and bereft of an explanation, before Roberto, whom I revere and whom I have lied to repeatedly. Now there is only the truth, which is more outrageous than any of my lies.

"All right, Henry," says Roberto. "Let's have it."

HENRY: It's a perfect September morning. I'm a little late to work because of Alba (she refused to get dressed) and the El (it refused to come) but not terribly late, by my standards, anyway. When I sign in at the Main Desk there's no Roy, it's Marsha. I say, "Hey Marsha, where's Roy?" and she says, "Oh, he's attending to some business." I say, "Oh," and take the elevator to the fourth floor. When I walk into Special Collections Isabelle says, "You're late," and I say, "But not very." I walk into my office and Matt is standing at my window, looking out over the park.

"Hi, Matt," I say, and Matt jumps a mile.

"Henry!" he says, going white. "How did you get out of the Cage?"

I set my knapsack on my desk and stare at him. "The Cage?"

"You—I just came from downstairs—you were trapped in the Cage, and Roberto is down there—you told me to come up here and wait, but you didn't say for what—"

"My god." I sit down on the desk. "Oh, my god." Matt sits down in my chair and looks up at me. "Look, I can explain . . . ," I begin.

"You can?"

"Sure." I think about it. "I—you see—oh, fuck."

"It's something really weird, isn't it, Henry?"

"Yeah. Yeah, it is." We stare at each other. "Look, Matt . . . let's go downstairs and see what's going on, and I'll explain to you and Roberto together, okay?"

"Okay." We stand up, and we go downstairs.

As we walk down the east corridor I see Roy loitering near the entrance to the stairs. He starts when he sees me, and just as he's about to ask me the obvious, I hear Catherine say, "Hi, boys, what's up?" as she breezes past us and tries to open the door to the stairs. "Hey, Roy, how come no can open?"

"Hum, well, Ms. Mead," Roy glances at me, "we've been having a problem with, uh . . ."

"It's okay, Roy," I say. "Come on, Catherine. Roy, would you mind staying up here?" He nods, and lets us into the stairwell.

As we step inside I hear Roberto say, "Listen, I do not appreciate you sitting in there telling me science fiction. If I wanted science fiction I would borrow some from Amelia." He's sitting on the bottom stairs and as we come down behind him he turns to see who it is.

"Hi, Roberto," I say softly. Catherine says, "Oh my god. Oh my god." Roberto stands up and loses his balance and Matt reaches over and steadies him. I look over at the Cage, and there I am. I'm sitting on the floor, wearing my white shirt and khakis and hugging my knees to my chest, obviously freezing and hungry. There's a cup of coffee sitting outside the Cage. Roberto and Matt and Catherine watch us silently.

"When are you from?" I ask.

"August 2006." I pick up the coffee, hold it at chin level, poke the straw through the side of the Cage. He sucks it down. "You want this sweet roll?" He does. I break it into three parts and push it in. I feel like I'm at the zoo. "You're hurt," I say. "I hit my head on something," he says. "How much longer are you going to be here?" "Another half hour or so." He gestures to Roberto. "You see?"

"What is going on?" Catherine asks.

I consult my self. "You want to explain?"

"I'm tired. Go ahead."

So I explain. I explain about being a time traveler, the practical and genetic aspects of it. I explain about how the whole thing is really a sort of disease, and I can't control it. I explain about Kendrick, and about how Clare and I met, and met again. I explain about causal loops, and quantum mechanics and photons and the speed of light. I explain about how it feels to be living outside of the time constraints most humans are subject to. I explain about the lying, and the stealing, and the fear. I explain about trying to have a normal life. "And part of having a normal life is having a normal job," I conclude.

"I wouldn't really call this a normal job," Catherine says.

"I wouldn't call this a normal life," says my self, sitting inside the Cage.

I look at Roberto, who is sitting on the stairs, leaning his head against the wall. He looks exhausted, and wistful. "So," I ask him. "Are you going to fire me?"

Roberto sighs. "No. No, Henry, I'm not going to fire you." He stands up carefully, and brushes off the back of his coat with his hand. "But I don't understand why you didn't tell me all this a long time ago."

"You wouldn't have believed me," says my self. "You didn't believe me just now, until you saw."

"Well, yes—" Roberto begins, but his next words are lost in the odd noise vacuum that sometimes accompanies my comings and goings. I turn and see a pile of clothes lying on the floor of the Cage. I will come back later this afternoon and fish them out with a clothes hanger. I turn back to Matt, Roberto, and Catherine. They look stunned.

"Gosh," says Catherine. "It's like working with Clark Kent."

"I feel like Jimmy Olsen," says Matt. "Ugh."

"That makes you Lois Lane," Roberto teases Catherine.

"No, no, Clare is Lois Lane," she replies.

Matt says, "But Lois Lane was oblivious to the Clark Kent/ Superman connection, whereas Clare . . ."

"Without Clare I would have given up a long time ago," I say. "I never understood why Clark Kent was so hell bent on keeping Lois Lane in the dark."

"It makes a better story," says Matt.

"Does it? I don't know," I reply.

Friday, July 7, 2006 (Henry is 43)

HENRY: I'm sitting in Kendrick's office, listening to him explain why it's not going to work. Outside the heat is stifling, blazing hot wet wool mummification. In here it's air-conditioned enough that I'm hunched gooseflesh in this chair. We are sitting across from each other in the same chairs we always sit in. On the table is an ashtray full of cigarette filters. Kendrick has been lighting each cigarette off the end of the previous one. We're sitting with the lights off, and the air is heavy with smoke and cold. I want a drink. I want to scream. I want Kendrick to stop talking so I can ask him a question. I want to stand up and walk out. But I sit, listening.

When Kendrick stops talking the background noises of the building are suddenly apparent.

"Henry? Did you hear me?"

I sit up and look at him like a schoolchild caught daydreaming. "Um, no."

"I asked you if you understood. Why it won't work."

"Um, yeah." I try to pull my head together. "It won't work because my immune system is all fucked up. And because I'm old. And because there are too many genes involved."

"Right." Kendrick sighs and stubs out his cigarette in the mound of stubs. Tendrils of smoke escape and die. "I'm sorry." He leans back in his chair and clasps his soft pink hands together in his lap. I think about the first time I saw him, here in this office, eight years ago. Both of us were younger and cockier, confident in the bounty of molecular genetics, ready to use science to confound nature. I think about holding Kendrick's time-traveling mouse in my hands, about the surge of hope I felt then, looking at my tiny white proxy. I think about the look on Clare's face when I tell her it's not going to work. She never thought it would work, though.

I clear my throat. "What about Alba?"

Kendrick crosses his ankles and fidgets. "What *about* Alba?"

"Would it work for her?"

"We'll never know, will we? Unless Clare changes her mind about letting me work with Alba's DNA. And we both know perfectly well that Clare's terrified of gene therapy. She looks at me like I'm Josef Mengele every time I try to discuss it with her."

"But if you had Alba's DNA," I say, "you could make some mice and work on stuff for her and when she turns eighteen if she wants she can try it."

"Yes."

"So even if I'm fucked at least Alba might benefit someday."

"Yes."

"Okay, then." I stand and rub my hands together, pluck my cotton shirt away from my body where it has been adhered by now-cold sweat. "That's what we'll do."

Friday, July 14, 2006 (Clare is 35, Henry is 43)

CLARE: I'm in the studio making gampi tissue. It's a paper so thin and transparent you can see through it; I plunge the su-ketta into the vat and bring it up, rolling the delicate slurry around until it is perfectly distributed. I set it on the corner of the vat to drain, and I hear Alba laughing, Alba running through the garden, Alba yelling, "Mama! Look what Daddy got me!" She bursts through the door and clatters toward me, Henry following more sedately. I look down to see why she is clattering and I see: ruby slippers.

"They're just like Dorothy's!" Alba says, doing a little tap dance on the wooden floor. She taps her heels together three times, but she doesn't vanish. Of course, she's already home. I laugh. Henry looks pleased with himself.

"Did you make it to the post office?" I ask him.

His face falls. "Shit. No, I forgot. Sorry. I'll go tomorrow, first thing." Alba is twirling around, and Henry reaches out and stops her. "Don't, Alba. You'll get dizzy."

"I like being dizzy."

"It's not a good idea."

Alba is wearing a T-shirt and shorts. She has a Band-Aid over the skin in the crook of her elbow. "What happened to your arm?" I ask her. Instead of answering she looks at Henry, so I do, too.

"It's nothing," he says. "She was sucking on her skin and she gave herself a hickey."

"What's a hickey?" Alba asks. Henry starts to explain but I say, "Why does a hickey need a Band-Aid?"

"I dunno," he says. "She just wanted one."

I have a premonition. Call it the sixth sense of mothers. I walk over to Alba. "Let's see."

She hugs her arm close to her, clutching it tight with her other arm. "Don't take off the Band-Aid. It'll hurt."

"I'll be careful." I grip her arm firmly. She makes a whimpering noise, but I am determined. Slowly I unbend her arm, peel off the bandage gently. There's a small red puncture wound in the center of a purple bruise. Alba says, "It's sore, *don't*," and I release her. She sticks the Band-Aid back down, and watches me, waiting.

"Alba, why don't you go call Kimy and see if she wants to come over for dinner?" Alba smiles and races out of the studio. In a minute the back door of the house bangs. Henry is sitting at my drawing table, swiveling slightly back and forth in my chair. He watches me. He waits for me to say something.

"I don't believe it," I finally say. "How could you?"

"I had to," Henry says. His voice is quiet. "She—I couldn't leave her without at least—I wanted to give her a head start. So Kendrick can be working on it, working for her, just in case." I walk over to him, squeaking in my galoshes and rubber apron, and lean against the table. Henry tilts his head, and the light rakes his face and I see the lines that run across his forehead, around the edges of his mouth, his eyes. He has lost more weight. His eyes are huge in his face. "Clare, I didn't tell her what it was for. You can tell her, when . . . it's time."

I shake my head, no. "Call Kendrick and tell him to stop."

"No."

"Then I will."

"Clare, don't—"

"You can do whatever you want with your own body, Henry, but—"

"Clare!" Henry squeezes my name out through clenched teeth.

"What?"

"It's over, okay? I'm done. Kendrick says he can't do anything more."

"But—" I pause to absorb what he's just said. "But then . . . what happens?"

Henry shakes his head. "I don't know. Probably what we thought might happen . . . happens. But if that's what happens, then . . . I can't just leave Alba without trying to help her . . . oh, Clare, just let me do this for her! It may not work, she may never use it—she may love time traveling, she may never be lost, or hungry, she may never get arrested or chased or raped or beat up, but what if she *doesn't* love it? What if she wants to just be a regular girl? Clare? Oh, Clare, don't cry . . ." But I can't stop, I stand weeping in my yellow rubber apron, and finally Henry stands up and puts his arms around me. "It's not like we ever were exempt, Clare," he says softly. "I'm just trying to make her a safety net." I can feel his ribs through his T-shirt. "Will you let me at least leave her that?" I nod, and Henry kisses my forehead. "Thank you," he says, and I start to cry again.

Saturday, October 27, 1984 (Henry is 43, Clare is 13)

HENRY: I know the end, now. It goes like this: I will be sitting in the Meadow, in the early morning, in autumn. It will be overcast, and chilly, and I will be wearing a black wool overcoat and boots and gloves. It will be a date that is not on the List. Clare will be asleep, in her warm twin bed. She will be thirteen years old.

In the distance, a shot will crack across the dry cold air. It is deer-hunting season. Somewhere out there, men in bright orange garments will be sitting, waiting, shooting. Later they will drink beer, and eat the sandwiches their wives have packed for them.

The wind will pick up, will ripple through the orchard, stripping the useless leaves from the apple trees. The back door of Meadowlark House will slam, and two tiny figures in fluorescent orange will emerge, carrying matchstick rifles. They will walk toward me, into the Meadow, Philip and Mark. They will not see me, because I will be huddled in the high grass, a dark, unmoving spot in a field of beige and dead green. About twenty yards from me Philip and Mark will turn off the path and walk towards the woods.

They will stop and listen. They will hear it before I do: a rustling, thrashing, something moving through the grass, something large and clumsy, a flash of white, a tail perhaps? and it will come toward me, toward the clearing, and Mark will raise his rifle, aim carefully, squeeze the trigger, and:

There will be a shot, and then a scream, a human scream. And then a pause. And then: *"Clare! Clare!"* And then nothing.

I will sit for a moment, not thinking, not breathing. Philip will be running, and then I will be running, and Mark, and we will converge on the place:

But there will be nothing. Blood on the earth, shiny and thick. Bent dead grass. We will stare at each other without recognition, over the empty dirt.

In her bed, Clare will hear the scream. She will hear someone calling her name, and she will sit up, her heart jumping in her ribcage. She will run downstairs, out the door, into the Meadow in her nightgown. When she sees the three of us she will stop, confused. Behind the backs of her father and brother I will put my finger to my lips. As Philip walks to her I will turn away, will stand in the shelter of the orchard and watch her shivering in her father's embrace, while Mark stands by, impatient and perplexed, his fifteen-year-old's stubble gracing his chin and he will look at me, as though he is trying to remember.

And Clare will look at me, and I will wave to her, and she will walk back to her house with her dad, and she will wave back, slender, her nightgown blowing around her like an angel's, and she will get smaller and smaller, will recede into the distance and disappear into the house, and I will stand over a small trampled bloody patch of soil and I will know: somewhere out there I am dying.

The Episode of the Monroe
Street Parking Garage

....

Monday, January 7, 2006 (Henry is 43)

HENRY: It's cold. It's very, very cold and I am lying on the ground in snow. Where am I? I try to sit up. My feet are numb, I can't feel my feet. I'm in an open space with no buildings or trees. How long have I been here? It's night. I hear traffic. I get to my hands and knees. I look up. I'm in Grant Park. The Art Institute stands dark and closed across hundreds of feet of blank snow. The beautiful buildings of Michigan Avenue are silent. Cars stream along Lake Shore Drive, headlights cutting through night. Over the lake is a faint line of light; dawn is coming. I have to get out of here. I have to get warm.

I stand up. My feet are white and stiff. I can't feel them or move them, but I begin to walk, I stagger forward through the snow, sometimes falling, getting back up and walking, it goes on and on, finally I am crawling. I crawl across a street. I crawl down concrete stairs backwards, clinging to the handrail. Salt gets into the raw places on my hands and knees. I crawl to a pay phone.

Seven rings. Eight. Nine. "'Lo," says my self.

"Help me," I say. "I'm in the Monroe Street Parking Garage. It's unbelievably fucking cold down here. I'm near the guard station. Come and get me."

"Okay. Stay there. We'll leave right now."

I try to hang up the phone but miss. My teeth are chattering uncontrollably. I crawl to the guard station and hammer on the door. No one is there. Inside I see video monitors, a space heater, a jacket, a desk, a chair. I try the knob. It's locked. I have nothing to open it with. The window is wire reinforced. I am shivering hard. There are no cars down here.

"Help me!" I yell. No one comes. I curl into a ball in front of the door, bring my knees to my chin, wrap my hands around my feet. No one comes, and then, at last, at last, I am gone.

FRAGMENTS

••••••••••••••••••••••••••••••••

Monday, Tuesday, Wednesday, September 25, 26, and 27, 2006
(Clare is 35, Henry is 43)

CLARE: Henry has been gone all day. Alba and I went to Mc-
Donald's for dinner. We played Go Fish and Crazy Eights; Alba
drew a picture of a girl with long hair flying a dog. We picked out
her dress for school tomorrow. Now she is in bed. I am sitting on
the front porch trying to read Proust; reading in French is making
me drowsy and I am almost asleep when there is a crash in the living room and Henry is on the floor shivering, white and cold—
"Help me," he says through chattering teeth and I run for the
phone.

Later:

The Emergency Room: a scene of fluorescent limbo: old people full
of ailments, mothers with feverish small children, teenagers whose
friends are having bullets removed from various limbs, who will
brag about this later to admiring girls but who are now subdued
and tired.

Later:

In a small white room: nurses lift Henry onto a bed and remove his blanket. His eyes open, register me, and close. A blond intern looks him over. A nurse takes his temperature, pulse. Henry is shivering, shivering so intensely it makes the bed shake, makes the nurse's arm vibrate like the Magic Fingers beds in 1970s motels. The resident looks at Henry's pupils, ears, nose, fingers, toes, genitals. They begin to wrap him in blankets and something metallic and aluminum foil-like. They pack his feet in cold packs. The small room is very warm. Henry's eyes flicker open again. He is trying to say something. It sounds like my name. I reach under the blankets and hold his icy hands in mine. I look at the nurse. "We need to warm him up, get his core temperature up," she says. "Then we'll see."

Later:

"How on earth did he get hypothermia in September?" the resident asks me.

"I don't know," I say. "Ask him."

Later:

It's morning. Charisse and I are in the hospital cafeteria. She's eating chocolate pudding. Upstairs in his room Henry is sleeping. Kimy is watching him. I have two pieces of toast on my plate; they are soggy with butter and untouched. Someone sits down next to Charisse; it's Kendrick. "Good news," he says, "his core temp's up to ninety-seven point six. There doesn't seem to be any brain damage."

I can't say anything. *Thank you, God,* is all I think.

"Okay, um, I'll check back later when I'm finished at Rush St. Luke's," says Kendrick, standing up.

"Thank you, David," I say as he's about to walk away, and Kendrick smiles and leaves.

Later:

Dr. Murray comes in with an Indian nurse whose name tag says Sue. Sue is carrying a large basin and a thermometer and a bucket. Whatever is about to happen, it will be low-tech.

"Good morning, Mr. DeTamble, Mrs. DeTamble. We're going to rewarm your feet." Sue sets the basin on the floor and silently disappears into the bathroom. Water runs. Dr. Murray is very large and has a wonderful beehive hairdo that only certain very imposing and beautiful black women can get away with. Her bulk tapers down from the hem of her white coat into two perfect feet in alligator-skin pumps. She produces a syringe and an ampoule from her pocket, and proceeds to draw the contents of the ampoule into the syringe.

"What is that?" I ask.

"Morphine. This is going to hurt. His feet are pretty far gone." She gently takes Henry's arm, which he mutely holds out to her as though she has won it from him in a poker game. She has a delicate touch. The needle slides in and she depresses the plunger; after a moment Henry makes a little moan of gratitude. Dr. Murray is removing the cold packs from Henry's feet as Sue emerges with hot water. She sets it on the floor by the bed. Dr. Murray lowers the bed, and the two of them manipulate him into a sitting position. Sue measures the temperature of the water. She pours the water into the basin and immerses Henry's feet. He gasps.

"Any tissue that's gonna make it will turn bright red. If it doesn't look like a lobster, it's a problem."

I watch Henry's feet floating in the yellow plastic basin. They are white as snow, white as marble, white as titanium, white as paper, white as bread, white as sheets, white as white can be. Sue changes the water as Henry's ice feet cool it down. The thermometer shows one hundred and six degrees. In five minutes it is ninety degrees and Sue changes it again. Henry's feet bob like dead fish. Tears run down his cheeks and disappear under his chin. I wipe his face. I stroke his head. I watch to see his feet turn bright red. It's like waiting for a photograph to develop, watching for the image slowly graying into black in the tray of chemicals. A flush of red appears at the ankles of both feet. The red spreads in splotches over the left heel, finally some of the toes hesitantly blush. The right foot remains stubbornly blanched. Pink appears reluctantly as far as the ball of the foot, and then goes no farther. After an hour, Dr. Murray and Sue carefully dry Henry's feet and Sue places bits of cotton between his toes. They put him back in bed and arrange a frame over his feet so nothing touches them.

The following night:

It's very late at night and I am sitting by Henry's bed in Mercy Hospital, watching him sleep. Gomez is sitting in a chair on the other side of the bed, and he is also asleep. Gomez sleeps with his head back and his mouth open, and every now and then he makes a little snorting noise and then turns his head.

Henry is still and silent. The IV machine beeps. At the foot of the bed a tent-like contraption raises the blankets away from the place where his feet should be, but Henry's feet are not there now. The frostbite ruined them. Both feet were amputated above the ankles this morning. I cannot imagine, I am trying not to imagine, what is below the blankets. Henry's bandaged hands are lying above the blankets and I take his hand, feeling how cool and dry it is, how the pulse beats in the wrist, how tangible Henry's hand is in my hand. After the surgery Dr. Murray asked me what I wanted her to do with Henry's feet. *Reattach them* seemed like the correct answer, but I just shrugged and looked away.

A nurse comes in, smiles at me, and gives Henry his injection. In a few minutes he sighs, as the drug envelopes his brain, and turns his face toward me. His eyes open so slightly, and then he is asleep again.

I want to pray, but I can't remember any prayers, all that runs through my head is *Eeny-meeny miney moe, catch a tiger by the toe, if he hollers, let him go, eeny meeny miney moe.* Oh, God, please don't, please don't do this to me. *But the Snark was a boojum.* No. Nothing comes. *Envoyez chercher le médecin. Qu'avez-vous? Il faudra aller à l'hôpital. Je me suis coupé assez fortement. Otez le bandage et laissez-moi voir. Oui, c'est une coupure profunde.*

I don't know what time it is. Outside it is getting light. I place Henry's hand back on the blanket. He draws it to his chest, protectively.

Gomez yawns, and stretches his arms out, cracking his knuckles. "Morning, kitten," he says, and gets up and lumbers into the bathroom. I can hear him peeing as Henry opens his eyes.

"Where am I?"

"Mercy. September 27, 2006."

Henry stares up at the ceiling. Then, slowly, he pushes himself up against the pillows and stares at the foot of the bed. He leans forward, reaching with his hands under the blanket. I close my eyes.

Henry begins to scream.

Tuesday, October 17, 2006 (Clare is 35, Henry is 43)

CLARE: Henry has been home from the hospital for a week. He spends the days in bed, curled up, facing the window, drifting in and out of morphine-laced sleep. I try to feed him soup, and toast, and macaroni and cheese, but he doesn't eat very much. He doesn't say much, either. Alba hovers around, silent and anxious to please, to bring Daddy an orange, a newspaper, her Teddy; but Henry only smiles absently and the small pile of offerings sits unused on his nightstand. A brisk nurse named Sonia Browne comes once a day to change the dressings and to give advice, but as soon as she vanishes into her red Volkswagen Beetle Henry subsides into his vacant-lot persona. I help him to use the bedpan. I make him change one pair of pajamas for another. I ask him how he feels, what he needs, and he answers vaguely or not at all. Although Henry is right here in front of me, he has disappeared.

I'm walking down the hall past the bedroom with a basket of laundry in my arms and I see Alba through the slightly open door, standing next to Henry, who is curled up in bed. I stop and watch her. She stands still, her arms hanging at her side, her black braids dangling down her back, her blue turtleneck distorted from being pulled on. Morning light floods the room, washes everything yellow.

"Daddy?" Alba says, softly. Henry doesn't respond. She tries again, louder. Henry turns toward her, rolls over. Alba sits down on the bed. Henry has his eyes closed.

"Daddy?"

"Hmm?"

"Are you dying?"

Henry opens his eyes and focuses on Alba. "No."

"Alba said you died."

"That's in the future, Alba. Not yet. Tell Alba she shouldn't tell you those kinds of things." Henry runs his hand over the beard that's been growing since we left the hospital. Alba sits with her hands folded in her lap and her knees together.

"Are you going to stay in bed all the time now?"

Henry pulls himself up so he is leaning against the headboard.

"Maybe." He is rummaging in the drawer of the nightstand, but the painkillers are in the bathroom.

"Why?"

"Because I feel like shit, *okay*?"

Alba shrinks away from Henry, gets up off the bed. "Okay!" she says, and she is opening the door and almost collides with me and is startled and then she silently flings her arms around my waist and I pick her up, so heavy in my arms now. I carry her into her room and we sit in the rocker, rocking together, Alba's hot face against my neck. What can I tell you, Alba? What can I say?

*Wednesday and Thursday, October 18 and 19,
and Thursday, October 26, 2006 (Clare is 35, Henry is 43)*

CLARE: I'm standing in my studio with a roll of armature wire and a bunch of drawings. I've cleared off the big work table, and the drawings are neatly pinned up on the wall. Now I stand and try to summon up the piece in my mind's eye. I try to imagine it 3-D. Life size. I snip off a length of wire and it springs away from the huge roll; I begin to shape a torso. I weave the wire into shoulders, ribcage, and then a pelvis. I pause. Maybe the arms and legs should be articulated? Should I make feet or not? I start to make a head and then realize that I don't want any of this. I push it all under the table and begin again with more wire.

Like an angel. *Every angel is terrifying. And yet, alas, I invoke you, almost deadly birds of the soul* . . . It is only the wings that I want to give him. I draw in the air with the thin metal, looping and weaving; I measure with my arms to make a wingspan, I repeat the process, mirror-reversed, for the second wing, comparing symmetry as though I'm giving Alba a haircut, measuring by eye, feeling out the weight, the shapes. I hinge the wings together, and then I get up on the ladder and hang them from the ceiling. They float, air encompassed by lines, at the level of my breasts, eight feet across, graceful, ornamental, useless.

At first I imagined white, but I realize now that that's not it. I open the cabinet of pigments and dyes. Ultramarine, Yellow Ochre, Raw Umber, Viridian, Madder Lake. No. Here it is: Red Iron Oxide. The color of dried blood. A terrible angel wouldn't be white, or would be whiter than any white I can make. I set the jar on the counter, along with Bone Black. I walk to the bundles of fiber that stand, fragrant, in the far corner of the studio. Kozo and linen; transparency and pliancy, a fiber that rattles like chattering teeth combined with one that is soft as lips. I weigh out two pounds of kozo, tough and resilient bark that must be cooked and beaten, broken and pounded. I heat water in the huge pot that covers two burners on the stove. When it is boiling I feed the kozo into it, watching it darken and slowly take in water. I measure in soda ash and cover the pot, turn on the exhaust hood. I chop a pound of white linen into small pieces, fill the beater with water, and start it rending and tearing up the linen into a fine white pulp. Then I make myself coffee and sit staring out the window across the yard at the house.

At that moment:

HENRY: My mother is sitting on the foot of my bed. I don't want her to know about my feet. I close my eyes and pretend to be asleep.

"Henry?" she says. "I know you're awake. C'mon, buddy, rise and shine."

I open my eyes. It's Kimy. "Mmm. Morning."

"It's 2:30 in the afternoon. You should get out of bed."

"I can't get out of bed, Kimy. I don't have any feet."

"You got wheelchair," she says. "Come on, you need a bath, you need a shave, pee-yoo, you smell like an old man." Kimy stands up, looking very grim. She peels the covers off of me and I lie there like a shelled shrimp, cold and flaccid in the afternoon sunlight. Kimy browbeats me into sitting in the wheelchair, and she wheels me to the door of the bathroom, which is too narrow for the chair to pass.

"Okay," Kimy says, standing in front of me with her hands on her hips. "How we gonna do this? Huh?"

"I don't know, Kimy. I'm just the gimp; I don't actually work here."

"What kind of word is that, *gimp*?"

"It's a highly pejorative slang word used to describe cripples."

Kimy looks at me as though I am eight and have used the word *fuck* in her presence (I didn't know what it meant, I only knew it was forbidden). "I think it's 'sposed to be *disabled*, Henry." She leans over and unbuttons my pajama top.

"I've got *hands*," I say, and finish the unbuttoning myself. Kimy turns around, brusque and grumpy, and turns on the tap, adjusts the temperature, places the plug in the drain. She rummages in the medicine cabinet, brings out my razor, shaving soap, the beaver-hair shaving brush. I can't figure out how to get out of the wheel-chair. I decide to try sliding off the seat; I push my ass forward, arch my back, and slither toward the floor. I wrench my left shoulder and bang my butt as I go down, but it's not too bad. In the hospital the physical therapist, an encouraging young person named Penny Featherwight, had several techniques for getting in and out of the chair, but they all had to do with chair/bed and chair/chair situations. Now I'm sitting on the floor and the bathtub looms like the white cliffs of Dover above me. I look up at Kimy, eighty-two years old, and realize that I'm on my own, here. She looks at me and it's all pity, that look. I think *fuck it, I have to do this somehow, I can't let*

Kimy look at me like that. I shrug out of my pajama bottoms, and begin to unwrap the bandages that cover the dressings on my legs. Kimy looks at her teeth in the mirror. I stick my arm over the side of the tub and test the bath water.

"If you throw some herbs in there you can have stewed gimp for supper."

"Too hot?" Kimy asks.

"Yeah."

Kimy adjusts the faucets and then leaves the bathroom, pushing the wheelchair out of the doorway. I gingerly remove the dressing from my right leg. Under the wrappings the skin is pale and cold. I put my hand at the folded-over part, the flesh that cushions the bone. I just took a Vicodin a little while ago. I wonder if I could take another one without Clare noticing. The bottle is probably up there in the medicine cabinet. Kimy comes back carrying one of the kitchen chairs. She plops it down next to me. I remove the dressing from the other leg.

"She did a nice job," Kimy says.

"Dr. Murray? Yeah, it's a big improvement, much more aerodynamic."

Kimy laughs. I send her to the kitchen for phone books. When she puts them next to the chair I raise myself so I'm sitting on them. Then I scramble onto the chair, and sort of fall/roll into the bathtub. A huge wave of water sloshes out of the tub onto the tile. I'm in the bathtub. Hallelujah. Kimy turns off the water, and dries her legs with a towel. I submerge.

Later:

CLARE: After hours of cooking I strain the kozo and it, too, goes into the beater. The longer it stays in the beater, the finer and more bonelike it will be. After four hours, I add retention aid, clay, pigment. The beige pulp suddenly turns a deep dark earth red. I drain it into buckets and pour it into the waiting vat. When I walk back to the house Kimy is in the kitchen making the kind of tuna fish casserole that has potato chips crumbled over it.

"How'd it go?" I ask her.

"Real good. He's in the living room." There is a trail of water between the bathroom and the living room in Kimy-sized footprints. Henry is sleeping on the sofa with a book spread open on his chest. Borges' *Ficciones.* He is shaved and I lean over him and breathe; he smells fresh, his damp gray hair sticking up all ways. Alba is chattering to Teddy in her room. For a moment I feel as though *I've* time traveled, as though this is some stray moment from *before,* but then I let my eyes travel down Henry's body to the flatnesses at the end of the blanket, and I know that I am only here and now.

The next morning it's raining. I open the door of the studio and the wire wings await me, floating in the morning gray light. I turn on the radio; it's Chopin, rolling etudes like waves over sand. I don rubber boots, a bandanna to keep my hair out of the pulp, a rubber apron. I hose down my favorite teak and brass mold and deckle, uncover the vat, set up a felt to couch the paper onto. I reach down into the vat and agitate the slurry of dark red to mix the fiber and water. Everything drips. I plunge the mold and deckle into the vat, and carefully bring it up, level, streaming water. I set it on the corner of the vat and the water drains from it and leaves a layer of fiber on the surface; I remove the deckle and press the mold onto the felt, rocking it gently and as I remove it the paper remains on the felt, delicate and shiny. I cover it with another felt, wet it, and again: I plunge the mold and deckle down, bring it up, drain it, couch it. I lose myself in the repetition, the piano music floating over the water sloshing and dripping and raining. When I have a post of paper and felt, I press it in the hydraulic paper press. Then I go back to the house and eat a ham sandwich. Henry is reading. Alba is at school.

After lunch, I stand in front of the wings with my post of freshly made paper. I am going to cover the armature with a paper membrane. The paper is damp and dark and wants to tear but it drapes over the wire forms like skin. I twist the paper into sinews, into cords that twist and connect. The wings are bat wings now, the tracing of the wire is evident below the gaunt paper surface. I dry the paper I haven't used yet, heating it on sheets of steel. Then I begin to tear it into strips, into feathers. When the wings are dry I will sew these on, one by one. I begin to paint the strips, black and gray and red. Plumage, for the terrible angel, the deadly bird.

A week later, in the evening:

HENRY: Clare has cajoled me into getting dressed and has enlisted Gomez to carry me out the back door, across the yard, and into her studio. The studio is lit with candles; there are probably a hundred of them, more, on tables and on the floor, and on the windowsills. Gomez sets me down on the studio couch, and retreats to the house. In the middle of the studio a white sheet is suspended from the ceiling, and I turn around to see if there's a projector, but there isn't. Clare is wearing a dark dress, and as she moves around the room her face and hands float white and disembodied.

"Want some coffee?" she asks me. I haven't had any since before the hospital. "Sure," I reply. She pours two cups, adds cream, and brings me one. The hot cup feels familiar and good in my hand. "I made you something," Clare says.

"Feet? I could use some feet."

"Wings," she says, dropping the white sheet to the floor.

The wings are huge and they float in the air, wavering in the candlelight. They are darker than the darkness, threatening but also redolent of longing, of freedom, of rushing through space. The feeling of standing solidly, *on my own two feet*, of running, running like flying. The dreams of hovering, of flying as though gravity has been rescinded and now is allowing me to be removed from the earth a safe distance, these dreams come back to me in the twilit studio. Clare sits down next to me. I feel her looking at me. The wings are silent, their edges ragged. I cannot speak. *Siehe, ich lebe. Woraus? Weder Kindheit noch Zukunft/ werden weniger . . . Überzähliges Dasein/ entspringt mir Herzen. (Look, I am living. On what? Neither childhood nor future/ grows any smaller . . . Superabundant being/ wells up in my heart.)*

"Kiss me," Clare says, and I turn to her, white face and dark lips floating in the dark, and I submerge, I fly, I am released: being wells up in my heart.

FEET DREAMS

••••••••••••••••••••••••••••••••

October/November 2006 (Henry is 43)

HENRY: I dream that I am at the Newberry, giving a Show and Tell to some graduate students from Columbia College. I'm showing them incunabula, early printed books. I show them the Gutenberg Fragment, Caxton's *Game and Play of Chess*, the Jensen *Eusebius*. It's going well, they are asking good questions. I rummage around on the cart, looking for this special book I just found in the stacks, something I never knew we had. It's in a heavy red box. There's no title, just the call number, CASE WING f ZX 983.D 453, stamped in gold under the Newberry insignia. I place the box on the table and set out the pads. I open the box, and there, pink and perfect, are my feet. They are surprisingly heavy. As I set them on the pads the toes all wiggle, to say Hi, to show me they can still do it. I begin to speak about them, explaining the relevance of my feet to fifteenth century Venetian printing. The students are taking notes. One of them, a pretty blonde in a shiny sequined tank top, points at my feet, and says, "Look, they're all white!" And it's true, the skin has gone dead white, the feet are lifeless and putrid. I sadly make a note to myself to send them up to Conservation first thing tomorrow.

In my dream I am running. Everything is fine. I run along the lake, from Oak Street Beach, heading north. I feel my heart pumping, my lungs smoothly rising and falling. I am moving right along. What a relief, I think. I was afraid I'd never run again, but here I am, running. It's great.

But things begin to go wrong. Parts of my body are falling off. First my left arm goes. I stop and pick it up off the sand and brush it off and put it back on, but it isn't very securely attached and it comes off again after only half a mile. So I carry it in my other arm, thinking maybe when I get it back home I can attach it more tightly. But then the other arm goes, and I have no arms at all to even pick up the arms I've lost. So I continue running. It's not too bad; it doesn't hurt. Soon I realize that my cock has dislodged and fallen into the right leg of my sweatpants, where it is banging around in an annoying manner, trapped by the elastic at the bottom. But I can't do anything about it, so I ignore it. And then I can feel that my feet are all broken up like pavement inside my shoes, and then both of my feet break off at the ankles and I fall face-first onto the path. I know that if I stay there I will be trampled by other runners, so I begin to roll. I roll and roll until I roll into the lake, and the waves roll me under, and I wake up gasping.

I dream that I am in a ballet. I am the star ballerina, I am in my dressing room being swathed in pink tulle by Barbara, who was my mom's dresser. Barbara is a tough cookie, so even though my feet hurt like hell I don't complain as she tenderly encases the stumps in long pink satin toe shoes. When she finishes I stagger up from my chair and cry out. "Don't be a sissy," says Barbara, but then she relents and gives me a shot of morphine. Uncle Ish appears at the door of the dressing room and we hurry down endless backstage hallways. I know that my feet hurt even though I cannot see them or feel them. We rush on, and suddenly I am in the wings and looking onto the stage I realize that the ballet is *The Nutcracker,* and I am the Sugar Plum Fairy. For some reason this really bugs me. This isn't what I was expecting. But someone gives me a little shove, and I totter on stage. And I dance. I am blinded by the lights, I dance without thinking, without knowing the steps, in an ecstasy of pain. Finally I fall to my knees, sobbing, and the audience rises to their feet, and applauds.

Friday, November 3, 2006 (Clare is 35, Henry is 43)

CLARE: Henry holds up an onion and looks at me gravely and says, "*This* . . . is an onion."

I nod. "Yes. I've read about them."

He raises one eyebrow. "Very good. Now, to peel an onion, you take a sharp knife, lay the aforementioned onion sideways on a cutting board, and remove each end, like so. Then you can peel the onion, like so. Okay. Now, slice it into cross-sections. If you're making onion rings, you just pull apart each slice, but if you're making soup or spaghetti sauce or something you dice it, like this . . ."

Henry has decided to teach me to cook. All the kitchen counters and cabinets are too high for him in his wheelchair. We sit at the kitchen table, surrounded by bowls and knives and cans of tomato sauce. Henry pushes the cutting board and knife across the table to me, and I stand up and awkwardly dice the onion. Henry watches patiently. "Okay, great. Now, green peppers: you run the knife around here, then pull out the stem . . ."

We make marinara sauce, pesto, lasagna. Another day it's

chocolate chip cookies, brownies, crème brûlée. Alba is in heaven. "More dessert," she begs. We poach eggs and salmon, make pizza from scratch. I have to admit that it's kind of fun. But I'm terrified the first night I cook dinner by myself. I'm standing in the kitchen surrounded by pots and pans, the asparagus is overcooked and I burn myself taking the monkfish out of the oven. I put everything on plates and bring it into the dining room where Henry and Alba are sitting at their places. Henry smiles, encouragingly. I sit down; Henry raises his glass of milk in the air: "To the new cook!" Alba clinks her cup against his, and we begin to eat. I sneak glances at Henry, eating. And as I'm eating, I realize that everything tastes fine. "It's good, Mama!" Alba says, and Henry nods. "It's terrific, Clare," Henry says, and we stare at each other and I think, *Don't leave me.*

WHAT GOES AROUND
COMES AROUND

••••••••••••••••••••••••••••••••

Monday, December 18, 2006/Sunday, January 2, 1994 (Henry is 43)

HENRY: I wake up in the middle of the night with a thousand razor-toothed insects gnawing on my legs and before I can even shake a Vicodin out of the bottle I am falling. I double up, I am on the floor but it's not our floor, it's some other floor, some other night. Where am I? Pain makes everything seem shimmery, but it's dark and there's something about the smell, what does it remind me of? Bleach. Sweat. Perfume, so familiar—but it couldn't be—

Footsteps walking up stairs, voices, a key unlocking several locks *(where can I hide?)* the door opens, I'm crawling across the floor as the light snaps on and explodes in my head like a flashbulb and a woman whispers, "Oh my god." I'm thinking *No, this just can't be happening,* and the door shuts and I hear Ingrid say, "Celia, you've got to go," and Celia protests, and as they stand on the other side of the door arguing about it I look around desperately but there's no way out. This must be Ingrid's apartment on Clark Street where I have never been but here is all her stuff, overwhelming me, the Eames chair, the kidney-shaped marble coffee table loaded with fashion magazines, the ugly orange couch we used to—I cast around wildly for something to wear, but the only textile in this minimal room is a purple and yellow afghan that's clashing with the couch, so I grab it and wind it around myself, hoist myself onto the couch and Ingrid opens the door again. She stands quietly for a long moment and looks at me and I look at her and all I can think is oh, Ing, why did you do this to yourself?

The Ingrid who lives in my memory is the incandescent blond angel of cool I met at Jimbo's Fourth of July party in 1988; Ingrid Carmichel was devastating and untouchable, encased in gleaming armor made of wealth, beauty, and ennui. The Ingrid who stands looking at me now is gaunt and hard and tired; she stands with her head tilted to one side and looks at me with wonder and contempt. Neither of us seems to know what to say. Finally she takes off her coat, tosses it on the chair, and perches at the other end of the couch. She's wearing leather pants. They squeak a little as she sits down.

"Henry."

"Ingrid."

"What are you doing here?"

"I don't know. I'm sorry. I just—well, you know." I shrug. My legs hurt so much that I almost don't care where I am.

"You look like shit."

"I'm in a lot of pain."

"That's funny. So am I."

"I mean physical pain."

"Why?" For all Ingrid cares I could be spontaneously combusting right in front of her. I pull back the afghan and reveal my stumps.

She doesn't recoil and she doesn't gasp. She doesn't look away, and when she does she looks me in the eyes and I see that Ingrid, of all people, understands perfectly. By entirely separate processes we have arrived at the same condition. She gets up and goes into another room, and when she comes back she has her old sewing kit in her hand. I feel a surge of hope, and my hope is justified: Ingrid sits down and opens the lid and it's just like the good old days, there's a complete pharmacy in there with the pin cushions and thimbles.

"What do you want?" Ingrid asks.

"Opiates." She picks through a baggie full of pills and offers me an assortment; I spot Ultram and take two. After I swallow them dry she gets me a glass of water and I drink it down.

"Well." Ingrid runs her long red fingernails through her long blond hair. "When are you coming from?"

"December 2006. What's the date here?"

Ingrid looks at her watch. "It *was* New Year's Day, but now it's January 2. 1994."

Oh, no. Please no. "What's wrong?" Ingrid says.

"Nothing." Today is the day Ingrid will commit suicide. What can I say to her? Can I stop her? What if I call someone? "Listen, Ing, I just want to say . . ." I hesitate. What can I tell her without spooking her? Does it matter now? Now that she's dead? Even though she's sitting right here?

"What?"

I'm sweating. "Just . . . be nice to yourself. Don't . . . I mean, I know you aren't very happy—"

"Well, whose fault is that?" Her bright red lipsticked mouth is set in a frown. I don't answer. Is it my fault? I don't really know. Ingrid is staring at me as though she expects an answer. I look away from her. I look at the Moholy-Nagy poster on the opposite wall. "Henry?" Ingrid says. "Why were you so mean to me?"

I drag my eyes back to her. "Was I? I didn't want to be."

Ingrid shakes her head. "You didn't care if I lived or died."

Oh, Ingrid. "I do care. I don't want you to die."

"You didn't care. You left me, and you never came to the hospital." Ingrid speaks as though the words choke her.

"Your family didn't want me to come. Your mom told me to stay away."

"You should have come."

I sigh. "Ingrid, your *doctor* told me I couldn't visit you."

"I asked and they said you never called."

"I called. I was told you didn't want to talk to me, and not to call anymore." The painkiller is kicking in. The prickling pain in my legs dulls. I slide my hands under the afghan and place my palms against the skin of my left stump, and then my right.

"I almost died and you never spoke to me again."

"I thought you didn't want to talk to me. How was I supposed to know?"

"You got married and you never called me and you invited Celia to the wedding to spite me."

I laugh, I can't help it. "Ingrid, *Clare* invited Celia. They're friends; I've never figured out why. Opposites attract, I guess. But anyway, it had nothing to do with you."

Ingrid says nothing. She's pale under her makeup. She digs in her coat pocket and brings out a pack of English Ovals and a lighter.

"Since when do you smoke?" I ask her. Ingrid hated smoking. Ingrid liked coke and crystal meth and drinks with poetic names. She extracts a cigarette from the pack between two long nails, and lights it. Her hands are shaking. She drags on the cigarette and smoke curls from her lips.

"So how's life without feet?" Ingrid asks me. "How'd that happen, anyway?"

"Frostbite. I passed out in Grant Park in January."

"So how do you get around?"

"Wheelchair, mostly."

"Oh. That sucks."

"Yeah," I say. "It does." We sit in silence for a moment.

Ingrid asks, "Are you still married?"

"Yeah."

"Kids?"

"One. A girl."

"Oh." Ingrid leans back, drags on her cigarette, blows a thin stream of smoke from her nostrils. "I wish I had kids."

"You never wanted kids, Ing."

She looks at me, but I can't read the look. "I always wanted kids. I didn't think *you* wanted kids, so I never said anything."

"You could still have kids."

Ingrid laughs. "Could I? Do I have kids, Henry? In 2006 do I have a husband and a house in Winnetka and 2.5 kids?"

"Not exactly." I shift my position on the couch. The pain has receded but what's left is the shell of the pain, an empty space where there should be pain but instead there is the expectation of pain.

"*'Not exactly,'*" Ingrid mimics. "How not exactly? Like, as in, 'Not exactly, Ingrid, really you're a bag lady?'"

"You're not a bag lady."

"So I'm not a bag lady. Okay, great." Ingrid stubs out her cigarette and crosses her legs. I always loved Ingrid's legs. She's wearing boots with high heels. She and Celia must have been to a party. Ingrid says, "We've eliminated the extremes: I'm not a suburban matron and I'm not homeless. Come on, Henry, give me some more hints."

I am silent. I don't want to play this game.

"Okay, let's make it multiple choice. Let's see . . . A) I'm a stripper in a real sleazy club on Rush Street. Um, B) I'm in prison for ax-murdering Celia and feeding her to Malcolm. Heh. Yeah, ah, C) I'm living on the Rio del Sol with an investment banker. How 'bout it Henry? Do any of those sound good to you?"

"Who's Malcolm?"

"Celia's Doberman."

"Figures."

Ingrid plays with her lighter, flicking it on and off. "How about D) I'm dead?" I flinch. "Does that appeal to you at all?"

"No. It doesn't."

"Really? I like that one best." Ingrid smiles. It's not a pretty smile. It's more like a grimace. "I like that one so much that it's given me an idea." She gets up and strides across the room and down the hall. I can hear her opening and shutting a drawer. When she reappears she has one hand behind her back. Ingrid stands in front of me, and says, "Surprise!" and she's pointing a gun at me.

It's not a very big gun. It's slim and black and shiny. Ingrid holds it close to her waist, casually, as though she's at a cocktail party. I stare at the gun. Ingrid says, "I could shoot you."

"Yes. You could," I say.

"Then I could shoot myself," she says.

"That could also happen."

"But does it?"

"I don't know, Ingrid. You get to decide."

"Bullshit, Henry. Tell me," Ingrid commands.

"All right. No. It doesn't happen that way." I try to sound confident.

Ingrid smirks. "But what if I want it to happen that way?"

"Ingrid, give me the gun."

"Come over here and get it."

"Are you going to shoot me?" Ingrid shakes her head, smiling. I climb off the couch, onto the floor, crawl toward Ingrid, trailing the afghan, slowed by the painkiller. She backs away, holding the gun trained on me. I stop.

"Come on, Henry. Nice doggie. *Trusting* doggie." Ingrid flicks off the safety catch and takes two steps toward me. I tense. She is aiming point blank at my head. But then Ingrid laughs, and places the muzzle of the gun against her temple. "How about this, Henry? Does it happen like this?"

"No." *No!*

She frowns. "Are you sure, Henry?" Ingrid moves the gun to her chest. "Is this better? Head or heart, Henry?" Ingrid steps forward. I could touch her. I could grab her—Ingrid kicks me in the chest and I fall backward, I am sprawled on the floor looking up at her and Ingrid leans over and spits in my face.

"Did you love me?" Ingrid asks, looking down at me.

"Yes," I tell her.

"Liar," Ingrid says, and she pulls the trigger.

Monday, December 18, 2006 (Clare is 35, Henry is 43)

CLARE: I wake up in the middle of the night and Henry is gone. I panic. I sit up in bed. The possibilities crowd into my mind. He could be run over by cars, stuck in abandoned buildings, out in the cold—I hear a sound, someone is crying. I think it is Alba, maybe Henry went to see what was wrong with Alba, so I get up and go into Alba's room, but Alba is asleep, curled around Teddy, her blankets thrown off the bed. I follow the sound down the hall and there, sitting on the living room floor, there is Henry, with his head in his hands.

I kneel beside him. "What's wrong?" I ask him.

Henry raises his face and I can see the shine of tears on his cheeks in the streetlight that comes in the windows. "Ingrid's dead," Henry says.

I put my arms around him. "Ingrid's been dead for a long time," I say softly.

Henry shakes his head. "Years, minutes . . . same thing," he says. We sit on the floor in silence. Finally Henry says, "Do you think it's morning yet?"

"Sure." The sky is still dark. No birds are singing.

"Let's get up," he says. I bring the wheelchair, help him into it, and wheel him into the kitchen. I bring his bathrobe and Henry struggles into it. He sits at the kitchen table staring out the window into the snow-covered backyard. Somewhere in the distance a snowplow scrapes along a street. I turn on the light. I measure coffee into a filter, measure water into the coffee maker, turn it on. I get out cups. I open the fridge, but when I ask Henry what he wants to eat he just shakes his head. I sit down at the kitchen table opposite Henry and he looks at me. His eyes are red and his hair is sticking out in many directions. His hands are thin and his face is bleak.

"It was my fault," Henry says. "If I hadn't been there . . ."

"Could you have stopped her?" I ask.

"No. I tried."

"Well, then."

The coffee maker makes little exploding noises. Henry runs his hands over his face. He says, "I always wondered why she didn't leave a note." I am about to ask him what he means when I realize that Alba is standing in the kitchen doorway. She's wearing a pink nightgown and green mouse slippers. Alba squints and yawns in the harsh light of the kitchen.

"Hi, kiddo," Henry says. Alba comes over to him and drapes herself over the side of his wheelchair. "Mmmmorning," Alba says.

"It's not really morning," I tell her. "It's really still nighttime."

"How come you guys are up if it's nighttime?" Alba sniffs. "You're making coffee, so it's morning."

"Oh, it's the old coffee-equals-morning fallacy," Henry says. "There's a hole in your logic, buddy."

"What?" Alba asks. She hates to be wrong about anything.

"You are basing your conclusion on faulty data; that is, you are forgetting that your parents are coffee fiends of the first order, and that we just might have gotten out of bed in the middle of the night in order to drink MORE COFFEE." He's roaring like a monster, maybe a Coffee Fiend.

"I want coffee," says Alba. "I am a Coffee Fiend." She roars back at Henry. But he scoops her off of him and plops her down on her feet. Alba runs around the table to me and throws her arms around my shoulders. "Roar!" she yells in my ear.

I get up and pick Alba up. She's so heavy now. "Roar, yourself." I carry her down the hall and throw her onto her bed, and she shrieks with laughter. The clock on her nightstand says 4:16 a.m. "See?" I show her. "It's too early for you to get up." After the obligatory amount of fuss Alba settles back into bed, and I walk back to the kitchen. Henry has managed to pour us both coffee. I sit down again. It's cold in here.

"Clare."

"Mmm?"

"When I'm dead—" Henry stops, looks away, takes a breath, begins again. "I've been getting everything organized, all the documents, you know, my will, and letters to people, and stuff for Alba, it's all in my desk." I can't say anything. Henry looks at me.

"When?" I ask. Henry shakes his head. "Months? Weeks? Days?"

"I don't know, Clare." He does know, I know he knows.

"You looked up the obituary, didn't you?" I say. Henry hesitates, and then nods. I open my mouth to ask again, and then I am afraid.

HOURS, IF NOT DAYS

••••••••••••••••••••••••••••••••

Friday, December 24, 2006 (Henry is 43, Clare is 35)

HENRY: I wake up early, so early that the bedroom is blue in the almost-dawn light. I lie in bed, listening to Clare's deep breathing, listening to the sporadic noise of traffic on Lincoln Avenue, crows calling to each other, the furnace shutting off. My legs ache. I prop myself up on my pillows and find the bottle of Vicodin on my bedside table. I take two, wash them down with flat Coke.

I slide back into the blankets and turn onto my side. Clare is sleeping face down, with her arms wrapped protectively around her head. Her hair is hidden under the covers. Clare seems smaller without her ambiance of hair. She reminds me of herself as a child, sleeping with the simplicity she had when she was little. I try to remember if I have ever seen Clare as a child, sleeping. I realize that I never have. It's Alba that I am thinking of. The light is changing. Clare stirs, turns toward me, onto her side. I study her face. There are a few faint lines, at the corners of her eyes and mouth, that are the merest suggestion of the beginnings of Clare's face in middle age. I will never see that face of hers, and I regret it bitterly, the face with which Clare will go on without me, which will never be kissed by me, which will belong to a world that I won't know, except as a memory of Clare's, relegated finally to a definite past.

Today is the thirty-seventh anniversary of my mother's death. I have thought of her, longed for her, every day of those thirty-seven years, and my father has, I think, thought of her almost without stopping. If fervent memory could raise the dead, she would be our Eurydice, she would rise like Lady Lazarus from her stubborn death to solace us. But all of our laments could not add a single second to her life, not one additional beat of the heart, nor a breath. The only thing my need could do was bring me to her. What will Clare have when I am gone? How can I leave her?

I hear Alba talking in her bed. "Hey," says Alba. "Hey, Teddy! Shh, go to sleep now." Silence. "Daddy?" I watch Clare, to see if she will wake up. She is still, asleep. "Daddy!" I gingerly turn, carefully extricate myself from the blankets, maneuver myself to the floor. I crawl out of our bedroom, down the hall and into Alba's room. She giggles when she sees me. I make a growling noise, and Alba pats my head as though I am a dog. She is sitting up in bed, in the midst of every stuffed animal she has. "Move over, Red Riding Hood." Alba scoots aside and I lift myself onto the bed. She fussily arranges some of the toys around me. I put my arm around her and lean back and she holds out Blue Teddy to me. "He wants to eat marshmallows."

"It's a little early for marshmallows, Blue Teddy. How about some poached eggs and toast?"

Alba makes a face. She does it by squinching together her mouth and eyebrows and nose. "Teddy doesn't like eggs," she announces.

"Shhhh. Mama's sleeping."

"Okay," Alba whispers, loudly. "Teddy wants blue Jell-O." I hear Clare groan and start to get up in the other room.

"Cream of Wheat?" I cajole. Alba considers. "With brown sugar?"

"Okay."

"You want to make it?" I slide off the bed.

"Yeah. Can I have a ride?"

I hesitate. My legs really hurt, and Alba has gotten a little too big to do this painlessly, but I can deny her nothing now. "Sure. Hop on." I am on my hands and knees. Alba climbs onto my back, and we make our way into the kitchen. Clare is standing sleepily by the sink, watching coffee drip into the pot. I clamber up to her and butt my head against her knees and she grabs Alba's arms and hoists her up, Alba giggling madly all the while. I crawl into my chair. Clare smiles and says, "What's for breakfast, cooks?"

"Jell-O!" Alba shrieks.

"Mmm. What kind of Jell-O? Cornflake Jell-O?"

"Nooooo!"

"Bacon Jell-O?"

"Ick!" Alba wraps herself around Clare, pulls on her hair.

"Ouch. Don't, sweetie. Well, it must be oatmeal Jell-O, then."

"Cream of Wheat!"

"Cream of Wheat Jell-O, yum." Clare gets out the brown sugar and the milk and the Cream of Wheat package. She sets them on the counter and looks at me inquiringly. "How 'bout you? Omelet Jell-O?"

"If you're making it, yeah." I marvel at Clare's efficiency, moving around the kitchen as though she's Betty Crocker, as though she's been doing this for years. She'll be okay without me, I think as I watch her, but I know that she will not. I watch Alba mix the water and the wheat together, and I think of Alba at ten, at fifteen, at twenty. It is not nearly enough, yet. I am not done, yet. I want to be here. I want to see them, I want to gather them in my arms, I want to live—

"Daddy's crying," Alba whispers to Clare.

"That's because he has to eat my cooking," Clare tells her, and winks at me, and I have to laugh.

·······································

Sunday, December 31, 2006 (Clare is 35, Henry is 43)
(7:25 p.m.)

CLARE: We're having a party! Henry was kind of reluctant at first but he seems perfectly content now. He's sitting at the kitchen table showing Alba how to cut flowers out of carrots and radishes. I admit that I didn't exactly play fair: I brought it up in front of Alba and she got all excited and then he couldn't bear to disappoint her.

"It'll be great, Henry. We'll ask everyone we know."

"Everyone?" he queried, smiling.

"Everyone we *like,*" I amended. And so for days I've been cleaning, and Henry and Alba have been baking cookies (although half the dough goes into Alba's mouth if we don't watch her). Yesterday Charisse and I went to the grocery store and bought dips, chips, spreads, every possible kind of vegetable, and beer, and wine, and champagne, little colored hors d'oeuvres toothpicks, and napkins with HAPPY NEW YEAR printed in gold, and matching paper plates and Lord knows what else. Now the whole house smells like meatballs and the rapidly dying Christmas tree in the living room. Alicia is here washing our wineglasses.

Henry looks up at me and says, "Hey, Clare, it's almost show-time. Go take your shower." I glance at my watch and realize that yes, it's time.

Into the shower and wash hair and dry hair and into underwear and bra, stockings and black silk party dress, heels and a tiny dab of perfume and lipstick and one last look in the mirror (I look startled) and back into the kitchen where Alba, oddly enough, is still pristine in her blue velvet dress and Henry is still wearing his holey red flannel shirt and ripped-up blue jeans.

"Aren't you going to change?"

"Oh—yeah. Sure. Help me, huh?" I wheel him into our bedroom.

"What do you want to wear?" I'm hunting through his drawers for underwear and socks.

"Whatever. You choose." Henry reaches over and shuts the bedroom door. "Come here."

I stop riffing through the closet and look at Henry. He puts the brake on the wheelchair and manuvers his body onto the bed.

"There's no time," I say.

"Right, exactly. So let's not waste time talking." His voice is quiet and compelling. I flip the lock on the door.

"You know, I just got dressed—"

"Shhh." He holds out his arms to me, and I relent, and sit beside him, and the phrase *one last time* pops into my mind unbidden.

(8:05 p.m.)

HENRY: The doorbell rings just as I am knotting my tie. Clare says nervously, "Do I look all right?" She does, she is pink and lovely, and I tell her so. We emerge from the bedroom as Alba runs to answer the door and starts yelling "Grandpa! Grandpa! Kimy!"

My father stomps his snowy boots and leans to hug her. Clare kisses him on both cheeks. Dad rewards her with his coat. Alba commandeers Kimy and takes her to see the Christmas tree before she even gets her coat off.

"Hello, Henry," says Dad, smiling, leaning over me and suddenly it hits me: tonight my life will flash before my eyes. We've invited everyone who matters to us: Dad, Kimy, Alicia, Gomez, Charisse, Philip, Mark and Sharon and their kids, Gram, Ben, Helen, Ruth, Kendrick and Nancy and their kids, Roberto, Catherine, Isabelle, Matt, Amelia, artist friends of Clare's, library school friends of mine, parents of Alba's friends, Clare's dealer, even Celia Attley, at Clare's insistence. . . . The only people missing have been unavoidably detained: my mother, Lucille, Ingrid. . . . Oh, God. Help me.

(8:20 p.m.)

CLARE: Gomez and Charisse come breezing in like kamikaze jet fighters. "Hey Library Boy, you lazy coot, don't you ever shovel your sidewalks?"

Henry smacks his forehead. "I knew I forgot something." Gomez dumps a shopping bag full of CDs in Henry's lap and goes out to clean the walks. Charisse laughs and follows me into the kitchen. She takes out a huge bottle of Russian vodka and sticks it in the freezer. We can hear Gomez singing "Let It Snow" as he makes his way down the side of the house with the shovel.

"Where are the kids?" I ask Charisse.

"We parked them at my mom's. It's New Year's; we figured they'd have more fun with Grandma. Plus we decided to have our hangovers in privacy, you know?" I've never given it much thought, actually; I haven't been drunk since before Alba was conceived. Alba comes running into the kitchen and Charisse gives her an enthusiastic hug. "Hey, Baby Girl! We brought you a Christmas present!"

Alba looks at me. "Go ahead and open it." It's a tiny manicure set, complete with nail polish. Alba is open-mouthed with awe. I nudge her, and she remembers.

"*Thank you*, Aunt Charisse."

"You're welcome, Alba."

"Go show Daddy," I tell her, and she runs off in the direction of the living room. I stick my head into the hall and I can see Alba gesturing excitedly at Henry, who holds out his fingers for her as though contemplating a fingernailectomy. "Big hit," I tell Charisse.

She smiles. "That was my trip when I was little. I wanted to be a beautician when I grew up."

I laugh. "But you couldn't hack it, so you became an artist."

"I met Gomez and realized that nobody ever overthrew the bourgeois capitalist misogynist corporate operating system by perming its hair."

"Of course, we haven't exactly been beating it to its knees by selling it art, either."

"Speak for yourself, babe. You're just addicted to beauty, that's all."

"Guilty, guilty, guilty." We wander into the dining room and Charisse begins to load up her plate. "So what are you working on?" I ask her.

"Computer viruses as art."

"Oooh." Oh, no. "Isn't that kind of illegal?"

"Well; no. I just design them, then I paint the html onto canvas, then I have a show. I don't actually put them into circulation."

"But someone could."

"Sure." Charisse smiles wickedly. "I hope they do. Gomez scoffs, but some of these little paintings could seriously inconvenience the World Bank and Bill Gates and those bastards who make ATM machines."

"Well, good luck. When's the show?"

"May. I'll send you a card."

"Yeah, when I get it I'll convert our assets into gold and lay in bottled water."

Charisse laughs. Catherine and Amelia arrive, and we cease to speak of World Anarchy Through Art and move on to admiring each other's party dresses.

(8:50 p.m.)

HENRY: The house is packed with our nearest and dearest, some of whom I haven't seen since before the surgery. Leah Jacobs, Clare's dealer, is tactful and kind, but I find it difficult to withstand the pity in her gaze. Celia surprises me by walking right up to me and offering her hand. I take it, and she says, "I'm sorry to see you like this."

"Well, you look great," I say, and she does. Her hair is done up really high and she's dressed all in shimmery blue.

"Uh-huh," says Celia in her fabulous toffee voice. "I liked it better when you were bad and I could just hate your skinny white self."

I laugh. "Ah, the good old days."

She delves into her purse. "I found this a long time ago in Ingrid's stuff. I thought Clare might want it." Celia hands me a photograph. It's a photo of me, probably from around 1990. My hair is long and I'm laughing, standing on Oak Street Beach, no shirt. It's a great photograph. I don't remember Ingrid taking it, but then again, so much of my time with Ing is kind of a blank now.

"Yeah, I bet she would like it. *Memento mori.*" I hand the picture back to her.

Celia glances at me sharply. "You're not dead, Henry DeTamble."

"I'm not far from it, Celia."

Celia laughs. "Well, if you get to Hell before I do, save me a place next to Ingrid." She turns abruptly and walks off in search of Clare.

(9:45 p.m.)

CLARE: The children have run around and eaten too much party food and now they are sleepy but cranky. I pass Colin Kendrick in the hall and ask if he wants to take a nap; he tells me very solemnly that he'd like to stay up with the grown-ups. I am touched by his politeness and his fourteen-year-old's beauty, his shyness with me even though he's known me all his life. Alba and Nadia Kendrick are not so restrained. "Mamaaa," Alba bleats, "you *said* we could stay *up!*"

"Sure you don't want to sleep for a while? I'll wake you up right before midnight."

"*Nooooo.*" Kendrick is listening to this exchange and I shrug my shoulders and he laughs.

"The Indomitable Duo. Okay, girls, why don't you go play quietly in Alba's room for a while." They shuffle off, grumbling. We know that within minutes they'll be playing happily.

"It's good to see you, Clare," Kendrick says as Alicia ambles over.

"Hey, Clare. Get a load of Daddy." I follow Alicia's gaze and realize that our father is flirting with Isabelle. "Who is that?"

"Oh, my god." I'm laughing. "That's Isabelle Berk." I start to outline Isabelle's draconian sexual proclivities for Alicia. We are laughing so hard we can hardly breathe. "Perfect, perfect. Oh. Stop," Alicia says.

Richard comes over to us, drawn by our hysterics. "What's so funny, *bella donnas*?"

We shake our heads, still giggling. "They're mocking the mating rituals of their paternal authority figure," says Kendrick. Richard nods, bemused, and asks Alicia about her spring concert schedule. They wander off in the direction of the kitchen, talking Bucharest and Bartók. Kendrick is still standing next to me, waiting to say something I don't want to hear. I begin to excuse myself, and he puts his hand on my arm.

"Wait, Clare—" I wait. "I'm sorry," he says.

"It's okay, David." We stare at each other for a moment. Kendrick shakes his head, fumbles for his cigarettes. "If you ever want to come by the lab I could show you what I've been doing for Alba...." I cast my eyes around the party, looking for Henry. Gomez is showing Sharon how to rumba in the living room. Everyone seems to be having a good time, but Henry is nowhere in sight. I haven't seen him for at least forty-five minutes, and I feel a strong urge to find him, make sure he's okay, make sure he's *here*. "Excuse me," I tell Kendrick, who looks like he wants to continue the conversation. "Another time. When it's quieter." He nods. Nancy Kendrick appears with Colin in tow, making the topic impossible anyway. They launch into a spirited discussion of ice hockey, and I escape.

(9:48 p.m.)

HENRY: It has become very warm in the house, and I need to cool off, so I am sitting on the enclosed front porch. I can hear people talking in the living room. The snow is falling thick and fast now, covering all the cars and bushes, softening their hard lines and deadening the sound of traffic. It's a beautiful night. I open the door between the porch and the living room.

"Hey, Gomez."

He comes trotting over and sticks his head through the doorway. "Yeah?"

"Let's go outside."

"It's fucking cold out there."

"Come on, you soft elderly alderman."

Something in my tone does the trick. "All right, all right. Just a minute." He disappears and comes back after a few minutes wearing his coat and carrying mine. As I'm angling into it he offers me his hip flask.

"Oh, no thanks."

"Vodka. Puts hair on your chest."

"Clashes with opiates."

"Oh, right. How quickly we forget." Gomez wheels me through the living room. At the top of the stairs he lifts me out of the chair and I am riding on his back like a child, like a monkey, and we are out the front door and out of doors and the cold air is like an exoskeleton. I can smell the liquor in Gomez's sweat. Somewhere out there behind the sodium vapor Chicago glare there are stars.

"Comrade."

"Umm?"

"Thanks for everything. You've been the best—" I can't see his face, but I can feel Gomez stiffen beneath all the layers of clothing.

"What are you saying?"

"My own personal fat lady is singing, Gomez. Time's up. Game over."

"When?"

"Soon."

"How soon?"

"I don't know," I lie. Very, very soon. "Anyway, I just wanted to tell you—I know I've been a pain in the ass every now and then," (Gomez laughs) "but it's been great" (I pause, because I am on the verge of tears) "it's been really great" (and we stand there, inarticulate American male creatures that we are, our breath freezing in clouds before us, all the possible words left unspoken now) and finally I say, "Let's go in," and we do. As Gomez gently replaces me in the wheelchair he embraces me for a moment, and then walks heavily away without looking back.

(10:15 p.m.)

CLARE: Henry isn't in the living room, which is filled with a small but determined group of people trying to dance, in a variety of unlikely ways, to the Squirrel Nut Zippers. Charisse and Matt are doing something that looks like the cha-cha, and Roberto is dancing with considerable flair with Kimy, who moves delicately but steadfastly in a kind of fox trot. Gomez has abandoned Sharon for Catherine, who whoops as he spins her and laughs when he stops dancing to light a cigarette.

Henry isn't in the kitchen, which has been taken over by Raoul and James and Lourdes and the rest of my artist friends. They are regaling each other with stories of terrible things art dealers have done to artists, and vice versa. Lourdes is telling the one about Ed Kienholtz making a kinetic sculpture that drilled a big hole in his dealer's expensive desk. They all laugh sadistically. I shake my finger at them. "Don't let Leah hear you," I tease. "Where's Leah?" cries James. "I bet *she* has some great stories—" He goes off in search of my dealer, who is drinking cognac with Mark on the stairs.

Ben is making himself tea. He has a Ziplock baggie with all sorts of foul herbs in it, which he measures carefully into a tea strainer and dunks into a mug of steaming water. "Have you seen Henry?" I ask him.

"Yeah, I was just talking to him. He's on the front porch." Ben peers at me. "I'm kind of worried about him. He seems very sad. He seemed—" Ben stops, makes a gesture with his hand that means *I might be wrong about this* "he reminded me of some patients I have, when they don't expect to be around much longer. . . ." My stomach tightens.

"He's been very depressed since his feet . . ."

"I know. But he was talking like he was getting on a train that was leaving *momentarily,* you know, he told me—" Ben lowers his voice, which is always very quiet, so that I can barely hear him: "he told me he *loved* me, and thanked me . . . I mean, people, *guys* don't say that kind of thing if they expect to be around, you know?" Ben's eyes are swimming behind his glasses, and I put my arms around him, and we stand like that for a minute, my arms encasing Ben's wasted frame. Around us people are chattering, ignoring us. "I don't want to outlive anybody," Ben says. "Jesus. After drinking this awful stuff and just generally being a bloody *martyr* for fifteen years I think I've earned the right to have everybody I know file past my casket and say, 'He died with his boots on.' Or something like that. I'm counting on Henry to be there quoting Donne, *'Death, be not proud, you stupid motherfucker.'* It'll be beautiful."

I laugh. "Well, if Henry can't make it, I'll come. I do a mean imitation of Henry." I raise one eyebrow, lift my chin, lower my voice: "'*One short sleep past, we wake eternally, And Death shall be sitting in the kitchen in his underwear at three in the morning, doing last week's crossword puzzle—*'" Ben cracks up. I kiss his pale smooth cheek and move on.

Henry is sitting by himself on the front porch, in the dark, watching it snow. I've hardly glanced out the window all day, and now I realize that it's been snowing steadily for hours. Snowplows are rattling down Lincoln Avenue, and our neighbors are out shoveling their walks. Although the porch is enclosed it's still cold out here.

"Come inside," I say. I am standing beside him, watching a dog bounding in the snow across the street. Henry puts his arm around my waist and leans his head on my hip.

"I wish we could just stop time now," he says. I'm running my fingers through his hair. It's stiffer and thicker than it used to be, before it went gray.

"Clare," he says.

"Henry."

"It's time . . ." He stops.

"What?"

"It's . . . I'm . . ."

"My God." I sit down on the divan, facing Henry. "But—don't. Just—stay." I squeeze his hands tightly.

"It has already happened. Here, let me sit next to you." He swings himself out of his chair and onto the divan. We lie back on the cold cloth. I am shivering in my thin dress. In the house people are laughing and dancing. Henry puts his arm around me, warming me.

"Why didn't you tell me? Why did you let me invite all these people?" I don't want to be angry, but I am.

"I don't want you to be alone . . . after. And I wanted to say goodbye to everyone. It's been good, it was a good last hurrah . . ." We lie there silently for a while. The snow falls, silently.

"What time is it?"

I check my watch. "A little after eleven." Oh, God. Henry grabs a blanket from the other chair, and we wrap it around each other. I can't believe this. I knew that it was coming, soon, had to come sooner or later, but here it is, and we are just lying here, waiting . . .

"Oh, why can't we *do* something!" I whisper into Henry's neck.

"Clare—" Henry's arms are wrapped around me. I close my eyes.

"Stop it. Refuse to let it happen. *Change it.*"

"Oh, Clare." Henry's voice is soft and I look up at him, and his eyes shine with tears in the light reflected by the snow. I lay my cheek against Henry's shoulder. He strokes my hair. We stay like this for a long time. Henry is sweating. I put my hand on his face and he's burning up with fever.

"What time is it?"

"Almost midnight."

"I'm scared." I twine my arms through his, wrap my legs around his. It's impossible to believe that Henry, so solid, my lover, this real body, which I am holding pressed to mine with all my strength, could ever disappear:

"Kiss me!"

I am kissing Henry, and then I am alone, under the blanket, on the divan, on the cold porch. It is still snowing. Inside, the record stops, and I hear Gomez say, "Ten! nine! eight!" and everyone says, all together, "seven! six! five! four! three! two! one! *Happy New Year!*" and a champagne cork pops, and everyone starts talking all at once, and someone says, "Where are Henry and Clare?" Outside in the street someone sets off firecrackers. I put my head in my hands and I wait.

III

....

A Treatise on Longing

His forty-third year. His small time's end. His time—
Who saw Infinity through the countless cracks
In the blank skin of things, and died of it.

—A. S. Byatt, Possession

She followed slowly, taking a long time,
as though there were some obstacle in the way;
and yet: as though, once it was overcome,
she would be beyond all walking, and would fly.

—from Going Blind,
Rainer Maria Rilke
translated by Stephen Mitchell

Saturday, October 27, 1984/Monday, January 1, 2007
(Henry is 43, Clare is 35)

HENRY: The sky is blank and I'm falling into the tall dry grass *let it be quick* and even as I try to be still the crack of a rifle sounds, far away, surely nothing to do with me but no: I am slammed to the ground, I look at my belly which has opened up like a pomegranate, a soup of entrails and blood cradled in the bowl of my body; it doesn't hurt at all *that can't be right* but I can only admire this cubist version of my insides *someone is running* all I want is to see Clare before *before* I am screaming her name *Clare, Clare*

and Clare leans over me, crying, and Alba whispers, "Daddy..."

"Love you..."

"Henry—"

"Always..."

"Oh God oh God—"

"World enough..."

"No!"

"And time..."

"Henry!"

CLARE: The living room is very still. Everyone stands fixed, frozen, staring down at us. Billie Holiday is singing, and then someone turns off the CD player and there is silence. I sit on the floor, holding Henry. Alba is crouching over him, whispering in his ear, shaking him. Henry's skin is warm, his eyes are open, staring past me, he is heavy in my arms, so heavy, his pale skin torn apart, red everywhere, ripped flesh framing a secret world of blood. I cradle Henry. There's blood at the corner of his mouth. I wipe it off. Fire-crackers explode somewhere nearby.

Gomez says, "I think we'd better call the police."

DISSOLUTION

••••••••••••••••••••••••••••••••••

Friday, February 2, 2007 (Clare is 35)

CLARE: I sleep all day. Noises flit around the house—garbage truck in the alley, rain, tree rapping against the bedroom window. I sleep. I inhabit sleep firmly, willing it, wielding it, pushing away dreams, refusing, refusing. Sleep is my lover now, my forgetting, my opiate, my oblivion. The phone rings and rings. I have turned off the machine that answers with Henry's voice. It is afternoon, it is night, it is morning. Everything is reduced to this bed, this endless slumber that makes the days into one day, makes time stop, stretches and compacts time until it is meaningless.

Sometimes sleep abandons me and I pretend, as though Etta has come to get me up for school. I breathe slowly and deeply. I make my eyes still under eyelids, I make my mind still, and soon, Sleep, seeing a perfect reproduction of himself, comes to be united with his facsimile.

Sometimes I wake up and reach for Henry. Sleep erases all differences: then and now; dead and living. I am past hunger, past vanity, past caring. This morning I caught sight of my face in the bathroom mirror. I am paper-skinned, gaunt, yellow, ring-eyed, hair matted. I look dead. I want nothing.

Kimy sits at the foot of the bed. She says, "Clare? Alba's home from school . . . won't you let her come in, say hi?" I pretend to sleep. Alba's little hand strokes my face. Tears leak from my eyes. Alba sets something, her knapsack? her violin case? on the floor and Kimy says, "Take off your shoes, Alba," and then Alba crawls into bed with me. She wraps my arm around her, thrusts her head under my chin. I sigh and open my eyes. Alba pretends to sleep. I stare at her thick black eyelashes, her wide mouth, her pale skin; she is breathing carefully, she clutches my hip with her strong hand, she smells of pencil shavings and rosin and shampoo. I kiss the top of her head. Alba opens her eyes, and then her resemblance to Henry is almost more than I can bear. Kimy gets up and walks out of the room.

Later I get up, take a shower, eat dinner sitting at the table with Kimy and Alba. I sit at Henry's desk after Alba has gone to bed, and I open the drawers, I take out the bundles of letters and papers, and I begin to read.

A Letter to Be Opened in the Event of My Death

December 10, 2006

Dearest Clare,

As I write this, I am sitting at my desk in the back bedroom looking out at your studio across the backyard full of blue evening snow, everything is slick and crusty with ice, and it is very still. It's one of those winter evenings when the coldness of every single thing seems to slow down time, like the narrow center of an hourglass which time itself flows through, but slowly, slowly. I have the feeling, very familiar to me when I am out of time but almost never otherwise, of being buoyed up by time, floating effortlessly on its surface like a fat lady swimmer. I had a sudden urge, tonight, here in the house by myself (you are at Alicia's recital at St. Lucy's) to write you a letter. I suddenly wanted to leave something, for *after.* I think that time is short, now. I feel as though all my reserves, of energy, of pleasure, of duration, are thin, small. I don't feel capable of continuing very much longer. I know you know.

If you are reading this, I am probably dead. (I say probably because you never know what circumstances may arise; it seems foolish and self-important to just declare one's own death as an out-and-out fact.) About this death of mine—I hope it was simple and clean and unambiguous. I hope it didn't create too much fuss. I'm sorry. (This reads like a suicide note. Strange.) But you know: you know that if I could have stayed, if I could have gone on, that I would have clutched every second: whatever it was, this death, you know that it came and *took* me, like a child carried away by goblins.

Clare, I want to tell you, again, I love you. Our love has been the thread through the labyrinth, the net under the high-wire walker, the only real thing in this strange life of mine that I could ever trust. Tonight I feel that my love for you has more density in this world than I do, myself: as though it could linger on after me and surround you, keep you, hold you.

I hate to think of you waiting. I know that you have been waiting for me all your life, always uncertain of how long this patch of waiting would be. Ten minutes, ten days. A month. What an uncertain husband I have been, Clare, like a sailor, Odysseus alone and buffeted by tall waves, sometimes wily and sometimes just a plaything of the gods. Please, Clare. When I am dead. Stop waiting and be free. Of me—put me deep inside you and then go out in the world and live. Love the world and yourself in it, move through it as though it offers no resistance, as though the world is your natural element. I have given you a life of suspended animation. I don't mean to say that you have done nothing. You have created beauty, and meaning, in your art, and Alba, who is so amazing, and for me: for me you have been everything.

After my mom died she ate my father up completely. She would have hated it. Every minute of his life since then has been marked by her absence, every action has lacked dimension because she is not there to measure against. And when I was young I didn't understand, but now, I know, how absence can be present, like a damaged nerve, like a dark bird. If I had to live on without you I know I could not do it. But I hope, I have this vision of you walking unencumbered, with your shining hair in the sun. I have not seen this with my eyes, but only with my imagination, that makes pictures, that always wanted to paint you, shining; but I hope that this vision will be true, anyway.

Clare, there is one last thing, and I have hesitated to tell you, because I'm superstitiously afraid that telling might cause it to not happen (I know: silly) and also because I have just been going on about not waiting and this might cause you to wait longer than you have ever waited before. But I will tell you in case you need something, *after.*

Last summer, I was sitting in Kendrick's waiting room when I suddenly found myself in a dark hallway in a house I don't know. I was sort of tangled up in a bunch of galoshes, and it smelled like rain. At the end of the hall I could see a rim of light around a door, and so I went very slowly and very quietly to the door and looked in. The room was white, and intensely lit with morning sun. At the window, with her back to me, sat a woman, wearing a coral-colored cardigan sweater, with long white hair all down her back. She had a cup of tea beside her, on a table. I must have made some little noise, or she sensed me behind her . . . she turned and saw me, and I saw her, and it was you, Clare, this was you as an old woman, in the future. It was sweet, Clare, it was sweet beyond telling, to come as though from death to hold you, and to see the years all present in your face. I won't tell you any more, so you can imagine it, so you can have it unrehearsed when the time comes, as it will, as it does come. We will see each other again, Clare. Until then, live, fully, present in the world, which is so beautiful.

It's dark, now, and I am very tired. I love you, always. Time is nothing.

Henry

DASEIN

• •

Saturday, July 12, 2008 (Clare is 37)

CLARE: Charisse has taken Alba and Rosa and Max and Joe roller skating at the Rainbo. I drive over to her house to pick Alba up, but I'm early and Charisse is running late. Gomez answers the door wearing a towel.

"Come on in," he says, opening the door wide. "Want some coffee?"

"Sure." I follow him through their chaotic living room to the kitchen. I sit at the table, which is still littered with breakfast dishes, and clear a space large enough to rest my elbows. Gomez rambles around the kitchen, making coffee.

"Haven't seen your mug in a while."

"I've been pretty busy. Alba takes all these different lessons, and I just drive her around."

"You making any art?" Gomez sets a cup and saucer in front of me and pours coffee into the cup. Milk and sugar are already on the table, so I help myself.

"No."

"Oh." Gomez leans against the kitchen counter, hands wrapped around his coffee cup. His hair is dark with water and combed back flat. I've never noticed before that his hairline is receding. "Well, other than chauffeuring her highness, what are you doing?"

What am I doing? I am waiting. I am thinking. I am sitting on our bed holding an old plaid shirt that still smells of Henry, taking deep breaths of his smell. I am going for walks at two in the morning, when Alba is safe in her bed, long walks to tire myself out enough to sleep. I am conducting conversations with Henry as though he were here with me, as though he could see through my eyes, think with my brain.

"Not much."

"Hmm."

"How 'bout you?"

"Oh, you know. Aldermanning. Playing the stern paterfamilias. The usual."

"Oh." I sip my coffee. I glance at the clock over the sink. It is shaped like a black cat: its tail twitches back and forth like a pendulum and its big eyes move in time with each twitch, ticking loudly. It's 11:45.

"Do you want anything to eat?"

I shake my head. "No, thanks." Judging from the dishes on the table, Gomez and Charisse had honeydew melon, scrambled eggs, and toast for breakfast. The children ate Lucky Charms, Cheerios, and something that had peanut butter on it. The table is like an archeological reconstruction of a twenty-first-century family breakfast.

"Are you dating anybody?" I look up and Gomez is still leaning on the counter, still holding his coffee cup at chin level.

"No."

"Why not?"

None of your business, Gomez. "It never occurred to me."

"You should think about it." He sets his cup in the sink.

"Why?"

"You need something new. Someone new. You can't sit around for the rest of your life waiting for Henry to show up."

"Sure I can. Watch me."

Gomez takes two steps and he's standing next to me. He leans over and puts his mouth next to my ear. "Don't you ever miss . . . this?" He licks the inside of my ear. *Yes, I miss that.* "Get away from me, Gomez," I hiss at him, but I don't move away. I am riveted in my seat by an idea. Gomez picks up my hair and kisses the back of my neck.

Come to me, oh! come to me!

I close my eyes. Hands pull me out of my seat, unbutton my shirt. Tongue on my neck, my shoulders, my nipples. I reach out blindly and find terrycloth, a bath towel that falls away. *Henry.* Hands unbutton my jeans, pull them down, bend me back over the kitchen table. Something falls to the floor, metallic. Food and silverware, a half-circle of plate, melon rind against my back. My legs spread. Tongue on my cunt. "Ohh . . ." *We are in the meadow. It's summer. A green blanket. We have just eaten, the taste of melon is still in my mouth.* Tongue gives way to empty space, wet and open. I open my eyes; I'm staring at a half-full glass of orange juice. I close my eyes. The firm, steady push of Henry's cock into me. Yes. *I've been waiting very patiently, Henry. I knew you'd come back sooner or later.* Yes. Skin on skin, hands on breasts, push pull clinging rhythm deeper yes, oh—

"Henry—"

Everything stops. A clock is ticking loudly. I open my eyes. Gomez is staring down at me, hurt? angry? in a moment he is expressionless. A car door slams. I sit up, jump off the table, run for the bathroom. Gomez throws my clothes in after me.

As I'm dressing I hear Charisse and the kids come in the front door, laughing. Alba calls, "Mama?" and I yell "I'll be out in a minute!" I stand in the dim light of the pink and black tiled bathroom and stare at myself in the mirror. I have Cheerios in my hair. My reflection looks lost and pale. I wash my hands, try to comb my hair with my fingers. *What am I doing? What have I allowed myself to become?*

An answer comes, of sorts: *You are the traveler now.*

Saturday, July 26, 2008 (Clare is 37)

CLARE: Alba's reward for being patient at the galleries while Charisse and I look at art is to go to Ed Debevic's, a faux diner that does a brisk tourist trade. As soon as we walk in the door it's sensory overload circa 1964. The Kinks are playing at top volume and there's signage everywhere:

"*If you're really a good customer you'd order more!!!*"
"*Please talk clearly when placing your order.*"
"*Our coffee is so good we drink it ourselves!*"

Today is evidently balloon-animal day; a gentleman in a shiny purple suit whips up a wiener dog for Alba and then turns it into a hat and plants it on her head. She squirms with joy. We stand in line for half an hour and Alba doesn't whine at all; she watches the waiters and waitresses flirt with each other and silently evaluates the other children's balloon animals. We are finally escorted to a booth by a waiter wearing thick horn-rimmed glasses and a name tag that says SPAZ. Charisse and I flip open our menus and try to find something we want to eat amidst the Cheddar Fries and the meatloaf. Alba just chants the word *milkshake* over and over. When Spaz reappears Alba has a sudden attack of shyness and has to be coaxed into telling him that she would like a peanut butter milkshake (and a small order of fries, because, I tell her, it's too decadent to eat nothing but a milkshake for lunch). Charisse orders macaroni and cheese and I order a BLT. Once Spaz leaves Charisse sings, "Alba and Spaz, sitting in a tree, K-I-S-S-I-N-G . . ." and Alba shuts her eyes and puts her hands over her ears, shaking her head and smiling. A waiter with a name tag that says BUZZ struts up and down the lunch counter doing karaoke to Bob Seger's "Old Time Rock & Roll."

"I hate Bob Seger," Charisse says. "Do you think it took him more than thirty seconds to write that song?"

The milkshake arrives in a tall glass with a bendable straw and a metal shaker that contains the milkshake that couldn't fit into the glass. Alba stands up to drink it, stands on tiptoe to achieve the best possible angle for sucking down a peanut butter milkshake. Her balloon wiener dog hat keeps sliding down her forehead, interfering with her concentration. She looks up at me through her thick black eyelashes and pushes the balloon hat up so that it is clinging to her head by static electricity.

"When's Daddy coming home?" she asks. Charisse makes the sound that one makes when one has accidentally gotten Pepsi up one's nose and starts to cough and I pound her on the back until she makes hand gestures at me to stop so I stop.

"August 29th," I tell Alba, who goes back to slurping the dregs of her shake while Charisse looks at me reproachfully.

Later, we're in the car, on Lake Shore Drive; I'm driving and Charisse is fiddling with the radio and Alba is sleeping in the back seat. I exit at Irving Park and Charisse says, "Doesn't Alba know that Henry is dead?"

"Of course she knows. She saw him," I remind Charisse.

"Well, why did you tell her he was coming home in August?"

"Because he is. He gave me the date himself."

"Oh." Even though my eyes are on the road I can feel Charisse staring at me. "Isn't that . . . kind of weird?"

"Alba loves it."

"For you, though?"

"I never see him." I try to keep my voice light, as though I am not tortured by the unfairness of this, as though I don't mourn my resentment when Alba tells me about her visits with Henry even as I drink up every detail.

Why not me, Henry? I ask him silently as I pull into Charisse and Gomez's toy-littered driveway. *Why only Alba?* But as usual there's no answer to this. As usual, that's just how it is. Charisse kisses me and gets out of the car, walks sedately toward her front door, which magically swings open, revealing Gomez and Rosa. Rosa is jumping up and down and holding something out toward Charisse, who takes it from her and says something, and gives her a big hug. Gomez stares at me, and finally gives me a little wave. I wave back. He turns away. Charisse and Rosa have gone inside. The door closes.

I sit there, in the driveway, Alba sleeping in the back seat. Crows are walking on the dandelion-infested lawn. *Henry, where are you?* I lean my head against the steering wheel. *Help me.* No one answers. After a minute I put the car in gear, back out of the driveway, and make my way toward our silent, waiting home.

Saturday, September 3, 1990 (Henry is 27)

HENRY: Ingrid and I have lost the car and we are drunk. We are drunk and it is dark and we have walked up and down and back and around and no car. Fucking Lincoln Park. Fucking Lincoln Towing. Fuck.

Ingrid is pissed off. She walks ahead of me, and her whole back, even the way her hips move, is pissed off. Somehow this is my fault. Fucking Park West nightclub. Why would anyone put a nightclub in wretched yuppieville Lincoln Park where you cannot leave your car for more than ten seconds without Lincoln Towing hauling it off to their lair to gloat over it—

"Henry."

"What?"

"There's that little girl again."

"What little girl?"

"The one we saw earlier." Ingrid stops. I look where she is pointing. The girl is standing in the doorway of a flower shop. She's wearing something dark, so all I see is her white face and her bare feet. She's maybe seven or eight; too young to be out alone in the middle of the night. Ingrid walks over to the girl, who watches her impassively.

"Are you okay?" Ingrid asks the girl. "Are you lost?"

The girl looks at me and says, "I *was* lost, but now I've figured out where I am. Thank you," she adds politely.

"Do you need a ride home? We could give you a ride if we ever manage to find the car." Ingrid is leaning over the girl. Her face is maybe a foot away from the girl's face. As I walk up to them I see that the girl is wearing a man's windbreaker. It comes all the way down to her ankles.

"No, thank you. I live too far away, anyhow." The girl has long black hair and startling dark eyes; in the yellow light of the flower shop she looks like a Victorian match girl, or DeQuincey's Ann.

"Where's your mom?" Ingrid asks her. The girl replies, "She's at home." She smiles at me and says, "She doesn't know I'm here."

"Did you run away?" I ask her.

"No," she says, and laughs. "I was looking for my daddy, but

I'm too early, I guess. I'll come back later." She squeezes past Ingrid and pads over to me, grabs my jacket and pulls me toward her. "The car's across the street," she whispers. I look across the street and there it is, Ingrid's red Porsche. "Thanks—" I begin, and the girl darts a kiss at me that lands near my ear and then runs down the sidewalk, her feet slapping the concrete as I stand staring after her. Ingrid is quiet as we get into the car. Finally I say, "That was strange," and she sighs and says, "Henry, for a smart person you can be pretty damn dense sometimes," and she drops me off in front of my apartment without another word.

Sunday, July 29, 1979 (Henry is 42)

HENRY: It's sometime in the past. I'm sitting on Lighthouse Beach with Alba. She's ten. I'm forty-two. Both of us are time traveling. It's a warm evening, maybe July or August. I'm wearing a pair of jeans and a white T-shirt I stole from a fancy North Evanston mansion; Alba is wearing a pink nightgown she took from an old lady's clothesline. It's too long for her so we have tied it up around her knees. People have been giving us strange looks all afternoon. I guess we don't exactly look like an average father and daughter at the beach. But we have done our best; we have swum, and we have built a sand castle. We have eaten hotdogs and fries we bought from the vendor in the parking lot. We don't have a blanket, or any towels, and so we are kind of sandy and damp and pleasantly tired, and we sit watching little children running back and forth in the waves and big silly dogs loping after them. The sun is setting behind us as we stare at the water.

"Tell me a story," says Alba, leaning against me like cold cooked pasta.

I put my arm around her. "What kind of story?"

"A good story. A story about you and Mama, when Mama was a little girl."

"Hmm. Okay. Once upon a time—"

"When was that?"

"All times at once. A long time ago, and right now."

"Both?"

"Yes, always both."

"How can it be both?"

"Do you want me to tell this story or not?"

"Yeah . . ."

"All right then. Once upon a time, your mama lived in a big house beside a meadow, and in the meadow was a place called the clearing where she used to go to play. And one fine day your mama, who was only a tiny thing whose hair was bigger than she was, went out to the clearing and there was a man there—"

"With no clothes!"

"With not a stitch on him," I agree. "And after your mama had given him a beach towel she happened to be carrying so he could have something to wear, he explained to her that he was a time traveler, and for some reason she believed him—"

"Because it was true!"

"Well, yes, but how was she going to know that? Anyway, she did believe him, and then later on she was silly enough to marry him and here we are."

Alba punches me in the stomach. "Tell it *right*," she demands.

"Ooof. How can I tell anything if you beat on me like that? Geez."

Alba is quiet. Then she says, "How come you never visit Mama in the future?"

"I don't know, Alba. If I could, I'd be there." The blue is deepening over the horizon and the tide is receding. I stand up and offer Alba my hand, pull her up. As she stands brushing sand from her nightgown she stumbles toward me and says, "Oh!" and is gone and I stand there on the beach holding a damp cotton nightgown and staring at Alba's slender footprints in the fading light.

RENASCENCE

• •

Thursday, December 4, 2008 (Clare is 37)

CLARE: It's a cold, bright morning. I unlock the door of the studio and stamp snow off my boots. I open the shades, turn up the heat. I start a pot of coffee brewing. I stand in the empty space in the middle of the studio and I look around me.

Two years' worth of dust and stillness lies over everything. My drawing table is bare. The beater sits clean and empty. The molds and deckles are neatly stacked, coils of armature wire sit untouched by the table. Paints and pigments, jars of brushes, tools, books; all are just as I left them. The sketches I had thumbtacked to the wall have yellowed and curled. I untack them and throw them in the wastebasket.

I sit at my drawing table and I close my eyes.

The wind is rattling tree branches against the side of the house. A car splashes through slush in the alley. The coffeemaker hisses and gurgles as it spits the last spurt of coffee into the pot. I open my eyes, shiver and pull my heavy sweater closer.

When I woke up this morning I had an urge to come here. It was like a flash of lust: an assignation with my old lover, art. But now I'm sitting here waiting for . . . something . . . to come to me and nothing comes. I open a flat file drawer and take out a sheet of indigo-dyed paper. It's heavy and slightly rough, deep blue and cold to the touch like metal. I lay it on the table. I stand and stare at it for a while. I take out a few pieces of soft white pastel and weigh them in my palm. Then I put them down and pour myself some coffee. I stare out the window at the back of the house. If Henry were here he might be sitting at his desk, might be looking back at me from the window above his desk. Or he might be playing Scrabble with Alba, or reading the comics, or making soup for lunch. I sip my coffee and try to feel time revert, try to erase the difference between now and then. It is only my memory that holds me here. Time, let me vanish. *Then what we separate by our very presence can come together.*

I stand in front of the sheet of paper, holding a white pastel. The paper is vast, and I begin in the center, bending over the paper though I know I would be more comfortable at the easel. I measure out the figure, half-life-sized: here is the top of the head, the groin, the heel of the foot. I rough in a head. I draw very lightly, from memory: empty eyes, here at the midpoint of the head, long nose, bow mouth slightly open. The eyebrows arch in surprise: oh, it's *you.* The pointed chin and the round jawline, the forehead high and the ears only indicated. Here is the neck, and the shoulders that slope into arms that cross protectively over the breasts, here is the bottom of the rib cage, the plump stomach, full hips, legs slightly bent, feet pointing downward as though the figure is floating in midair. The points of measurement are like stars in the indigo night sky of the paper; the figure is a constellation. I indicate highlights and the figure becomes three dimensional, a glass vessel. I draw the features carefully, create the structure of the face, fill in the eyes, which regard me, astonished at suddenly existing. The hair undulates across the paper, floating weightless and motionless, linear pattern that makes the static body dynamic. What else is in this universe, this drawing? Other stars, far away. I hunt through my tools and find a needle. I tape the drawing over a window and I begin to prick the paper full of tiny holes, and each pin prick becomes a sun in some other set of worlds. And when I have a galaxy full of stars I prick out the figure, which now becomes a constellation in earnest, a network of tiny lights. I regard my likeness, and she returns my gaze. I place my finger on her forehead and say, "Vanish," but it is she who will stay; I am the one who is vanishing.

ALWAYS AGAIN

....

Thursday, July 24, 2053 (Henry is 43, Clare is 82)

HENRY: I find myself in a dark hallway. At the end of the hall is
a door, slightly open with white light spilling around its edges. The
hall is full of galoshes and rain coats. I walk slowly and silently to
the door and carefully look into the next room. Morning light fills
up the room and is painful at first, but as my eyes adjust I see that
in the room is a plain wooden table next to a window. A woman sits
at the table facing the window. A teacup sits at her elbow. Outside is
the lake, the waves rush up the shore and recede with calming repetition which becomes like stillness after a few minutes. The woman
is extremely still. Something about her is familiar. She is an old
woman; her hair is perfectly white and lies long on her back in a
thin stream, over a slight dowager's hump. She wears a sweater the
color of coral. The curve of her shoulders, the stiffness in her pos-
ture say *here is someone who is very tired,* and I am very tired, myself.
I shift my weight from one foot to the other and the floor creaks;
the woman turns and sees me and her face is remade into joy; I am
suddenly amazed; this is Clare, Clare old! and she is coming to me,
so slowly, and I take her into my arms.

Monday, July 14, 2053 (Clare is 82)

CLARE: This morning everything is clean; the storm has left branches strewn around the yard, which I will presently go out and pick up: all the beach's sand has been redistributed and laid down fresh in an even blanket pocked with impressions of rain, and the daylilies bend and glisten in the white seven a.m. light. I sit at the dining room table with a cup of tea, looking at the water, listening. Waiting.

Today is not much different from all the other days. I get up at dawn, put on slacks and a sweater, brush my hair, make toast, and tea, and sit looking at the lake, wondering if he will come today. It's not much different from the many other times he was gone, and I waited, except that this time I have instructions: this time I know Henry will come, eventually. I sometimes wonder if this readiness, this expectation, prevents the miracle from happening. But I have no choice. He is coming, and I am here.

ACKNOWLEDGMENTS

·····································

Writing is a private thing. It's boring to watch, and its pleasures tend to be most intense for the person who's actually doing the writing. So with big gratitude and much awe, I would like to thank everyone who helped me to write and publish *The Time Traveler's Wife*:

Thank you to Joseph Regal, for saying Yes, and for an education in the wily ways of publishing. It's been a blast. Thank you to the excellent people of MacAdam/Cage, especially Anika Streitfeld, my editor, for patience and care and close scrutiny. It is a great pleasure to work with Dorothy Carico Smith, Pat Walsh, David Poindexter, Kate Nitze, Tom White, and John Gray. And thank you also to Melanie Mitchell, Amy Stoll, and Tasha Reynolds. Many thanks also to Howard Sanders, and to Caspian Dennis.

The Ragdale Foundation supported this book with numerous residencies. Thank you to its marvelous staff, especially Sylvia Brown, Anne Hughes, Susan Tillett, and Melissa Mosher. And thank you to The Illinois Arts Council, and the taxpayers of Illinois, who awarded me a Fellowship in Prose in 2000.

Thank you to the librarians and staff, past and present, of the Newberry Library: Dr. Paul Gehl, Bart Smith, and Margaret Kulis. Without their generous help, Henry would have ended up working at Starbucks. I would also like to thank the librarians of the Reference Desk at the Evanston Public Library, for their patient assistance with all sorts of wacko queries.

I am grateful to Random House for the use of the quote on page 235, a translation by R. L. Wing of a poem by Wu Chen. The translation appears in the *Illustrated I Ching*. Likewise, I am pleased to be able to include material from A. S. Byatt's marvelous book *w*.

Thank you to papermakers who patiently shared their knowledge: Marilyn Sward and Andrea Peterson.

Thanks to Roger Carlson of Bookman's Alley, for many years of happy book hunting, and to Steve Kay of Vintage Vinyl for stocking everything I want to listen to. And thanks to Carol Prieto, realtor supreme.

Many thanks to friends, family, and colleagues who read, critiqued, and contributed their expertise: Lyn Rosen, Danea Rush, Jonelle Niffenegger, Riva Lehrer, Lisa Gurr, Robert Vladova, Melissa Jay Craig, Stacey Stern, Ron Falzone, Marcy Henry, Josie Kearns, Caroline Preston, Bill Frederick, Bert Menco, Patricia Niffenegger, Beth Niffenegger, Jonis Agee and the members of her Advanced Novel class, Iowa City, 2001. Thanks to Paula Campbell for her help with the French.

Special thanks to Alan Larson, whose unflagging optimism set me a good example.

Last and best, thanks to Christopher Schneberger: I waited for you, and now you're here.

PERMISSIONS ACKNOWLEDGMENTS

....

1981) 2120 S. Michigan Avenue, Chicago, Il 60616. (312) 808-1286, www.bluesheaven.com

Excerpt from "Gimme the Car" written by Gordon Gano ©1980, Gorno Music (ASCAP). Used by permission from Gorno Music. Administered by Alan N. Skiena, Esq.

Excerpt from "Add It Up" written by Gordon Gano ©1980, Gorno Music (ASCAP). Used by permission from Gorno Music. Administered by Alan N. Skiena, Esq.

References to pharmaceutical products credited to the 2000 edition of the *Physicians' Desk Reference.* Used by permission of Thomson Medical Economics.

Lines by Emily Dickinson reprinted by permission of the publishers and the Trustees of Amherst College from *The Poems of Emily Dickinson*, Ralph W. Franklin, ed., Cambridge, Mass.: The Belknap Press of Harvard University Press, copyright ©1998 by the President and Fellows of Harvard College. Copyright ©1951, 1955, 1979 by the President and Fellows of Harvard College.

Quotations from the *Dictionary of Given Names* by Flora Haines Loughead. Copyright ©1933. Used by permission of the Arthur H. Clark Company.

Excerpt from "Pussy Power" written by Iggy Pop. Copyright ©1990 James Osterberg Music (BMI)/Administered by BUG. All rights reserved. Used by permission.

Excerpt from "Yellow Submarine" copyright ©1966 (renewed) Sony/ATV Tunes LLC. All rights administered by Sony/ATV Music Publishing, 8 Music Square West, Nashville, TN 37203. All rights reserved. Used by permission.

Excerpt from *Homer: The Odyssey* translated by Robert Fitzgerald. Copyright ©1961, 1963 by Robert Fitzgerald. Copyright renewed 1989 by Benedict R.C. Fitzgerald, on behalf of the Fitzgerald children. Used by permission of Farrar, Straus and Giroux, LLC.

READING GROUP GUIDE

· ·

1. On the novel's first page Clare declares, "I wait for Henry." In what way does this define her character, and how is the theme of waiting developed throughout the book?

2. Just as Clare is defined by her waiting, so Henry is defined by his unpredictable comings and goings. That—along with his hard drinking and proclivities for stealing and beating people up—might be described as stereotypically masculine behavior, just as waiting might be called stereotypically feminine. What keeps these characters from being stereotypes? In what ways does the author give them depth and nuance? For example, at what points in the book do Henry and Clare reverse roles?

3. Niffenegger portrays Henry's time traveling as the result of a genetic disorder, which is explained at some length later on. How plausible is this explanation—not from a scientific point of view, but from a dramatic or literary one? Do you think that Henry's condition requires an explanation?

4. How has Henry's personality been shaped by his bouts of chrono-displacement? How does his time traveling affect Clare? In addition, how is Clare affected by meeting her future husband when she is six and seeing him repeatedly throughout her childhood and adolescence before they become lovers? How does the author manage to make their relationship seem eccentric—and even enchanted—rather than sinister?

5. What is the particular significance of Henry's job as a librarian? What connection do you see between his choice of career and his childhood fascination with the Field Museum (pp. 27–34)?

6. Along with his frequent trips backward and forward in time, the critical event in Henry's early life is the hideous death of his mother, which he witnesses as a child and revisits compulsively as an adult (pp. 111–115). How has this event helped shape him and how does it foreshadow other events in the novel?

7. How does the author manage her novel's fantastically intricate time scheme? For example, where in her narrative does she relate the same incident from different perspectives in order to supply missing information? How does she foreshadow such developments as Ingrid Carmichel's suicide, the birth of Alba DeTamble, and Henry's death?

8. Among the curiosities of the book is the way chrono-displacement occasionally causes its protagonists to split and double. At the age of nine Henry is taught pickpocketing by his twenty-seven-year-old self (pp. 50–53); Henry returns to his thirty-three-year-old wife after making love to her on her eighteenth birthday (pp. 428–430). After Henry has a vasectomy at the age of thirty-seven, Clare becomes pregnant by a thirty-three-year-old "surrogate" (pp. 377–379). How do Henry and Clare view their younger and older selves? Why, for one thing, aren't they ever jealous of them? And what are this novel's implications about the relationship between time and the self?

9. In theory Henry's time traveling should make him omniscient—at least as far as his own timeline is concerned—but Clare knows things about him that he does not. What accounts for this? What role does the characters' knowledge—and the gaps in their knowledge—play in the novel?

10. Closely related to the theme of foreknowledge is the idea of free will. Does Henry's chrono-instability give him a freedom that Clare lacks, or does it make him more powerless? Discuss Henry's observation that "there is only free will when you are in time, in the present" (p. 57).

11. When Henry asks her to describe her artwork, Clare tells him that it's about birds and longing (p. 12). How do the themes of birds—along with wings and flight—and longing figure elsewhere in this book?

12. What is the List that Henry makes for Clare, and how does it give the book dramatic momentum? Does Niffenegger employ other devices to similar effect? One of the things that makes a story suspenseful is the reader's sense that events are reaching a climax, that time is running out. How is Niffenegger able to impart this sense to her readers, given Henry's seemingly inexhaustible supply of time?

13. Both Gomez and Celia warn Clare about Henry. "This guy would chew you up and spit you out . . . He's not at all what you need," says Gomez (p. 436). Can we simply chalk those warnings up to jealousy,

or might the observers be correct? Is Henry more ruthless and amoral than he appears to Clare? How do you interpret Henry's statement: "I'm not exactly the man she's known from earliest childhood. I'm a close approximation she is guiding surreptitiously toward a me that exists in her mind's eye" (pp. 152–153)?

14. How does Henry and Clare's relationship change following their marriage? How is it affected by their desire for a child?

15. Would you call *The Time Traveler's Wife* a comedy or a tragedy, or are such classifications relevant to a work that plays havoc with time and allows one character to appear periodically after his death?

16. How does the author use time travel as a metaphor: for love, for loss and absence, for fate, for aging, for death? To what extent are Clare and Henry a "normal" couple?